Cor

Corsets & Clockwork:

13 Steampunk Romances

Edited by Trisha Telep

RP|TEENS
PHILADELPHIA · LONDON

Constable & Robinson Ltd
3 The Lanchesters
162 Fulham Palace Road
London W6 9ER
www.constablerobinson.com

First published in the UK by Robinson,
an imprint of Constable & Robinson, 2011

A copy of the British Library Cataloguing in Publication
Data is available from the British Library

UK ISBN 978-1-84901-658-2

1 3 5 7 9 10 8 6 4 2

First published in the United States in 2011 by Running Press Book Publishers
All rights reserved under the Pan-American and International Copyright Conventions

9 8 7 6 5 4 3 2 1
Digit on the right indicates the number of this printing

Library of Congress Control Number: 2010941311
US ISBN 978-0-7624-4092-4

Published by Running Press Teens
an imprint of Running Press Book Publishers
2300 Chestnut Street
Philadelphia, PA 19103-4371

Visit us on the web!
www.runningpress.com

Cover image and design: Joe Roberts.co.uk

Printed in the United States

Contents

Introduction

THERE ARE MILLIONS of stories in the Clockwork City; here are thirteen of them.

Human hearts are delicate things. They are not made of gears and cogs, or pistons and steam-driven hydraulics. Place the human heart next to a technological marvel of scientific industry created by the lurid imaginations of the Victorians and it will seem weak, useless, good for nothing—easily punctured, torn, or broken. It obviously needs sturdier parts and could use a lesson in physics. A human heart will not, for example, win a war or power a factory or light a city or fuel a demonic industry. A clockwork heart would certainly be a better idea—sturdier, more useful, sound, and reliable. It would not get so easily bruised and battered, nor would it be a slave to emotion. But would a finely tuned wonder of engineering be able to love?

Fortunately, none of our heroes and heroines has a clockwork heart (well, okay, one does, but that's unavoidable). You might get away with a clockwork heart for the "steam" portion of our entertainment, but you'll never make the "punk" contingent with anything less than a gory, flesh-and-gristle muscle that is pumping blood and taking prisoners. The devil may be in the mechanized technological details, but the story is firmly in the human. Victorian science fiction is

1

not much without a healthy dose of the incorrigible, brave, hysterical Victorians themselves, is it? You may yearn for the infernal devices but it's the heroine who breaks your heart. Where would the story be without the kick-ass rebellion . . . in an airship under goggles, in a corset that's simply impossible to swim in, fighting Lovecraftian monsters in a 1958 T-bird, or dodging metal Nazis? Come for the steam, stay for the punk.

In this book you'll find magical outcasts and kindred spirits, feisty heroines and genius inventors, war zones and supernatural rituals, darkness and dystopia. A tonic of forgetfulness helps keep the real world under wraps; a misunderstood murderer is on the lookout for love in the City of Gold. There is an eternal struggle between science and magic, logic and beauty, technology and intuition. Lovelorn stage managers, oppressed Siamese twins, and idealistic young bombers skulk through the dangerous streets of the soot-choked city of industry. This is a sprawling, diverse, fantasy-heavy, unashamedly promiscuous steampunk collection that takes giddy pleasure in throwing the rule book out the window and detouring drunkenly like some many-tentacled Great One with ADD.

So, what *do* you get when you cross steampunk with romance? Say hello to my little friend—steampunk's younger sister, the romantic baby of the family who refuses to pay attention and who, when you dress her up in all her steampunk finery, invariably takes her safety scissors to her epaulettes and trades all her cool weapons to a cute boy in homeroom for a lunchbox full of Twinkies (she'll just make more in shop class next period). And although she might seem a tad light-hearted to the steampunk purist, beneath her too-tight corset, intricate infernal hairstyle (which can be reduced to cinders by a well-placed bomb), and optimistic desire for love beats the heart of a true pioneer adventurer and a suitably fierce addition to the steampunk family tree.

TRISHA TELEP

Rude Mechanicals

by Lesley Livingston

> . . . A crew of patches, rude mechanicals,
> That work for bread upon Athenian stalls,
> Were met together to rehearse a play . . .
>
> *A Midsummer Night's Dream*, William Shakespeare

QUINTILLIUS FARTHING SAT on the high stool at the stage manager's post in the darkened wings of his uncle's theatre, contemplating murder. Or perhaps suicide.

No . . . no . . . a murder-suicide. *Yes*, he thought, *that seems the most elegant solution to this, my present dilemma.* After all, wasn't that how Romeo and Juliet worked things out? Maybe this could be one of those cases of Life imitating Art . . .

Out on the stage—standing *just* out of her light, as usual—Marjorie Dalliance blanked on a line, stood blinking dumbly for a long moment as if waiting for the forgotten words to magically appear in the air in front of her, and then laughed like a braying ass when they didn't. Just to let the meagre audience know, in case they hadn't already figured it out for themselves, that this particular production of *Romeo and Juliet* was—contrary to the marquee billing overtop the Aurora Theatre's front doors—a comedy.

Or maybe it was a joke. A long, cruel joke.

Quint ground his teeth together and his thoughts swung back into the just plain "murder" camp. For a while, sitting there in the darkness, he'd idly considered feeding his cue script to the blue-glassed gas lamp at his elbow, a page at a time. Once the entire thing was consumed, Quint fancied he would just up and leave the performers—if such they could be genuinely called—to their own devices.

He sighed and took the silver fob watch from his vest pocket, glancing at the faintly luminous face. There was still plenty of time left before the second-act curtain fell. He could probably manage to track down that shifty fellow he'd seen earlier that afternoon peddling gas-powered pistols and auto-shooters from a cart in the Narrow Market.

A bit of luck and Quint could be there and back again in time to spectacularly, and with *great* realism, remind Marjorie Dalliance—and the theatre's whole, buffoon-ridden patronage—that this particular play was *supposed . . . to be . . . a . . . tragedy*.

Instead, it was just tragic.

He hazarded a glance back at the stage where "Romeo" approached the balcony and tripped over a bit of foliage that "Juliet" had knocked loose in her out-of-character merriment. Quint shook his head woefully and settled back onto his perch in resignation, signalling another lighting cue up to the booth with his hooded lamp. He couldn't leave. The troupe probably wouldn't survive his absence long enough for him to exact his bloody vengeance. And besides, his uncle did truly need him to—

"Moon!" Quint hissed to himself in a whisper, suddenly having realized that Marjorie had—yet again—forgotten to trip the lever switch that activated a specific mechanism of the scenery apparatus before she'd made her entrance. "She's forgotten the ruddy moon again . . ."

"Lady!" Honorius Clement, the actor playing Romeo, sadly hadn't noticed and was already barrelling on through his next line: "By yonder blessed moon I swear . . ."

The guffaws from the boorish few souls sprawled about the audience seats drowned out Clement's voice as the hapless twit gestured to an empty space above the balcony where the risen moon was, most definitely, not.

Quint dropped his head into his hands and groaned.

On it went. For almost another two whole hours, and it was mostly all downhill. When the final curtain fell, Quint felt it almost as a blessing.

• • •

Once he'd finished sweeping the empty house and setting the gas lamp ghost light to keep lonely vigil in the middle of the darkened stage, Quint left by the stage door, turning the key in the big brass lock, and headed over to the Deus Ex Machina—the pub up the street—for a bit of liquid consolation. His uncle, Agamemnon Wentworth Farthing—once the greatest theatre impresario the City had ever known—would already be there. He hadn't even had the heart to stick it out for curtain call. And that, Quint thought, had been mercifully brief, the actors offering only perfunctory bows before leaving the stage, shedding bits of costume in their collective wake as they headed toward the dressing rooms. Mostly, they'd all been in a hurry to get to the place Quint found himself now, too.

The Deus Ex Machina—as the Mac was formally proclaimed by the soot-begrimed sign that hung swaying over the doorway—had become in recent years a kind of eccentric shrine of sorts. A memorial for all of the theatres and all of the productions that had met their deaths along the once-grand "Palace Row." The Row was an area of the City comprising four long blocks of increasingly dilapidated edifices, crumbling buildings housing stages—referred to in the better days of recent memory as "theatre palaces"—where scintillating performances of the thespian craft seen in times past had mostly given way to the creeping depredations of the "popular arts."

As, over the years, the crowds had thinned, one by one the theatres had begun closing their doors. And as they had, the owner of the Deus Ex Machina had bought up the most interesting bits of sets and props—at ridiculously low prices—and mounted them on the walls and posts and beams of the rabbit-warren public house. The best ones he hung suspended from the rafters above the long oak bar.

Quint was, admittedly, conflicted about the practice. On the one hand, he appreciated the memorializing—these were productions that *should* be remembered—but, on the other, it sometimes seemed to him . . . macabre. Like theatrical taxidermy. He didn't like to think of all the living breathing performances he'd marvelled at in his youth as something to be skinned and stuffed and mounted like the carcasses of hunting trophies.

He shook off his gloomy thoughts and pulled open the heavy oak and bronze door of the pub. A rush of warm, greasy air tumbled over him, dissipating in the cool, wet night, and he stepped into the noisy closeness of the Mac's innards. He elbowed his way toward the very back corner to the long, low table where his uncle always sat slumped after a performance, surrounded by a bevy of theatrical cronies, to discover that talk had already turned to "the problem with theatre."

That's a bad sign, Quint thought. That topic didn't usually rear its ugly head until the second or third round of ales. He signalled the barmaid for a small beer and sat down, turning only half an ear to the same familiar conversation. It was like

7

listening to one of those old circular songs where one party began and everyone picked up the tune in turn and it just went round and round with no end and no beginning. Often the discussions would chug away into the wee hours, until Quint was forced to drag his uncle out into the street and help him stumble up the steps of the late-run trolley-tram.

Always, the topic was the same. The problem with theatre.

"Bums in the seats" was the problem. Or, rather, the increasing *lack* thereof. Over the past few years, the Aurora (in particular, but all of the Palace Row houses in general) had been losing audiences to other forms of popular entertainment. *"Entertainment" being an entirely subjective term*, Quint thought bleakly. He'd trodden the boards beneath the soaring gilded arches of the Aurora's proscenium since he was old enough to toddle about upright, fetching props and costumes, bringing the actors jugs of water and flasks of whisky. Eventually he'd been allowed to take on bit parts now and then—he had a natural talent for acting and an eye for directing, his uncle had told him—when he wasn't stage managing the productions.

But now, at the ripe old age of nineteen, Quintillius Farthing was beginning to despair for the future of his chosen profession. The Chalice, one block over on the Row, was the first to give up on producing actual plays. Its owner now ran nightly revues of assorted novelty acts instead. Quint had gone to see the show—if "show" it could rightly be called—out of pure, bloody-minded curiosity one night when the Aurora had been dark. Afterwards he'd cursed himself and heartily wished he hadn't gone. The headline act had consisted of a chorus of dancing girls in peek-a-boo underthings, jiggling and bobbing alongside a fire-breathing dwarf on stilts wearing break-away suspenders . . . and *no* underthings whatsoever. Quint shuddered at the memory.

But the Chalice wasn't the only one, either. A few houses further up, for instance, there was a theatre that had recently opened a larger-than-life—and *entirely* obscene—marionette puppet show that was running three performances a day and drew large, rowdy, drunk crowds. In between that tarnished venue and the Aurora, there was another boarded-up theatre that had gone permanently dark where, outside on the street, a tramp ran an act with a marmoset on a pneumatic pogo stick.

A marmoset. Of all things.

The last time he'd walked past, Quint's heart had sank to discover that the marmoset was pulling in more cash than his uncle's theatre. Getting better crowds than a performance of Shakespeare, for pity's sake.

A marmoset.

"Spectacle!" one of the old boys down the table in the Mac suddenly roared. "We need more spectacle!"

"Bigger sets!"

"Explosions!"

"What about *art*?" Quint said finally, tiring of the wrongheadedness of it all. "What about artistry?"

"Aye, lad." The roaring chap gave him a sharp glare. "What about it?"

"We could try hiring some real actors, you know." Quint shrugged. "Instead of that ridiculous bawd we've got playing Juliet—"

"Oy! Watch'r mouf, Farving!" the delicate ingénue in question yowled from the next table over, where she sat on Old Capulet's lap, quaffing from a pewter mug. "Or I'll give you a rose by any ovva name!" She shook her fist at him.

Quint sighed and turned away from the raucous laughter at that table. He had no actual fear of offending the base creature. She probably wouldn't remember most of that

9

night's proceedings by the next morn, anyway. "Just like she can't remember most of her lines," Quint grumbled to himself.

Agamemnon smiled gently in the face of his nephew's seething frustration. He nodded his chin at the table full of actors. "We've got her for the same reason we've got most of them, except for the few old-timers. We've got her because she's cheap."

"She is that," Quint agreed, but quietly enough so that Marjorie didn't hear him this time. The last thing he wanted, ironically enough, was to make a scene. He sighed. It was the crux of the problem. Smaller audiences meant less money coming, which meant less money to pay for real talent, which in turn, ensured even smaller audiences. "I should go back to the Aurora, Uncle. The box office receipts are in need of counting . . ."

"Twenty in the audience today, Tilli, old chap," Agamemnon patted his nephew's knee. "I already counted. And five of those were comps."

"Uncle, I thought we'd agreed—no more complimentary tickets?"

"You worry too much, Quintillius," the old sage who still ran the Orpheum said from across the table as he pushed a mug toward him. "You need a lass, my boy. Some lovely doll who'll take your mind off the work."

In the corner, the gaggle of chorus dancers from the naughty revue sent up an unrelated shriek of laughter and Quint shuddered.

A lass.

He was certainly not opposed to the idea. But he'd grown up steeped in the classics. The great love stories. And he'd decided long ago—somewhere around the age of nine or ten (he'd been a terribly precocious child)—that the girl who managed to capture the heart of Quintillius Farthing would be . . . extraordinary. He would settle for nothing less.

Never mind that. He shook the silly fantasy of a lady love from his thoughts, frowning. No. The work was the only thing Quint cared about. He didn't want a girl to take his mind off it. Through the haze of pipe and hookah smoke, Quint gazed up at the ceiling of the Mac. Above him, a harpy-wing apparatus from his uncle's last truly successful performance— Shakespeare's *The Tempest*—hung suspended from wires, stretched out as if in phantom flight.

Quint distinctly remembered the thrill of watching an actor wearing the magnificent wings descend to the stage from the Aurora's fly-tower through a rolling cloud of dry-ice fog to the accompaniment of crashing thunder and lightning, speaking those marvellous lines . . .

Agamemnon had been forced to sell off the contraption to the Mac's owner when his bar tally had grown too long. Quint stared at the iridescent feathers, wired with such care to the frame, and wondered at the artistry that had made them seem so lifelike on stage, under the lights.

Suddenly, the bench beside him creaked, shaking Quint out of his reverie. He turned to find himself looking into the eyes of a compact, wiry little man with iron-grey hair curling out from under a velvet top hat, and wearing an immaculate, if slightly old-fashioned, frock coat and cravat. The man leaned forward and Quint saw his own eyes reflected in the convex lenses of the delicate brass pince-nez perched on the other man's long, hawkish nose.

"Call me Kingfisher," the man said. His breath was hot, pungent with the tang of absinthe. "Young Master Farthing . . . I have something you should see. You and your uncle."

• • •

They left the Mac, travelling by hired coach up the hill until the streets became too narrow and perilously rutted for the high, thin wheels of the carriage to navigate. The man, Kingfisher, paid the driver with carefully counted-out coins— silver, Quint thought, impressed—and then led the way down a winding side street.

At ground level, a thickening coal-dust dirty fog swirled about their boots as they walked along the cobbled streets. High overhead, Quint saw the gleaming metal skin of a TransAtlantica Flights intercontinental dirigible reflecting silver-blue moonlight as it made its stately way westward through the night skies. Toward America, on the other side of the vast ocean, Quint sighed wistfully. He wondered for a brief moment about the theatrical possibilities in a city like New York, where the airship would dock in a mere few days. Perhaps that was what he should do. Pack up and head for the New World!

Excitement, romance . . .

Who are you trying to fool, Quintillius? he thought. *You'll never leave London.* It was his home. The City. The theatre. The loneliness.

The trio walked side by side until the way became so narrow that they had to trudge along one behind the other and the upper floors of the houses they passed seemed to lean menacingly in toward them, blocking out the sliver of indigo sky with dark, looming brick facades. Quint began to suspect that the mysterious Mister Kingfisher was leading them into some sort of nefarious trap—that he and his uncle were on the verge of being accosted and robbed of their belongings, or perhaps their very lives—when the old man suddenly stopped before the narrow door to a tall, neat house. A small blue flame burning in the lantern above the door illuminated a series of elaborate brass locks that

Kingfisher unlatched, one by one, with the keys on a large ring he brought forth from some inner pocket. The keys on the ring were like none Quint had ever seen before. One of them seemed to glow when the old man inserted it into the keyhole.

"My own invention, this security system. Top notch. One can never be too cautious." Kingfisher grinned at them over his shoulder. "Especially not with the treasures hoarded in *my* particular stores . . ."

Once over the threshold, Quint gazed around in astonishment. He was hard-pressed to imagine how anyone could find *anything* of value in amongst the unidentifiable junk and clutter that towered in teetering piles, lining walls and obscuring furniture. Sitting room, dining room, tiny kitchen —all were virtually un-navigable on account of the masses of paraphernalia.

Coils of wire, glass bulbs, sheets of what looked like hammered tin and copper, gears and cogs of all sizes, fine linens, a dressmaker's dummy, and tools ranging from an industrial-grade riveter to cases lined with tiny precision instruments for watchmaking were stacked about as though a crazed gathering of Santa's elves had gone on break in the middle of an assemblage of nightmarish toys. In the corner, there was a fully articulated human skeleton hanging from a pole. A pair of what looked like welder's goggles were perched at a jaunty angle on its bleached skull. There were books everywhere. Scrolls. Tablets. Palimpsests. Some new, some positively ancient.

"Have you ever heard of the Library of Alexandria?"

"Of course I have," Quint snorted. "It burned to the ground in ancient times, taking a vast accumulated wealth of knowledge with it."

"Yes! Yes, it did." Kingfisher's eyes grew a touch unfocused for a moment. "Well, some of it survived. *Some*. Enough. Heron, for example . . ."

"I've heard of Heron of Alexandria," Agamemnon piped up from where he'd been crouched down on the floor, examining some sort of spring-loaded curiosity that resembled a tiny catapult. "An inventor, he was. Built one of the first steam turbines, didn't he? And mechanical things. Whirligigs and such. Doors that opened on their own and wind-powered musical thingamies. Clever bloke."

"Clever. Oh, my, yes." Kingfisher nodded and clapped his hands. "Hydraulics, pneumatics, automation. You might even call him the father of cybernetics, in fact."

"Cyber . . . what?" Quint frowned. He'd understood the other words, but . . .

Kingfisher's eyes twinkled. "Follow me," he said, and crooked a long finger, beckoning the two Farthing gentlemen toward a door, which he opened. Through the archway, Quint saw the darkness beyond suddenly disperse and become filled with light from what must have been cleverly recessed lamps. The soft, golden illumination seemed to come from everywhere as they descended a circular staircase down into a basement that was as pristine and organized as the rooms above were cluttered and chaotic.

Kingfisher trotted eagerly over to a shapeless bulk in the middle of the room, covered with a canvas drop cloth. "As I say, I've something to show you," he said, drawing aside the tarp with a magician's flourish. "Something men of your quality may find . . . of use."

• • •

It's not some*thing*, Quint thought to himself as he stepped off the bottom rung of the iron spiral staircase. It's some*one*. A girl. And she was beautiful in the light of a dozen oil lamps.

14

The lambent glow of the flames rendered her skin golden-hued. It gleamed, almost as if it were polished—

"Metal . . ." The word whispered from between Quint's lips, but as he approached the exquisite statue of the girl perched on the high stool in the corner of the workroom, he realized that it wasn't an illusion. No trick of the light. Her skin looked as if it were, indeed, fashioned out of precious electrum.

Her auburn tresses gleamed like fine-spun copper. No. Not *like* fine-spun copper . . . her hair *was* copper. Quint felt his eyes grow wide. Thousands of coiled and coiffed filaments, dressed in careful ringlets cascading down her back, shimmered like flame.

"I needed the conductivity to power her synapticulator," Kingfisher said, following Quint's gaze. "Copper was just the ticket."

"Her . . . uh . . ." Agamemnon stammered. "Her *what* is it you say?"

"Her artificial mind. The thought-processors consume a dreadful lot of energy," Kingfisher talked as he walked in a circle around the stool where the statue perched, "and then there's all the motivators that move her limbs and gears . . . but I had help with the design from an Austrian fellow—very clever, lives in New York now—and we managed to miniaturize the power source enough so that we could internalize it."

"I don't understand." Quint stood there blinking dumbly. "It's just a statue."

"Oh, ho!" Kingfisher grinned impishly and patted the "statue's" shoulder. "Now you don't want to say anything to offend her, Master Farthing! She is no statue. She's a *performer*."

"You mean . . . like a . . . simulacrum?" Quint had heard

15

of such things, only he'd always imagined them clumsy, bulky constructs. This . . . this thing looked positively human.

The old inventor chuckled. "A simulacrum—no! Heavens. My girl here is to those crude clunkers what the Sistine Chapel ceiling is to . . . to finger painting!" He gestured with a proud flourish. "I call her my Actromaton."

"I see," Quint's uncle said, a tiny amused smile twitching beneath his moustache.

Quint shook his head slightly. His uncle was obviously humouring the poor old fellow. Who was—quite obviously—stark raving mad. Still . . . Quint took a step toward the inanimate thing. It was really quite lovely. Her sculpted features were delicately pretty. She even had tiny, finely spun copper eyelashes.

"What's her name?" Agamemnon asked.

"Oh—she only responds to her *character* name, of course," Kingfisher answered. "Anything else would just confuse her programming."

"Ah. I see . . ." Quint's uncle *harrumphed* in wry amusement. "Her . . . her programming, is it? She's not one of those Stanislavsky disciples, is she? They take everything so seriously!"

"No, no." Kingfisher laughed along with Agamemnon's joke about the controversial Russian. "I simply meant that she is presently attuned to respond initially at the mention of her character's name—as in her first scene in the play. Otherwise, she reverts to a state of dormancy, as you see her now, to conserve power."

Quint took another step forward, drawn as if by an unseen force. "'Oh, she doth teach the torches to burn bright!'" he murmured one of Romeo's lines that, in the moment, struck him as particularly fitting for such a charming whimsy. "'It

16

seems she hangs upon the cheek of night like a rich jewel in an Ethiop's ear—'"

Suddenly, the Actromaton raised her delicate chin and turned her head toward Quint. Bright green eyes fluttered open and the shadow of a smile curved her shimmering lips.

"Oh!" Kingfisher blinked, a confused frown shadowing his brow. "Well, my dear! You are awake, it seems . . ."

"I thought you said she was in a state of dormancy!" Quint's uncle exclaimed, taking a step back.

"Well, I . . ." The old inventor paused for a moment, thinking, and then his expression suddenly cleared. "Ah! Of course! Nurse calls her 'Jule' in the play. That's what she must have thought she heard when you said 'jewel.'"

The Actromaton turned her head toward her creator, her movements graceful as a dancer's. Precise and lyrical. She turned her head back toward Quint and her leaf-green eyes seemed to sparkle with vitality.

"Made of Viennese glass," Kingfisher said proudly. "The finest."

Quint was enchanted. "Can I call her Jewel then?" he asked. "It seems so . . . fitting."

"I suppose it couldn't hurt," Kingfisher said. Then he winked. "I think she likes you, Master Farthing."

"That's not really possible," Agamemnon said, knotting his arms across his chest and regarding the marvellous mechanical construct with some scepticism. "Is it? Her . . . er . . . *liking* someone?"

"Oh, no," Kingfisher smiled. "That was a little joke. She's just responding with a series of pre-programmed responses. It's all algorithms and such. An illusion, if you will—although a damned fine one, if I do say so myself. And, after all . . . isn't that what the best actors do?"

Jewel had slid off her perch and taken a step toward Quint,

raising one slender hand, as if she would reach out and touch his face. Quint mirrored the gesture. Their fingertips touched and he could feel the slight, gentle whirring of the tiny gears and servos that operated her joints and limbs beneath the paper-thin, flexible covering of her metal skin. Truly, the Actromaton was a marvel. More than a feat of engineering she was almost . . . alchemy. Magic.

For a fleeting moment, Quint felt as though he should have been repulsed. She wasn't real. She was a mockery. A machine. But then a thought occurred to him.

Well, what else are you, Quint, but a biological machine? You're not so different. Just muscles and tendons instead of gears and pulleys.

What was it Shakespeare had called his troupe of actors in *A Midsummer Night's Dream*? "Rude mechanicals"? And Quint was far more rudely mechanical than the Actromaton when it came right down to it! He laughed a little at his silent joke and Jewel noticed. She parroted the gesture and her voice was like the chiming of silver bells, musical and wondrous.

Quint pressed his rough palm against her cool smooth one and said, "'If I profane with my unworthiest hand, the gentle sin is this: my lips, two blushing pilgrims ready stand to smooth that rough touch with a tender kiss . . .'"

It was Romeo's first line to Juliet in the banquet scene—the first time the two characters spoke—and Jewel responded with a swift, startled intake of "breath." Just as a proper Juliet would. Quint could almost imagine he perceived a slight, hectic blush brightening her gleaming cheeks. She opened her mouth as if to answer back when Kingfisher stepped forward to interrupt them. Quint had almost forgotten that the two other men were in the room.

"Now, now," the inventor patted his creation on the shoulder. "Let's not go too far down that road just yet. Time enough for banquets and balconies. Masters Farthing, let me show you something." He beckoned Agamemnon forward and smiled in a fatherly way at Jewel. "My dear? If you'd be so kind?"

She smiled serenely and lifted her arms over her head like a ballerina. Her costume, Quint saw, was not so much a costume as a *casing*. A housing for machinery. Kingfisher gently pushed aside the copper curls hanging down between the Actromaton's shoulders, revealing a series of rivets and intricate brass buckling that fastened up the back of her delicate corset instead of lacing.

"She runs on an electromagnetic engine, you see." The inventor beamed at his captive, captivated audience. "She's wireless! And these are her hydraulics, her pneumatics . . ."

What Quint had taken to be nothing more than the stays of Jewel's corsetry was actually piping; thin pneumatic tubing that ribbed her garment in vertical stripes like whalebone. Up close, he could hear the hiss and gentle gurgle of gases and fluids that gave her motion. Simulated life. Kingfisher unlatched a hidden, lace-covered panel in her bodice and showed them the chambered, fluid-pumping apparatus of Jewel's "circulatory pump"—her heart.

Quint stared at the intricate mechanism, utterly intrigued. It was beautiful.

Agamemnon, for his part, was seemingly a touch overwhelmed. "I could use a wee dram to help me take all this in, Mister Kingfisher."

"Yes, yes. Of course! Help yourself." The inventor waved in the direction of an oaken sideboard as he adjusted his creation's marvellous corsetry. The sideboard held an assortment of cut crystal decanters holding liquids of various colours. "Just anything but the . . . No! Agamemnon, stop!"

Quint's uncle froze, a liqueur glass full of something that

looked like crème de menthe or green chartreuse, poised beneath his moustaches.

"Heh . . ." Kingfisher bustled over and plucked the bilious green concoction from the other man's fingers. "Not *that* one."

"What the deuce? I thought it was plain old absinthe!"

"No. Although the 'green fairy' *is* part of the base liquid, this is no ordinary aperitif. No, this particular tonic takes a good deal of getting used to, you see. That is, if you want to avoid instant paralysis, followed by a slow, creeping death. Oh yes. One must . . . build up a resistance over years and years of ingesting tiny amounts . . ." He was muttering almost to himself now.

"And then?"

"Hm?"

"After the years and years?" Quint asked. "Why would one wish to partake of such a substance over a protracted period of time, sir, unless the benefits were unusually rewarding?"

The old man's timeless gaze swept back across the room to where Jewel waited patiently for her master to finish his tinkering with her mechanics. "One devotes one's life to the creation of such a thing, wouldn't you say? And if that life isn't long enough . . . one finds ways to get . . . more life." Kingfisher downed the contents of the glass himself with a grimace.

Agamemnon frowned deeply. "Sounds like a Devil's bargain, old man."

Kingfisher's grin returned. "But . . . But . . . it has, in a small way, allowed me to play not the Devil, but God—if you will allow the blasphemy." His laughter sounded slightly unhinged. "At least I didn't make her in my own image! Ha . . . that would have been a terrible burden now, wouldn't it?" He closed the panel over Jewel's heart again and tapped it gently with a fingertip.

"What about her . . ." Quint gestured vaguely toward the Actromaton's head.

"Her synapticulator? Her brain is—well, I assure you—it's just as finely made as the rest of her. And I've filled it full of the complete works of the Bard. Every word. She's a Shakespearean encyclopaedia! She'll never miss a cue or jump a line!"

"You really mean to put her on the stage?" Quint's uncle's jaw dropped open almost until it was touching his chest. "You think she can actually act?"

"She *will*. Once you teach her. Train her." Kingfisher was staring at the Farthings now with a feverish glare. "I've given her the raw materials. She only needs the fine-tuning that a director—a mentor—can give her. I want that teacher to be young Master Farthing."

"I . . ."

Quint felt suddenly very unsure of himself. Of this whole strange endeavour. He backed away—right into his uncle who stood at his elbow. Agamemnon grasped his arm before he could turn and bolt up the stairs and out into the night.

"Think of it," his uncle murmured in his ear, "no more Marjories up on our stage. No more gaffed lines or botched blocking! Every performance just as perfect as the one that went before. And just the way you want it to be. Think of it, Tillie, my lad. Even those newfangled infernal pictie-shows still need human actors to pull off a real performance. We won't need real actors at all anymore once they see what it—what this, er, what *she* can do!"

"Quintillius," the inventor said, "I beseech you. Will you do the honours of teaching her nuance? Of directing her, as it were? I know it is in your soul, young man. The words are in her *mind*, she just needs a taste of what they should sound like in her *heart*," Kingfisher argued persuasively. "Much like your own mind is simply the end result of an accumulation of knowledge and then the interpretation of that knowledge, she simply needs to be guided in the art of that interpretation. Shape her performance, Quintillius. And then, together, we three will present her to the world. The finest Juliet to ever grace a stage. And that stage will be the Aurora!"

"Agamemnon?" Quint said quietly, turning to his uncle. "What do you think about all this? Truly?"

His uncle's gaze had lost its wariness. In its place, Quint could see the dreams of the erstwhile impresario kindling to fevered life. This could be just the very thing the theatre needed to revive. Their fortunes could be looking rosier within a month. Word of the Actromaton's novelty would guarantee a sold-out show. Quint knew that in his bones.

Arms still raised gracefully over her head, Jewel turned and winked at Quint. Neither of the other men noticed and— for some reason—Quint did not feel inclined to tell them. It was like a little secret. It made him feel less apprehensive about the undertaking. Slightly.

He winked back . . . and then reluctantly agreed to be Jewel's tutor. And more than that.

He told them he would only do it if he could also be her Romeo.

• • •

Marjorie Dalliance had responded just as expected when told she would be getting the boot in favour of a machine. And that Quint would be taking over the part of Romeo. "Cor lumme!" she crowed. "You? Romeo! Ha! You what? never been kissed? Snoggin' it up wiv this bucket o' bolts? Ain't that fittin'. Carn't handle a real woman, this one. Well, good luck t'yer, sweeting. Hope she don't break yer pansy wee 'art!" She spat on the stage at his feet and turned on the heel of her high, laced boot to flounce off up the aisle of the theatre, bustle bouncing absurdly in her wake.

Honorius Clement, the actor who'd played Romeo opposite Marjorie, took the news a good deal better. He'd always had a sort of laconic spirit anyway. And he'd seemed a bit alarmed when he'd thought for a moment that he'd have to be the one playing opposite the Actromaton.

Marjorie was one thing, he said, but he'd played Pygmalion once in an operetta and the story of the man who'd fallen in love with the beautiful statue had struck him as just slightly . . . sad. He wished Quint luck. Quint instantly offered to make Honorius the stage manager of the production.

He was glad he did so, too, because Quint had his hands more than full with a rehearsal period that turned out to be only a few weeks long. The minute word leaked out of Kingfisher's and Farthing's daring new enterprise, the whole of the City, it seemed, was clamouring for tickets to the rumoured one-night-only exclusive gala showing. The price his uncle was charging was utterly exorbitant—and yet they sold like proverbial hot cakes.

Quint barely had time to take notice of the kerfuffle, though. All of his time was spent in rehearsal sessions with Jewel. And those moments seemed to pass in a kind of dream-like haze. Kingfisher marvellous creation soaked up Quint's direction like a thirsty sponge. The subtlety and nuance of her performance grew exponentially, a balm to his artistic soul. And her grace and beauty touched his heart. When, in a dress run of the balcony scene, she reached out to him and asked, "Dost thou love me?" Quint felt a twinge in his chest, and a deep, strange happiness.

It was a joy that was only compounded by the fact that, when he turned to swear his love to her by the light of the moon, it was to see that—thanks to Jewel's precise memory—

the moon was indeed shining down over the Aurora's stage.

• • •

The week before opening was one of great excitement. There were new and ingenious set pieces built for the production, designed—of course—by Kingfisher himself. It would make all of the backstage machinations so much easier. Not that the actors wouldn't be kept busy. In such a small company, everyone had a part to play, off stage as well as on. Quint handled all the masks and cloaks and random bits of scenery. The actor playing Mercutio took care of swords and torches. Jewel, along with her moon duties, would be responsible for preparing the props table each night. For that, Quint was inordinately grateful. When Marjorie had done it, she'd always forgotten half of the items and the other actors would have to run around looking for things or go onstage empty-handed.

When it finally came time for the curtain to rise, Quint's pre-show jitters gave way to a kind of euphoria. And more than halfway through the performance, he realized that the show was progressing better than he'd even dared hope. Not a single hitch so far and not just where Kingfisher's star was concerned. In fact, it seemed that Jewel's presence onstage, instead of overshadowing them, had actually caused the other actors in the company to step up their game. They were all bloody brilliant. Quint could feel the over-capacity crowd hanging on every word. Just as he was.

Standing in the darkness of the wings, in the midst of Act IV, he heard Jewel say, "'I have a faint cold fear thrills through my veins that almost freezes up the heat of life,'" and he felt a shiver run up his own spine. The coaching sessions he'd done with the Actromaton really had worked wonders for her. With her flawless command of the lines and—thanks to his work with her—a precise understanding of how to act them, she was scintillating. She was perfect. She was Juliet.

And Quint suddenly, utterly, understood why Romeo loved her so.

Loved her enough to take poison in her tomb when he thought she was dead, so that he could lie there with her for all eternity. " 'Thus, with a kiss, I die!' " Quint proclaimed, drinking off the potion in the black glass vial that Jewel had left prepared for him backstage. Onstage under the lights, he noticed that the liquid stained his fingertips bright green . . . and then Quint fell to the ground beside Juliet's bier, quite paralysed, unable even to close his eyes as he felt his heart begin to slow throughout the remainder of the scene.

Oh, God, he thought as Juliet woke, banished the Friar from her tomb, and knelt over his body. His barely breathing body.

We've taught her too well, he thought.

Somewhere along the line, somewhere during rehearsals, it had ceased to be a play for her. In Jewel's mind, Romeo took poison and Romeo died for love of her. For love of Juliet. And so, knowing that as a certainty, she had set the props table with a vial of Kingfisher's "tonic." And now Quint was going to die.

Because of the simple fact that as human—*more* than human—as she seemed to be . . . his Jewel was not. She was an illusion.

She knelt at his side and bent over him, smiling sadly. Her beautiful eyes were incapable of producing moisture and yet, in that moment, they sparkled so brightly—as if with unshed tears—that the effect was more convincing than if Marjorie Dalliance had cried out a river. Women in the audience, maybe men too, were sobbing into handkerchiefs.

Quint felt Jewel's pain. Her love. He just couldn't feel

anything else. His body had gone numb. Nerveless. He tried to speak, to tell her, *No! this isn't real!*

But it was. It was the most convincing performance that his uncle's warped and weathered stage had ever played host to.

Jewel leaned down to caress his face with her cool, smooth fingertips.

He was really going to die. She was, too.

Real death. Real . . . love?

Quint's slowing heart ached, even as—with a wrenching cry—Jewel drove an all-too-real dagger through her own, destroying the delicate, irreplaceable mechanism that kept her functioning. Dark, honey-red hydraulic fluid seeped through the brocaded fabric of her costume in a widening stain, and she fell across his body with a last, lingering sigh of pure contentment.

· · ·

It was almost a full month before Quint could stand without holding on to a chair or the wall for support. His uncle told him that he was very lucky indeed to have survived. Kingfisher had been convinced that he would be dead within the hour. The dram Jewel had given him should have stopped his heart that very night. Just as hers had. Quint secretly wondered if some part of the Actromaton's programming had fought with her driving need for realism. He imagined that maybe she had diluted the deadly stuff—perhaps even in spite of herself. He would never know. Days later, Kingfisher had vanished, taking his now-defunct creation with him. When Agamemnon had gone round to his house, it was only to find the place deserted. As empty as if it had never been occupied.

At any rate, Quint was alive.

In fits and starts, he had regained first consciousness and

then his mental faculties—although he still tended to drift a bit in conversations if he didn't concentrate very hard. The paralysis had dissipated, eventually, and his muscles regained their strength and suppleness. But Quintillius Farthing's wasn't the only miraculous recovery.

The Aurora was back in business. The over-capacity crowd that had paid wildly inflated prices to see the spectacle of the Actromaton's first—and, sadly, last—performance had given the company a tremendous boost. And not just financially. While Quint had been convalescing, Agamemnon had announced a casting call for an entirely new production. Still Shakespeare, of course, but a comedy this time—*All's Well That Ends Well*. Actors and actresses—real ones, talented ones—had returned to Palace Row to sign up for auditions now that the Aurora once again had the money to pay.

Agamemnon asked Quint to run them.

It was near the end of the day when she walked in. Silhouetted in the dwindling light of the late afternoon, all Quint saw was a glint of coppery curls underneath a stylish feather bonnet, and the hourglass contours of corset and skirts. His breath caught in his throat. But then the young woman stepped inside the doorway and he blinked and took a slow step toward her.

"I hope I'm not too late," said the girl in a sweetly musical voice.

Quint rushed forward, extending a hand. "Not at all . . . Miss . . . ?"

"My name is Sapphy," she said, smiling, reaching forward to take Quint's hand in her own small, warm one. "It's short for Sapphire . . ."

A jewel, Quint thought. The pang in his heart was fleeting as he bent low over her hand and then raised his eyes. She blushed prettily and he led the lovely young actress toward the stage saying, "And what piece would you like to read for me today, Miss Sapphire?"

He smiled when she chose something *not* from *Romeo and Juliet*, and he settled back in his seat to watch.

The Cannibal Fiend of Rotherhithe

BY FREWIN JONES

PART THE FIRST

Hector MacAlindon and the North Sea Mermaid

NOW, WHEN A person hears the word *mermaid*, certain images will probably unfurl themselves across the mythic canvas of their mind, perhaps of silky sirens frolicking amidst the billows of the cobalt-blue sea, laughing and sporting with dolphins and flying fish. Or maybe they might conjure a picture of a beautiful woman seated upon a rock contemplatively combing her flowing tresses, her lips rich and red, her eyes ocean-green and filled with arcane knowledge, her long tail iridescent with shining scales, the pale flukes spread like webbed fingers, slapping idly at the foam.

Or if they're of a mind to fear such things, perhaps they will imagine a dark and stormy night, the moon shrouded in a veil of lace, mariners peering with puckered brows into a deep booming darkness flecked with white: the grinning teeth of surf on oil-black and sharp-fanged rocks. And they cock an ear and hear sweet dulcet voices calling, calling. And they leap overboard for the heady delight of it and are seen nevermore.

The reality, as it turns out, is somewhat different, as Hector MacAlindon discovered one dark night.

Not that Hector Mac ever had a mind for the fantastic or the wonderful. Hector was a dull, grimy, grim, gloomy, practical shred of a man. He lived alone in a cottage on a cliff that overlooked the bitter wastes of the English North Sea. Well, I call it a cottage, but hovel would be a better word for the dilapidated heap of mouldering stone and slate where he lived in dour isolation. The cracks between the stones were stuffed with rags and clods of mud, but the wind still fingered its way in on cold winter nights, plucking at Hector's threadbare blankets, insinuating its way into bed beside him, holding him in its arctic embrace and freezing his feet to shards of blue ice.

And he had no wife to warm his thin bones, no woman to light his lamps and heat the grey stew in his Crock-pot, no gentle hand to soothe his brow when he came home after a long shift, dog-tired and sick at heart. No fleshy body to lie between him and the biting north wind. He was quite alone, and it gnawed at him.

Hector MacAlindon eked out a meagre existence as an undersea trawler-man. Every evening he'd make his way down the cliff path to the long strand where the massive black submersibles stood like beached whales between the wooden groynes, their high, thin smokestacks lifting to the clouded heavens like the lone and mute pipes of some broken-down old church organ. The ugly submersibles stank of stale brine and rotting seaweed, and of engine oil and coal, their great copper-clad hulks stamped with barnacles and crawling with crabs and starfish.

Every evening it would be Hector's duty to climb the slimy rail to the porthole door and clamber in and spin the wheel to make the seal watertight.

Then he would make his way through the labyrinth of machinery, ducking the hanging hawsers, avoiding the hissing and spitting steam pipes, checking the dials and meters and gauges and the pistons and cylinders and pumps to make sure the stokers had done their jobs right, and that the furnaces were blazing.

Finally, he'd settle into the pilot's seat and pull the levers and trim the gyres and set the ratchets clanking. The engines would begin to rumble and roar and grey smoke would belch from the tall smokestacks as the undersea trawler crawled its way down the filthy sand and slowly sank beneath the waves until all that remained above the water were the five black chimney-tops trailing their thick ashy plumes.

He remembered, years back, when he'd been an apprentice—in those days the undersea trawlers had names and personalities and were crewed by a jolly bunch of old salts. But these days there was just him and the weary, complaining engines and the gaping bell-shaped mouth of the trawler and the catch-tanks that filled with the swirl of black water, and the corroding filters and the holding pens into which the fish were spat. And there was the noise, of course: the never-ending, mind-shredding noise of the steam engines clanking and clanging and shrieking and raving.

And no hope of a cool hand to soothe his brow at the end of his twelve-hour shift. No wife to give him ease. No joy.

Except for that one unbelievable night when something large and fierce came shooting into the catch-tank, screaming and thrashing and writhing and wailing.

Hector slammed his hand down on the KILL button and the whole shuddering and booming contraption came to a sudden halt on the seabed. At first he thought a person had been caught by the suction pumps. A swimmer, dragged under by the rip of the in-drawn water. But at night? At this depth? In winter?

More alarmed that he might get the blame for the person's

death than fearing for the safety of the victim, Hector scuttled down the vertical iron stair and ran breathlessly along the ramps and gantries and corridors in the guts of the machine until he stood staring down into the rush and flurry of the half-filled catch-tank.

A pale, fearful face peered up at him from the belly of the water. Long dark hair hung lank about the head. The eyes were huge and luminous. A hand reached up pitifully.

Hector leaned as far over the rail as he dared and snatched at the hand. Cold! Cold as death! But he held on and lugged the terrified woman up out of the water, his eyes filling with salt spray so that he could hardly see. He managed to grab the woman around the waist as she came over the rail and a moment later the weight of her threw him onto his back and the air was beaten out of his lungs. She felt strangely slimy in his grip. She floundered about on top of him for a moment then he heard a dull thud and the woman became still. He guessed she had bumped her head on some hard iron protuberance and that the jolt had rendered her unconscious.

Gathering his wits, Hector pushed the limp form off himself and got to his feet. The light was not good down there, the wall lamps occluded by years of grime and oily smears. But the illumination was adequate enough for Hector MacAlindon to trust his eyes as he stared down at that sinuous, supine shape, still shedding water as it lay immobile at his feet.

From the waist up, she was of human shape, but from the hips down she was all fish, grey-scaled and limned with pale phlegm-coloured fins. Trembling from the shock, Hector Mac crouched at the thing's side and turned her onto her back. His stomach churned and he started away.

Close up, the face was far from human. In fact, he found the sight of the mermaid's face all the more disgusting because it was neither pure fish nor—Watt help him—pure human! It was an ugly, blue-skinned, blubber-lipped, goggle-eyed mixture of human and fish, with long thin tentacles or feelers twitching at the side of the down-curved mouth. And the hair was rank and flat like shredded seaweed, and she stank and froth bubbled down her chin. A necklace of blue periwinkle shells hung about her thick neck, but otherwise, she was naked.

Recovering a little, Hector Mac came down on his knees at her side, brushing the slithery hair away from her blue upper body and gazing ruminatively at the small blue-tipped bosom that was revealed. He lifted her limp arm and examined the bony white fingers with their translucent webbing in between.

The mermaid was breathing. He watched her for a while, wondering whether she would drown of air, like fish did.

Time passed and she did not. A thought burrowed through his brain like a satanic weevil. A smile crooked the corner of his mouth.

"You stay there, my girl," he said, his voice creaky because he had not used it for so long. "You're a gift from the deep, that's what you are. I'm going to take you home. You're not many a man's idea of the perfect wife, but I'm not a fussy fellow, and you'll do for me, oh, yes you will. You'll do for me just fine."

And with that, he went lurching along the gantry in search of some stout rope and a large canvas sack.

• • •

I'll not dwell too much on the life Hector MacAlindon and his new-trawled wife led in the cottage on the cliffs. They had little in common and he had to keep a rope around her tail to stop her from escaping. She had no language, so far as he could make out, communicating in high-pitched squeaks and clicks and whoops, and showing her displeasure with snapping teeth and pinching fingers and sometimes with a whack of her thick, strong tail that would tip her husband base over apex and throw him across the room. But she learned quickly not to do that. Hector wasn't much of a man, but he knew how to wield a burning stick, and the mermaid was terribly afraid of fire and screamed like a banshee when her skin sizzled.

But it taught her to be dutiful and Hector found that she did not need to be kept wet, which was a blessing when he came home in the weary morning and slipped into bed beside her.

And here's where I draw a veil, except to say that somehow the mermaid became pregnant, and after four swollen months of pain and grief and shrieking a girl-child was born and the mermaid died of it and her husband dragged her to the cliff edge and tipped her over so that she fell, rag-limp, down into the foaming brine without even a whispered farewell from her cold-hearted spouse.

The mermaid's child seemed more human than aquatic, with white skin and two legs and no fins that her father could see. Hector cut raw seal blubber into thin strips to feed her, and she seemed to like it. He made her a playpen prison of wooden slats and chicken wire, and clamped a chain around her left leg and fed her on fish heads and entrails and on snails and slugs and stagnant water, working on the basis that even this squalling brat was better company than none at all. And although there was little about her that gave away the secret of her fishy maternal line, when she teethed, the teeth were white and needle-thin and pointed like the teeth of a pike, and her mouth was full of them.

He found the periwinkle shell necklace among the folds of his bedclothes and he gave it to the babe to play with, and it quietened her crying. To assuage his solitude he would speak to the infant, and so he learned that she could understand him and form words. And he called her Silka and grew a little fond of her, so long as she behaved herself and did exactly as she was told. He kept her captive in the cottage as her infancy passed and she turned into a young girl with skin like blue-veined ivory and hair so black that in a certain light it seemed almost ultramarine.

And she took to wearing her mother's necklace about her slender throat. And she had quick wits and learned fast and was deft with her long slender nimble fingers. And she had large grey eyes and wide cheekbones and a narrow little chin, and sometimes she even smiled and looked almost pretty as she peered out between the curtains of her oil-black hair. Just so long as she smiled with her lips closed and kept her dreadful teeth hidden away.

The years passed and Silka was fifteen-years-old and still she had never left the cottage, although she often gazed wistfully through the small windows at the sky and the cliffs and the rolling green hills. When he was in a good mood, her father would set a fire of beech wood in the hearth and he would cut herrings longwise and open them up like butterflies and hang them in the aromatic smoke and feed her portions of smoked kipper, while he told her far-fetched tales of the wide and wonderful world. She loved the taste of the smoked fish and wished she got to eat it more often.

He spoke to her of her mother, although never the truth, saying instead that she was a fine lady from a big house and that evil misfortune had sundered them, and that all there was of her now was the necklace of blue periwinkle shells. And when her father told these stories, Silka would clutch at the necklace and weep for the mother she had never known.

At other times, he would speak of the filthy fishing port of Grimsby that lay to the north, but more often of the wonderful sun-baked southlands and of London Town where the streets were paved with gold and where everyone could find their true love.

Hector had no real idea of what a true love might be, but he had heard tell of it once, and coveted the idea of it in his hard and leathery heart.

"I would like to see the wide world," she'd say. "I would like to go to London Town and find my true love. When will I get to go there, Papa? Will you take me some day?"

"In good time," he would reply, meaning never.

And then Hector MacAlindon made a fatal mistake.

One bright spring morning, when the wicked sap was rising in him, he mistook his daughter for his wife and Silka reacted badly. Affronted and enraged, she snatched up a kitchen knife and plunged it three times into her father's neck. Then she sat back on her heels, watching the gush of blood turn to a thick trickle. She dabbled her fingers in the red ooze, and not having been taught better, licked the blood off and rather liked it. Then she leaned down to her dead father's neck and bit and chewed and liked that even more.

I draw another veil here, except to say that once she had eaten her fill, it took Silka some hours to finally prize herself loose of the leg shackles. Able to move freely at last, she went through her father's belongings, discovering his best Sunday suit, tucked away and reeking of camphor. He was a small man, and she was a lanky girl, and while the white shirt and black waistcoat and trousers were too big for her, they weren't *so* much too big that she couldn't wear them. She looped a black tie at her neck and pulled the black frockcoat over all, regarding her reflection in the dull shine of a tin plate.

"Quite the dandy," she said tonelessly, remembering how her father had sometimes put this suit on and paraded up and down in front of her, saying those very words. "Who'd have thought it to see me in my work clothes? Quite the dandy!"

Then she tied up some raw fish and meat in a piece of rag, kicked the cottage door off its rusty hinges and stepped out on a lovely, glowing, clear-skied noontide and saw daffodils dancing and heard seagulls calling.

She walked to the cliff edge. For a moment she gazed out wistfully over the sea. Her fingers slipped inside the collar of her shirt and caressed the tiny ridges of her lost mother's periwinkle shell necklace. But even on a bonny spring day, the North Sea is grey and dispiriting, so with a melancholy feeling that she did not quite understand, she turned her face to the south and set forth to learn about the wide world.

PART THE SECOND

Silka Sallies Forth to London Town

Silka strode the wild hills with a light heart and a spring in her step, hoping and expecting to catch a glimpse of London Town as she crested each hilltop, disappointed that she did not but determined that it would lie beyond the next. Or the next. Or—please Watt—the *next*!

Her father had often described London Town to her—its soaring steeples and lofty domes, its teeming streets, its wise and courteous citizens, gliding from mansion house to coffee shop, tipping their hats, smoking cigars and speaking of philosophy and of the natural sciences. And he had told her of the mechanical marvels of the great dirigible harbour at Alexandra Palace and of the ornithopter ports at Biggin Hill and Croydon. Of river bridges that rose to let the steamships through to the wharfs and quays—steamships laden to the portholes with all the treasures of the British Empire.

She could see it in her mind already. She could almost feel the golden paving stones under her bare feet. Alas, but her trammelled life had not given her any real sense of the size of the world, and so she suffered disappointment after dis- appointment as the day dwindled and the evening came gliding in on feathered wings.

The first human habitation she came upon was the village of Scartho, although she didn't know its name. She stood on a hilltop in the deepening twilight and looked down on a small cluster of buildings with windows that shone with yellow and white gaslight.

Full of hope, she made her way down the long hill and found a beaten and rutted road that led a winding way into the heart of the village.

She approached a stable and discovered a man grooming a horse by the light of a hanging oil lamp. She had never seen a horse. It was very large. Very extraordinary. Oh, the marvels of the world! She wondered what it would taste like.

She stood in front of the man, waiting for him to look at her. She had been taught not to speak until spoken to. She had no wish to be beaten.

After a short while the man turned from his work with the grooming brushes. He stared her up and down, his face growing puzzled.

"Do you want something, lass?" he asked.

"My name is Silka MacAlindon and I am going to London Town to find my true love," she replied.

The man grinned. "Are you, indeed?" he said. "You've a fair old step ahead of you, if that's your aim."

"Truly?" Silka replied, a little crestfallen. "Is it very far, then?"

The man rubbed his stubbly chin, staring down at her

grimy bare feet. "If you're walking, lass, you'll be ten days on the road, for sure," he told her. "But if you took a road train, I dare say you could be there within a day," he added. "But the road trains don't run through Scartho. You'd need to get to Scunthorpe and pick up the Iron Road there."

Silka looked solemnly at him. "I don't know what a road train is," she said. "And I have never heard of Scunthorpe. Is it far?"

"Far enough, if you're on foot," said the man.

"How do I get there?"

He pointed westwards. "Scunthorpe lies that way," he said. "Follow the road through Keelby Town and Limber and Kirmington, through Wrawby and Brigg and Sawby Brook, and you will get to Scunthorpe . . . in the end."

"Thank you, I will," said Silka.

The man took a step forward, looking closely at her. "You've a bonny face, Silka MacAlindon. Are you travelling alone?"

"I am," Silka replied.

He smiled. "Dressed in your big brother's cast offs, eh? I'll bet there's a story there, lass. Are you a runaway? Are you hungry? Would you like a bite to eat before you set off?"

"I am and I would!" Silka declared, spreading her lips and giving the man a wide, friendly smile.

Alarm flashed across his face and he took a stumbling step backwards. "Watt save us! What are you?" he gasped.

"I am Silka MacAlindon," she said, confused.

"You're some manifestation," cried the man, clearly frightened now, starting to panic. "You're the Pale Girl of Accrington or the ghost of Anne Mort, you are! Some evil thing from out the hills! Get away from me!"

Silka reached out a hand, unsettled by the man's behaviour.

He backed off, stumbled and fell. "Demons!" he howled at the top of his voice. "Demons from hell! Help! Help me!"

Doors and windows opened, feet began to run. Voices called from out of the gloaming.

"It's Nathan Switcher! He sounds fair frit to death!"

"Is that you, Nathan? What's the matter, lad?"

Silka spun, her eyes darting from side to side as a ring of people closed in on her from all directions in the twilight. One or two carried pitchforks, another clutched a meat cleaver, and one glowering man held an odd contraption of iron and wood in his hands.

Silka lowered her head, hissing and spitting, her eyes narrowed in watchful fear, her fingers curled. She had no idea, of course, of what a fearsome sight she made to the disturbed populace of that small village.

The circle of terrified people halted at the full sight of her in the lamplight. Surely she had to be some demonic thing spewed up from the bowels of the earth. For sure and certain, she was not human. Just take a look at those *teeth*!

The man with the iron and wooden contrivance lifted it to his shoulder, pointing a bell-shaped black tube toward her. There was a flash of blue light and a loud bang. Something hot slashed past Silka's face, grazing her cheek. Hurting her.

She howled and threw herself away from the fiery contraption. A man with a wooden club barred her way. She sprang high like a leaping salmon, coming down on him with all her weight. He collapsed under her. She dipped her head to his neck and bit hard. There was blood and flesh in her mouth for an instant, then she bounced to her feet and fled away along the darkened street and off up into the high hills again.

• • •

She was in the hills, lying on her back under a starry sky, panting still from her exertions. She had run a very long way before finally collapsing in the grass. She rubbed the sore spot on her cheek where the hot thing had scorched her skin. She would be wary of approaching people again. They were not to be trusted—and they carried dangerous weapons.

But a lesson had been learned. Don't smile at people—you have the teeth of a pike! Your father told it to you often enough, you fool! Keep those teeth behind closed lips unless you want the whole world to scream bloody murder whenever they see you.

She caught a hare and ate it raw and still warm, then slept, curled among tree-roots. The night was cold, but she was hardened to that. Tomorrow she must seek Scunthorpe and learn what road trains were.

• • •

The little huddled villages were threaded along the slushy spring-wet road like knuckles of flint stamped into the green land. Silka skirted them, preferring to avoid any more encounters than was strictly necessary for her to get to London Town. Once there, she felt sure the cultured and courteous people of the sun-drenched City of Gold would help her to find her true love. And then all would be well.

It was the foul air that first alerted her to the fact that she was closing in on the industrial town of Scunthorpe. She sniffed, not knowing what she was smelling, but not liking it much.

Nothing Silka had encountered so far prepared her for the sight and smell and din of Scunthorpe. It lay in a wide valley, black as evil, shrouded in a cowl of dense swirling cloud. Iron and brick structures thrust up like broken fists and fingers into the underbelly of the smoggy sky, belching more filth, spreading their stain over the cerulean blue of the heavens. And like a vile effulgence, red and yellow fires would spurt up at random from various parts of the hellish place, briefly staining the cloud with a hectic, horrible brightness before sinking back down again like dragons spent of flame.

Through the haze, bulbous shapes drifted to and fro above the town. Silka guessed they were the dirigibles of which her father had sometimes spoken—great elongated bags of gas, ribbed and hung with gondolas, powered by grinding engines, gouting steam and sparks as they cruised like airborne pigs, filled with passengers and cargoes.

And other, smaller flying things buzzed through the clouds, like black beetles, hovering and darting, rising and dipping. Ornithopters ferrying folk about, their curved wings beating the air, their exhaust pipes spewing more filth into the polluted sky.

Silka stood stark on a hilltop on a sweet spring afternoon and stared into the gaping maw of hell on earth. But for good or bad, she must enter the black pit of Scunthorpe to get to London Town.

She made her way down the road. Be polite. Don't smile. And be ready to run if things go awry.

• • •

There were few people on the cobbled streets, and those she met ignored her or moved away to avoid her as she approached them. And they hadn't even seen her teeth! They simply distrusted strangers, she decided.

At length she came to the mouth of a narrow alley. She heard singing and was drawn to it. A straggle of men and women stood around an open doorway. A rank, peculiar smell billowed out. It was an inn and the smell was beer, but Silka knew nothing of either. Her father had been a gin drinker. When he could afford it.

"I'm sorry to bother you," Silka began, approaching a man with his arm around the shoulders of a buxom woman with copper-coloured hair and a bloated, painted face. "Could you direct me to the road train, please."

The man and the woman stared at her for a moment then laughed. They called the others over and soon Silka was surrounded by people, grinning and staring and occasionally plucking at her clothes as though she was a great curiosity to them.

"Where have you come from, my girl?" asked one man, running dirty fingers along the lapel of her frock coat.

"From the north," Silka replied. "My name is Silka MacAlindon and I am going to London to seek my true love. I am told I should use the road train. Could you direct me to the road train?"

"Well, you're a strange one," said the painted woman. "London, indeed! I never did! And what's with the clothes, dearie? You look neither one thing nor another! A little he-she, that's what you are—and barefoot to boot."

There was more laughter and it sounded mocking to Silka and she did not much like it. She lost her temper a little.

"I ate my father because he angered me," she said quietly, looking hard at the woman. "But I would not eat you, woman, I think you would taste rank and rancid. I wouldn't drink your blood if I was dying of thirst!"

There was laughter at this as well, but it sounded more hesitant, and the painted woman did not laugh at all, but stared at Silka in astonishment. "Well, I never!" she declared at last. "What a thing to say. The saucy minx."

"I'll box her ears!" announced the man at her side. "That'll teach her to give cheek to her elders and betters."

He squared up to Silka and was about to launch a blow at her—which may have been the last action he ever took in this world—when a loud voice sounded from beyond the boozy congregation.

"What's all this? Leave the girl alone!" A tall, wide-shouldered man pushed through the small throng. He had a rugged, handsome face and crinkly blue eyes. "Get inside, you blowsy good-for-nothings, before I take a piston rod to the lot of you."

Grumbling and muttering, the crowd slunk away through the doorway and Silka was left alone with the big man.

"Don't mind them, lass," he said. "They don't mean any harm." He eyed her with a faint smile. "Now then, what's your tale? You look no more than a child, despite wearing your father's Sunday best. Off to London to find wealth and fame, are you?"

Silka smiled cautiously at him, lips pressed together. "I am going to London, but not for wealth or fame." She looked hopefully at him. "First I must find the road train that will take me there."

The man tapped his broad chest. "I'm Royston Hoof, I am—and I can tell you all there is to know about road trains, lass, if you've a mind." His face opened up into a big friendly smile. "And how can that be, you're asking yourself? It's plain enough, lass. I drive one!"

• • •

The Marshalling Yard was huge under the cloud-clogged night sky. Great lamps shone down from tall posts set at intervals along the perimeter fence, smearing shadows in all directions.

"We're not allowed passengers," Royston Hoof had told her as they had slipped together through a side gate in the high wire fence. "So keep quiet and out of sight till they've finished loading my train." He had pointed to one of several vast dark iron snakes that stretched along the yard. "That's the *William Murdoch*. My train. I'm going to leave you now. When you hear two blasts from the horn, you'll know I'm good to go. Make your way quietly to the gateway yonder, and with luck, we'll be on the road as sweet as a whistle."

He had left her and she had settled herself on a heap of plump sacks on a pallet in between two of the beaming lamps. The Marshalling Yard was a ferment of activity. Wheeled and tracked vehicles scampered and scurried here and there, laden with freight for the trains. Men laboured by the dozen, winding winches and hauling crates and swinging cranes as they filled the gaping mouths of the long string of black carriages attached to each of the rumbling and steaming road trains.

The engines themselves were great snub-nosed machines, their backs higher than the rooftops of the nearby ware-houses, squatting like immense fat black sows on rows of iron wheels, enveloped in veils of white steam, shuddering and grumbling as though eager to be on their way.

Silka found the sight of them both exciting and scary. Less scary, though, when she saw Royston Hoof climbing up to the high cab that projected above the back of the engine of the *William Murdoch*. He looked tiny as he clambered into the cab, like a flea crawling into a dog's ear.

One by one the carriages of the *William Murdoch* were slammed closed and bolted. A jet of white steam spurted up. A moment later there was a haunting double hoot, deep and resonant. Silka got to her feet as she watched the road train begin to inch forward. More steam. Rumbling and roaring. The grind and clank of iron wheels on an iron floor.

She slipped along the fence and watched the road train

coming. She cringed a little as it ground past her, its wheels taller than her, the black bulk creeping alongside her like a moving mountain. She snatched at the lowest iron staple and hung on for grim life as her feet were whipped from under her. Steam eddied around her body, hot and wet. She climbed swiftly like a fly on a wall.

Feeling a little dizzy, she came to the cab and dragged herself inside. Royston Hoof smiled at her and yanked on a chain. The horn let out three melancholic blasts.

"All aboard who's coming aboard," Royston declared, pulling a lever that brought an iron shutter down over the entrance Silka had used. "Next stop, London Town."

The large black leather seat was easily wide enough to accommodate both Royston and Silka. She sat at his side, feeling the engine vibrating under her as he explained the banks of controls that spread in front of them.

He spoke of running gears and of axel rods and driving wheels. He pointed to levers and treadles and knobs and triggers, explaining how they operated the tender's conveyer belts, bringing coal to the fireboxes, and he pointed out more gauges and dials that showed the automated steam pressure and water levels in the storage tanks.

And all the while that he spoke, she did her best to pay attention and nod and look like she understood even a shred of what he was telling her. And all the while, she had one eye cocked through the wide window above the bank of controls, seeing how the houses and factories of Scunthorpe flew by faster and ever faster as the road train gathered momentum and went roaring away into the night.

"In the old days, there was always a crew of two on a road train," Royston continued. "But then they automated this and mechanized that and pretty soon the machinery was doing half the work." He cocked his head over his shoulder. "See the bunk bed? That was so that one man could catch a nap on longer journeys. Not needed now." He smiled into her face. "Not while we're on the road."

Soon, the thundering road train came out from under the ugly pall of Scunthorpe and Silka was delighted to see a wide starry sky spreading above them, hazed with white steam, of course, and made glorious and spectacular by sparks from the smokestack, looking like shooting stars spat out from the roaring belly of the beast.

There was light enough for Silka to see the iron road that stretched out ahead of them across the rolling countryside. It was twenty feet wide and constructed of jointed slabs of black cast iron. It skirted the hills and vaulted valleys and rivers on high viaducts of wrought iron. Occasionally it would plunge into a black tunnel, and the darkness would roar and seethe and smoke would filter into the cab and all conversation would be rendered impossible.

"What is that?" Silka asked, pointing to a flare of eerie blue light that whisked and wavered on a far hilltop ahead of them.

"Do you not know, Silka?" Royston asked in obvious surprise. "Why, that's Teslagraph, that is. Have you never seen it before?"

"Never," breathed Silka, enchanted and intrigued. As they closed in on the lights, she saw that they were atop a dark tower—the flaring electric-blue lights attached to the far ends of long moving arms. The four arms were in constant motion, spinning this way and that, leaving a bright blue stain in the air that shimmered and died, flared, shimmered and died. And far off, another set of lights swished and swept in the darkness. And another, and another, all across the countryside.

"What are they for?" Silka asked.

"They send messages," said Royston, looking askance at

her. "Silka? Where do you come from that you've never seen Teslagraph before?"

"I would rather not speak of it," Silka said. "It's enough to say I will never go back there. My mother died giving birth to me, and my father . . . died . . . of . . . of *sin*. I have no one. I am going to London to find my true love." She looked at him and smiled carefully. "And you are my friend for taking me there. My only friend."

"I hope I shall be, Silka," said Royston. "I hope you'll let me be a good friend to you. I truly do."

There was a slightly odd light in his eyes as he said this, but Silka decided it was just the reflections of the swirling blue Teslagraph and thought nothing more of it.

• • •

The road train thundered on through the night, its plume of steam outdoing the clouds, its gush of sparks outshining the stars as it hammered its way down the spine of England. Silka became used to the noise and the endless vibration and she even dozed off.

She awoke at the touch of a hand moving spiderlike on her thigh.

She sat up from an unintentional sleep. Royston Hoof smiled at her and his hand was gone from her leg.

"It's almost dawn, sleepyhead," Royston said. "We'll be in London soon." His eyes pierced her. "And how might you wish to recompense me for bringing you all this way, Silka?"

She rubbed her eyes, trying to gather her drowsy wits. "I have no money," she replied uneasily. "I have nothing."

His smile widened and he seemed heartily entertained by her. "I don't want your money, my pretty," he laughed. "And it's not true to say you have nothing. You have something I would like very much indeed."

Silka frowned at him. "And what might that be?"

"The smile of a pretty girl," said Royston Hoof, a thin white light coming into his eyes as the sun crept over the horizon and the shadows of night fled into the west. "I have kept the throttle on full all the way, and we're an hour early. What say we stop for a while and . . ." he tipped his head toward the bunk bed behind the big leather seat, ". . . and you let me be your friend a while longer."

Oh, the wickedness and perfidy of the world! Would she never learn?

"And if I say no?" Silka asked quietly.

"I am stronger than you, my pretty." His eyes hardened to blue diamond. "I will be your friend, Silka, whether you wish it or no. Did you not come to London to find true love? I'll show it to you, by my lights, I will."

Silka lowered her head and for a moment her black hair fell over her face. She wasn't afraid of him, but she was terribly disappointed.

"You want a smile, do you?" she asked in a subdued voice. "A smile and a kiss?"

"For starters," said Royston Hoof.

Silka lifted her face and the dark curtain of her hair was swept back as she spread her lips. "Then you shall have them!" she said. "You shall have them in abundance!"

• • •

It occurred to Silka that she might have been wiser to have let Royston Hoof bring the road train to a halt before the smile and the kiss. She stood in the cab, wiping her bloody mouth on her sleeve and watching the world flash past. They were climbing a long hillside into a dawn-white sky. The horizon was closing in on her and she had no idea how to stop the road train.

But she did remember the lever Royston had used to bring the shutter down over the entrance. She pushed it and heard it click and saw the slab of dark iron rise. More early light flooded the cab, turning the spilled blood to copper and making the train driver's eyes glow with fake life.

She moved to the entrance. The wind whipped her hair and tore at her clothes. The crest of the hill was fast approaching. She climbed down the ladder of iron hoops. Steam hissed at her and sparks flew past. At the side of the iron trackway, grass grew thick and lush.

Silka hung for a moment then leaped. She hit the ground hard, rolling and rolling, her limbs tucked up as she bounced and bounded like a flung stone in the road train's wake.

She got to her feet, dizzy and aching. The last of the carriages were thundering past her; the front of the train had dipped over the breast of the hill.

She jogged along the black iron track, smelling hot iron and coal dust and smoke.

A wonderful sight met her eyes as she came to the hilltop. Nestled in a deep river-threaded valley, glowing like gold in the day's early light, was a huge city of towers and spires and steeples and domes. And sailing gloriously above the town in skies of purest blue were a host of dirigibles and steam-balloons and airships and ornithopters, brightly coloured, trailing flags and pennants, shining in the new-risen sun and more miraculous and beautiful and alluring than Silka had ever dared to hope.

"London Town!" she sighed, for truly the vision before her eyes could be none other.

And as she stood there astounded and amazed and delighted and thrilled, the road train went thundering down the black iron track, gathering speed all the time, and with its dead driver at the helm.

PART THE THIRD

Tobias Hart and the Beadle of Bow

Illustrated London News, 25 April:

HORRIFIC ROAD TRAIN CRASH AT ST. PANCRAS
A most terrible accident occurred on Friday last when the
William Murdoch, *a fully laden road train travelling over-*
night from Scunthorpe, dashed into St. Pancras Terminus in
North London at high speed, smashing through the barriers and
exploding, killing fourteen officers and workers and causing an
extensive fire. The crash of the collision was heard throughout
North London and the dreadful light of the resulting con-
flagration could be seen for many miles. The body of the driver,
Mr. Royston Emanuel Hoof, an experienced road train engineer,
was utterly destroyed in the disaster, and to date no explanation
has been forthcoming with regards to how this terrible event could
have come to pass.

• • •

London Times, 9 August:

CANNIBALISTIC FIEND AT LARGE IN ROTHERHITHE
The police investigation of the deaths of up to fifteen male
residents of the Rotherhithe area of London took a gruesome turn
in the early hours of Monday morning when officers were called
to an address in Stew Lane. The building was an abandoned
warehouse from which strange-smelling smoke had been exuding
for several days. Upon entering an upper room in the building,
police officers were confronted by an appalling sight. The bodies
of several men were found, hanging upside down over a low fire
and engulfed in the rising smoke. Initial reports from the shaken

officers suggested that the scene resembled nothing less than a food-curing smokehouse, and that the bodies appeared to be in the process of being prepared for consumption. The perpetrator of this abomination was not at the scene at the time of the police incursion, and although several officers secreted themselves in the building, he did not return.

Although no proof has been forthcoming, the more sensational organs of the gutter press have already termed the killer "Jack the Kipper," ghoulishly referencing the Whitechapel murders of the recent past.

If these remains are indeed the work of the same cannibalistic killer whose fearful activities have blighted the streets of Rotherhithe over the summer months, then we urge the Beadle of Bow to redouble his efforts in capturing this fiend and bringing him to swift and final justice.

• • •

"I have you this time, Toby Hart. I have you to the rightabouts, sure and simple!"

The Beadle's fruity voice, aggrandized to a bullish roar by a megaphone, reached Toby as he squatted precariously on the sloping rooftop. "Give yourself up, or face the consequences, Toby Hart. I will not warn you a second time!"

Toby inched closer to the forty-foot drop and peered down into the dark alley. Large, tripod-mounted teslights beamed up at him, blue and eerie in the deep of the night. There had to be a dozen or more Runners down there with the dratted Beadle—and he guessed even more of the Bluebottles were probably already in the building, swarming up the stairs—cutting off his retreat.

And all for a Kennedy's pork pie.

Toby licked his lips. It had almost been worth it. Almost.

"Toby Hart, surrender yourself now!"

Toby leaned a little further over the edge. "I thought you weren't going to warn me again," he called down. "Make your mind up." He could see the Beadle's big tricorn hat of office, its silver badge shining in the electric blue light. He plucked a clod of muck from the gutter and slung it down.

"Rats!" It missed the Beadle, splatting instead on the tunic of some lesser Runner.

He heard a scraping noise at his back. He snapped his head around. The helmet, face and shoulders of a bearded Bluebottle were emerging through the skylight a little way up the roof. An arm came up and a blue spark flickered.

The Bluebottle was armed with a vorpal lance. Nasty things. They could send lightning crackling through the air—accurate to twenty feet or more in experienced hands.

The Bluebottle aimed the vorpal lance and a thin tongue of flickering blue-white electricity stabbed through the air. Toby flung himself flat and the searing lash of electricity exhausted itself a fraction above his head.

Good. Now he had a short amount of time while the Bluebottle had to rewind the lance to recharge it. He saw the man's arm working as he twisted the key. He heard the familiar clockwork whizzing noise.

He got to his feet. He took three wobbly steps away from the edge of the roof, his eyes fixed on the guttering on the roof opposite. It was a long jump, but if he hesitated he might as well resign himself to a life chained up in the Floating Hulks—the prison dirigibles that hung like black-hearted storm clouds above the Thames Estuary—because that would be his only other option.

"Don't do it, lad!" he heard the Bluebottle call.

"I think I will," he shouted back.

And then he did. His heart pounding, he bounded forward

and leaped. For a long, long while he hung over fathoms of blue air, windmilling his arms, pedalling furiously with his feet, willing his thin body to keep moving forward.

Then the far rooftop came smacking hard into his chest. He snatched at a rusty iron spike. He scrambled and scrabbled and somehow slithered up onto the roof. Through the ringing in his ears, he heard shouting and bellowing from below.

He went up the slope of slate on all fours like a monkey. He straddled the spine of the roof, waved once to the infuriated Bluebottle behind him, then drew his trailing leg over and went racing off into the night, rooftop to rooftop, cupola to gable to parapet to peak, bounding away over the smoky roofscapes of London Town until all fear of capture was far behind him.

Grinning to himself, he spotted a handy skylight, blinded by a century of grime. He took out his knife and prised it open. He could see nothing through the black hole. But he'd already faced down death and worse this night—what did he have to fear here?

He lowered himself into the square hole. Finally he hung for a few moments by his fingers before releasing his grip and dropping into the dense darkness.

It was not a long fall, and he landed, fortunately, on something soft.

Or maybe not so fortunately.

The soft thing let out a high-pitched yell and twisted under his feet, tossing him headlong to the floor and sending the knife spinning out of his hand. Something quick and lithe and very strong pinned him down. The narrow beam of a hand-held teslight burned into his face, making him blink and pull his head away from the sudden brightness.

"I mean you no harm!" he choked, uncomfortably aware of a vice-like grip at his throat. "On my word!"

"Is that so?" said a sharp female voice. "And what if I mean harm to *you*?"

Toby couldn't see the face behind the teslight, but he saw the shadowed head dip toward his throat. He heard the girl sniffing him in a very similar way to how he had sniffed the Kennedy's pork pie that he had so unwisely stolen only a few hours previously.

That was disturbing in so many ways.

"And are you tasty, boss?" asked the girl. "Is your blood sweet?"

There was cold laughter and warm breath on his neck.

And it was in this manner that Tobias Hart made first contact with the Cannibal Fiend of Rotherhithe.

• • •

A rank smell filled Silka's nostrils and she bridled back from the boy's neck. If he tasted as bad as he smelled, she'd rather take a swig from a chamber pot!

"Watt's Wheels, but you stink." she gasped, lifting her head and loosening her grip a fraction. "What is that foul reek?"

"That's low-tide Thames River mud, that is," said the boy.

"It's putrid!" said Silka. "How do you bear it?"

"With honour and fortitude!" replied the boy, and before she could make another move, he jerked his knees up, striking her hard in the stomach and sending her tumbling head over heels across the floor. The beam of her teslight swung wildly, flashing over peeling walls and a mould-encrusted ceiling, over bare rotten boards and over the bundle of ragged blankets upon which Silka had been sleeping.

They were both on their feet and ready for combat in less time than it takes to tell. Silka held the teslight beam steadily on his face. A slither of blue light glinted in his fist. A knife. He was crouching, arms spread, watching her carefully. She had the feeling he would know how to defend himself if it came to a fight between them.

"Were you going to bite me?" the boy asked.

"What's that to you?" Silka retorted.

"A great deal, I'd say," he responded. "I apologize if I frightened you, but I really meant no harm. It was all quite accidental, I assure you."

"Why did you attack me?" asked Silka. "Are you a Runner sent by the Beadle?" She narrowed her eyes. "You don't look like a Runner."

"I'm no Bluebottle, I'll have you know. I was in the act of escaping from them when I came upon you." The boy sounded affronted, and she had to admit he did seem young to be a Runner—in fact, he seemed to be no older than her. His eyes narrowed calculatingly. "And why would the Beadle be sending Runners after you?" he asked slyly.

"For that matter, why would he be sending them after *you*?" asked Silka.

There was a pause, and she got the impression he was thinking hard. "Because I am the Cannibal Fiend of Rotherhithe," he announced. "I kill people and I eat them. So you'd be wise to show me the door and let me go, before I feast on your flesh!"

Silka gave a gasp. "You are *not*!" she declared. "That is such a colossal fib."

"And why are you so certain of that?" the boy asked. "Anyone would think . . ." His voice trailed off. "Oh," he said, as though enlightenment had struck him hard between the eyes. "Ohhh . . ."

There was a protracted silence between them.

"My name is Tobias Hart," the boy said at last. "Toby to friends and enemies alike. I'm a Thames Mudlark, and I can assure you I taste as bad as I smell."

"Silka MacAlindon," Silka replied, bobbing her head politely.
"The Cannibal Fiend of Rotherhithe?"

Silka gave a great sigh. "Apparently so," she said. "But in my own defence, I have eaten almost no one who didn't deserve it." She peered into the boy's bright eyes, shining as blue as sapphire in the teslight beam. "And I have to tell you that I am very disappointed in London Town. The streets are most certainly not made of gold—and I have come nowhere close to finding my true love!"

There was another pensive silence. "Do you dine exclusively on men?" Toby asked. He slid a hand into some pocket in his clothing and drew out a wedge of pie. "Kennedy's make the best pork pies in London," he said, holding out the portion of pie on the flat of his hand. "Try it. It'll taste better than me by far."

Silka edged toward him and snatched the pie out of his hand.

She sat back on her heels and bit into the pie. She chewed thoughtfully.

"Well?" Toby asked.

"Somewhat bland," said Silka. "But pleasant enough in its way." She eyed him. "What is a Thames Mudlark?"

Toby grinned a wide, rascally grin. "We're the lowest of the low, the outcasts of the gutters, the sewer rats, pickpockets, cutthroats and thieves. And I'm one of the best, I am. The fat old Beadle of Bow has been after me for years, but he's never caught me yet. And he never will." He cocked his head like a curious bird. "And what's your story, Silka MacAlindon? Who ever told you the streets of London were paved with gold?"

"My father did, the big liar," said Silka.

"You should pay him back for putting such falsehoods into your head!"

"I already have."

57

"I see," said Toby, and he sounded as if he entirely understood what she meant. "And what about your true love? Does he have a name?"

She frowned at him. "What do you mean?"

"What is the name of the man you love? Surely he has a name?"

"You're talking nonsense," snapped Silka. "My true love is not a person. Why would you think that?"

"If not a man, then what?" Toby asked.

Silka lowered her head. "I don't know," she said.

"Ahhh," said Toby, very quietly. "Ahhh . . ."

• • •

The two young outcasts sat silently at opposite ends of the small shabby attic as the light of dawn began to filter down through the skylight. There were no windows, and the angles of the roof pressed the walls in. A small door crouched under the sloping ceiling.

Silka and Toby eyed each other with wary interest, sensing some affinity between them—understanding instinctively that they both walked a dangerous and dark path. Then Toby pocketed his knife and Silka switched off her teslight and let herself relax a little.

"So," Toby began. "I have an important question for you, Silka MacAlindon."

"And what is that?"

"Are you intending to eat me?"

"Not while you smell the way you do," Silka replied.

"Then I'd best not wash!" he replied, quick as a whip.

Unbidden, a laugh burst out of Silka at the way in which Toby had responded, half in earnest and half in jest.

He started back, his wide eyes fixed on the teeth that her laughter had revealed.

"Well now," he said breathlessly. "You're something different, I must say."

Annoyed with herself, she pressed her lips together, throwing one hand up over her mouth.

He looked solemnly at her and shook his head, lifting his hand to wag an admonishing finger. "Never be ashamed of who you are, Silka. That's the only true rule of this life."

"My teeth repel people," she mumbled.

"My smell revolts people," laughed Toby. "What of it?" He tilted his head and regarded her thoughtfully. "You are not repellent to me, Silka MacAlindon. For three years I earned my crust as a roustabout with Monsewer Pierre Gris and his Caravan of Marvels." His eyes sparkled. "It was a travelling freak show. I'd be with them still if the dratted Beadle hadn't felt my collar at an inappropriate moment." He spread his hands. "So you see, Silka, you're nothing strange to me. I've broken bread and supped porter with people stranger by far than you could ever imagine."

She smiled again, and for the first time she didn't care that her dreadful teeth showed.

"From what I have read in the newspapers about your dietary habits," Toby continued, "do you not like men very much, then?"

Silka felt strangely at ease with this malodorous Mudlark. "I like them well enough," she replied. "I like them fine, smoked for a few days over a fire of beech wood and cut into strips."

There was a long silence between them. Toby was the first to speak. "Eating people is beyond the pale, Silka. It's not done, you know?"

"Then someone should have told me so," said Silka. "I have lived a very sheltered life. I do not know the rules you people live by."

Toby gave her an incredulous look. "It did not occur to you that killing and eating human beings might be a bad thing to do?" he asked.

Silka grinned sheepishly at him. "I did wonder about it," she admitted. "But I only ate unkind men who had evil intent." She gave him a guilty look. "At least, that was how it was at the beginning. The last few men I ate did me no actual harm, but . . ." Her voice trailed away.

". . . but they might have done, yes?" Toby finished her sentence for her. "Men have treated you badly in the past," he added, and it was a statement not a question. "I can see you have consorted with quite the wrong sort of person, Silka. You want to learn the rules we live by? Fine—I'll teach them to you. But you have to stop eating people—beginning with me."

Silka smiled again, her teeth gleaming like a hundred slender knives in the growing daylight. "I will try," she said. "I will try especially hard when it comes to you."

"You must have eaten other things," Toby said. "What else do you like?"

"I like kippered herrings," said Silka.

"Kippered herrings are good," agreed Toby. "How about jellied eels?"

"I don't know."

"You'll like them, for sure. And whelks and cockles and oysters, if we can get them. I'll find good food for you, Silka. Don't worry, I won't let you go hungry. We will be quite the team, you and I. And we'll run rings around the fat Beadle and all of London Town will be our playground." He grinned a wide grin. "What do you say, Silka? Shall we be friends?"

Silka smiled again for joy and nodded and wondered whether in the end at least some of the things her father had told her of London Town might be true. And as she thought of her old life in the cottage on the cliffs, her hand moved to her throat and her fingers reached inside her collar to touch her mother's periwinkle shell necklace.

But the necklace was gone.

She gave a cry as she remembered that the string had snapped as she had attacked her last victim and she had thrust the necklace into the pocket of her frock coat, meaning to mend it later. But then the Beadle's Runners had come and she had fled—leaving the frock coat in a heap on the floor with the precious necklace still in the pocket.

"What's wrong?" asked Toby.

"I left my necklace behind," Silka wailed. "I must go back and get it."

"Go back where?"

"To my room . . . with the fire and the curing meat," Silka said, getting up and heading for the door.

Toby leaped to his feet, snatching at her arm. "Whoa there!" he cried. "Silka—you can't do that. The Beadle has the place staked out. They're waiting for you to go back. They'll nab you for sure."

"I don't care, I must have my necklace," said Silka, tugging at Toby's grip.

"No!"

"*Yes!*"

He looked at her with big, anxious eyes. "Are you cunning, Silka?" he asked. "Are you sly and sneaky and slick and perfidious? Can you arrive like a shadow and leave like a draught of air? Could you pluck the gold teeth from a man's mouth at noon and not have him know they were gone till supper time?" She stared unblinkingly at him. "Are you larcenous, crooked, piratical, and plunderous?" His voice became even more urgent. "In short, Silka MacAlindon, are you a natural-born sticky-fingered thief?"

"I should not imagine so," Silka replied.

"Well, I am," Toby said. "If you are determined to get into your old smokehouse under the beery noses of the Beadle's Bluebottles, and to escape undetected with your mother's necklace, then you need a well-seasoned crook with you." He released her and gave a low, sweeping bow. "I am that malefactor, Silka, and I will help you get your necklace."

She frowned. "Why would you do that?" she asked.

He smiled. "Say it's because I'm a whimsical rapscallion who revels in perilous adventure," he replied. "Or, say it's because I like you. Or, if you prefer, say it's because I want to get one over on the fat Beadle. Take your pick."

She eyed him. "You are a strange fellow," she said. There was a pause and then a wide, crooked grin. "Agreed." she said. "Let's bamboozle the Beadle."

Toby laughed and caught her hand. "Yes," he said. "Let's do exactly that."

• • •

Much against her instincts, Silka allowed Toby to convince her to lie low in the abandoned attic all through the long hours of daylight. Given her way, she would have stormed her old smokehouse and used her murderous teeth to retrieve her necklace. But Toby thought otherwise. Stealth by night was his preferred option, and to be fair, she could see the sense in that.

Making her promise to stay put, he disappeared around mid-morning and returned with his pockets full of swag. It was mostly sausage, cheese, and bread. She quite liked the sausage, and devoured it in great hunks, but the cheese tasted to her like something that had gone bad, and the bread tasted of nothing at all.

They chatted amiably through the afternoon of this and that, and to his astonishment, Toby learned of Silka's part in the Great St. Pancras Road Train Disaster of the early summer. Silka also learned several wonderful and astounding things about her pungent new friend, but as they do not come into this story, and as this yarn is long enough already, I'll leave those revelations for another time.

Often, through the day, they would hear the crackling beat of ornithopter wings above the rooftops, or the steady low hum and whir of a passing dirigible, but apart from that, their little room was oddly quiet, considering that it stood in the heart of the teeming metropolis, and that the people of London Town swarmed all around them like distracted ants.

Dusk came drifting over the city like the ghost of night. As the day died, Silka switched on the teslight she had stolen from her first victim, but its power was running down and it only gave a thin light. Toby kept them there till the sky was as dark as pitch. Then he led Silka out through the small door and down many a winding stair until they came out into a narrow alley.

He turned to her. "Take me to your old home," he said. "And when we get there, trust me to get us in and out safely, and do exactly as I say."

"I will," Silka agreed.

"I will procure for us a length of rope, and then we'll be off." With a grin and a wink and a roguish upturned flip of his collar, Toby slipped away along the cobbled alley with Silka following close behind.

• • •

Silka had never seen the rooftops of London Town by night before. There was a kind of stark beauty to it, she thought, as their thin figures stole, silent as cats, along a high slate ridge and came to rest up against a tall brick-built chimney stack.

The sky was white with low clouds, their plump rounded bellies reflecting the city's light downwards with a soft sheen.

And there were many lights, scattered like jewels over the hard-edged silhouettes of the city. A thousand lights. At least a thousand. There was rosy firelight through windows, bright gas lamps on the streets, Teslagraph arms whirling on towers and hilltops. And slow and majestic above all were the bright coloured lights of the airships that cruised the night sky like fluorescent slugs against the cloud-wrack.

Toby crawled to the edge of the roof. Far below, he saw two men standing in deep shadow. Two men in Bluebottle helmets with vorpal lances at the ready. Smiling, he made his way to the other side of the roof. There was another of the Beadle's men down there, thinking himself so very smart as he lurked in a doorway assuming he could not be seen.

In all, Toby counted seven Bluebottles on watch around the building. And he guessed there would be others inside. He rubbed his hands together and went back to where Silka was waiting for him.

He had already chosen their method of entry. Time and wind and bad weather had prodded a hole in the slate roof. He went to it and used his pocketknife to loosen a few more slates, handing them to Silka as he leaned into the hole with the teslight in his fist. The weak blue beam showed a landing, some twelve feet below his perch.

"Hold my belt," he instructed Silka, and she did so while he leaned further into the opening and secured one end of his rope to a handy beam. He let the rope down and slipped feet-first into the hole, catching the rope between the instep of one shoe and the side of the other. Lowering himself, he signalled Silka to climb down behind him.

They stood together on the landing. Toby brought his lips close to her ear. "Which room?" he whispered.

She pointed along a dark corridor. There was a closed door at the far end.

Again, the lips at her ear and the warm breath on her neck. "Keep close to me and be as quiet as you can."

They padded down the corridor by spectral beam of the teslight. The silence was so intense that Silka's head felt full of thunder. Toby halted and pressed his ear to the door panels. He remained immobile for so long that Silka was about to give him a prod to see that he hadn't dropped dead on his feet, when he turned his face to her and winked. "I hear nothing," he whispered. "Let's go."

He turned the handle. There was creaking and grinding as he pushed the door open. The acrid smell of cold old smoke wafted from the black pit of the room. Along with it came the more pleasant aroma of cured meat, faint now, but still sweet enough to make Silka's mouth water.

No! Bad Silka. Toby says you're not to eat people anymore. Be content with kippers and sausage.

Following close on Toby's heels, Silka entered her old lair.

"The coat," Toby hissed. "Where is it?"

Silka ran to where she remembered dropping the coat. Toby trained the blue light on the floor. There it was, a bundle of black on the carious boards. She hunkered down and rummaged and in a few moments she had the precious necklace in her hand.

She turned, holding it up, seeing with joy how the periwinkle shells shone and sparkled in the teslight beam.

"I have it!" she declared, thrusting it into a pocket.

"Good. Now, let's get out of here before we get caught."

"I think not," boomed a fruity voice.

The door slammed shut like a bomb going off. A blinding teslight beam raked across the room, sending shadows flying. And from every direction, Silka saw the Beadle's Runners closing in on them.

Toby gave a wild yell and threw himself toward the door.

Silka twisted and turned, crouching, hissing, and showing her teeth.

She saw Toby disappear under several Runners. More came for her. She sprang at the first one and her teeth met in his throat before the others could get to her. Then she saw lashes of blue-white light, whipping toward her through the air. She felt the burning agony of the vorpal lances. With a scream, she arched backwards into darkness and knew no more.

• • •

Silka awoke, hurting in every bone and with a headache that was ripping her brain apart inside her skull. She was lying down, tied hand and foot, and the floor was vibrating under her and the air was humming in her ears She opened her eyes a crack.

It took her a moment or two to focus, the light being so dim and grainy. Toby was lying next to her, his eyes open, looking into her face.

"I am so sorry," he whispered. "I should have known."

She screwed her eyes closed and opened them again, seeing more clearly now. "Where are we?" she asked.

"In the Beadle's Flying Black Maria," murmured Toby. "On our way to the Bow Street Lockups. And from there it's but a short step to the Bailey, and for the likes of you and me, the only road out of there leads to the hangman's noose or the Floating Hulks." He gave a sad, rueful grin. "Neither of them delightful prospects."

Silka lifted her head. They were in some kind of metal pit or trough with a ceiling of latticed iron. Dull light filtered down from above, and she could hear distant muffled voices over the steady humming noise.

"We ought to escape, then," she said.

"I agree. Do you have any thoughts on the matter?"

"Turn over and bring your hands up to my mouth," Silka said.

Toby squirmed onto his back and then onto his other side in the confined space. It was difficult and it took a while for him to wriggle and writhe so that the ropes binding his wrists were close enough to Silka's mouth for her to gnaw at them. But once her teeth got going, the ropes quickly frayed and unwound and came loose.

Toby untied his ankles then worked swiftly and silently to let Silka free.

They crouched together in their prison hole, backs bent under the iron grille. "It will be held shut with a simple bolt," whispered Toby. "But escaping from this coffin is only the start of it. We're in an airship, Silka—the only way off is to jump. I have many skills, but flying isn't one of them."

"Shall we tie ourselves up again then, and await our fate?" Silka asked.

"I'm not saying that," Toby replied. "I was simply pointing out . . ."

"Hush!" said Silka. "Let's try our luck." She squeezed her long thin hand out through the grille. Feeling blindly with her nimble fingers, she discovered the iron bolt and quietly and slowly eased it back.

Inch by stealthy inch they lifted the heavy grating. Silka's eyes emerged at floor level. They were in a long, narrow, gloomy iron cabin with curved walls and a ceiling made from riveted metal plates. Round portholes punctuated the sides, revealing discs of dark cloud.

There were no guards down there, but an iron stairway led to an open hatch in the ceiling.

Silent as mice, Silka and Toby slid out of their pit and lowered the grid.

Silka could hear the boasting and laughing voices of the Runners filtering down through the hatch.

"We're in the prison hold," Toby said, stretching and arching his back. He cocked his head upwards. "Can you hear them up there—congratulating themselves on capturing two of London's most desperate felons?"

"They'll be less cheery with my teeth in their wretched necks," growled Silka.

"No, no," warned Toby. "There will be far too many of them. Stealth is our best ally in this fix." He tugged at her sleeve. She turned and saw that he was pointing to a round hatchway set in the rear of the cabin. A way out, it seemed, so long as they learned the art of flight between the airship and the ground.

"We may as well gauge the level of the challenge facing us," said Toby, moving to the doorway. He twisted the handle and a moment later the hatch swung open and a blast of cold night air was beating into Silka's face, sending her hair flying.

Toby tottered on the brink of the hatch. He stared downwards.

"Like my old Mum always said, it's better to be born lucky than rich!" he declared, grinning as he looked back at her. "Can you swim, Silka?" The wind tore at his words, shredding them so she could hardly understand what he was saying.

She stared downwards. The airship was cruising above the Thames River, the thick body of slow-moving water winding like a dour black snake between the teeming buildings of London Town.

"I don't know," she shouted back.

"Neither do I," Toby howled. "What say we find out?"

She nodded and hand in hand they launched themselves into the shrieking air.

The wind of their fall tore at Silka's clothes and sent her

hair upwards in a fountain. She clung hard to Toby's hand, vaguely aware that he was yelling as they plummeted.

The black river came racing up to meet them. Scenes from Silka's short, strange life flashed in front of her eyes like Teslagraph: her father dead upon the cottage floor. Royston Hoof's treacherous smile. Bodies hung smoking over wood-fires. Toby's smiling face—the face of her only true friend. How sad that she should not live to know him better. But there was comfort in the knowledge that they would perish together. Assailed by these thoughts, her eyes dazzled by the whirling blades of a hundred beckoning Teslagraphs, she gripped Toby's hand all the tighter and prepared herself for oblivion.

She knifed into the river, sending up a great white fluke of water. She sank like a stone, blinded by bubbles, surrounded by the swirl and churn of black river water. There was a moment of intense, biting cold, then suddenly all her fear and trepidation were gone.

As they plunged into the river, she had lost grip of Toby's hand. Fearful for him, she opened her eyes and found she could see perfectly well under the dark tide.

Toby was beneath her, dropping away into the deeps, his pale face turned up toward her, his eyes blank, his arms hanging as though already lifeless.

She twisted lithely in the water and swam down toward him. Snatching hold of his collar, she flipped her legs under her and made for the surface.

She trod water as she held his face to the air. He gasped and gulped and choked and floundered.

"Stop your panicking!" she told him. "I've got you."

And she did have him. It was the strangest sensation. She felt completely at ease in the water, able to move naturally in it, almost as though it was her native element.

"Hold onto me," she commanded. He looped his arms around her neck and she swam fish-swift for the shadows of a nearby bridge. She held him up till he caught his breath and was able to support himself in the water by clinging to gaps between the brickwork.

"You said . . . you didn't . . . know whether . . . you . . . could swim . . ." he panted.

"I didn't." Silka declared. "It seems I can!" She swam away from him, diving deep, twisting and turning in the water like an aquatic dancer, instinctively knowing how to shift her limbs and arch her back to send her down to the deep or to bring her exultantly to the surface.

She knew it in every fibre of her body; she knew it to the deep places of her soul. Her true home was in the water.

She surfaced, grinning like a shark.

"You're a mermaid!" Toby cried. "For sure, you're a mermaid!"

"A half-mermaid, at least," Silka replied.

"You would make a fine addition to Monsewer Pierre's Caravan of Marvels." Toby said. "You would be the star."

"And where would we find Monsewer Pierre?" Silka asked.

"Last I saw him, they were heading for France on a grand tour of Europe and the Russias."

"Can we get to France by water?" asked Silka, frolicking and sporting and laughing in the delightful embrace of the river.

"Eventually, I imagine," said Toby. "But you will need to help me a great deal if I'm to get there alive."

"Show me the way," said Silka. "I will teach you to swim as we go."

Toby grinned, pointing under the dark arch of the bridge and away into the watery east. They waved a brief farewell to the Beadle's airship, hovering impotently far above them, and then they struck out together down the sinuous throat of the mighty River Thames and were never seen in London Town again.

And that is the story of how Silka MacAlindon found her true love, but whether that true love was a stinky but loyal London Mudlark or the deep and all-encompassing bosom of the eternal and maternal oceans of the world, you will have to decide for yourself.

Wild Magic

BY ANN AGUIRRE

ONE

I CAME TO the artists' promenade every second Friday, no matter the weather. Today threatened snow, the sky gray as my father's eyes, darker than my own. Against the bitter winter wind, those who could afford it bundled in cashmere cloaks and fine wool jackets. The unfortunates who could not, made do with ragged layers of lesser fabrics. Along this busy avenue, house bondsmen and paid lackeys hurried, heads down, running other people's errands.

I sympathized. As a scion of House Magnus, my time was heavily committed—lessons in dancing, comportment, and languages (my father felt that a true lady must be fluent in Old Ferisher) as well as the arts and sciences. He respected history, but not magic; studying the dead language was mere lip service to the old ways.

They hadn't wanted me studying Atreides' infernal devices either, but as I hadn't balked at anything demanded of me, my father permitted the unwomanly pursuits. Atreides was the greatest inventor of our day, responsible for the steam-puffing carriages, clockwork mechanisms, and other technical wonders. He had harnessed the magic powering the mirrors that permitted messages to be sent through the ether to government buildings and the great houses. Since possession of a mirror merely required an exorbitant licensing fee, they weren't illegal for others to possess, just out of reach for financial reasons. I studied his work because the puzzles fascinated me, even if they were not thought suitable for a fragile female mind.

In any event, my brother Viktor occupied most of our sire's attention, as he wasn't interested in being a good heir for various reasons. Which meant my parents appreciated my dutiful behavior and chose to overlook my small rebellions . . . such as spending an icy-bright winter afternoon on the artists' promenade.

Even wearing my least expensive cloak, sewn of simple black velvet and no fur trim at all, I still drew the eye; it was the distinctive silver-blond Magnus hair and the equally identifiable nose. The bridge of mine had more of an arch than most, leading my peers to judge me supercilious and unfriendly before I'd spoken a word to them. At this juncture, it was unlikely I ever would.

I preferred it here anyway. As I strolled, I marveled at the artists' stalls. That was why I came—to admire the talents of those who did what I could not. I admired beauty but had no flair for its creation. Some might argue that my lineage offered the only gifts I needed. Like any scion of a great house, I could trace my bloodline back to the original ten princes and princesses, those who sacrificed themselves for the greater good and married into the barbarian families who came from across the seas, through the mists, and into our green hills. With that pedigree, came responsibility and, sometimes, actual power. In my family, I was the first in three generations who could do more than cast a faint glamour—and the horde of official Magnus tutors didn't know what to do with me. Most days, I didn't either.

The great houses frowned on such abilities, preferring to rely on technology instead. They considered magic barbarous and uncivilized, a throwback to primitive days. They didn't like the reminder that they'd come as invaders to this land and had been forced to intermarry as a means of survival.

I might like being different, if that meant I fit somewhere. Unfortunately, I didn't; there was no special school for unexpectedly powerful scions. My father just had to keep the rumors about me to a minimum while he attempted to contract an advantageous marriage. That would be years off yet, of course, presuming we could settle upon a mutually agreeable candidate. There would be contracts to negotiate and counteroffers to run past our elite cadre of legal advisors. This might occur before I got so much as a glimpse of my intended; I'd heard of girls who married without ever spending a moment alone with their betrothed. I didn't look forward to that future, but it was the one fate had granted me.

Smothering a sigh, I stopped before a display of cut-crystal and clockwork gears. In the most cunning fashion, the artist had married science and splendor to create a dancing couple that caught the wan winter light with each studied pirouette. The vendor was no more than eighteen, certainly. Although with my pale face and funereal attire, I doubtless looked older than sixteen to her. She smiled at me as I paused, an anxious *will you buy it, so we can eat* sort of look. It was a useless thing, prone to appeal only to someone like me, who had empty rooms in want of filling.

"How much?" I asked.

She named a sum that made me laugh. It appeared she had correctly judged my house, but I wasn't a fool. We dickered amiably until we reached the center, which was what she'd wanted for the piece all along. I paid that without complaint and pretended I didn't see my watcher on the opposite corner, monitoring my activities. Even my little "freedoms" came with a hidden thorn to prick the flesh and leave it tenderly torn.

The girl wrapped my purchase and handed me the dancing clockwork couple; they would occupy a place of honor on my dresser, along with the gilt hairbrushes and expensive perfumes. I had so many luxuries and wanted so few. But this one, I did. I'd chosen it for myself, after all.

As I moved on, my minder followed me, discreetly, of course. With a quirk of mischief, I swept the hem of my skirt away from the melting snow and crossed toward the painters, leaving his line of sight. A broad-shouldered fellow like Bertram would find it difficult to pass where I had.

Most of the canvases depicted scenes in the popular style— romantic realism, with women poised before mirrors in a cloud of glamour, faces half-obscured by the drape of a gauze veil. *Woman in a White Hat* had been inspiring imitations for the past two years and these were lackluster at best. Artists occasionally glamoured their works to charm a patron's eye; this was one reason my parents distrusted my affinity for the promenade.

Of course, the consequences for that magic use could be dire. Even four stalls away, I saw the gentle glow, almost an echo of my thoughts. And if I noticed, others would too, including those committed to enforcing the law.

Don't do that. It's not worth it.

But the artisan couldn't hear my silent warning, and across the way, two blue-breasted constables pounced. He called to his neighbors for help, but they turned their faces away. Bully boys came with clubs to smash all of his tainted merchandise, and then they hauled him away. I couldn't catch my breath.

That could so easily be me.

The lower-classed Ferishers who made their way with charms and glamours had been at odds with the great houses for a long while. I saw them on street corners sometimes, scraping a living of odds and ends. Sometimes they didn't look altogether human, and civilized folk muttered they ought to be ashamed and restrict themselves to back alleys. But like anyone else, they only wanted to live as best they could.

With some effort, I put the grim spectacle from my mind and continued shopping.

At the next stall, a small portrait caught my eye. Unlike its neighbors it had been rendered with bold, religiously faithful detail. There was no hint of magic, nothing but the face of this young man with angry eyes and sullen mouth. He had a shock of dark hair, a thin face, sharply pointed chin, and a cruelly beautiful mouth. But his patchwork velvet jacket, all black and gray squares, captivated me as much as his aspect; he looked dangerous and disreputable, not someone I would ever meet.

"How much?" I asked the dealer, though it was rare for me to make two purchases in one outing.

She studied me as if looking for something specific, and then answered, "Thirty talons."

A small price, in all honesty. I felt uneasy with her scrutiny, but I had the coin, and so why not? If only I'd known.

I bought the painting without haggling then because I was in a hurry to take it home to see how it looked on my bedroom wall . . . and whether those icy-starlight eyes would seem to follow me, even in my private sanctuary. As I tucked the parcel beneath my arm, I had the uncanny sense I was being watched.

Well, of course. My minder was never far away. As I strolled along the promenade, the crowd thinned. Bertram should have been visible—a tall, hulking figure in House Magnus colors. I turned in a slow circle, expecting to spot him, but I'd apparently lost him as I took the shortcut through the stalls. For the first time in my life, I was completely alone in the crowd. Bodies surged around me, jostling me; somehow, somewhere along the way, I had lost my untouchable Magnus air. The prospect was both exhilarating and terrifying. I had been trying to achieve some privacy on these outings for two years, but this was the first time I'd succeeded.

I was supposed to meet the family hansom one block away, but the driver might well report me to my father if I arrived without Bertram at my back. Still, I had no more business on the promenade, so I took my two small packages and picked a path across the square toward the busier thoroughfare where my coach waited.

But before I got there, as I passed twin brick buildings with a gap too narrow between them to qualify as a proper alley, a boy sprang out in front of me. Instinctively, I clutched my purchases to my chest, but that left my beaded purse hanging free over the crook of my arm. I expected him to cut the strings and run, but instead, he only studied me with a mocking lift of his brows.

"So you bought me, did you, House Magnus?"

It was only then that I realized—he'd modeled for the portrait. The initial fright had blinded me to the fey sharpness of his features, those unmistakable moonlight eyes and the rakish swathe of midnight hair. Instead of the patchwork velvet jacket, he wore a white shirt with dirty lace at the cuffs and a leather vest that was a little too large. His skin should be blue, dressed so on a winter's day, but perhaps he had enough Ferisher blood to charm the cold away. He sported a leather thong about his neck, strung with beads in thalassic hues, here a glimmer of cerulean, there beryl, shimmers of vert and viridian. Though I had precious gemstones aplenty, I didn't think I'd ever seen anything so lovely as the necklace about his pale throat.

Moreover, I'd never spoken to a boy my father had not vetted and approved prior; I wasn't sure whether I had the nerve . . . until I did.

"It's a lovely picture."

"Is it?" He sauntered about me in a slow circle, as though I were livestock he might intend to buy. "Will you hang me on your wall, Magnus?"

Suddenly, fiercely, I hated the reminder of my status and my fate and the subtle disdain he showed for me, as if I had done wrong in coming to the artists' promenade, as if I were a well-bred nothing who ought to remain in marble halls without ever feeling the wind on my face. There were birds, I knew, bred in captivity, who chose the security of bars over any chance at freedom. I did not wish to be such a creature, though I feared I might be; I did not appreciate his mockery. I wanted to say something stern and cutting that would make him sorry.

I didn't.

"My name is Pearl," I said.

"You have the skin for it. Like you've never seen the sun, Lily-pale."

From his tone, I took that for a nickname, and not a kind one. Hurt coiled through me that this boy, whose face I had liked well enough to want to take home, would go out of his way to make sport of me. It shamed me on an instinctive level, and I tried to brush past him. But he caught my elbow, an *unspeakable* liberty. I felt the heat of his touch clear through my cloak, and gazed up at him, wide-eyed.

"What do you want?" I demanded.

People passed all around us, indifferent to my plight. Someone should care that a house scion was being importuned, but nobody seemed to notice the embroidery of our crest on the hem of my gown. Pretending I felt no fear at all, I stiffened in his grip and stared pointedly at his hand on my arm.

"Will you have me whipped for my temerity? Now there's a word, innit?"

"I could."

"But then you'd never discover what I'm after, precious Pearl." The laughter in his voice lost the mocking edge. Then he smiled truly, and it was the most painfully beautiful thing I'd ever seen—painful because it made my heart seize in my chest; it had never behaved that way before.

"A donation," I guessed, "or perhaps patronage."

His approach was unorthodox, but I would recommend him to my father, whatever his trade, so long as he let me go unscathed. I had no desire for my parents to receive of this little adventure by any means.

"A valiant try, but no, my price is much higher. I want your secrets."

A startled laugh escaped me. How ridiculous—I had none. And then I realized he might mean the strength of my wild, untaught magic. But how could a boy I'd found in a painting know that I could make my palms crackle with fire? Neither my father, nor Viktor, did. I eyed him with wariness now, more than when I thought him a simple cutpurse. He could do me great harm, should he so desire.

"Who are you?"

"Pick," he answered.

"That tells me nothing at all."

"A name *given* means nothing," he corrected. "A name *earned* means everything, and mine tells you what you need to know . . . or at least it will, once you're wise enough to hear it."

Riddles, I thought in disgust.

But it made no matter. He peeled his fingers from my arm with deliberate grace, and stepped back. After bowing low, he sprang away as he'd come, like a storm that takes your breath with its speed and strength. I tried to follow him and found that the buildings now seemed to touch; there was no true passage there at all.

I pressed my fingertips to the brick and found it solid, though it tingled as well, kindling my own magic in response. Someone had spelled the area, but I didn't know what was the illusion—then or now. Either way, I couldn't follow him, as Bertram finally located me, sweat pouring down his red face.

"Please, m'lady, don't run off like that again."

"It was a simple misunderstanding, was it not?" I smiled up at him, willing him to take the excuse I offered. If they replaced him with someone faster and sharper, I might never know another moment's peace. "No one needs to know."

"Aye," he said, nodding slowly. "No one needs to know."

Ah, lovely. I had a conspirator.

TWO

Despite my misgivings about our encounter, I hung the portrait of Pick on my wall. Or rather, the staff did. I certainly was not to be trusted with hammer and nails. I might crush one of my thumbs, and that would render me unattractive to the prospective suitors my father intended to bring home the following week. I wondered whether he would line them up for me and let me choose according to the cut of their coats or the shape of their skulls.

Unlikely. I would play no role in their selection at all. They would be assembled by bloodline, property holdings, and how badly they wanted to join House Magnus. Certainly, the majority of suitors would come from lesser houses, or perhaps younger sons with no hope of inheritance. Otherwise they would not be so willing to renounce their own names and take mine.

Supper that night was a gloomy affair. My parents both had social engagements, and Viktor—well, my brother never dined at home if he could help it. He was forever chasing sin in opera houses and dark theaters. Not that I was supposed to know, but I had ears and I couldn't help but overhear the gossip. Once a week, my father rang him a thundering scold about his general lack of regard for the Magnus name. Yet by the morrow, they would be drinking together whereas if I enacted even a quarter of my brother's mischief, I would be sent to the country for all eternity. Rules of gender were wretchedly unfair.

So I sat alone at the long dining room table, the chandelier throwing harsh shadows overhead. I would much prefer to eat in my room, but if I did, my mother would hear of it and chide me for avoiding the obligations inherent in my station. I had been hearing about such responsibilities for most of my life.

For reasons I could not have named, I was in a hurry to return to my room, so I could stare at the face of the boy who had, by turns, unnerved and excited me. At last, the staff cleared the final course and I hastened back to my chamber. Ordinarily I might stop in the library to find a book, so I could curl up to read until I felt sleepy. Tonight, I thought only of Pick.

When I returned, the bed was already turned down, a merry fire crackling in the hearth. The maid had laid my nightgown—a demure white lawn with pearl buttons, edged in ecru lace—across the pillows in anticipation of my usual routine. And from across the room, I gazed at the portrait. Somehow it seemed even more vital than it had before, almost as though he could *see* me, and I felt loath to change in front of the picture—nonsense, no doubt, just girlish fancy.

Yet I drew nearer to gaze into those eyes, like moonlight on the ocean, and I murmured, "What is it you want of me, hmm, Pick?"

To my astonishment, silver light blazed from the frame and it shivered, becoming simultaneously less and more, expanding—no, unfolding—into a doorway. Shimmering darkness lay beyond and the enchanted chime of fey music. Unearthly laughter echoed in the distance, and I took a step forward, thrumming with curious enticement. My heart thumped as I drew close to the passage that had not existed before I spoke his name.

I hesitated. Many times, I had railed against the constant nature of my life and the lack of surprises. Each day was much the same as the next, and I, a creature of unshakable routine. If I craved adventure, here it was.

Making a swift decision, I took up the beaded purse that contained the remainder of my pin money and the letter opener on my writing desk. I did not fool myself I could do much with it in the event of physical harm, but it seemed better to attempt to be prepared. I also snatched my second-best shawl in case it was cold where I was going, and then I stepped through.

The air felt thick on my skin, almost like honey, and it carried an indistinct sweetness that drifted across my senses in a drugging swirl. From behind me came a soft pop as though the world had corked itself. I whirled and put my hands up against the now solid wall. Unthinkable. And yet, not so surprising. I could conjure fire, after all. There was magic in my world, but most citizens had long ago lost the art of its mastery. The great houses governed now, not the Ferisher courts.

Ahead, a party seemed to be in full swing. I hid the letter opener in my purse and went forward as if this weren't the most daring thing I'd ever done. *Pearl Magnus*, I thought, *intrepid adventuress*. How Viktor would laugh—*he* was the wild one, always in search of the greatest thrill. And yet the memory of the timorous creature I had been did not prevent me from taking those last steps down the dark corridor toward the circle of golden light.

Within, I found the most amazing spectacle—a court of dancers, some in harlequin rags and leather masks, others in torn velvet and donkey ears. The music I had heard came in part from a giant music box, its immense gears ticking over with metronomic precision, but there were also more vibrant airs granted by live musicians on pipes and flutes, spurring the carousers to greater exuberance. The scent of honey lingered in the air, as I'd first noticed when I crossed, and it came from great shining goblets—wine, perhaps.

In my ordinary, at-home gown, I did not fit this scene, but I didn't have a way back either. For a moment, I merely watched them, unsure what revel I had joined. And then a lean figure broke from the throng; I recognized the patchwork gray and black jacket first. Before I raised my eyes to his, I knew who it would be.

"You unlocked the door and you came," Pick said, removing his mask.

A hiss of disapproval surged from the proximate crowd. A few dancers broke away, encircling us, and their merriment assumed a threatening air. One creature wore no mask; its own features were warped enough, its body bent, twisted into unspeakable lines. Another held a gleaming knife and it cut patterns into the air.

"Take care of her," one of them sang. "Take *care* of her, Pick. Or we shall."

"Enough." He threw up a hand, subtly imperious despite his patchwork coat.

A chill spilled through me. He put his hand on my arm and towed me away to a quiet corner, where only the music surrounded us. They followed his lead, though I did not know why, and left me to his guidance.

"Did you glamour my picture?" I asked.

He shook his head. "Not I, precious Pearl. But my name did serve as the key. You spoke to my picture, then? What did you say?"

Heat flushed my cheeks and I ducked my head. How humiliating for him to know I had stood before his image and done *precisely* that. And how could they know I would? Yet with his sharp, wild beauty, I supposed it was only natural I would play the fool for him.

I ignored his query, mustering some composure. "Why have you drawn me here? And *where* is here for that matter?"

His lovely smile flared. "If I am to answer you, we must have a bargain."

"Of what sort?"

"The reasonable sort, of course."

Traps and snares might as well litter the ground between us. With more bravado than courage, I said, "State your terms, and we'll come to some arrangement."

"An answer for an answer."

I considered, and that did not seem too dire. "Very well, with two rights of refusal if the inquiries become too personal."

"And the game is done once both refusals are used."

"Certainly."

"Then I will give your two answers with the understanding you owe me in turn. We are the Wild, in whom Ferisher blood burns the brightest. We use our magic without shame or fear

84

of condemnation. We are freedom, and we have *drawn you here*, as you say, because you belong with us. I see the fire beneath your skin."

The intensity of his regard sent shivers through me. *Can you, indeed?* I had never heard of such a thing, but in the great houses, potent Ferisher blood had long since diluted from marriage with other nobles, whom put secular power ahead of arcane gifts. Yet I knew without question that I was a cuckoo in the nest.

I lost my breath at the idea he could see inside me. The pleasure at being recognized also carried a dark edge with its base in fear. I was not ready to be identified when I did not even know myself.

Personal uncertainties aside, I'd never heard of the Wild, so curiosity frothed as I watched the dancers. He followed my gaze and read my interest; for some reason, he answered without my needing to ask, outside the parameters of the game.

"They're just like me," he said quietly. "That girl sells oranges on the other side, near where we met. And that gentleman—" He nodded at a man in donkey ears, "if I may be so bold as to use the term—he runs a rag-and-bone shop."

"This is their escape," I surmised.

From the world the great houses stole, turning to clockwork and steam engines in place of magic, and driving away anyone who cast a glamour.

"It is where we plot and plan and host our revels. There used to be great magic here, but it has long since fallen into disrepair, like so many of the old ways. But they were not all wicked."

"I expect not. And history ought not to be discarded completely."

"No, indeed." His gaze caught mine then with such sweetness that I momentarily forgot our planned exchange.

It took me long moments to recollect what I'd meant to ask next.

"And the answer to where?" I asked softly.

"The barbarians once called this place Under the Hill, though of course there is no hill. And only those with strong blood can survive the crossing."

A strange sickness seized me. "That doorway could have *killed* me?"

"Not you, Pearl. Another, yes. But not you." His sharp features gained an impish cast. "But that is three questions answered, and so I believe it is my turn."

"Ask. I will honor the bargain." But my fingers were cold; there was no question I was, now, elsewhere.

Pick gazed down at me in the flickering gaslight, and the otherworldly dancers faded from my perception. Though they still snared and snarled and drank their wind in this wild revel, there was only him with his looming height, his ragged elegance, and his brilliant eyes.

"The first question is: does House Magnus realize how powerful you are?"

"They suspect I'm stronger than most, but I've never been tested or trained."

A pleased look fluttered beneath his lashes, a softening like that of wax applied to a strong flame. I didn't know what I'd done to kindle such an expression, but by the warmth in my belly, I wouldn't mind seeing it again.

"Have you practiced your own tricks in private?" Something about the way he stressed the word *tricks* sent warmth streaming through me. I knew he was teasing me, but I couldn't put a finger on precisely how.

I swallowed twice before I could speak. "Of course. But I

don't know what I'm doing, and I've been afraid of calling more magic than I could discharge."

In the library, I'd found old texts, cautioning Ferisher images. They were spotty on the "hows" and instead focused on the "you mustn't" aspects of casting a glamour. There were confusing bits about energy exchanges in place of true creation, and if one place pulled too much, then the world shifted to restore the balance. It hinted at dire consequences of that return to equilibrium without articulating what those might be. At the time, I'd been frustrated in my attempts to learn, but caution had gotten the best of me, so I'd stopped trying.

"Then I suppose I've only one question left," he said. "I had best make the most of it."

"Ask."

"Have you ever been kissed, precious Pearl?" His starlight eyes, fringed in sooty lashes, twinkled at me.

I could use my right of refusal here, but I sensed I would lose his respect if I did. So I lifted my chin. "I have not."

"Would you like to be?"

Heat spilled through me, setting my cheeks aflame. My lips tingled, though he stood a full handspan away from me. Oh, but he had a mouth made for kissing—superbly shaped, lovely as a sunrise. I struggled to keep my wits; that might itself constitute a glamour, if he could make sensible young women like myself feel so.

"That's a fourth question. I believe I should hear another answer before you receive yours."

"Truth," he admitted.

Oddly giddy, I felt as if I'd won more than an answer from him. The dancers twirled on, though I did notice a few studying us in their spins. It wasn't a look I'd seen before—measuring, calculating, as though they pictured me as a sacrifice—an odd sensation, to be sure. The bent thing bared yellow teeth at me, playfully snapping, and I drew back, forcing myself to focus on the game.

"What purpose do you intend me to serve here?" It was another version of the question I had asked before, but this time, shaped so he could not wriggle out of it.

"You're clever," he said. "That will help."

"That's not an answer."

"No, it's an observation. It is simple, my precious Pearl. I intend for you to use your magic to circumvent the infernal devices protecting the archives of Atreides."

THREE

"You're mad."

He grinned. "So they say."

"Never mind that it's impossible—"

"A frontal assault would be suicide," he agreed. "But I know another way in."

"And why do you want to get into Atreides' vault?" Too late, I realized I owed him an answer.

"My query first, if you please."

"Of course." Those two words served as reply to both his statement and his question, and it took him a minute to realize this.

For a moment, I thought he would grant my first kiss, there and then, but instead, he filed away the information with an inscrutable nod. "To retrieve old records, spells and incantations, locked away as too dangerous for public knowledge."

"I'd like to end the game and have a conversation now," I said.

His smile grew roguish. "You trust me enough to dispense with your own rules? I take that as a good sign."

He might be playful as a cat with a rodent, but I didn't feel mousey. "Take it as you like. Tell me more about this alternate way in."

"Long ago, there were passages within the city, traveled by the princes and princesses of the two courts."

I nodded. That much I'd heard in stories, but I hadn't believed in such magic, not as more than just a legend anyway. "But doesn't it take an artifact to control the hidden doors?"

"Precisely. And I shall find the one keyed to the old prince, who once controlled these corridors."

"Can you *do* that?" I didn't mean to sound doubtful; it was just all so overwhelming.

"Absolutely. They'll never expect it. In fact, I'll wager they've forgotten about those passages entirely."

So he expected to locate a lost key and raid the archives.

"How do you think I can help? Without those forbidden tomes, I don't know how to use my magic as you require. That leaves us in something of a paradoxical situation."

"I shall tutor you. I possess the theoretical knowledge necessary for our purpose."

"So why can't you undo the glamours yourself?" I tried to ask intelligent questions; I didn't want to rush into a foolish decision.

"I lack the power."

"I see." I sensed he wasn't being completely candid with me. "Is there no one else who can do this then?"

"It must be a sorceress from one of the ten great houses."

"And the magic has nearly died out among the nobility."

"You understand why you're so valuable to us."

Indeed. Someone finally found me invaluable due to the freakish aptitude I displayed. It was the combination of my blue blood and my rare power they required. It would undoubtedly be dangerous, no matter how forgotten this route might be.

"So, for a fool's errand, one needs only a suitable fool."

"You could change everything," he said, cajoling. "Don't you want to?"

Hm. Lessons in magic from a mysterious boy who belonged to a hidden Ferisher court called the Wild—I couldn't think of anything that would horrify my parents more. Therefore, the proposition became exponentially more enticing.

"I can't be gone from home too long at one time."

"Tell me when, and I can come to you."

"But only if I open the door first?"

"Certainly. The power is all yours."

Though I didn't believe the latter statement, I nonetheless turned the idea over in my mind. Did I want this—an adventure, a minor rebellion, culminating in an impossible task? *Of course.* It was like something straight out of the stories, and I would be a poor specimen indeed if I refused. My heart fluttered at the notion of having him alone in my bedchamber; I'd need to bar the door during our lessons. Anything might happen.

"Come to me tomorrow evening," I said softly. "At this same time."

"I will await you on the other side of the wall."

The music rushed back into my ears then—as if we'd occupied a space apart—coupled with my cognition of the dancers watching us. Seeming as though he didn't wish to leave me alone with them, Pick took my elbow and escorted me from whence I'd come. The hall was dark, ancient crumbling stone walls on either side.

He placed a blue, graven token in my hand. "This permits you to open the door on this side, should you ever become stranded here. There are no others keyed to my portrait."

I didn't know if I could believe him. Perhaps I might awaken some night to find him perched on the side of my bed.

"You'll find a key like this to get into the archives?"

"By the time you complete your lessons, I will have it," he promised.

I curled my fingers around the item. As soon as I did, silver light sprang up around us. He backed up a step as the doorway opened, and I went home.

• • •

Things should've been different, given the pact I'd made, but no. My bedchamber remained the same. I sank onto the mattress and gazed at the disc in my palm. Taking a deep breath, I dropped the boundaries in my head that penned in my magic to keep it hidden from my parents, who cringed at any reminder of it. In response, the fire rushed from my skin, pale as moonlight, and the token crackled in reaction. *Truth.* I had an artifact from the old courts. I banished the energy then and found the perfect hiding place for it.

By the ornate pendulum clock on my mantel, it was nearly midnight, so I got into my nightgown. With the events of the day, I should have found it impossible to sleep. I didn't. In the morning, I awoke and trudged through the routine: breakfast and lessons. This time, however, I paid special attention to my tutor's remarks on Old Ferisher. If I was to acquire ancient tomes for the Wild, then they might, conceivably, also need my aid in translating them.

By the time I went up to my room after supper that eve, impatience bubbled in my blood. I could have spent the next half hour preparing in other ways, but instead I donned my prettiest blue gown and dressed my hair in matching ribbons. Silly and vain, as I would always be pale and plain with an unfortunate nose, but I could not resist the impulse. Finally, I locked my bedroom door.

At last I felt ready to face my would-be teacher, so I stopped before his portrait and murmured, "Come to me, Pick."

Light. No matter how many times I saw the doorway open, it would never grow less than marvelous. But on this occasion, I stood back so he could cross, my heart pounding in my chest like a mad thing. His appearance in my bedchamber offered a splendid spectacle—deliciously forbidden.

Tonight, he wore again his black trousers, white shirt, and black vest as he had when I met him in the market. Unlike that day, he also radiated focus, no teasing in his moonlit eyes. A tremor of disappointment curled through me, but I crushed it. The dress had been a ridiculous impulse; his flirtation had doubtless been calculated to win my cooperation, and once he had it, he needed waste no more time on any aspect of me but my magic. I tried not to let that hurt.

"Are you ready to begin?" he asked.

For the next seven nights, Pick was all business in my room, even when his beauty distracted me—the slope of his nose and the dagger-sharp line of his cheekbones, to say nothing of his mouth. For all my wistful stares, he did nothing but instruct me, and so I gleaned our mission must be of the utmost import. The rest of my life seemed a dream, though I ate my dinners with prospective young men under my father's watchful eye. I lived for those stolen hours with Pick, fey lightning streaming from my fingertips.

To my sorrow, he treated me only as a promising pupil. I stopped wearing my prettiest dresses and tying garlands in my hair.

We drilled on the spells I would need to pass the traps safeguarding the Atreides archive, and within two weeks, I mastered glamours he could cast only in theory, though he had some power of his own. Yet he didn't waste our limited time with displays of his showmanship, however great my curiosity.

On our twenty-second night of training, I felt I'd achieved enough to ask, "What is your sphere of influence?"

Mine was, unquestionably, air. Lightning came to my fingertips, and I could stir the winds with a whisper. With each subsequent session, my precision improved. With this mastery came greater confidence. What did it matter that I wasn't pretty if I possessed such power? In any dynastic alliance my father arranged for me, the advantage would always be mine.

Pick curled long fingers around a tumbler on the desk. He exhaled in a soft white cloud, so that ice crackled atop the surface of the water, frosting the glass outside as well.

"Water," I guessed. "That must have many applications."

He took my measure with a long, considering look, before saying softly, "The body needs it to survive, precious Pearl."

A chill took me. "Does that mean you can kill with your magic?"

I wish he'd denied it. Instead he replied, "As can you."

"But I wouldn't."

"Not even to save your own life?"

I didn't want to think about that question tonight. "Are we finished then?"

"Nearly. We need one final glamour to attempt the labyrinth."

"We? You're coming with me, then?"

"I'd hardly ask you to do brave the dangers alone."

I tilted my head. "Wouldn't you?"

Pick put his hand atop mine, and his touch carried such a sweet shock that I lost my breath. "Never. You are important."

"Because of my magic and my bloodline."

"That's not the only reason."

"Isn't it?" I drew my hand from beneath his.

Don't touch me. Don't give me expectations. I understand the arrangement.

"What's the matter?"

"Let's return to the subject at hand. How long will it take to learn this final glamour?" I wasn't sure whether I could continue lessons indefinitely without my parents noticing. Then again, so long as I did as they asked without argument, they paid little enough attention to me. The social requirements of a ruling house scion were steep indeed.

He pulled away, somewhat reluctantly, I thought. "Another week, perhaps. You're a good student."

"I should be," I said with a trace of bitterness. "I have no other occupation at the moment."

Apart from those occasional dinners at home, I'd begged off the entertainments where I once accompanied my parents. In truth, my mother wasn't sorry to lose my company. She didn't like others being reminded she had a daughter my age. It interfered with maintaining the illusion of eternal youth, like those of the most powerful Ferisher blood.

For the first time since I'd known him, his brows drew together in a display of tangible dismay. "And you miss the soulless entertainments, I take it? The endless parties where you're paraded like a pedigreed pony."

"That's my life you're disparaging."

"It's not the one you should have."

"And who decides that?"

"It's not my place. I understand."

"Your *place*?"

"Do you think it's easy for me to sit in your bedchamber, surrounded by your fine things, and know that you'd never have spoken to me of your own free will?"

I stared at him, nonplussed. It came to me then—Pick felt as if I were superior for being born a Magnus. For the first time, I put myself in his shoes—hiding in my room, teaching me forbidden glamours. If anyone found him here, he would be put to death. No questions. No trial. Perhaps, then, his lack of interest had nothing to do with my prettiness or any lack thereof. Instead, he was acutely conscious of the social chasm between us. But to me, he was fascinating and beautiful, no matter where he'd been born.

"Is that why you stopped—" I broke off the question because it was embarrassing and presumptuous.

"Flirting," he finished. "Yes. I can't show interest *here* of all places. We're not equals, precious Pearl, however much I wish we were."

"We are, you know. Equals."

"In your eyes?" he asked.

Somehow, I knew the answer mattered. It might well change everything. "It doesn't matter to me where you were born or to whom. You're my friend."

Not wholly a lie, that. But I wanted so much more. I wasn't learning these glamours for the adventure anymore; I wanted to please him and make him proud.

He softened, then. His smile lost its diamond edge, and his eyes went luminous. "I think that's the kindest thing anyone's ever said to me."

What had his life been like—that my regard could mean so much? My heart ached. I laced my hands together to hide their sudden unsteadiness and summoned a challenging smile. "But if you're to be punished regardless if we're caught, wouldn't it be better to have done something worth the price?"

His breath caught, his starlit gaze fixed on my mouth. "What would you suggest?"

Could I truly be this bold? It seemed so. "A month ago you mentioned a kiss."

Pick rose then and took my hands in his, drawing me to my feet. I became aware of the disparity in our heights, and despite his affinity for water, he radiated heat until I felt the space around us ought to swirl with steam. And then—it *did*. I glanced down at my fingers, entwined with his, and saw the crystalline sparks flashing—unearthly beauty, wherever our skin touched.

He leaned down, a lock of raven hair spilling over his face, and his lips brushed mine—once, twice, just the barest caress, and our magic swelled, the sparks and steam becoming radiant. Though he barely touched me, I was breathless when he drew back. But as if he was reluctant to let me go entirely, he traced my cheek. Then he lifted the necklace I'd admired over his head and dropped it around my throat.

"For you. So you don't forget about me."

I stretched up on tiptoe, kissing him again. "I could never."

"I'd better go."

"Why?"

"I can't keep my mind on business now," he said gently. "Good night."

FOUR

The next night, I made my usual excuses to avoid being dragged to a party, but this time, my mother refused to accept that I had too many lessons to complete and couldn't attend a formal dinner at House Thorgrim. It seemed she'd taken the time to talk with my tutor, and his story didn't align with mine. Since I'd been using him as a pretext, discovery was inevitable, and the only reason it had taken this long was my mother's preference for traveling unencumbered.

"Really, Pearl. Next, you'll be following in your brother's footsteps. I couldn't stand the shame."

With a sigh, I donned my evening clothes. The hours dragged with excruciating tedium, as my parents attempted, none too subtly, to match me with a sullen, spotty-faced younger son. While I made polite conversation, I thought of Pick waiting for the door to open on his side—and he might imagine the kiss had something to do with my absence. I fingered the necklace beneath my gown and willed time to flow faster.

It was after midnight by the time I got back in my room and later still when I banished my maid and bolted the door behind her. There was no point in saying his name; he wouldn't be there. Yet I'd already made up my mind; if he wasn't, then I'd go looking for him. I fetched the blue token that would permit me to return. With the glamours he'd taught me, I could handle myself in the Wild court.

Squaring my shoulders, I whispered his name and waited for the portal to unfold. For a moment I imagined someone passing my room at this precise moment and wondered what they would make of the lights glimmering from beneath my door. As I'd expected, Pick didn't step in, so I did. Unlike the last time, I heard no enchanting music, nor smelled any sweet wine. Under the Hill was quiet and dark tonight, eerie with long, spindly shadows.

I followed the corridor down to the big room where the others had been dancing, but it too was empty. This room felt vast, many hallways leading off into pitch-black uncertainty. Turning slowly, I considered each passage. He would surely sense the magic of my crossing and come in search of me ere long.

When I spun back toward the center, a creature appeared—huge, bulbous eyes and green-brown skin, covered in warts, with spines bristling from its neck. Legends had spoken of them, of course, but it had been ages since anyone believed they were real, more than the stories in a child's primer. *Spriggan*. They must shadow walk because I didn't hear it approaching.

It bared its teeth at me in what definitely was not a smile. And then it sang, "Come! Fresh meat, fresh meat, and *oh so* sweet."

From deeper in the darkness, something stirred. Four more appeared, melting from the darkness in swirls of knobby flesh. They carried the stench of carrion. My heart thudded in my ears, but instead of letting fear overwhelm me as I would have not long before, I called Ferisher fire to my hand.

"I'm looking for Pick. You'd be wise not to detain me."

I'd never cast an offensive glamour but I could. So I didn't back up. *They need you. They won't hurt you*, I told myself. *They just want to frighten you.* Sadly, it was working. As they advanced, I slammed the ground before me in an explosion of magic that made them growl and fall aside. Since I didn't know what the punishment might be for hurting them, I directed the flames around me in a ring. To get to me, they had to cross through it, and it was too bright for a shadow walk. Of course, it also meant I was trapped until Pick noticed the commotion. The stalemate didn't trouble me over much. With more courage than I felt, I crossed my arms and stared at them over the blue flicker. They hissed and circled several times, but as I'd suspected, they weren't willing to burn to cinders to use me as the night's entertainment.

Fortunately, their noisy complaints drew more of the Wild court. Soon, I had a veritable party of interested onlookers. It shouldn't be long before Pick arrived to sort this all out.

They'd listened to him before, after all. With some effort, I squared my shoulders and tried to look as though I was accustomed to such attention.

I'd never been gladder to see him than when he pushed through the milling crowd in his black and gray patchwork jacket. He wore braids in his hair tonight, twined with white ribbons, and he looked both beautiful and fearsome, though why that word should come to mind—well, it could only be his expression rather than his long raven hair. I'd beheld thunderclouds with more brightness.

"Begone," he growled at the others.

"Have you forgotten at whose orders you serve?" a spriggan growled. "You smell of her, her perfume on your skin. Perhaps we'll eat you as well."

Pick turned, his fingers smoky with frost. "Do you wish to test me? I still hold the authority here."

The spriggan snarled, showing jagged teeth. "We shall let you pass. But do not imagine we shall forget."

They melted into the side corridors with angry mutters; the spriggans were the last to depart. It gave me a little chill to think of them watching us from the shadows, but he cast some minor glamour that sparked one who tried to linger. When he signaled it was safe, I let the flames die away. *Just in time, too.* My head felt queer and painful, as I'd held the power much longer than I ever had before. I took a step toward him and my knees went soft.

He caught me before I hit the ground; his arms were as gentle as his face was furious. "What're you *doing* here?"

"Looking for you," I said muzzily.

"And quite a job you made of it, didn't you? That was as fine a spectacle as any I've seen outside the theatre."

I smiled up into his face, wondering why he was so blurry. "I'm pretty proud of it. Better than being eaten by spriggans."

He sighed. "I suppose it was. But don't you understand how dangerous the Wild court can be? Why in the world did you risk this?"

"Didn't want you to think I'd forgotten you."

At those ill-conceived words, his whole aspect lit from silver-edged darkness to the live light of stars raining down on a face upturned for a kiss. "I knew you didn't, my precious Pearl. I gathered something came up."

"But I had no way to cancel our plans properly. It wasn't polite."

A startled laugh escaped him, and I realized he was trembling. A fine, low trembling, to be sure, but he'd been frightened. That set heat blazing in my belly.

"Polite," he repeated. "Only you would worry about hurting my feelings. Nobody else imagines I have any. I sometimes forget what a princess you are, all the way down to your pretty feet."

"I'm not." I pushed at his shoulder, wishing to recover some of my dignity, but he didn't let me go.

Instead, he strode with me down the long corridor. He paused while I retrieved the token from my beaded purse. After the doorway opened, Pick carried me into my room and deposited me on my bed. Yet he did not let me go, his brow against mine.

"Oh, Pearl," he whispered, his thin face tight with torment. "How will I do what must be done?"

My head still felt thick and dizzy. "I'm doing it, am I not? You're only going to watch out for me."

"Yes." He combed his fingers through my loose hair, so gentle that I rested my cheek on his chest, though I'd no intention of doing any such thing. "Of course."

"Thank you for finding me," I said softly.

Eventually, he let go and pushed to his feet, pacing with

agitation. "Promise me you won't do that again. I won't see you harmed by any of the Wild." But his expression reflected such conflict; it bewildered me.

"Why would they harm me? Don't they need me? I thought we were allies."

"Some cannot help it," he said softly. "In the Wild court, there are those born of darkness, just as there are the beautiful and bright. And the ones who challenged you bear the shadow in their souls. They must act as their natures drive."

"Then perhaps I should not acquire tomes and scrolls that will make them more powerful." It was a valid statement, I thought.

He ran a hand through his hair. "We're not all like the spriggans. If you knew where I lived, how I fought for every scrap of food as a child, you wouldn't question why I want more power."

It hurt me imagining him starving and cold, huddling for warmth as I'd seen street children do. There was only one possible response. "When will we go after the Atreides archives?"

"Two nights hence. You need a night to rest after this evening, but if standing down half the Wild court doesn't prove you're ready, I don't know what does."

"So I won't see you tomorrow?" How I hated the wistful trail of that question.

"I'm sorry. I must get ready." Yet he sensed my forlorn air, or he saw it in my eyes. He sat beside me on the bed again and tipped my chin up. "Perhaps I shouldn't admit it, but . . . it means a great deal that you came looking for me."

This is why I came, I thought. *Not because it wasn't polite.*

I wanted his kiss more than my next breath, and this time, it wasn't sweet or gentle, as if he thought I might break into shards in his fingers. His mouth felt hot and hungry; he ran his hands down my back, and I wished I wasn't wearing this cursed corset so I might feel his fingers at my waist. He kissed my throat and my jaw, that fine trembling still in him like an earthquake of the spirit. Pick traced the curve of my ear with his mouth and I shivered, sinking my fingers into his silky dark hair. I toyed with the ribbons and the plaits, his beauty every bit as mesmerizing as it had been when I bought his portrait.

Curling into his arms, I kissed him, feeling as though I'd die if we stopped. My frustrating feminine armor prevented us from sharing greater intimacies and yet he danced about the edges of my corset, his fingers first on my ankles, and then gliding up toward my knee. My breath caught as our gazes locked. His eyes gleamed molten silver in his thin face.

"Stop me," he whispered against the curve of my throat.

I wasn't ready to let him unlace my bindings and remove my gown. But someday I would be—and it was to *him* I would give myself when the time came, not some boy of my father's choosing. Making that resolution, I sat back.

"You were that frightened for me?" I asked. This was the first time he'd lost his composure when he touched me, the first time he'd shown more intensity than he intended.

Before, I'd felt he controlled every aspect of our relationship, and so I couldn't help but feel a little delighted that I roused strong, bewildering emotions in him as well. Pride flared through me at this realization.

"I was. I cannot fight the Wild without harsh consequences, but I would've killed for you tonight, had they not stood down."

Pure warmth filled me like a shot of my father's liquor, stolen from his study. "I love you, Pick."

He squeezed his eyes shut as if I had stabbed him through

the heart instead of spoken from mine. "Pearl. You undo me utterly."

"Oh." It wasn't the response for which I'd hoped.

"And now I must go before I forget my good intentions and remember only the sweetness of your kiss."

Oh, to perdition with familial alliances and great houses. If he asked, right then I'd run away to the Wild court and let Father persuade Viktor to do his duty. No more tutors, no more lessons. It would be dark and dangerous, all adventure and mysterious glamour. I made no decisions then, though I had some idea that a confrontation was coming—between my parents and me, between the life I had and the one I wanted for myself.

Lips still tingling, I opened the doorway and watched him go, my heart unsettled as the seas surrounding Uí Breasail.

FIVE

I met with my father's favorite the night I was to go questing for the archive. Somehow I managed to make intelligent conversation, though the boy was dull as an old meat pie. But I knew better than to attempt excuses; that would only arouse questions and give my parents an excuse to pry into my business.

At last the interminable meal ended, and I escaped to my room. Fortunately, I still had time to lock the door, change into a dark dress more suitable for adventuring, and then open the way for Pick. This time, he reached through and pulled me across into the darkness. It was quiet tonight; he led the way down the long corridor to where the spriggans had cornered me, and then down another hallway.

"You know the way?"

"These passages lead between . . . You can get anywhere in the city if you know where the exits lie."

"And you do?"

Pick laced his fingers through mine and gave a gentle squeeze. "Trust me."

I must, or I wouldn't be following him. We walked what seemed like miles in the dark, interspersed with the faint glow of lamps on the walls. At last he stopped and produced his own token. This one was red, and radiated an infernal glow in his palm. He pressed it to the wall, and cracks appeared in the mortar, a different sort of doorway from the one accessible by his portrait. The door swung inward, revealing a dim room beyond.

"This is the entry into the archives," he said. "You must lead from here, and disarm the glamours precisely as I taught you."

"What if I can't remember which one to use?"

"I'll remind you. I'm behind you, precious Pearl. We can do this."

I knew Pick wanted to give more power to those who had magical affinity instead of blue bloodlines. I wasn't just rebelling a little; this could change everything. For the first time, I considered what this would mean for my own family, but I couldn't turn back now.

I stepped through into the archives, remembering what he'd told me about wards. They had been constructed long ago when more citizens could cast a respectable glamour. Now they were remnants of a lost era, one Pick sought to restore. The ruling classes owned no particular merit or wisdom; too many centuries of privilege had spoiled the great houses. Now it was time to give the lower classes a touch of equality, magical skill in place of secular authority.

"The first test lies up ahead," he said quietly.

"I'm ready."

And I was. My doubts died away. I set off with bold strides, my dark skirt swirling about my ankles. Five feet away, I stopped and first cast the glamour that would confirm the sort of trap facing me. I needed to confirm that Pick's information had been correct. In response to my whispered words, the runes on the stones before me lit with a sickly green glow.

I traced the letters with my gaze and then glanced over my shoulder for confirmation. "It's the sigil for choking."

Pick nodded. "If we set foot on it without first drawing out the magic, we'll asphyxiate."

"I know what to do." I'd practiced this until I could cast it in my sleep.

In my mind's eye, I unpicked the weft of the spell; arcane energies sparked against the dark stones, but to no avail. Once I broke the cohesion, my lightning swept in and burned it clean, but just to be sure, I cast another glamour to see if any residual remained. The floor showed nothing now but the dust of long years.

"It's safe," I said. "Let's push forward."

So it went through four more tests. The drills I'd run with Pick had prepared me well, and the glamours laid in the tunnels were old and tattered. No one had come to bolster these defenses in years—and why would they? My birth was an anomaly. No one could've expected the Wild to find somebody like me.

Ahead of us lay only one more line of defense—the clockwork men. Between his ice and my lightning, we should be able to disable them. Yet fear still bubbled in my veins.

As if he felt the same, Pick laid his hand on my arm, staying me. "No matter what happens," he said softly, "never doubt you are important to me. I didn't answer you before, because I knew I shouldn't. But you should hear it, at least this once. I adore you, Pearl. You hold my heart in these two hands."

Then he took the hands of which he spoke and pressed his lips to each palm.

Afterward, he cupped my cheek and kissed me properly. It tasted faintly of salt; even without arcane means of divination, my heart twisted.

"What have you seen? Does something go wrong beyond these doors?"

He merely stared down at me with the most tormented expression I've ever seen. There were those with the ability to foresee the future, but if mine ended here, I would as soon not know it. So I did not press him for more. In answer, he merely laid his brow against mine, arms around me. In the silence I heard his heartbeat, and beyond the granite slabs of the portal before us, the faint clank of the guardians. Taking a deep breath, I stepped out of his arms, spun and called the fire to my hand. The doors were hewn of heavy rock, graven with symbols in old Ferisher.

"What does it say?" he asked.

"Here bide the old secrets, buried by imperial decree. It is best to let dead things lie."

"Do you agree?"

If I did, I wouldn't be standing here. "Back up."

Raising both palms, I slammed the doors with lightning, again and again, until they cracked and crumbled. A whoosh of air blew past us as the seal broke. Nobody had entered through these doors in so long, but the guardians still cleaved to their purpose. There were twenty of them in dull brass and mottled iron, all carrying weapons to rend our flesh.

Though blowing the doors cost me more power than I'd cared to admit, I summoned the fire again and let fly. Beside me, Pick coated the guardians with ice. The twin bursts of heat and cold warped the metal, yet the monstrous automatons came on, lurching forward. One fired a weapon and something struck the wall beside us, cutting me with the resultant spray of rock shards.

"Blow open their front panels," Pick called. "I need to get at the gears."

It took more concentration, but I managed to do as he asked. My fingers tingled, hot like fire, and my lips went numb. My vision sparkled from the constant outpouring of magic; even when I'd faced down the spriggans, I hadn't pulled like this. But I didn't stop, knowing failure here meant our lives. These heartless creatures would run us through and leave our bodies for rats and mice, until we were nothing but an unanswered question in the world above and dusty bones down below.

I ran as I opened their chests. They were inexorable, but not fast, and Pick laid down a sheet of ice on the stones, so their metal feet slid and they fell into clanking, crawling piles. We fought on, ice and lightning, until their mechanisms bent and shot sparks, grinding against one another.

But I hit the ice as well, trying to escape the last two. I went down on my knees and the creature lunged for me with jutting blades. The knives pierced my skirt, slicing against my thigh. The pain startled me so I lost my focus, and the Ferisher fire died. Pick had long since lost his ability to cast; his power wasn't as great as mine. Now we were defenseless—and the men were still moving. I crawled backward, kicking out with both feet, but my slippers were small and ineffective.

Pick swooped in with a heavy metallic arm ripped from one of them and bludgeoned the automatons until even their gears stopped spinning. We knelt together amid so much wreckage and the shakes took me. That had been much closer than I'd expected when I played at adventure in the safety of my bedroom. He wrapped his arms around me and buried his face in my disheveled hair.

"Are you hurt?"

I nodded, unable to speak.

"I'm going to raise your skirt and look at the wound on your calf. I won't do anything improper, I promise."

"Other than lift my skirts," I managed to joke.

An answering smile lit his starlight eyes. "It's an ugly slash," he said a few seconds later, "but I can bandage it for you. Can you go on?"

"Yes. We're almost there now."

He worked on me with efficient expertise, tying my leg with a strip from my petticoat. The scrolls in the next chamber should be free and clear from here—and if they weren't, we were as good as done. I was hurt, and I had no magic left. With Pick's help, I levered to my feet. He kept his arm around me even after I showed I could maneuver on my own, and we passed through the final doorway together. Beyond, in the dark, lay shelf after shelf of forbidden secrets.

SIX

Pick left me beside the door. Since he knew what we needed, it made sense for him to perform the actual thievery. The low throb in my leg made me wonder how I was going to explain the injury—obtained in my bedroom, alone—to my parents. But that was a distant worry, a low buzz of concern that didn't touch the pride and elation I felt at succeeding in this impossible task.

Some moments later he returned, his pack bulging with ancient scrolls and tomes. I pushed away from the wall and turned back the way I'd come at a slow, limping pace. The outer room was still a mess; if anyone ever came down here, they'd know at once that there had been a break-in, but there was nothing to be done. I continued into the dark hallways beyond, which were now clear of magic.

"Pearl," he said.

I turned with an inquiring look. Pick stood with upraised hand, ice smoking from his palm, and anguish in his eyes. "What's wrong?" I asked.

As he drew closer, I thought back to his exchanges with the spriggans, his conflicted expression, the declaration he'd made to me just before we arrived at the archives. After combining all the disparate elements, I *knew* . . . and marveled that I had been so stupid.

"I'm not meant to leave here. You're supposed to kill me."

"No witnesses," he said brokenly. "That was the Wild court's plan. They don't trust anyone from the great houses."

They'd needed me, and so they used me. They probably selected him because he would prove irresistible to a girl like myself.

"And so everything you did and said was designed to gain my trust." I closed my eyes, heartbreak tearing me in two.

"At first."

"Don't lie to me. Not now. Whatever you intend, do it swiftly."

I'd given everything, all my power, to circumventing the defenses, and then reserves I hadn't known I possessed to defeating the clockwork men. Now I had no magic with which to defend myself. Doubtless he'd been counting on that, saving his last burst for my demise. It was a wonder he'd bothered to patch up the wound on my leg.

The long silence made me uneasy, so I opened my eyes. His suffering seemed so real, and I hated feeling sympathy for him. For my murderer.

"I can't," he said, setting his bag on the ground.

To my astonishment, he dropped to his knees before me. "Get one of the blades from the iron soldiers. Use it to gut me, for I deserve no mercy."

Did he really think I could do that? I *loved* him, heartless liar that he was. "I know now why you took the name Pick. It's the weapon you used to tear my heart from my chest." I ruffled his hair.

He bowed his head. "Mine too. You cared about me, Pearl. You didn't ask who my father was—not that I know in any case. You worried about my feelings. How could I *not* return such honest affections? I cannot do as the Wild wants, and so I'd rather die here at your hand than be hunted by theirs. Please."

I was already shaking my head. Tears sprang up in my eyes at both the physical and emotional pain. My hand trembled when I rested it on his head. There had to be a way out of this maze. My parents would kill him for dallying with me, and I would be exiled if they discovered what I'd done.

And the Wild court would execute him for refusing to comply with their demands.

"We can disappear." The words slipped out before I fully formed them in my mind. "You, certainly, know where to hide in this city. We can find a safe place and study these texts. Surely there's something in them that will give us an advantage in the struggle to come."

It might come to war between the Wild court and the great houses. The Wild would fight with glamour and the houses with foot soldiers, heavy weapons, and more clockwork men. It would be best if Pick and I got out of the way. Perhaps then after the smoke settled, we could come out of hiding and put some of our new skills to use. I had no doubt that with him by my side, I could do anything, even lead House Magnus, should it come down to it. But it seemed the cleverest move was to wait out the fighting and see who was left standing at the end.

"You're willing to give up everything for me?" he asked, his heart in his eyes.

"It's nothing I ever wanted anyway."

"It may be difficult. We'll have to scrape and steal."

"That will better equip me to lead," I said. "One day. If I know how the other half lives."

"You're thinking that far ahead?" There was a touch of awe in his voice, as he gazed up at me, and for the first time, I thought I deserved it.

I answered with a simple nod.

"I know a place by the water. The Wild will never find us."

"Come," I said. "We cannot linger here."

Slowly he eased to his feet. "I will be your loyal man until death."

That kind of devotion I did not want from him. So I cupped his cheek in my hand and kissed him, as he had taught me. "Only like this, dear Pick. If I ever rise to queenly stature, you will stand beside me, not kneel at my feet."

"I love you," he said. "Beyond reason."

"And I, you." Then I bade him pick up the bag and led him toward our next adventure. I had a feeling it would be glorious.

Deadwood

BY MICHAEL SCOTT

"WOULD YOU CARE to read this, miss?" The young man sitting opposite looked over the top of his newspaper and smiled at the girl.

Martha Burke blinked at him in surprise.

"I noticed you were staring at the front page," he said softly, folding down the newspaper and resting it across his thighs. His eyes, she noticed, were a startling cornflower blue.

"It was the date," she said, momentarily unnerved by his directness.

"The date?" Turning over the crumpled newspaper, the *Omaha Bee*, he looked at the date just below the masthead. "The first of May, 1868."

"I've just remembered that today is my birthday," Martha Burke admitted. She'd realized that there was something familiar about that date, but it had taken her a moment to make the connection.

"Well, congratulations, miss." He smiled again, the corners of his eyes crinkling. "I'll not ask your age. My mama told me it was impolite to ask a lady."

Martha dipped her head and smiled. She was sixteen . . . or maybe seventeen. Her mother had always been sure about the day and month, but never too clear on the year or the place.

Martha might have been born in 1852 in Missouri or maybe 1853 in Montana.

"I'm sixteen," she said, surprising herself. She rarely entered into conversation with strangers.

"No disrespect, miss, but you look older."

"So I've been told." Feeling a touch of warm color on her cheeks, she turned away to look out of the oval portal at the brown hard-baked landscape below. "I wonder how many other sixteen-year-olds are spending their birthday in the skies over Dakota?" she said quietly, not looking at the young man.

"Actually, quite a few," he said surprising her. Leaning forward, he lowered his voice. "When we touched down in St. Paul, I noticed what looked like a big school group boarding. Fifty, maybe sixty young men and women. One of the crew told me they were war orphans," he added, "heading out to a new school in San Francisco. They all looked around fifteen or sixteen."

"I haven't seen them," Martha said.

"They're riding Low, in steerage."

Martha shifted in her seat and craned her neck. Through the porthole, she could see back along the length of one side of the sky-blue Transcontinental airship. It was one of the older single-balloon airships—the latest models were twice the size and boasted two balloons fitted with a ring of turbine engines. Originally designed to transport supplies across the country above the battlefields, many of the airships had been remodeled to carry passengers. The wealthy rode High in steel-wrapped gantries and glass bubbles on the top of the balloon. Anyone with money rode Middle in layers of carriages fitted to the sides, while the poorest rode Low in steerage in draughty and noisy metal containers slung under the balloons that were originally designed to carry freight.

Martha had ridden Low only once; she'd never been so cold in all her life.

"I would have said eighteen maybe."

She turned, suddenly conscious that the young man was still talking to her.

"I beg your pardon."

"Eighteen. I would have said you were eighteen. That's meant as a compliment," he added hastily.

"I'll take it as a compliment."

Martha Burke was tall for her age—taller than most girls—and had passed for a boy on many occasions. It was safer that way now that she was on her own. When she dressed like a man no one ever gave her a second glance, but when she put on a skirt and bonnet and added a little rouge and powder, she was pretty enough to get attention . . . especially when it was noted that she was traveling unaccompanied. Martha had learned to put a stop to that quickly enough. She had been on the road for almost two years, moving ever westwards, by road and rail and air. It was a hard life and it had taught her a few neat tricks and a couple of choice phrases for dissuading those men who wouldn't take the hint that she wasn't interested. She'd met a French girl in Boston who told her that the best way to get rid of a boy was to throw up all over them. She kept a little packet of salt tucked into her corset for that very purpose, though she'd never had to use it. She carried a tiny double-barrel dart gun in the lining of her hat and a six-inch steel-bladed knife strapped high on her thigh. She'd cut a slit in the seam of her skirt to allow her easy access to it. Today, she was traveling as a girl, dressed in one of her two sets of women's clothing. In a little valise tucked under her seat were her entire worldly possessions: a change of women's clothing, two men's shirts, denim trousers and a pair of men's steel-toed work boots.

"I was born in September, myself," the young man continued. "September fifth, in Clay County, Missouri."

Martha sat back in surprise. "I'm a Missouri girl. I was born in Mercer County, I believe."

The blue-eyed young man sat forward, coat falling open and, for a moment, the late afternoon light ran across his gray waistcoat and she realized that it was not made of cloth, it was woven from the new metal threads. She wondered why he'd need a bullet-proof vest. "Seems impolite not to introduce ourselves, since we were born practically neighbors." His smile lit up his face. "I'm JW."

She held out her gloved hand. "Martha," she said, noting that he did not give his surname and deciding not to reveal hers in return.

"Pleased to meet you, miss."

"Pleased to meet you too, JW." They shook hands politely and then both sat back in their chairs.

Martha guessed that he was maybe four or five years her senior. He was tall—as tall as she was—and while he was not handsome, his astonishingly blue eyes lent his face a dramatic intensity. His nose was straight and unbroken, his top lip so thin it was almost invisible and when he pressed his lips together, it gave his face an ugly, sour expression. He wore his thick hair swept straight back off his head in the latest fashion. His clothes were tailored and relatively new, except for his boots, which were battered and scarred and looked at least a decade old. He was dressed entirely in black, in the style popularized by the last president. Unlike the president, who favored bow ties, JW preferred a string tie. His looked like it was made from two strands of woven gold. And now that she'd seen the metal-weave vest, she noticed the bulges beneath both arms and the hint of a sheath knife on his belt.

"You're staring at me as intently as you were at the newspaper."

"I'm shortsighted," Martha admitted. "I broke my glasses. Sat on them a couple of days ago. I'll get a new pair in San Francisco."

"I heard everything is expensive there." He stretched out his legs and crossed them at the ankles. "There's so much money flowing out of the mines, the miners don't know what to do with it, and have no qualms about spending it. A new pair of glasses could be costly."

"I'm sure I can afford it," Martha said tightly. She had two dollars in her pocket and another four hidden in the sole of her shoe.

"Of course." JW sat back in the chair fiddling with the gold band on his little finger. She realized that he had rings on every finger, an enormous gold watch on his right wrist and a second timepiece on his left.

The only piece of jewelry she owned—her mother's rose gold wedding ring—was sewn into the hem of her skirt for safekeeping. She used to have an English pocket watch that, for a long time, she believed was her father's, but she'd sold it a couple of weeks ago in Chicago for the price of the airship tickets. A year ago she met a man who had fought with her father, Robert, in the First Canadian War. The man claimed that Robert Burke was so anti-British that he refused to eat English food or even drink tea. When he was wounded in the Battle of the Lakes, he'd been captured by the Britannica forces. Refusing to accept treatment from an English doctor, he had died of his wounds. When Martha discovered that the pocket watch had been made in London, she immediately knew her father would never have carried an English watch and had no qualms about selling it for the price of the Transcontinental tickets.

JW, she decided, was probably a gambler, or a shootist. She'd come across them before on her travels. None of them had been older than twenty-five, and most died a lot younger.

"What brings you out west, Miss Martha?" JW asked.

"I was about to ask you the same question," she smiled.

"I asked first."

There was a moment when she thought about lying, but finally settled on the truth. "I'm looking for someone," she said quietly.

"Parent?"

"My brothers," she said.

JW said nothing.

"Two years ago, they started out west," Martha said. "Then they disappeared."

"It happens," JW said quietly, and something flickered behind his blue eyes. "People lose touch. Families fall apart."

Martha shook her head quickly. "No," she said fiercely. "Not this family. Not my family. We lost our mother on the trail from Missouri to Virginia City. I became mother to the boys. When they left they promised they'd write. And they did. They wrote to me every week for the first couple of months, even sent me a little money when they could afford it. Then the letters stopped."

"So you decided to go find them," JW said.

"I did."

"And you were, what—fourteen when you started?"

"I guess I was."

"That's a long time to be on the road, alone."

The young woman said nothing.

The young man's eyes twinkled. "You're something else, Miss Martha. You know that? Something else again." There was a note of genuine respect in his voice.

"You've got family, brothers . . . sisters?" she asked, shifting the conversation away from herself.

"I've a brother, Frank."

"And if he went missing, you'd go looking for him, wouldn't you?" Martha said quickly.

"In a heartbeat."

"Then we're not so different, are we?"

JW opened his mouth to reply, but a dull throbbing pulsed up through the floor as the airship's engines audibly slowed. Martha looked out of the window again. The ground looked a little closer. Unfolding the ship's schedule tucked into her glove, the young woman traced the airship's route across the United States and Native Nations. She looked up to find JW staring at her.

"Something's wrong," she said. "We shouldn't be landing so soon."

The intercom whistled and the scattering of passengers in the carriage automatically looked up to the brass speaking tubes hanging over the seats. "Ladies and gentlemen, this is Captain Fontaine speaking." The accent was pure Boston. "As we are about to begin our descent into the Deadwood aerodrome, please return to your seats and fasten your harnesses."

The huge gas turbines rumbled again and the airship dipped. Further down the carriage, a woman screamed and then tried to turn it into a laugh.

The ship's steward moved down the aisle. "Next stop, Deadwood, South Dakota. Strap on your harnesses, ladies and gentlemen." He stopped alongside Martha and leaned down. He smiled, but his two front teeth were missing and his tongue wriggled in his mouth like a fat worm. "Are you doing all right, little lady? Do you need a helping hand there?"

"No, thank you," she said firmly and something in her expression made him turn away. The last person to call her "little lady" would walk with a limp for the rest of his life. "Why are we landing?" she asked loudly as he moved down the carriage.

The man shrugged elaborately. "We sometimes overnight in Deadwood if we're running out of daylight. We can get an early start in the morning." The steward tipped a finger to the brim of his peaked cap and moved on down the aisle.

"We've three hours of daylight left," JW said quietly.

The young man and woman leaned forward to look down at the quickly approaching town, their heads almost touching as they stared out of the porthole. "I don't recall a Deadwood stop on our schedule," he muttered.

"That's because there isn't one." Martha said quickly, focusing on the ground. The outskirts of the town had appeared, a smattering of adobe tenements clustered along a stretch of water that was too straight to be natural.

"Never heard anything good about Deadwood," JW said.

"Neither have I. Why are we landing, then?"

"The ship's captain probably has a deal with the local hotels and restaurants," he said. "Land the ship for the night and the passengers will pay well for a comfortable bed and a hot meal. The taverns will do a good business also. The rest of the crew might get a kickback too—free drinks, maybe."

Martha nodded very slowly.

"But you don't believe that, do you?" JW asked. Resting his elbows on his knees, he leaned forward and clasped his hands together. His face was inches from hers.

"I don't. Do you?" she countered.

JW's smile lit up his face. "Guess I don't."

There was the familiar banshee wail as gas vented from the balloon's flues and the ship swayed, then dipped.

119

"I guess you know what I am, Miss Martha?" JW said quietly.

"A shootist and a gambler."

Impressed, the young man nodded in agreement. "And you know what's kept me alive?"

"The same thing that's kept me out of trouble for the past two years," Martha Burke said softly.

"Instinct," JW said.

"Instinct," Martha agreed.

Heads pressed together, they stared through the porthole and watched as the airship sailed over the town, and out onto a field marked off in rectangles and squares. One side of the airfield was taken up by an enormous airship hangar. As it banked, the young couple saw a welcoming committee gathered around the base of the steps that would be positioned against the balloon. There were a dozen men, black metal clearly visible beneath their work clothes, heads concealed in globular mirrored helmets that gave them an almost insectile appearance. They were armed with long spears topped with ugly metal heads. Blue green flames flickered at the top of some of the lances, while others leaked gray smoke into the late afternoon air.

"That's not good," JW muttered. "This is too elaborate for a robbery."

The airship was close enough to the ground now that they could make out details in the costumes of the armed men. Their metal vests were emblazoned with the stylized logo of a crossed pickaxe and hammer, the symbol for the Federation of American Mine Owners, a ruthless cartel who controlled almost ninety percent of all America's mines.

JW focused on the weapons. "That's the latest technology: Canadian compressed-air flechette rifles and gas flame spears," he said. "Very, very expensive . . ." He looked over at

Martha and the expression on her face stopped him cold. "What?" he breathed.

"In the barn, behind the men," she whispered and moved back so that he could peer through the window.

"What am I looking for . . .?" he began. "Oh . . ." he breathed.

Wrapped in twisting steam and curling gray smoke, an enormous metal and glass object was visible through the open doors of the huge airship hangar. It looked like a bird, a cross between an eagle and a bat. Taller than a three-story house, broad at the base, narrowing to a jutting peak, it was constructed entirely of burnished red metal, polished white ceramics and gleaming glass. The head was a mirrored globe that matched the helmets of the men on the ground. One enormous wing was folded snug against the body of the creature, its twin was spread out while men crawled across it, torches and welding guns sparking and flashing.

"Thunderbird," Martha Burke and JW said together. "So they're not a legend," the young man added, unsnapping his seat harness. "We need to get . . ."

"You need to stay right where you are." The airship steward had reappeared behind the young man. He was accompanied by two crewmen. All of them were wearing black metal vests over their sky-blue uniforms. The three men were carrying old-fashioned gas-powered pistols. "Little miss," the steward said looking at Martha, "why don't you tell your friend here what I've got in my hand." The smile on his face was ugly.

Without taking her eyes off him, Martha said. "Probably one of the nastiest-looking guns I've ever seen," she said softly.

"You'll be giving me your pistols, young man," the steward said. "And you'll be doing it very slowly and carefully."

For a single instant Martha saw JW's lips turn white as he

pressed them tightly together. His eyes locked on hers and she shook her head, warning him not to do anything stupid. There was a moment when she thought he was going to try something anyway and then his head moved in the tiniest of nods and he smiled. Reaching under his coat, right hand under left arm, left hand under right, he produced a pair of matched black dart guns with ornate silver and bone handles.

"Very nice," the steward said with a wet-lipped grin, examining the weapons before stuffing them both into his belt.

"Take real good care of them," JW said, "I'll want them back."

"That's not going to happen," the steward said.

"We'll see," JW muttered, and the young woman could clearly hear the threat in his voice.

As the three men moved on down the cabin, relieving the male passengers of their weapons, Martha calmly pulled her valise from under her chair, opened it and brought out her scuffed steel-toed boots. Kicking off her flat-soled shoes, she pulled on a pair of worn socks before slipping into the boots. JW watched her, a bemused look on his face.

"Those are my best shoes," Martha explained, laying them carefully in her valise, "in fact, they're my only shoes. I don't want them destroyed in the mud."

Puzzled, JW said, "What mud?"

Martha nodded to the fast approaching ground. "That mud."

JW shook his head. "We'll not leave the airship," he said confidently.

The engines roared for a brief moment then fell shockingly quiet. In the silence, Captain Fontaine's voice echoed crisp and clear from the speaking tubes. "Move to the doors, ladies and gentlemen. You will disembark on the port side of the ship."

"Or maybe we will," JW said.

Martha managed not to smile as she pulled her bonnet out of her bag and fixed it on her head, tying the black ribbon in a neat bow under her chin.

The steward marched down the cabin, followed by the two crewmen carrying satchels full of pistols and knives taken from passengers. The ornate head of a swordstick poked through one of the bags. "Ladies and gentlemen, welcome to Deadwood. You'll never want to leave," he said. "And some of you probably won't either," he added nastily, glancing at JW.

• • •

There was a long scream of venting gas and then a series of thumps as the airship deployed its four anchors. On the ground, mechanics struggled to attach the four huge anchor hooks to the enormous circular rings set into the earth. When the anchors were in place, the huge craft shuddered before coming to a halt. The mechanics rolled a wooden cradle into place. It slotted beneath the balloon, keeping it ten feet off the ground. The Low and freight carriages were barely inches from the earth.

The wealthier passengers from High appeared first, men in fine suits, some in military or naval uniforms, though it was unlikely they had ever been in the services. All the women from High were in the latest fashions, which also favored a military theme this season. Then the Middle appeared, escorted out of their carriages by the insect-helmeted men. And finally the Low doors were opened to reveal the group of terrified children. They were unceremoniously bundled out onto the hard earth. Many were blue-lipped with the chill from the uninsulated carriage and so cold they could barely stand.

Surrounded by the helmeted guards, the airship's 120 passengers were marched across the muddy airfield, toward the streets of Deadwood.

"Have you any idea what's going on?" Martha asked.

"None," JW admitted. "Maybe we're going to be held for ransom."

Lifting up the hem of her skirt, Martha hopped over an oily puddle. "I'm not worth anything."

"I am," JW muttered.

Martha looked at him quickly. "There's a bounty on you?"

"A small one. Enough to entice a bounty hunter or two to try their hands, but not enough for something like this. And if they just wanted me, they could have taken me off the ship." He shook his head quickly. "No this is more, much more."

Martha stumbled and JW's hand shot out and caught her arm, steadying her. "Thank you," she said. When they both realized he still had his hand on her arm, they colored and immediately looked away. "What do you know about this place?" she asked quickly.

"Rumors . . ." he said, looking up as they passed under an arched sign that read "Deadwood," the letters picked out in scraps of twisted metal. The sign had been scorched by fire around the edges and was speckled with black flechette needles. "Campfire stories. It's said that once people enter the town, they never leave. It's also said there is no law in Deadwood."

The town's inhabitants had gathered to watch the passengers march in. Still and silent, they lined up on either side of the broad street, men and women in a peculiar mix of costumes and dress. Many were in fashionable attire—though few of the clothes fit properly—others were wearing cast-off army uniforms, still others were wearing clothes that were obviously homemade from scraps of cloth. None of the clothes were clean. The people were gaunt and unnaturally pale as if they rarely saw the sunlight.

"They seem like ghosts," JW said.

The helmeted guards were everywhere, lurking in the dark alleyways, positioned on the rooftops or gathered on street corners.

"At least the guards look human," Martha said quietly, staring at them in their frightening helmets.

"They are," JW muttered. "But I'm not sure about the creatures in the shadows."

Martha looked quickly left and right. Most of the wooden buildings lining the street were clustered close together with narrow, shaded alleyways running between some of them. Many were piled high with garbage, rotting food and scraps of timber, tumbled weed and burst bags of soiled cloth. Skinny dogs and large feral cats darted in and out of the alleys. "Where?" she asked.

"To your left," JW muttered, not looking at her.

It took Martha a moment to spot the cluster of black-painted automata standing flat against the walls.

"Automata: war machines," she breathed. "I thought most of them had been destroyed."

"That's what I heard too. Obviously, we heard wrong. Why does a nothing town in South Dakota need obsolete war machines?" JW asked.

Now that she had spotted them, Martha realized that the machines were everywhere, standing still and unmoving in the shadows. The automata were tall and thin, mismatched scraps of metal and wire, some obviously welded together from other machines. Each one was taller than a man, a vaguely human headless body set atop metal wheels or tracks.

When they were new, each one had four arms that ended in weapons, but most of these were missing some limbs. Ominously, although the automata were stained with rust and streaked with dirt, the wide-mouthed guns at the ends of their arms were bright and clean.

Martha had seen automata before. They had first been introduced in the War a decade earlier. The original clockwork versions had quickly been replaced by spring-powered and, finally, compressed-air and steam-driven models. Although they were terrifying-looking, they were unreliable and not suited to modern warfare and were eventually phased out or used exclusively as sentries or private security. Working models sometimes turned up at fairs and carnivals, and a famous model nicknamed the Colonel, had been redesigned and put to work as a traffic cop in Chicago.

They turned down another street and suddenly the nature of the town changed. The road turned from dirt to smooth black pitch and the buildings on either side—banks and mining offices, hotels and restaurants—were bright and clean, sheathed in shining metal and polished ceramic. Rows of ornately carved streetlights lined both sides of the street.

"I'm guessing we've just passed through the workers' part of town, and this is where the employers live," JW muttered.

"Metal, glass, and ceramic buildings," Martha said. "I've heard San Francisco is like this."

JW nodded.

The doors opened and more townspeople came out onto the street to watch the airship passengers and their guards pass by. It took Martha a few moments before she realized what was wrong about the whole place.

"I know," JW said, as she opened her mouth. "There are no children. I noticed it a moment ago."

Martha Burke nodded, suddenly realizing that from the moment she'd landed in Deadwood, she'd seen no children. And as she watched the townspeople, she discovered that they were all focused on the war orphans that had been taken off the ship.

The group were ordered to stop before a gleaming silver metal-sheeted building. The words "Deadwood Gaol" were etched deep into the metal over the huge double doors.

Martha saw JW look at the sign and watched his shoulders twitch uncomfortably. "Nervous?" she asked.

"Don't much like the idea of spending time in jail."

"You've done it before."

"Oh, that was a case of mistaken identity," he said quickly, and they both knew he was lying.

The jail doors opened and a ramrod-straight backed middle-aged man in the blue and black uniform of an airship captain appeared.

"Captain Fontaine," JW murmured. "Saw him greeting the High passengers when we were boarding."

The captain's uniform had once been pristine, but it was now stained and worn. His left sleeve hung empty and was pinned up against his collar. A series of straight scars reached from his left ear to his chin. The ship's steward joined the captain on the steps, his ugly guns held loosely by his side.

The captain looked over the assembled passengers and when he spoke, Martha recognized his accent from his announcements made on the airship.

"Ladies and gentlemen, allow me to welcome you to your new home: Deadwood." His smile was icy. "Let me tell you what is happening right now." He glanced at the chronograph strapped to his right wrist. "In the next few minutes, the airship will broadcast a distress message. Apparently, our instruments have failed and the balloon is losing pressure."

His smile broadened. "In an hour or so, the ship will be reported lost, with all hands. It will be a tragedy, of course. But every year, a dozen ships are lost across the Native Nations and the United States." His smile broadened. "Most of them are lost over Dakota in an area known as the Black Hills Triangle. All of them end up here," he added.

Fontaine came down off the steps and moved toward the passengers, who immediately backed away from him. "Unfortunately, ladies and gentlemen, you had the misfortune to book a flight with this group of children." He stopped before the orphaned boys and girls, most of them too shocked to be terrified. The captain waved his hand. "You, ladies and gentlemen, are a bonus. But these children—these are the prize."

Martha found JW's hand and squeezed tightly. Then she tugged him to one side, moving slowly through the crowd, toward the captain and the steward.

"Are we being held for ransom?" a red-faced man in a smart suit demanded. "We have money, we can pay."

"Money!" Fontaine laughed. "This is a mining town—no, this is *the* mining town. The wealthiest mining town in the United States. We don't need money. We have money. Look around you," he smiled. "Look at these buildings. They're made of solid metal sheets so thin they're almost transparent. The roofs are ceramic, impervious to cold and heat. These are some of the most expensive building materials in the world. This jail cost more than you earn in a year. This is most definitely not about money. This is about bodies. We need workers. In the mines." He took a moment to allow the sentence to sink in.

A confused murmur ran through the crowd. "But we can't work the mines . . ." someone began.

"We're not miners . . ."

"We have rights . . ."

"The law . . ."

"There is no law here," the captain snapped. "All of you now are citizens of Deadwood. You'll work for the mine owners, which means you work for me. I run Deadwood. Some of you—the ladies and the smaller men—will end up down in the mines, the rest will work on the surface, breaking rocks, hauling waste." His voice grew as ugly as the expression on his face. "You will do as you are told. That is not open to discussion. This is a company town. You'll never be able to leave it. And if you try, you'll not get more than five feet beyond the city limits. The graveyard on the hill is full of people who thought they could make it out."

Still clutching JW's hand, Martha called out. "What makes the children so special? Why are they the prize?"

"We got the idea from Britain where small children are sent up narrow chimneys to clean them. We send the children down into the deepest, narrowest tunnels, miles underground."

"But they'll die," Martha whispered, horrified.

"Some," he agreed. "But there are always more children."

Shocked, Martha took a step back. JW rested his hand on her shoulder and squeezed reassuringly.

"Most of the gold coming out of California is mined by children," the captain said slowly. "The mine owners have poured millions of dollars into the latest technology both above and below ground, but apparently nothing beats a very small human child with a pickaxe, chisel, and hammer."

"So that's where all the children have been going," a short red-haired woman said in a strong Irish accent. She looked around. "Children have been disappearing all across the West. Young boys mostly, but girls too."

"My brothers," Martha whispered to JW.

"That's a big assumption."

"That's what my instinct is telling me," she hissed.

"I believe you." JW added.

"Our Thunderbirds raided the Native villages first," Captain Fontaine said, "then the isolated towns and farmsteads, but there just weren't enough children. So we came up with a different plan: we bring the children to us. War orphans from the East Coast are offered places in schools along the West Coast." He shrugged. "Then we bring down the airships that are transporting them."

"This is slavery," Martha whispered, pulling off her hat to wipe her shining forehead. She had drawn JW with her to the front of the crowd.

The captain turned toward her, a look of disdain on his face. "This is business."

The hat slipped from Martha's hand to reveal her tiny double-barreled dart pistol she'd tugged from its hiding place in the lining. She pushed the barrel of the gun up against the captain's bobbing Adam's apple. "So is this."

The steward moved, bringing his gun to bear on Martha, but JW lunged forward and struck the man between the eyes with the heel of his hand, then grabbed his matched pistols from the steward's belt, pointing one at the steward, and the second at the captain.

JW nodded at Martha in admiration. "You're full of surprises," he whispered.

"You have no idea." She pressed her gun against the captain's throat for emphasis. "Now tell your men to hand over the weapons."

"I will not."

"I've got two darts in here. Now these are not ordinary darts. I got them from a shaman in the Native Nations. One is tipped with bee sting, the second with spider venom. Maybe, they'll not kill you, but they will really, really hurt. Tell him, JW."

The young man smiled at the captain. "I got hit in the neck by a bee dart a while ago. My face swelled up like a balloon. My throat closed. I could barely breathe," JW leaned forward and lowered his voice. "I have heard that the shaman darts are really powerful. You get stuck with one of those and soon you start to turn into the bee or snake or spider. I saw a guy in a traveling circus who was half-man, half-bee. He'd been shot with an Indian Native dart . . ."

"Hand over the guns," Fontaine ordered his men, "Do it . . . do it now."

Passengers snatched their weapons back from the crewmen. "What do we do now?" a short stout man asked JW.

He turned to Martha, eyebrows raised in a question.

"Now we leave," she said.

"You'll never get out of here alive," the captain yelled. "There is no way out of Deadwood. The automata will stop you if you try to leave the city limits."

"There's another way," Martha said. "The same way we got here in the first place."

The captain grunted a laugh. "None of my crew will fly you out."

"Then I'll fly it myself."

• • •

Martha and JW walked on either side of the captain, their weapons trained on him.

Behind them, the armed passengers guarded the others, with the children safe in the middle of the group. They had left the disarmed guards and the glowering steward on the steps of the jail.

"We need to get out of here," JW said, looking around warily.

"Too late," the captain shouted. "My steward will already have activated the town's guardians."

Even as he was speaking, the automata appeared, lumbering and lurching out from the side streets, leaking steam and dripping liquid. Their guns moved across the group, whirring and whining. And nothing happened.

"They daren't open fire in case they hit you," JW laughed at Fontaine. He looked across at Martha. "They're programmed not to fire on their own commanders."

Helmeted guards appeared on the roof and in doorways, guns levelled. JW put his mouth close to the captain's ear. "You better tell them not to shoot." He pressed his gun into the captain's ribs for emphasis.

"Don't shoot," Fontaine called out. "I'll order the automata to cut down any man who opens fire."

"Wait, please wait." A woman hurried out of a hardware shop and ran toward the group. Her once-fashionable skirt was frayed and patched. JW raised his gun and pointed it at her. "No closer."

"Let me come with you," she pleaded. "My ship was captured two years ago. My son was sent down the mine. He died there," she added.

JW looked at Martha. She nodded and he lowered his gun.

An elderly man limped out of the bank. "Let me come with you," he begged. "I've been here five years. If you don't take me, I'll die here," he added.

And suddenly more and more people were steaming out of the shops and begging to join the passengers. By the time they reached the airfield, the group had almost doubled in size. All the mismatched automata in Deadwood followed behind them.

"We can't take any more people," JW said. "We'll not get the ship off the ground."

"We're leaving no one behind," Martha said firmly.

"I knew you were going to say that," JW said. "You get everyone on board. I'll stand here with the captain to make sure no one takes a shot at us."

"Be careful," she whispered.

"I'm always careful," he replied.

"I don't believe that for a minute."

• • •

"So how good a shot are you?" Martha asked as the last passenger climbed the steps into the airship.

"Good. Real good. Why?" he asked.

Martha nodded to where the ship was anchored to the ground by four thick cables. "We'll not get into the air with them attached."

"What do we do with the captain here?"

"I say we should leave him," Martha smiled. "I'll bet his bosses won't be too pleased with him." She turned and hurried up the steps, but stopped at the door and looked down at JW. "I'm counting on you. We're all counting on you."

"It's been a long time since anyone said that to me," JW muttered. Shoving one gun back into its holster, he put his hand in the small of the captain's back and pushed him. "Get away from me."

"Wait," Fontaine said, "They'll kill me. You can't leave me here."

"Oh, yes, we can." JW's smile was chilling. "I think you should run." Then he turned and darted up the stairs. Kneeling in the doorway, he steadied the gun in his right hand with his left, took aim and fired at the nearest anchor cable. A second shot and then a third raised sparks off it. A fourth shot severed the thick cord, sending it hissing and whiplashing through the air. The airship lurched upward, freed on one side, and then the huge turbines roared to life.

The cheers from the passengers within was clearly audible.

Captain Fontaine turned and raced toward the automata. "Prisoners escaping," he screamed. "Fire. Open fire!"

Whirring and clicking, dozens of guns raised and fixed on the young man in the doorway.

• • •

Standing in the control room, Martha Burke faced a wall of levers. And all the labels were in German or Dutch.

There were many times when she'd wished for a better education, but never before now had she wanted as desperately to be able to read a foreign language.

A series of vacuum valves and glowing colored bulbs took up another wall. Most of the lights were dead, but in the bottom right-hand corner, one of a quartet of green bulbs turned red at precisely the same instant she heard JW's triumphant shout.

She grinned. Maybe he was as good as he said.

Then there was a dull whirring roar as dozens of guns opened fire at once. She actually felt the craft shudder with the force of what she guessed were hundreds of darts hitting the side.

"JW," she whispered, suddenly feeling sick to her stomach.

There was a highly polished battered leather seat in the center of the room, facing a large circular observation window. The leather was worn thin in places, horsehair stuffing poking through. Settling herself into the chair, Martha sat back and looked around. It stood to reason that the captain would control everything from this chair. Allowing her hands to fall naturally onto the arms, her hands came to a rest on two glass-topped levers. Looking closely, she discovered that there were bubble levels within the glass tops.

"Miss Martha, do something . . ." JW's distant shout was accompanied by a second green light turning red at the same moment that the ship lurched and shifted. He'd released a second cable.

She felt a physical wash of relief at hearing his voice and she suddenly found there were tears in her eyes.

"I wonder what would happen if I did this . . ." Gripping the levers in both hands, she pushed them forward.

A brass speaking tube was almost at the level of her mouth. She blew into it and could hear the tinny whistle through the rest of the ship. "This is Martha Burke, your captain speaking. Strap yourselves in. It's going to be a bumpy ride!"

The airship's huge gas turbines roared into action and the entire ship shuddered to life.

• • •

Darts whizzed and buzzed around JW.

He'd managed to shoot two of the anchor cables—the rear left and right—and the back of the airship rose up into the air. However, he was coming under sustained fire from the automata on the ground. Every time he raised his head and tried to get off a shot, dozens of hissing darts embedded themselves in the wooden doorframe. It now resembled a pin cushion. One had entangled itself in his hair and a ricochet had whined off his metal vest.

He wasn't sure how much ammunition he had left. It had taken five or six rounds to sever each cable and, even if he conserved every shot, he didn't think he had enough to cut the remaining two.

The engines howled again and the ship lurched dramatically, the free back end rising, the tethered nose dipping down.

JW sat back and reloaded his guns as more darts buzzed through the doorway like angry bees. The wall opposite him was thick with the black needles.

He should never have gotten involved with the girl. He made it a rule never to get involved with any girl. And now he'd broken that rule—and look where it had got him.

A quick smile curled his lips. She was worth it. Tough as nails, determined, and prepared to spend two years and more crossing the country looking for her brothers. He knew what that was like: he'd do the same for his brother, Frank, and he knew Frank would do it for him. He'd grown up believing that family was everything and loyalty was paramount. Experience and circumstances had nearly robbed him of that belief. But now, here he was with Miss Martha, determined to fight for the fate of a bunch of orphans she hadn't even met.

JW admired her. Even though he'd just met her, he liked her. If circumstances had been different, he would have liked to have taken the time to get to know her better. It was a pity he was not going to live very much longer.

• • •

On the ground, Captain Fontaine, his steward and a handful of crewmen raced towards the Thunderbird in the hangar. They would not let the airship escape.

• • •

The wall of valves was a blaze of red lights.

Every single light was illuminated, some flickering intermittently, others pulsing. Then, one by one, they burned

136

out. They exploded, sending speckles of hot glass sizzling across the room.

Martha had discovered a series of pedals by her feet. One was bigger than the rest and set off to the side. Strapping herself into the chair, and with nothing to lose, she put her foot on the pedal and pressed hard. The turbines howled, high pitched and terrifying, the entire airship lurching. All the light bulbs burned black and then they popped and exploded, leaving the room stinking of ozone.

Then she pushed hard on both levers.

The airship's nose dipped alarmingly and Martha found she was looking straight down at the ground. She could see the anchor cables stretched taut, the ground beneath them trembling.

Martha applied more power.

The right front anchor chain snapped close to the ground. A long length of metal chain whiplashed through the air. It struck one of the automata, reducing it to twisted metal. Then the second remaining anchor tore out of the earth, the curved hook still attached to its chain. It bounced along the ground, ripping long gouges in the hard-packed dirt, smashing a dozen of the automata to cogs and flattened metal. One exploded in a ball of steam, its internal wiring sparking and smoking.

"So if I do this . . ." Martha murmured. She pushed the lever to the right, and the airship's nose turned to the left.

JW burst into the control room, staggering left and right as the airship lurched from side to side. "If you had a plan," he began, then fell and spun across the floor to fall against the observation window. "Fontaine's heading for the Thunderbird," he yelled.

"Good idea," Martha shouted.

"No, it wasn't a suggestion."

JW crawled across the floor and struggled to his feet behind Martha's chair. He clung to it, fingers puncturing holes in the old leather.

The airship roared low over the converted barn. The dangling whip-like chain scything through the air, slicing automata in two, ripping them apart while the attached anchor on the other chain pulverized everything in its path. The wooden barn walls shredded as Martha deliberately changed course to take her directly over the enormous Thunderbird.

The flailing chain shattered the Thunderbird's glass dome while the anchor smashed through delicate metal, crushing glass windows and ceramic shields to powder. Steam vented from broken pipes.

Cautiously lifting her foot off the pedal, she allowed the airship to sink, dropping down until it was almost on top of the Thunderbird. The dangling chains settled onto the broken metal craft.

"Martha," JW began, "what are you . . ."

Then she hit the power pedal and pulled both levers back. The airship rose, and the anchor caught in the Thunderbird's extended wing. It hooked through the skeletal structure, wrapped around exposed wires, struts and cables. The airship throbbed, the weight of the other craft holding it down.

"Help me," Martha said. "We're stuck."

JW leaned across the chair and put his hands on top of Martha's, helping her pull the levers all the way toward her. Engines throbbed violently. Metal screamed and scraped . . . and then the Thunderbird's wing ripped off completely. The airship soared straight upward, the broken Thunderbird wing dangling precariously from the anchor, like a huge curved sword.

Martha tapped the controls and the ship shuddered. Vibrations rattled down the length of the chain onto the anchor. The Thunderbird wing shifted, then slipped free. The curl of metal plummeted back into the barn, striking the Thunderbird on its spine, punching straight through it. There was a dull explosion and thick, oily black smoke began to plume into the air. A second explosion rattled through the barn and then the fuel barrels detonated in a huge fireball. A pulse of warm air pushed the airship away from the town of Deadwood.

The passengers howled and cheered their applause.

"You can let go now," Martha said quietly.

JW lifted his hands off the girl's and gently rubbed the palms together. "Now what?" he asked.

"Get on the radio, let the authorities know what's been happening here. Deadwood's days are numbered."

"I meant what about you. What are you going to do?"

"Find my brothers," she said fiercely.

JW came around the chair and knelt down, so that his face was on a level with hers. "That was a good thing you did today, Miss Martha. I'm proud to know you."

She nodded, suddenly conscious of the heat in her cheeks. The last person who'd told her she was proud of her was her mother. Martha blinked hard, embarrassed by the prickling at the back of her eyes. "I couldn't have done it without you," she said shyly. "Thank you."

"We make a good team."

"We do."

JW suddenly stretched out his hand. "You know, I don't believe we were ever properly introduced. I'm Jesse Woodson James."

Martha took his hand in hers. "I'm Martha Jane Cannary Burke. My friends call me Calamity."

Jesse James looked back at the fireball rising over Deadwood and nodded.

"I can see why."

Code of Blood

by Dru Pagliassotti

La Reppublica di Venezia, 4 Maggio 1815—La Festa della Sensa

I: NIGREDO (THE HARROWING)

Chiara Dandolo was in disgrace, which is why she was leaning a ladder against the skylight of a large attic in the Old Prison instead of standing in the Piazzetta di San Marco next to her grandfather, preparing to head out to sea.

It was all a misunderstanding. Yes, she'd been in the Sala dello Scudo last night with the *cappelletto* Lucio Volpi, but he'd only been teaching her how to play the card game piquet. They hadn't even been wagering money, just buttons.

But her overprotective grandfather hadn't listened to a word of her explanation before forbidding her to participate in the next day's festivities—punishment for her "scandalous" behavior.

He never let her do anything. Sometimes she suspected he'd prefer to keep her wrapped in silk and locked away in the palazzo all her life, like some fragile ornament.

"Brezza?" she asked, looking up. "Is it clear?"

The tiny *silfo* gusted through the open skylight and danced around her shoulders, playfully disturbing her curls of dark hair. Chiara blew a puff of air at it and Brezza stole her breath a moment, making her gasp and laugh.

Reassured, Chiara adjusted the fabric bag that hung from her shoulder, hiked up her gold-and-crimson silk skirts, and began to climb.

Her dress hadn't been designed for calisthenics. Chiara had considered pilfering a pair of men's breeches and stockings, but only women of ill repute paraded around showing their legs, and she was in enough trouble already.

If she got caught—well, most likely, *when* she got caught—she only wanted to irritate her grandfather, not shame him.

At last she reached the top of the ladder. Dirt covered the slanted, sun-warmed lead-sheathed roof, but Brezza swooped down to blow it away and clear a spot for Chiara to crouch.

"Thank you," she said, panting a little from the climb. Since nobody else was on the roof, she tugged at the edges of her corset. She'd inhaled that morning while her maid had tightened its laces, wanting it to be a little looser than usual for this adventure, but the stiffened fabric still dug into her flesh.

Music and voices sounded from the piazza below. To her right, beyond the edge of the palazzo roof, rose San Marco's brick bell tower, crowned by its golden clockwork archangel Gabriel. Directly ahead, across the glittering water of the Bacino di San Marco, gleamed the white church of San Giorgio Maggiore.

The breeze off the lagoon still bore an early spring chill, but the skies were bright and clear.

It was a beautiful day for the Festival of the Ascension and the Sposalizio del Mare, the ceremony in which her grandfather ceremonially wed the Adriatic and reaffirmed Venezia's alchemical pact with the *ondine* who protected the lagoon.

Disgrace or no disgrace, Chiara was not going to be left out of her favorite day of the year. So she'd taken a page from Venezia's most infamous scoundrel, spy, and alchemist, Giovanni Giacomo Casanova, planning an escape *over* her guards rather than *through* them.

She was luckier than Casanova. His familiar had been a *gnomo*, a spirit of earth—useful for breaking through a lead roof but not much help getting from roof to ground.

Chiara, on the other hand, had an affinity for the silfi, the spirits of the air.

She slipped off her embroidered morocco slippers and crossed the palazzo roof, heading away from the lagoon. She stopped close to the basilica. The Rio di Palazzo, that shadowy canal that ran beneath the Ponte dei Suspiri and adjacent to the palazzo's eastern wall, narrowed here. On the other side was a little street by Sant'Apollónia that was, at the moment, empty.

She set out five small brass trays from her bag, making sure they wouldn't slide off the slanted roof into the canal below. A tiny pinch of tinder on each, and then she thrust an alchemical match into a phial of igniting liquid. Its tip burst into flame. She touched the flame to the tinder and dropped the match, which guttered out on the lead roof.

After re-capping the phial, she sprinkled grains of resin incense over the trays.

Frankincense, myrrh, cassia, and benzoin—the perfumed smoke coiled into the air, and curious silfi began to gather. Air elementals were capricious things, harder to please than earth and fire but less demanding than water. Chiara knew the smoke would win their attention for a minute or two.

"Brezza," she murmured, respectful of the spirits' presence, "would you ask them to carry me down to the street across the canal?"

Her familiar gusted past her face in reply. Chiara set down the bag and picked up her shoes. She'd have to leave the bag and trays; either she'd retrieve them another day or they'd be swept off the roof in one of Venezia's rainstorms.

Wind began to whip around her. The silfi had agreed. She drew in a deep breath and lifted her face. Her exhale began long and slow, but then the air spirits began to drink, greedily sucking the air from her lungs. She closed her eyes against her sharp, instinctive fear of suffocation, trusting Brezza to keep the silfi from taking too much.

Then, without warning, she rose into the air, free again to gasp for breath. Clutching her shoes with one hand and holding down her skirts with the other, Chiara was lifted across the canal and set down, none too gently, on the street on the other side.

She staggered, grabbing a wall to steady herself, and then laughed and straightened up.

"Thank you!" she shouted, beaming and waving. The dust around her feet whirled into the air a moment, leaving a sheen of dirt on her skirts.

"Although I could have done without *that*," she muttered, brushing it off. When the gold-embroidered silk looked respectable again, she slipped on her shoes and walked around Sant'Apollónia back to the masses who thronged the edges of the Canale di San Marco.

Pushing through the shoulder-to-shoulder mob was impossible. Everybody in the city seemed to have collected along the *fondamenta*, from fishmongers to foreigners to fashionably-dressed nobles, all pressed together without concern for rank or gender. Nobody seemed inclined to make room for anybody else.

Chiara squirmed and twisted to the water's edge. Ornate, gilded boats bobbed around the massive bulk of the Bucintoro like cygnets around a mother swan. The Bucintoro itself, its great, two-decked body adorned with a riot of gilded clockwork sirens, hydras, *putti*, and zephyrs, loomed over the Molo. A removable walkway draped with flags and ribbons and wreaths swung from its top deck to the piazzetta.

And there, in the piazzetta, she spotted a crowd of ceremonially-robed councilors surrounding her grandfather, the doge of Venezia, Carlo Dandolo.

Somebody jostled her and she nearly lost her footing. Grabbing the nearest arm, Chiara pulled herself away from the water with a quick apology and then darted from the bystander's merry attempt to catch her around the waist. His laughter followed her as she hid behind a group of heavyset grandmothers who were barreling their way through the crowd with the implacable dignity of age and righteousness. Chiara meekly followed in their wake.

Crossing the Ponte di Paglia was another struggle, but her advance guard of *nonne* battled through, spitting dire imprecations in fierce Veneziano. Chiara stayed close behind.

She had just set foot on the other side of the bridge when she heard a series of sharp reports. For a moment she thought somebody had set off fireworks, but then an explosion ripped through the air and people began screaming.

The panicked press of the mob physically shoved her backward. Alarmed, Chiara grabbed the bridge's stone railing, holding on tightly. Her eyes instinctively went to the piazzetta, searching for her grandfather.

"Save us, Mother of God!" one of the black-veiled grand-mothers cried out, clutching a crucifix close to her bosom. "It's Napoleon!"

Napoleon. Chiara's eyes widened. Impossible. He'd recently escaped from Elba, but the republic had doubled its guard along every border and kept its Three Great Hermetic

Gates sealed, banning foreign traffic from the lagoon. Venezia couldn't risk another near-disaster like 1797, when Doge Lodovico Manin had trembled on the edge of surrender. The city was saved only after the Guild of Alchemical Engineers raised the Three Gates and whipped the ondine into a wild April tempest that had driven the invading French fleet aground.

Manin had stepped down, and Chiara's fiercely nationalist grandfather was elected in his place.

Napoleon had detested and coveted Venezia ever since.

"The doge!" someone shouted. "They're after the doge!"

"It's the Austrians!"

"It's the French!"

"Terrorists!"

"Protestants!"

"Grandfather!" Chiara's heart sped up. Her grandfather—the only family she had left—was he alive? She pushed herself away from the railing, fighting against the crowd. Fugitives from the shooting were pouring out of the piazzetta, some of them leaping into the lagoon in their terror. "Grandfather!"

The crowd was a montage of shouting, fear-filled faces, flailing arms, and pumping legs. For every two steps Chiara took forward, she was shoved back one. At last she lurched forward through a gap in the mob, but her foot caught on an irregular paving stone and she nearly fell. As she regained her balance, Chiara recognized the granite columns on either side of her. The one on her left was topped with a statue of St. Theodore and his crocodilian dragon, and the one on her right with a statue of St. Mark's winged lion.

She shuddered and crossed herself. It was bad luck to pass between Venezia's execution pillars.

Shots fired again and she twisted, spotting two dark shapes standing at the top of the campanile, holding rifles aimed down into the crowds. More shots sounded from the other side of the piazza. The attackers, whoever they were, must have climbed into the clock tower or stationed themselves between the four bronze horses of the basilica.

Praying to Theodore and Mark for protection, Chiara wrapped her arms around her shoulders and pushed forward again. Seconds later she stumbled over broken pavement stones and a black-robed body. She cringed. Fallen council members surrounded her, some groaning and crawling for shelter and others lying prone and glassy-eyed.

Trembling, Chiara knelt next to one of the Corner heirs, pulling aside the somber gown of office to reveal blood-stained finery beneath. The young man groaned. Pain-filled brown eyes fastened on her.

"Help—"

"Where's Nonno Carlo?" she demanded, reverting back to the nickname she'd used as a child. "Where's the doge?"

"Ah . . ." Blood bubbled against the man's pale lips as he gave her a despairing look. "No."

Her trembling increased.

"Be strong—somebody will come for you," she whispered, touching his cheek. He coughed. Tiny droplets of blood sprayed over her sleeve, staining the fabric.

Swallowing hard, she moved deeper into the wreckage of shattered stone and flesh.

There—she spotted the brilliant scarlet, purple, and white of her grandfather's ceremonial *dogalina* and the glitter of the pearls and precious stones on his *corno ducale*.

"Nonno!" She threw herself past a russet-robed man and onto the broken pavement. Her hands flew to her fallen grandfather's head and she pushed his white hair aside. Blood from a gash in his scalp streaked his narrow, wrinkled face and stained the piazza's pale stone.

Her grandfather blinked once, his dark eyes unfocused. One thin hand rose, bloodstained and weighted down by its heavy gold signet ring, to touch her face.

"Chiara . . ." his voice was like a sigh. "Why are you here?"

More shots filled the air. She flinched, throwing herself protectively over his chest. The robed man turned, frowning.

Through momentary gaps in the crowd, Chiara spotted blue-and-white uniformed men pushing into the piazza holding rifles with affixed bayonets. Brave citizens, some military and others civilian, rushed the invaders. Knives, rapiers, and bayonets flashed as the two sides clashed.

Somewhere, somebody began ringing a church bell, sounding the alarm at last.

"Get up," she urged her grandfather. "We have to hide!" If they could get to the colonnaded arcade of the palazzo and take cover behind one of its marble pillars, they might be safe.

The doge struggled to focus on her.

"Go," he said, his voice faint. "The Guild will help you."

Chiara shook her head, standing.

"No. Come, Nonno, we—"

She heard a report and the whine of a bullet that passed close to her head. With a gasp she sat down hard next to her grandfather.

"Stop!" the robed man threw out a hand and shouted a word in Latin. The piazza burst into flame as three large, fiery salamandre materialized, looking much like St. Theodore's squat dragon as they snarled and spat sparks. They lumbered forward toward the startled French invaders as Veneziani cheered and backed out of the way.

Chiara's grandfather took her hand.

"Run," he said. "I'll be all right. It's just my leg."

She looked at him, disbelieving.

"Nonno . . ."

"Chiara!" He sucked in a painful breath and turned his head toward her, scowling just as he had earlier that morning, when he'd forbidden her to leave the palazzo. "Stop arguing and obey. You must go, before it's too late. *Maestro!*"

"*Illustrissimo* . . ." the robed man left his salamandre to their work and turned, kneeling again. Chiara recognized him as Jacopo Lezze, the grand master of the Guild of Alchemical Engineers.

"Protect my granddaughter," the doge whispered, his voice weak but still imbued with the tenor of command.

"Of course." Lezze met her eyes for the first time. "Come, *eccellentissima*, we should go."

"We can't leave my grandfather here!"

"He was shot in the leg. He can't run but, God willing, he won't die from the wound."

"But his head—"

"A scrape from the fall." Her grandfather closed his eyes. "I'll be well, Chiara. Now, go."

"We will send his cappelletti for him once you're safely in the palazzo," Lezze said. "Come. You can't do any good sitting here."

Chiara reluctantly nodded. He was right.

"All right."

Lezze held out a hand and she took it, allowing him to help her back up to her feet. His skin was summoning-cold, as if he'd bathed in ice water.

"*Assassini!*" somebody screamed behind them, from the palazzo.

Lezze yanked her aside, shielding her with his body. Chiara peered over his shoulder. French soldiers were pouring through the second-story loggia of the palazzo, pointing rifles down at the piazza from the colonnade.

The enemy had infiltrated the ducal palace.

Shock, indignation, and fear warred within her as the deadly rifle barrels rose. For one endless moment she stared up at the weapons, certain they would be the last thing she'd ever see.

Lezze yanked a narrow-bladed dagger from his belt and plunged it into his arm, twisting out a chunk of flesh.

"*Venite!*"

To Chiara's amazement, the sculpted figures on the columns twisted and began to climb, their stubby fingers sinking into stone as though it were cotton. The French soldiers leaped back, training their guns on the *gnomi*, and began to fire. Marble shattered, stone shards flying everywhere.

"Come." Lezze grabbed her shoulder, pulling her away.

"Your arm!"

"Later!" He drew her into the mass of people who had stopped to cheer the elementals. Chiara bit down on her protests and let the alchemist lead her through the piazza to the *sottoportego* beside the church of San Geminiano. They ducked through the narrow passage and dodged into an alley, panting.

"A minute," Lezze gasped, leaning against a brick wall and clutching his wounded arm. He pulled out a handkerchief.

"Let me." Chiara took it as he rolled up his sleeve, revealing a bloody gouge. His entire arm was scarred with old wounds and new scabs. "Did you have to cut so deeply?"

"Fast work means crude sacrifices." He stood still as she wrapped the fabric around his arm. She pulled the knot tight and he winced.

"Will your elementals keep Grandfather safe?"

"They'll keep the French busy." He opened his eyes again. "But there will be more soldiers in the city. This was a carefully planned attack."

"They're barbarians, attacking on Ascension Day."

"They're infernally clever." He drew a deep breath. "And they'll be looking for you, *magnifica*."

"Why? Grandfather's the doge—I'm nothing."

"You have your grandfather's blood, and because of that, they'll do anything in their power to capture you today."

II: ALBEDO (THE PURIFICATION)

"Go to the Guild in Murano and tell them what's happened," he continued. With his good arm, he pulled off his heavy bronze chain and medallion and held it out. "Take this with you. My apprentice is there; he'll know what to do."

"You aren't coming with me?"

"I'll distract the soldiers as long as I can. It'll buy you some time—you'll need as much as you can get."

Chiara started to protest, but then she thought of her grandfather, lying with a bullet in his leg. She fell silent.

Elsewhere in the city, the church bells kept ringing and shots were fired, but the noise faded around her as she listened to her heart.

Her grandfather was helpless; she wasn't. And if Lezze said she could help by warning the Guild, then it was her duty to go.

She lifted her eyes.

"Don't die, Maestro," she said gravely, meeting his gaze. "You need to keep my grandfather safe and make sure he's seen by a physician."

"I'll do everything I can," Lezze promised.

"All right." She took the heavy medallion and wrapped it in her own lace-edged silk handkerchief. The alchemist nodded.

151

"Good luck," he said, as she turned and plunged back out of the alley.

She ran to Campo Santa Maria di Giglio, where she found men and women gathered in alarmed clusters. As soon as she appeared they surged forward, shouting questions.

"It's the French," she said, clutching her precious bundle. "They shot my . . . they shot the doge!"

Cries of protest and outrage rose from the listeners.

"It's Napoleon!" somebody cried out. "I knew he would return!"

"What about the Gates? Did they get past the Gates?"

"How dare they attack on a holy day?"

"Please, *cittadini illustri*," Chiara pleaded, "we have to do something. We can't let Venezia fall."

Curses and roars of "no!" met her words. A group of young bravos carrying knives and clubs broke away, running toward the piazza. The crowd cheered.

Chiara worked her way through the campo, forgotten, until she reached the Giglio dock. A roughly dressed middle-aged man was leaning on an oar, watching.

"Excuse me, *signor*. I need to go to Murano to warn the Guild. Will you take me?"

His dark eyes flickered up and down, taking in her rich garments and jewelry.

"It's for the safety of Venezia," she added, hoping to appeal to his patriotism. "The Guild can drive the invaders out."

"Yes, of course, *gentildonna*," he replied sourly. "But you understand, a man has to make a living."

Not at the republic's expense, she thought, but she fought to keep her disapproval off her face. She hadn't brought any money, so she tugged off a gold-and-amber ring that had been a birthday present two years ago, handing it to him.

"This should be enough," she said.

152

He gave her a mocking smile and gestured toward one of the *batèle*, the city's traditional shallow-bottomed boats. With a touch of trepidation, Chiara swept her skirts off the ground and carefully made her way across the wood dock to the boat. The man strode past her and stepped in, turning to offer his hand.

"Thank you," she said, hoping her distaste for the way his hand squeezed hers wasn't too obvious.

"My pleasure," he said. "You can sit on the prow, if you want."

The polished wood that covered the front of the boat looked clean enough. The salt spray from the lagoon's waves would probably ruin her dress, but that hardly mattered anymore.

"What's your name, *signor*?" she asked, arranging her skirts as the boatman untied the ropes and used his oar to push away from the dock.

"Lucco, *gentildonna*." He stepped up onto the stern, set his oar in the twisted *forcola* oarlock, and maneuvered the craft free of the others. "You want to avoid the French?"

"Of course."

"Then we'll take a shortcut." He turned the boat toward the narrow, shadowed canals that criss-crossed the city rather than rowing straight into the Great Canal.

Their route took them diagonally through Sestiere San Marco into Castello and up to Rio di San Giustina. As Lucco rowed, Chiara listened to shots and shouts and caught glimpses of people running back and forth through the streets. Once or twice she saw the white pants and blue jackets of the French, but the soldiers seemed intent on their own business and ignored the quiet batèla slipping past them.

As they drew close to Fondamenta Nuove, a cannon roared. They both flinched, rocking the boat.

"The Arsenale," Chiara guessed, her ears ringing.

"The whoresons haven't broken through the Gates," Lucco agreed as another cannon fired.

The batèla entered the open, unusually empty Canale delle Fondamenta Nuove. Chiara twisted around, searching for some sign of military activity by the great dockyards of the Arsenale. People and boats had gathered wherever the streets and campi opened up to the water, but it was hard to make out details against the bright sun. She didn't see any French ships, though. The Gates were still sealed.

As long as the lagoon was secure, Venezia had a chance.

She clutched the handkerchief-wrapped medallion and hoped her grandfather was all right. He was stern, proud, and sometimes arrogant, but every inch an heir of the fierce warrior-doge Enrico Dandolo who, at age ninety and virtually blind, had led an invasion of Constantinople and taken the city.

Chiara straightened her back. That was *her* birthright, too. The blood of four doges ran through her veins.

She didn't plan to shame any of them.

The batèla passed the island San Cristoforo, with its dark, rectangular church, and then its close neighbor San Michele, with its pale dome.

Beyond them rose the tall buildings and chimneys of Murano.

Murano was the home of Venezia's alchemical engineers, who had been sequestered there since 1291 in an attempt to keep the city safe from their volatile experiments. They'd put their mark on the island. Top-heavy iron chimney flues rose over Murano's high-walled, narrow stone buildings, which pressed against each other, bristling with sextants and turquets and telescopes and other, more mystifying instruments. The misshapen watercraft at their docks combined the elegant lines of Venezia's *sàndoli*, batèle, *caorlìne*, and *peàte* with bizarre, ungraceful mechanical engines and paddlewheels and, in one case, an articulated brass man holding a wooden oar.

Today, Murano seemed abandoned. Nobody was fishing; nobody was walking along the streets. No children were playing along the waterfront, and no seniors were taking in the sun.

Had everyone gone to the city for the festival?

"The Guild headquarters is by Palazzo Giustinian," she said, feeling uneasy. Lucco rowed them through the empty waters past Rio Alchimia toward the Canal Grande di Murano.

As they reached the mouth of the canal, they saw a line of flat-bottomed peàte strung across the water like beads on a necklace. French soldiers stood along the fondamenta in orderly ranks, holding rifles.

Lucco swore, shifting his weight and making their little batèla rock as he propelled it back around the curve of the island.

"Too late," he said. "They're here."

"The Guild can't have fallen! We'd have heard the fighting."

He shrugged, setting the dripping oar inside the boat. "Maybe they just arrived."

Chiara clutched the medallion tighter.

She had to get to the Guild. The alchemical engineers were the only ones in Venezia with the knowledge and resources to save her grandfather.

"Can . . . can you let me off somewhere close?"

"Well, now, *gentildonna*," Lucco said slowly, "I'm afraid the price has just gone up."

Chiara turned, drawing back as she saw the rapacious look on his face.

"What do you mean? That ring was worth a month's wages."

"But not your life." Lucco bared his teeth in a predatory smile. "I don't know who you are, little girl, or what you're holding so tightly, but I'm willing to bet those soldiers would be *very* happy with me if I handed you over to them right now. I wouldn't mind making the French happy, not if they're going to take over Venezia, do you understand?"

A cold knot formed in her stomach.

"You'd betray your own homeland?"

"Not if you give me what I want."

Chiara shot him a furious look. Traitor! Then, disdainfully, she pulled off the rest of her rings and unclasped her bracelet and necklace.

"There." She held out the handful of gold and jewels. "That's everything I have."

"Not everything." He jerked his chin toward the package in her lap. "What's that?"

"It belongs to the Guild."

"Open it."

She glared at him. He was bigger and stronger than she was, and if the boat overturned in a struggle, she'd be lucky to make it to shore in her heavy dress.

She was at his mercy.

Hating him as much as she hated the French, Chiara unwrapped the bronze medallion. Its thick central disk was covered with an odd jigsaw-patterned design of interlocking gears, and alchemical symbols had been carved into each link of its heavy ceremonial chain.

"Give it to me."

"It's unique—you could never sell it. The Guild would know."

"I could melt it down and sell the bronze." Lucco stepped

down from the stern and walked toward her. "Give it all to me and maybe, if you're lucky, I won't demand anything else."

Chiara bristled. Jacopo Lezze had entrusted her with his medallion.

She had to turn the tables on Lucco, somehow.

"This is plenty." She set the handkerchief and medallion next to her and held out the gold and jewels. "You could live on it for two years, if you wanted."

"Don't get uppity with me, you rich little—" He reached out and Chiara jerked her hand over the edge of the batèla, opening her fingers.

Lucco lunged, trying to catch the glittering jewels before they fell into the water. Chiara's other hand flew out, shoving him. He stumbled against the gunwale and teetered.

With an angry cry, she shoved him again.

The boat tilted as Lucco fell over the side, shouting. Chiara gasped as her handkerchief slid toward the water. Her fingers snagged the fabric, but the heavy medallion went overboard.

"No, no, no!" Horrified, she threw herself forward just as a sputtering, furious Lucco grabbed the gunwale with one hand, glaring at her.

"I'll kill you!" he hissed, pulling himself up. The boat tilted at a sharp angle again and the loose oar rattled.

Sobbing with frustration, Chiara snatched up the oar and slammed it against his knuckles.

He swore and she brought the oar down again. He yanked his hand back and his head vanished underwater.

She jammed the oar into the water, feeling the blade hit Lucco's shoulder, and pushed with all her strength. The batèla drifted a few feet away.

Lucco rose from the water again, gasping. She brandished her makeshift weapon.

"Come any closer and I'll hit you again!"

He glowered and called her every dirty name she knew and a few she didn't, but instead of swimming toward the boat, he headed toward the wooden docks along the fondamenta.

Relieved, Chiara leaned against the covered stern, her heart thudding against her ribs.

He would hunt for her, she was certain, or maybe even alert the French. Either way, she had to leave this part of the island and disembark someplace he couldn't find her.

But now she didn't have anything left to bribe authorities— or to prove she'd been sent by Jacopo Lezze. She'd lost it all.

Tears of frustration burned her eyes. Everything seemed to have gone wrong. She was worried about her grandfather and frightened for her city and she had nothing left to help either of them.

Brezza slipped past her face, drying her eyes. Chiara took a deep breath and tightened her jaws, fighting back her misery.

She might have lost everything, but she could still find the Guild and try to save her grandfather.

Grimly determined, she hiked up her skirts and clambered onto the batèla's stern. She hadn't rowed since she was a child, and then she hadn't been wearing a corset and dress. But the lagoon's water ran in her blood. She struggled to summon that ancestral knowledge as she set the long oar back into the forcola. Her feet slipped on the polished wood. She pulled off her silk slippers, now badly scuffed, soiled, and stained, and dropped them into the bottom of the boat.

The batèla's sun-warmed wood was oddly comforting under her bare feet.

Chiara slowly turned the prow of the batèla and began rowing toward Rio Alchimia, grateful to Brezza for keeping her cool. She struggled to keep her back straight and her feet solidly planted, just as her father had taught her years ago.

Bit by bit, the lessons were returning.

A shout made her look over her shoulder. Lucco had pulled himself out of the water and was shaking a fist, calling her names, of which "thief" was the least offensive.

And then, as though his cries were a signal, the shooting began, and a flock of startled pigeons rose from the city like a cloud of smoke.

III: CITRINITAS (THE ENLIGHTENMENT)

The gunfire hadn't stopped fifteen minutes later, when Chiara pulled herself gracelessly out of the batèla. After brushing yet more dirt off her skirts, she pulled on her slippers and nudged the boat back into the wide canal. She'd considered tying it up, but if Lucco was looking for it, she preferred that it drift as far away as possible.

"All right, Brezza," she whispered. "I'll bet you know where the Guild is, don't you?"

The silfo created a small whirlwind of dust and set it skipping forward.

The miniature storm led her through the abandoned streets, darting off every few minutes to flap through somebody's drying sheets, waft a discarded piece of paper into the air, or ruffle the fur of a sleeping cat. Chiara was patient. Air elementals were flighty; she was lucky to get as much from Brezza as she did.

Not that she needed much help. Street by street, they drew closer to the sound of fighting. At last it seemed straight ahead, and she slowed her pace, creeping through the narrow gaps between the alchemists' tall buildings and huddling close to the wall whenever a shot sounded nearby. She was skirting a tall, spike-tipped wall when a grinding sound reverberated through the ground, nearly knocking her off her feet. A roar like a lion's filled the air, followed by cries of alarm.

Her eyes rose. A great, sculpted metal-winged lion of St. Mark stood on the corner of the reinforced brick building she recognized as the Guildhall. The lion crouched as though ready to pounce, its massive front paws on top of a closed book and its hinged jaws gaping wide.

As she stared, another roar burst from it as it spewed liquid fire somewhere along Fondamenta Marco Giustinian. And, judging from the shouting and French curses, very close to the invading force.

A grin broke across her face. Three more lion sculptures were set along the top of the building, one at each corner. As she watched, they slowly rotated on huge metal turntables, their jaws opening.

Over them all proudly flapped the crimson-and-gold flag of the republic.

A splintering crash rose from beyond the wall beside her. Chiara crept forward and found a giant metal door in the wall standing open. Peering inside, she saw the Guild building itself, beyond a courtyard full of half-finished machines. People were shouting and shooting inside.

A tall man in a fine French-cut blue suit stood by the doorway to the building, frowning as he looked inside. He was carrying a polished walking stick instead of a gun, and he didn't bear himself like a military man.

A soldier appeared, clutching the collar of a chestnut-haired young man about Chiara's age who struggled in his grip.

"He was upstairs in the control room, working alone," the soldier reported in French. Chiara's grandfather had required her to learn French, saying that one could never know enough about one's enemies.

One more thing she owed him.

"An apprentice?" The tall man sounded unimpressed and switched to French-accented academy Italian. "Who else is up there? Where's Lezze?"

"Guillaume LeClerc." The boy sneered. "You dirty French dog—we never should have trusted you."

LeClerc made a dismissive gesture. "How many others are still in the Guild? Tell me the truth, and I will try to keep the bloodshed to a minimum."

The youth spat into LeClerc's face. The soldier threw him down into the courtyard and kicked him in the side. Chiara sucked in a breath. The boy was brave, but he was going to get himself killed.

"Should I take care of him?" the soldier asked, lifting his rifle suggestively.

"No, no, he may be of use at the Gate. Tie him up and take me to the control room. If they have a graphocaster, I'll signal our commander to tell him we've reached the Guild."

"Yes, sir." The guard kicked the young man again for good measure and unslung the small pack on his back, pulling out rope. A minute later, the apprentice was bound and gagged and left in the courtyard, and the guard and LeClerc vanished inside the building.

Chiara ran across the cobbles and knelt next to the young man. He gave her an amazed look.

"Shhh." She pulled the guard's balled-up handkerchief out of his mouth.

"Ah, you're an angel! What's your name?"

"I said 'shhh,' *signor*." She moved to one side and began plucking at the tight knots around his wrist. "Maestro Lezze sent me. He gave me his medallion as proof, but I lost it."

"*Il maestro*! Where is he? Does he know—"

"He stayed back to protect the doge."

161

"Is the doge all right?"

"The French shot him in the leg. I . . . I think he'll live." She swallowed a lump in her throat.

She hoped he'd live.

"I hope so, as well." The apprentice sounded worried. "Can you manage the knots?"

"They're tight." She stopped. "If there's a piece of sharp metal out here, maybe . . ."

"Move back, *signorina*. My familiar will help."

She sat back, curious.

"Tizzo," he whispered, "are you there?"

A flame ignited the rope around the youth's wrists.

Tizzo was a *salamandra*.

"You'll burn yourself," she warned.

"Maybe a little." He gave her a confident smile. "It's all right; I'm used to it."

Chiara glanced away, taken aback by his casual attitude. The metal lions had stopped roaring, but the soldiers inside the Guild were still shooting and shouting.

"Are there many engineers inside?"

"No, don't worry. Almost everyone was in Venezia for the festival." The boy couldn't hide his sudden wince as the flame reached his flesh.

"Tizzo, stop!" Chiara demanded. "I'll do the rest."

The spark wavered once and then obediently flickered out. She yanked on the charred rope, breaking the last strands.

The young man pulled his arms away and she caught his hands, turning them palm up to inspect the damage. His flesh was cool from commanding the little salamandra, but blisters had formed from the elemental's heat.

"Tizzo obeyed you," he observed with fascination. "Not many people can command elementals other than their own. Who are you, *signorina*?"

"Chiara." She met his rapt gaze and felt a shock run through her.

Nobody had ever looked so deeply into her eyes before. Her breath quickened and her pulse started to pound.

"You're very beautiful, *Signorina* Chiara," he said.

Flustered, she blushed and released him.

"Come on." Why was she letting him affect her like that, when they had more important things to do? "We have to get out of here before they see us."

"I'm Pietro," he said, standing. "I know where we can hide."

"What about—" she looked back at the building.

"I activated a few combat automata that ought to keep the soldiers busy for a while." He smiled again with the same calm, confident expression he'd shown before.

"But—the others?"

"There are no others. I sent all the other apprentices away to warn their families as soon as we saw the boats and the rifles." He took her hand and urged her through the courtyard and into the alley.

"You mean, you were the only one in there?"

"I'm Maestro Lezze's assistant. It was my duty to stay as long as I could."

"Then you're the one he sent me to meet!"

Pietro glanced back at her, his hand tightening on hers.

"Was my master all right when you left him?"

"He hadn't been shot, but he was cut and shivering from his summonings."

"Ah, stupid." Pietro sounded worried. "He keeps forgetting his age. His body can't handle that kind of strain anymore."

Chiara tugged her hand out of his. "He's not stupid. He jumped between me and the French, and he made sure I was safe before he headed back."

"Well," Pietro said, his smile returning, "at least he's not stupid enough to ignore a pretty girl."

She didn't know how to respond to that, so they wound through tight alleys and tiny campielli in silence for several minutes.

"Where are we going?" she asked at last.

"I can't take you to Maestro Lezze's house. LeClerc has been there before. But I know some smaller workshops, ones LeClerc never visited. We can hide in one of them until nightfall."

"Will a real alchemical engineer be there?"

"*I'm* a real alchemical engineer. Almost."

"Pietro!"

"No. They all went to the festival. I'm sure they'll stay to fight the French."

Chiara held her other questions as they skirted the milling invasion force and headed out to the city's borders. A narrow road along the outskirts led to a small stone building with a canal behind it.

Pietro pulled a strange-looking tubular key out of his pocket. He twisted and turned it until all the notches were in a particular order and then inserted the key into the metal lock on the door, opening it.

As Chiara entered, she realized that the door and the frame were both made of painted iron. This was more than a mere farmhouse.

Pietro pulled down a lantern and called Tizzo to light the wick, revealing a metal-reinforced laboratory filled with tables covered with ornate glass tubes and retorts, funnels, and flasks.

"Brezza, please be careful," Chiara warned as her familiar curiously swept from table to table, rattling the delicate tubing.

"Your familiar is a silfo." Pietro sounded pleased. "Perfect for an angel like you." He grabbed her right hand and brought it to his lips, his brown eyes warm as he gazed admiringly at her. "I haven't thanked you properly for rescuing me."

Chiara blushed. The skin on the back of her hand burned where his lips had brushed it, and she was suddenly aware that, despite his apprentice's uniform and callused hands, Pietro was a handsome young man.

She pulled her hand away.

"Stop it. This is no time to flirt."

"I'm not flirting; I'm stating a fact. I *hadn't* thanked you for rescuing me. We alchemical engineers always prefer facts to flirtation."

She shot him a look and saw the twinkle in his eyes.

"You're not an alchemical engineer; you're an apprentice."

"Only for two more years."

"And you need to be more serious," she scolded, turning away. "My grandfather was shot by those soldiers. People are dying out there."

His smile faded and he nodded, pulling around chairs for both of them.

"You're right." His expression darkened. "The Guild was wondering if Napoleon would make another attempt on Venezia after his escape, but we never heard a word. LeClerc knows us and our agents too well."

"Who is LeClerc?"

"A French alchemist who studied here in his youth. He's come back to visit several times, despite Napoleon. My master trusted him." Pietro ran a hand through his hair. "He knows too much about our defenses."

"Maestro Lezze told me to come to the Guild and tell you what happened. He said you'd know what to do. But I'm sure he never thought the Guild would be betrayed." Chiara rubbed her temples, feeling tense. "Now what?"

"You said he gave you his medallion?"

"Yes, but I lost it when I was attacked." She quickly explained what happened.

"I hope the French find that man and shoot him," Pietro exclaimed, angrily. "Threatening a desperate woman is despicable."

She leaned forward and touched his knee, shaking her head.

"No—if they find him, he'll tell them about me. It's better if he gets away."

Pietro gave her a puzzled look, his eyes flickering over her dress. Chiara self-consciously ran a hand over her dusty and salt-stained skirt and hid her feet beneath its hem. The soles of her shoes were getting holes in them; they'd never been intended for rough cobblestone streets.

She looked like a wreck.

"Why would the soldiers want to find you? Certainly, the French appreciate a beautiful woman, but—"

"My grandfather is the doge," she said, cutting him off before he could embarrass her further.

To her amazement, the color drained from his face. He stood, nearly stumbling over his chair in his haste.

"I . . . I . . ." he stammered, "I'm sorry. I didn't know."

Chiara rose. Pietro seemed scared to death, and it occurred to her that she should have mentioned her last name.

"It's all right," she said. "I should have said something. I forgot."

"I . . . I would never have brought you here . . ."

Oh! Chiara looked around, chagrined.

If she'd caused a minor scandal simply by being alone with a guard inside the palace, being alone with a young man in a remote farmhouse could ruin her reputation entirely.

Which, she thought with frustration, was absolutely ridiculous.

"Oh, stop it. You're not going to get into any trouble. My grandfather was the one who told me the Guild could help me in the first place. So relax and *help*, and everything will be all right."

He shifted from foot to foot, avoiding her eyes.

"I'm sorry. I don't even know how to address you. Nobody ever taught me court etiquette."

"It doesn't matter. The only thing that matters is getting my grandfather free and driving the French away."

He nodded but kept his eyes fixed on the dusty workroom floor.

"Look—Pietro—just sit down and act like you did before." She sank back down into her own chair. "I need you to help me figure out what to do next."

"All right." He gingerly sat and collected his thoughts. "You said your grandfather was shot."

"In the leg."

"Was he captured?"

"Not when I was there but . . . probably. The soldiers were all over Piazza San Marco, and they'd broken into the palazzo." She braced herself. "Do you think they'll kill him?"

"No! No, Chi—uh . . . I don't think they'd kill him. Napoleon's too smart to turn him into a martyr. Most likely he'll demand that your grandfather step down and turn the republic over to France, just like he did before."

He frowned.

"What?"

"You're the doge's only surviving relative?"

"In the direct line, yes. There are other Dandolos in Venezia and abroad."

"Ah." His frown deepened.

"Tell me!"

"Well . . . how much do you know about the Sposalizio del Mare?"

"The doge marries the Adriatic Sea on Ascension Day every year. It's how the republic maintains its pact with the ondine, so that they'll protect us from invaders." She paused. "Do you think—have the French broken the pact?"

"They can't break it, but if the ritual isn't completed today . . ."

Chiara's eyes widened.

"How much longer do we have?"

"Until sunset."

"Then we only have a few hours left to rescue him!"

"Ch—it's not that easy. We also need the ring."

"He didn't give it to me."

"It was locked inside Maestro Lezze's medallion. That's why he wanted you to bring it back here."

Chiara covered her mouth with one hand, shocked.

"He should have told me," she whispered. "It fell into the lagoon—does that count?"

"No. The ritual needs to take place outside the Lido Gate, and the ring needs to make contact with the water."

"Can we get another ring?"

"It's forged out of carmot, an alchemical metal made from the doge's blood."

Despair swept over her.

"Then I've failed." She buried her head in her hands, the tears she'd fought back all day spilling over at last. "I've doomed the republic."

After a minute she felt a tentative touch on her shoulder.

"Er—"

She shook her head, not wanting to hear any words of sympathy. By sunset the French would be free to sail into the lagoon and Venezia would fall.

"Chiara—there's still hope."

She sniffed and looked up. Pietro was kneeling on the floor next to her chair, staring intently at her again.

"What?" she whispered, wiping her eyes with her hands.

"The ring works because it holds the doge's *cifra di sangue*, his blood code. As his direct descendant, your blood might be accepted by the ondine in his place. It should be similar enough."

Chiara thrust out an arm. "Then take it!"

"We don't have time to make a ring." He met her eyes. "You'll have to go to the site yourself and bleed into the sea."

She swallowed, lowering her arm again.

"Just . . . cut myself and bleed?"

"Yes. It takes two pints to make a ring, so . . ."

She winced. The laborers setting up the festival had been drinking pints of beer in the piazza all week.

Two pints was a lot of blood.

"And you have to say the ritual words, of course. I'm sorry. You understand the principle of sympathetic exchange?"

"Earth to flesh, air to breath, fire to temperature, and water to blood."

"Right. Nothing in the world is lost; only exchanged. Tizzo serves me in exchange for my body heat. And Brezza serves you in exchange for your breath."

"But she never takes that much . . ."

"You never ask that much. But if we want the ondine to protect our waters, we need to make a sufficient sacrifice. Two pints and . . ."

"What?"

"Anyone who falls into the lagoon during a storm." He shrugged apologetically. "It's a little more humane than human sacrifice, at least."

She drew in a breath.

"Will you take me to the right place? We don't need to be in the Bucintoro, do we?"

"No." He gazed at her. "But it's going to be dangerous. Are you sure?"

She met his eyes, trusting their steady attentiveness.

"When do we leave?"

IV: RUBEDO (THE ASSIMILATION)

Taking the farmhouse's small rowboat, they worked their way around Murano to dock where some of the engineers' strange watercraft were tied. The three Great Hermetic Gates of Venezia were located at the ports of Lido, Malamocco, and Chiogga. Lido was the site of the Sposalizio ceremony, but to get there in time they'd need something faster than a rowboat.

"This is Maestro Lezze's boat," Pietro said, climbing into a large boat with side-mounted paddle wheels and a bright metal chimney. It was a beautiful craft, with brass-covered gunwales covered in alchemical symbols and all the wood polished to a shine. He reached down and threw a rope-and-board ladder over the side.

"Does it run by steam?" Chiara asked, climbing up. She hesitated at the gunwale, and Pietro held out a hand to assist.

With his help, she managed to get aboard with a reasonable amount of modesty.

It took him a moment to remember to let go of her hand.

"Um, yes," he said hastily, pulling up the ladder again. "It's

a French design, based on Marquis Jouffroy d'Abbans'
Pyroscaphe. We improved it, of course."

"Is it safe?"

"Well, it *is* a French design." Pietro shot her a grin. She
gave him a skeptical look, secretly relieved that he was
relaxing around her again. "No, it's safe as long as we don't
spill any of this." He pulled out the small jars of amber liquid
he'd taken from the farmhouse—liquid fire, in case the
French chased them. "Better keep them far from Tizzo."

She stowed them by the prow while Pietro and Tizzo began
to stoke up the furnace. A small chest in the prow contained
scrolls and pens, navigation instruments, and a spyglass. She
pulled out the spyglass and looked toward Venezia. A faint
cloud of dark smoke hung near the Arsenale. More boats were
in the water. She guessed that the Veneziani were rallying.

She turned the glass toward Murano and saw a few faces in
the windows, watching them. She moved the glass and
groaned as she saw a shape bobbing on the water as it
rounded the tip of Fondamenta Serenella.

"Pietro! Lucco has his boat back!"

"Who? Oh, *him*. Is he coming this way?"

"Maybe."

She should have thrown the batèla's oar into the water.
That would have slowed him down.

"We'll be gone before he gets here," the apprentice assured
her.

Chiara nodded, watching the hateful man. He eventually
raised his head and looked straight at her. Then, slowly, he
lifted a hand from the oar and pointed.

She couldn't quite make out his expression, but she
guessed it wasn't very friendly.

"He sees us."

"It's all right."

"Pietro . . ."

"Yes?"

"He's turning the batèla. He's heading back the way he came."

"Toward the French?"

"Yes. I think so."

"Then would you ask Brezza to help stoke the fire?"

"Of course!" Chiara lowered the spyglass and turned.

With the fire tended by the two elementals, Pietro closed the furnace door. When the steam pressure rose, he took the rudder, next to a panel of levers that were connected to the paddlewheels and furnace through a complicated system of gears, pistons, and pipes.

"Have you . . . worked on this thing often?" Chiara asked, not sure quite how to describe the process of maneuvering a steamship. It wasn't rowing or sailing, that was for certain.

"Never." He grinned and threw a lever. The wheels on the left and right began to turn, propelling the craft backward into open water.

"But you've seen it done before, right?" she shouted over the grinding of the gears, the splashing of the water, and the rumble of the steam engine.

"Twice!"

Chiara buried her face in her hands and prayed to the saints that she hadn't entrusted her voyage to another madman.

After they'd traveled long enough for her to be certain that they weren't going to explode, she moved forward and leaned against the gunwale. Broad expanses of blue water and green marshland spread before her gaze. The sun warmed her back while occasional water droplets from the paddlewheels moistened her cheeks, but she was oblivious, her thoughts fixed on the mission ahead.

As granddaughter of the doge, getting past the Lido Gates shouldn't be too hard. And the ritual wouldn't be too difficult, either. She'd always been impressed by the pomp and ceremony when she'd gone with her grandfather, but Pietro said most of it was show. All the doge really needed to do was declare his intention and reaffirm the pact with his *cifra di sangue*.

Her stomach fluttered as she touched the small knife she'd taken from the farmhouse and tucked into her dresswaist. She'd already seen too much blood today. Soon she'd be seeing a lot more. But Pietro had promised he'd be there to monitor the ritual and bandage her when she was done.

She shot him a quick glance. He was standing with one hand on the rudder, grinning happily as the breeze ruffled his chestnut hair. They could be going out to Lido for a picnic, for all the worry he showed.

Maybe someday they could do that, too.

Right. As if her grandfather would ever allow it.

Her eyes moved behind him and she straightened. A dark line of boats was moving away from Murano.

"Pietro—the French!" she shouted over the steamship's noisy engine. He gave her a puzzled look. She pointed behind him. He turned and the ship shuddered as his hand slipped on the rudder.

She moved to his side and lifted the spyglass.

"It's definitely the French," she reported. "That man in the blue coat is in the first boat."

"LeClerc." Pietro laid a hand on her shoulder, leaning closer so that he didn't have to shout so loud. She didn't mind. "He must have guessed where we were going when that traitor told him about us."

"Do you think he knows who I am?"

"He might have guessed." He squeezed her shoulder

173

gently. "I'll make sure you get to the ritual on time. I promise."

She looked up at him. Their faces were just inches apart, and for a breathless moment they both stood motionless, gazing at each other.

But then the boat shuddered and Pietro turned to correct the course. His cheeks were flushed, she saw, with a combination of embarrassment and satisfaction.

And so were hers. She raised the spyglass again to make it harder for him to tell.

"They're falling behind," she reported some time later. "But what happens when we get to the Gate? Won't they catch up then?"

"If they do, we'll have the rest of the alchemical engineers to help us." He glanced at her. "And *they* have guns and cannon."

She nodded, reassured.

Sure enough, the French boats fell back as the engineer's steam-powered watercraft chugged through the lagoon, frightening waterfowl and churning up the waters.

They reached Lido by late afternoon. Chiara lifted the spyglass again, studying the great wood-and-brass gate that towered over the water, encrusted with the immense pistons and gears that opened and closed it. The gate was flanked by a militant stone structure that stretched from the shore out into the water.

She lowered the glass to study the harbor.

Three large, flat-bottomed peàte were moored to the docks. And, his back propped against one of the brass-topped oak mooring posts, a French sentry lazily aimed his rifle at the seagulls overhead, pretending to fire.

Chiara grabbed Pietro's arm.

"The French are already here!"

174

"Impossible!"

She handed him the glass and he pointed it to the docks, then swung toward the gates. At last he lowered it, looking thoughtful.

"Maybe it was a three-pronged attack?" he asked. "One group attacks the city. One group attacks the Guild headquarters at Murano. And one group comes here. But that's so many soldiers . . ."

"And how could they get here?" Chiara protested. "Why didn't somebody fire on them?" She gestured to the crenellated walls, through which the muzzles of cannon glinted in the low sun.

"I don't know. Maybe they came in disguise?"

"The soldiers in San Marco and Murano were in uniform . . . Could there have been a traitor among the Gatehouse engineers?"

"Maybe, but how could one traitor keep the entire day-shift of engineers under control by himself? Especially on a day when everyone would be overly watchful and cautious?" Pietro stared at the sealed port. "Maybe they had a hostage."

"Everyone important was in the piazza with my grandfather for the festival." She looked up, alarmed. "What if they have him? What if they captured him and took him here?"

Pietro drew in a sharp breath. "Holding the doge hostage would keep us from firing."

"We need to hurry. Where do I have to go?"

"Wait. You can't get past that sentry by yourself!"

"I can't wait here, either. I need to go now. I can have the silfi carry me to the Gatehouse."

"It's too far. You'd pass out—they'd take too much breath." He looked around. "Can you swim?"

"Yes. But—" She gestured to her dress. "Not in this."

175

"Then you'll have to hold on to me for a little while we swim to shore. But I know how we can distract the guards."

"Hold on to you?"

He grinned. "I won't mind if you forget to let go when we get to shore."

She frowned, but her heart wasn't in it. "What are you going to do?"

He explained.

She *had* entrusted her voyage to a madman.

Ten minutes later, they were both in the water, clutching the rope ladder hanging over the back of the steamship as the craft dragged them toward the wharfs. Pietro had jammed the rudder in place and opened the valve to full power before they'd both climbed overboard.

The sentry soon heard the ship and turned, shouting in French and then in heavily accented Italian.

"Stop! Stop the boat!"

When nothing happened, he began to fire. Chiara winced as she heard a bullet ping off the exhaust vent and then, a minute later, another thud into the ship's hull.

The sentry began shouting in French again.

"Now!" Pietro exclaimed, letting go of the rope. Chiara released it, too, choking a moment as her head dipped under the water. Pietro grabbed her as she surfaced. Just as she'd feared, swimming was impossible in her skirts.

"Hold on!"

She threw her arms around his neck as he began swimming for shore under cover of the inexorably retreating steamship.

Chiara's feet touched ground just as a splintering crash heralded the craft's impact with the docks. Pietro scrambled upright, grabbing her hand and pulling her out of the water, one arm thrown over her back as if to protect her from—

A great booming explosion rattled through their bones and a ball of flame burst into the air as Tizzo followed through with his orders, igniting the liquid fire they'd poured over the craft.

For a moment they both knelt on the scrubby grass by the water, clutching each other in stunned silence. Somewhere out of sight they heard swearing and splashing. The sentry must have been thrown into the water.

Chiara shook herself and pulled away.

"Let's go!"

Pietro nodded, dragging his eyes from the fire.

"That was fantastic!" he declared, his face alight with enthusiasm.

Exasperated, Chiara grabbed her drenched skirts in both hands and began running toward the Gatehouse.

Soldiers in French uniforms were gathering on top of the battlements, attention caught by the flames destroying the dock and their transport ships. Nobody seemed to notice Chiara and Pietro as they raced up and flattened themselves against the wall, panting and dripping lagoon water.

"This way." Pietro took the lead and they crept like rats along the base of the giant walls, away from the water.

The Gatehouse was as much a military fortress as a building to house the complicated machinery that operated the Hermetic Gate. There was no hope of sneaking through the main doors, Pietro had said, but he knew of spillway reservoirs and sluice gates leading into the Gatehouse, and he had the maintenance combinations necessary to open them.

"How do you know so much about this place?" Chiara whispered as they slipped into one of the spillways. It was about six feet deep and three feet across, filled with a foot of stagnant water. She made a face as the stinking water soaked through her slippers and brownish-green algae clung to the hem of her dress.

"I work here sometimes."

"Is this where you want to go when you finish your apprenticeship?"

"Not really." He sighed. "I hate this place. Master Lezze sends me to clean the machinery every time I make a mistake."

"And you've made enough mistakes to memorize all the gate combinations?"

"Well—yes."

"Why does he keep you on as his apprentice?"

"Because when I *don't* make mistakes, I'm very impressive." He laughed as she kicked some greenish water at him.

"How long are you going to have to scrub gears now that you've blown up his ship?"

"Not at all, if the doge's beautiful granddaughter will vouch for me."

"Hmph. I see you aren't afraid of me anymore."

"Not while you have marsh grass in your hair."

She scowled and ran her fingers over her curls, dislodging several long, thin strands of dead grass. Pietro grinned and she flicked them onto his shirt as punishment.

"It's all right; you're still beautiful."

"And you're a shameless flirt."

"I prefer 'very impressive flirt,'" he said lightly, taking her hand and squeezing it a moment before releasing her. Then, turning serious again, he pointed. "We're almost there."

The sluice gate was a tall, nearly featureless metal door in the Gatehouse wall. A circular gearlock, each tooth numbered, held it shut.

Pietro twisted the gears back and forth until the lock

clicked. The gears dropped into a groove and continued to rotate as the door ground to one side.

"This way. Tizzo, where are you?" He rummaged in his bag and pulled out a tiny metal lamp.

Chiara slid inside as soon as the gate opened enough to let her pass. The only source of light was the little salamandra, burning like a candleflame in the lamp. Pietro held it up. Chiara got the impression of a vast space filled with machinery.

"Pumps and pipes," Pietro said, resetting the door's combination. It slid shut. "The Gate's primary purpose is to keep enemies out of the lagoon, but it also mediates the flow of the tides. The spillways divert excess water back out to sea to prevent flooding."

A giant rumbling sound made them both stop and look up.

"They're starting the engines," Pietro said.

They ran, their feet splashing through oily puddles of water and their ears deafened by the sound of rumbling pipes and slowly turning gears. Pietro led them up ladders and through narrow catwalks. Finally he threw open a door to reveal lantern light and two men in French uniforms examining a pressure gauge. Surprised, one of them reached for his rifle.

Pietro threw himself forward, knocking the soldier over. Chiara plucked up the rifle, turning and pointing it at the second soldier at the same time that he raised his own.

They stared at each other over the barrels.

"Put it down, little lady," the French soldier said.

"Put *yours* down," she replied.

Beside them, Pietro slammed a knee between the soldier's legs and rolled aside, lifting a hand.

"*Venite!*"

Fire burst over the soldier's sleeve as a large salamandra

materialized, its molten claws clutching his arm. The soldier howled and dropped his rifle, shaking his arm to try to jostle it free.

"Don't kill him!" Chiara grabbed the fallen rifle with her free hand.

The salamandra vanished.

"May I have one?" Pietro asked, shivering as he stood. She handed him the weapon and laid a hand against his face. His skin was cold.

"That wasn't Tizzo."

"No." He smiled, his cheek moving under her palm. "But it *was* very impressive, don't you think?"

"It wasn't bad," she allowed, dropping her hand and aiming the rifle again as the soldier finished slapping out the flames on his sleeve.

After Pietro locked the invaders in a room full of cleaning oil and rags, they advanced through the next corridor more carefully, holding the soldiers' rifles and lantern. In the brighter light, Chiara could see more of the machinery that ran the Grand Hermetic Gate of Lido—a vast, oily, sometimes dripping, tangle of metal and gears.

At last they came to two sets of stairs, one going up and the other down.

"The Gear Room is up there," Pietro said, pointing, "but the maintenance door that leads to the harbor is down here."

Chiara hesitated, torn between going up to find her grandfather and running down to complete the ritual.

"If they have my grandfather . . . What if they threaten to kill him to make me stop?"

Pietro gently took her rifle and then leaned over to press his lips against hers. She tried to draw in a startled breath, couldn't, and grabbed the front of his shirt for balance as she swayed.

They kissed for a long moment before pulling back, their eyes fastened wonderingly on each other.

Pietro finally smiled.

"You save the republic," he said. "I'll save your grandfather. With any luck, he'll be so grateful that he won't have me executed for falling in love with his granddaughter."

Heat rose in her cheeks.

She swallowed.

"Go on," he urged.

"But . . . but . . ." *Love?* "But I don't know what two pints of blood feels like! How will I know when to stop?"

"Let yourself bleed until you're dizzy," he said, his smile falling away. "But stop to bandage yourself as soon as you feel light-headed. You don't want to pass out while you're still bleeding."

Stop as soon as she felt light-headed? She already felt light-headed.

"Will you come find me?"

"As soon as I can."

She closed her eyes, trying to pull her thoughts into order. It would help a lot if her heart would stop beating so fast.

She hated to let him go, but Pietro had one shot in each rifle and his ability to summon elementals which, despite her teasing, *had* been impressive. All he needed to do was keep the soldiers from opening the Gate until she finished the ritual.

Then they'd be safe.

"All right," she said, opening her eyes again. "Be careful."

"You too, *bella*." He didn't show any intention of moving until she was gone, so she drew a deep breath and turned, heading down the stairs.

After the first turn she touched her lips.

If her overly protective grandfather ever learned of that stolen kiss, not even rescuing him from the French would keep Pietro safe.

She smiled and hurried down the stairs to open the maintenance door.

The outdoor light was momentarily blinding. She raised a hand and squinted at the broad expanse of the Adriatic. The massive construction of the Gatehouse and its Hermetic Gate rose on either side of the platform she was standing on. And straight ahead, dark and ominous, sailed a fleet of warships.

Their flags were dark silhouettes against the late afternoon sun, but she had no doubt that they displayed Napoleon's *tricolore*.

She turned and descended the ladder. Rust and dried sea salt crumbled beneath her hands, and the breeze off the ocean felt cold against her wet dress and hair. The giant engines that powered the Hermetic Gate's mechanisms were audible even out here, vibrating through the metal rungs.

"Brezza, are you there?"

The silfo brushed her face in reply.

At last she reached the narrow walkway, a precarious line between the Gatehouse wall and the open sea. Its large cut-stone blocks were slippery and covered with moss, threatening to pitch her into the water with one false step. She carefully turned, feeling salt spray soaking her. Down here, the engine's rumbling was drowned by the crash of waves against the towering Gate.

"I thought you might show up."

Chiara recoiled as the French alchemist LeClerc rose from the niche where he'd been resting. Fear weakened her knees and she clutched the ladder with one hand to steady herself.

"Signorina Chiara Dandolo, am I right? Or is there some sort of title I should be using? You Venetians have a surprising number of titles for an ostensible republic."

"How did you get here?"

"I had the silfi carry me over the gate, of course. I'm surprised you didn't do the same. But I suppose that apprentice you were with didn't have the stamina for it."

"You couldn't have had them carry you that far. You wouldn't be conscious."

He laughed.

"I didn't sacrifice my *own* breath. I sacrificed the breath of that odious water-rat we brought with us from Murano. I expect you won't shed any tears over him. He seemed thoroughly unpleasant."

"You're disgusting." Chiara tried to back up, but her shoulders hit the wall.

"Needs must, in times of war. They frown on me using our own soldiers, although the enemy is fair game. But you're in no danger, Signorina Dandolo, as long as you sit quietly and wait for the Gate to open."

Chiara swallowed. LeClerc was taller and stronger than she was, not to mention an elementalist. What if he summoned a salamandra on top of her, the way Pietro had atop that soldier? Or ordered a silfo to steal her breath?

Her heart pounded.

He could easily render her unconscious or even kill her, if he wanted. And that's all he needed to do to keep her from shedding her blood into the sea.

"Agreed?" LeClerc gave her a lazy smile. "And then we'll both go back and talk to your grandfather about handing over the republic. With Venice's warships and alchemically engineered armaments, the emperor should finally have the edge over the English he's been seeking for so long."

"You have my grandfather?"

"He should be upstairs, if he survived the initial attack. Our orders were to take both of you alive. Frankly, I think killing you would be safer but," he gestured dismissively, "as long as I get what I want, I don't really care."

"And what *do* you want?" Tucked out of his sight, her fingers curled around the hilt of the knife. Chiara sank into a crouch as if in pain.

"Control of your Guild, of course. Are you all right? Do you need a spot of brandy? I have a flask. Why don't we share it while we watch the fleet sail in?"

She shook her head, squeezing her eyes closed.

That morning, she'd awoken to the ringing of church bells and the light of a pale spring morning streaming through her casements. She'd had an exciting day planned—a day of adventure and disguise that she had guessed would probably end with another argument but, she'd hoped, would be worth the reprimand and punishment to come.

She hadn't expected to see men killed and her city invaded.

There was only one way to stop it.

Well, she thought with regret, *at least I got to have one first kiss before I died.*

I'm sorry, Pietro. I don't have a choice.

She dove forward, leaping as far as she could out into the water, and jammed the knife blade deeply into her arm.

Waves slammed into her and she went under, choking. Her eyes burned from the saltwater and the wound in her arm stung as a dark plume of blood stained the water around her.

Her head popped up and she gasped, kicking and thrashing. Her dress was dragging her down, just as she'd known it would.

"Stop! You little idiot, stop that!" LeClerc was tearing off his coat and kicking off his shoes, his face pale with anger. "Come back here!"

She opened her mouth to speak and swallowed a mouthful of seawater, instead. Gasping, she kicked hard, shaking her head.

"Brezza!"

The silfo swept around her face and she breathed deeply, then shouted the words she'd heard her grandfather intone, year after year, in these waters.

"*Desponsamus te, mare, in signum veri perpetuique dominii!*" We espouse you, oh sea, in sign of a true and perpetual leadership.

Translucent shapes like man-eating mermaids manifested around her. Chiara plunged the knife into her arm again, dragging it down into the water. She felt the ondine eagerly sucking her blood, their rough tongues lapping her flesh.

Then LeClerc was in the water, swimming toward her with strong, even strokes. Chiara gasped.

Beyond them, the Great Hermetic Gate shook and slowly, ponderously, divided. It began to draw to either side.

"No!" she shouted, horrified. If the Gate was opening—Pietro had failed.

The ondine surged toward the Gate, plunging Chiara underwater again. She didn't know if it was tears or salt burning her eyes as she slashed at her arm with short strokes like tally marks. Blood—she needed to give them blood. How much blood was two pints? How could she tell? How could she tell underwater?

LeClerc grabbed her wrist and yanked her to the surface. She twisted and tried to kick him, but her skirts were tangled around her legs.

"Stop them!" she shouted. "Ondine, stop the French! If they enter the lagoon, stop them, sink their ships, keep them from reaching shore!"

"Shut up!" LeClerc gave her wrist a sharp twist. Chiara cried out as the knife's hilt slipped from her wet fingers.

The weapon fell into the water and sank.

"It's too late!" she shouted defiantly as blood from her many deep wounds soaked his shirt sleeve and dripped into the water. "We won!"

"Do you really think this piss-poor travesty of a ritual—" LeClerc's words were cut off as the rough waters swept them both under.

Chiara fought to pull away, but the Frenchman's grip was like iron. She was starting to feel weak as the ondine continued to whirl around her, sucking her blood out of her body.

Her head broke the surface again and she choked, gasping for air. Dark spots swam before her eyes. Seawater poured through the gate and into the lagoon, sweeping them forward.

LeClerc pulled her to him.

"Do you see?" he shouted in her ear as they passed through the narrow gap in the Gate. "It's open! You failed!"

She'd failed. Her blood had been rejected, her heritage denied.

I'm sorry, she thought weakly. It was an apology to everyone—to Pietro, to her grandfather, to Venezia. *I'm sorry I wasn't good enough.*

The ondine had left her. Ribbons of blood curled around her arms, meaningless in their absence. She wanted to argue, but the Gate *was* open, and she was feeling very cold and tired.

So cold and tired that she was hardly even startled when, all of a sudden, the ondine turned on *him*. LeClerc's mouth opened in shock as the aquatic creatures wrapped slender fingers around his wrists and ankles, plunging into the depths with powerful strokes of their piscine tails and dragging him down with them.

Chiara stared through the water, chilled, as his eyes widened, fear entering them at last. A bubble of air burst from his throat, and then he was lost in the abyssal darkness of the deep.

She hadn't failed, after all.

Her eyes closed with a bone-deep weariness, and she felt herself sinking, as well.

She slammed abruptly into something hard. She dragged her eyes back open, weakly throwing an arm up out of the water. Her hand landed on a spar of wood and she desperately clung to it, shivering. One end of the spar was splintered and burned. It was a piece of Lezze's destroyed steamship.

She rested her face on the charred wood, barely noticing either the tiny gust of air that kept puffing and puffing around her, slowly blowing her and the spar closer to shore, or the young man running out the door of the Gatehouse, anxiously shouting her name.

V: MAGNUM OPUS (THE COMPLETION)

"You're cold," Chiara complained, after she'd coughed most of the water from her lungs while he was bandaging her arms. Pietro hugged her closer, resting his forehead against hers. His lips were blue from summoning salamandre, and his hands felt icy. "I thought you were trying to warm me up."

"Well, that's what I'll tell your grandfather if he sees us."

"Grandfather!" She pushed away from his chest and looked up at him. "Is he there? Is he all right?"

"He's there. Bruised and bandaged, but alive."

"And your maestro?"

"Apparently bound and gagged and thrown into prison."

"How did they capture him?"

"I didn't stop to ask for details." Pietro brushed a strand of wet hair from her face. "As soon as I saw you and that traitor swept through the Gates, I gave the rifles to the doge and ran out here to find you."

"Did Grandfather shut the Gate?"

They both turned. The Hermetic Gate was moving ponderously closed, fighting against the pressure of the incoming tide.

No French ships had made it through in the few minutes it had been open.

"They haven't even bothered firing," Pietro observed. "They know the plot failed. I'll bet they're already leaving, before we get our own ships assembled."

Chiara rested her head against his shoulder, shivering. "I think I killed LeClerc. I told the ondine to stop any Frenchmen who entered the lagoon. They drowned him."

"He deserved it."

"Pietro!" She raised her head, frowning. "It's a holy day."

"You'll be forgiven. It was war." He laid a finger on her forehead where her frown had creased it and then leaned forward to kiss her.

This time she was ready.

"I don't know about you, but I feel warmer already," he said after a breathless moment.

"So you'll tell my grandfather this is therapeutic, too?" she inquired, a smile tugging at her lips. Despite the chills that still wracked her, her heart was glowing with a completely internal, private heat of its own.

He climbed to his feet, reaching down to grasp her unbandaged arm and gently help her up.

"No," he said, "I'll tell your grandfather that it's a promissory note for the reward I plan to collect for helping to save the republic."

"What reward?"

"We can talk about it in two more years." He possessively tucked her arm close to his body as they began walking back to the Gatehouse.

"When your apprenticeship is over." She drew in a deep breath, considering that implicit promise as she looked up at the Gatehouse.

Her grandfather wasn't going to like it. He wasn't going to like seeing her walk in, exhausted, drenched, and bandaged, and he wasn't going to like the young man who'd helped her get into this state.

Her hand tightened on Pietro's arm.

But her grandfather was just going to have to learn to live with it. Because the blood of doges ran through Chiara's veins, too, and she was ready to stand up to him to get what she wanted.

"You'd better remember," she warned, "my grandfather can't give you everything."

"All I need is his permission to try." Pietro gave her a warm, secretive smile. "And after that all I need to do is to convince *you*. And I can be very persuasive."

She met his eyes and saw a strength and determination there that matched her own.

"Well," she said, "I suppose two years might be enough." And then she laughed, confidently turning her face up to the late afternoon sun as Pietro sputtered with indignation beside her.

It was a beautiful day, her favorite day of the year.

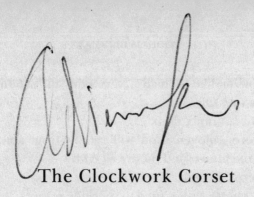

The Clockwork Corset

BY ADRIENNE KRESS

"IT HAS COME to my attention that you've been ambushing Rafe."

I looked at my father but said nothing.

"Imogen," he continued, "is it true?"

"What exactly do you mean by 'ambushing'?" I didn't feel his word choice accurately reflected my motives.

"I mean you've been hiding in trees and then jumping out and attacking him."

I thought about this for a moment. "If that's your definition, Father, then yes, yes I have." I couldn't understand what was wrong with that. After all, it had been Father who had taught me how to climb up trees in the first place. Surely jumping out of them was logically the next step. And if someone was standing beneath you, unaware of your presence, surely making him your target made perfect sense.

"I'd like you to stop."

His line of reasoning didn't make sense. I bit my bottom lip and squinted at him.

"You simply cannot attack people, Imogen. And especially not Rafe. I thought he was your friend."

He was my friend. My very best friend. That's why I would attack him. The thought of jumping on someone whom I

191

didn't know or like seemed a very odd thing. Sometimes Father was very silly.

"Father . . . I don't think . . ."

"No more, Imogen. You will refrain from ambushing anyone in the future, and there's an end."

And there's an end.

It was a phrase Father used to conclude matters. What was surprising was that, almost predictably upon his choosing to say it, the matter would be far from concluded. When, for example, Mother had told him that she was with child, he'd explained to her the importance of the final result being a boy. Mother had explained she had little control over the outcome, but Father had said, "I expect a boy, Margaret, and there's an end."

But it wasn't an end. For there I was, nine months later, swaddled in his arms. I don't recall his expression, I was too concerned with the nature of the universe and what on earth all this meant to notice his face. Mother had assured me, when I was a little older, that he had been so shocked at the result and yet so excited at the same time that his features had contorted into a strange open smile, almost a grimace. A horrific expression, she'd said, and she'd been greatly concerned what my opinion of him might be.

Again I assured her his expression was the last thing on my mind at the time.

They had tried again for a boy, when I was nine, and the tragedy of the thing was not only the loss of the little unknown soul, but my mother as well. A pain felt strongly by both husband and daughter.

Father, I think, at that point, blamed himself and his preoccupation with his wanting a boy for the loss of his wife. And so he set about making it right, spoiling me no end. He also was determined to teach me all the things he had longed to teach a boy. And so it was that we went quail hunting together, I learned to fence, and I could run a foot race as a serious threat to any male competitor. He had encouraged my friendship with Rafe from the start, seeing something positive in a boy's influence. The funny thing, of course, was that at this stage, the very mature age of eleven, I was far more masculine than he.

Rafe Wells was my age, the son of Father's clock winder, a job that described itself in its title. Father was rich. There was no mistaking that. Our home was so vast that once it had taken a week before I'd realized he'd returned from Europe. He had many servants that worked for us, employed half the county some said. We had maids and footmen, cooks and two chauffeurs. Even a pilot for the days Father rented an air machine for a lark. This massive home of his was filled with exotic furnishings and historic paintings. It also housed hundreds of ticking time pieces—beautiful, dainty things that kept us all at his rigorous schedule. And Mr. Wells was the man who wound them.

He would make his way through the home carefully seeing to each. By the time he reached the last in Father's study, it was time to call it a day. In the morning it all began again. He did more than just wind the clocks, though he performed that particular duty with all due seriousness. He repaired them when they broke, he kept them free from dust. Rafe was being trained to inherit the family business.

Darling Rafe. He had come to us as a bit of a surprise. A woman from town deposited him at Father's door when he was seven with a note around his neck addressed to Mr. Wells. Servants were not allowed families usually, but it was such a strange happening, and Mr. Wells was such a noble fellow, that, upon his attempt to quit so that he might care for the child, Mother had refused, insisting he keep his position and son. So it followed that Mr. Wells raised the boy in our home and trained him to be a clock winder like himself.

Rafe took to ticking things beautifully. He was so inspired by the devices that he would take any useless bits of wheels and winches and put them together to make the most fantastic creations. He had begun joining me in studies. This is how I discovered his talent. My father believed in education even for the masses, and had insisted Rafe be tutored by my governess along with me.

I'd been resentful at the start, but it turned out we rather got on. He liked how I'd tease him and thought I was terribly funny with my jokes. And I liked all his little inventions, the way his mind worked. For my twelfth birthday he'd made me a fantastic little train that, once wound up, would speed about the floor all on its own.

We could play for hours. Talk about matters of the day, or just act silly. He always liked it when we wrestled, though I inevitably won. So it made sense that I would feel rather frustrated being told that I was no longer allowed to jump out of trees at him. It made no sense. Our innocent pastime was amusing to both of us. Where was the harm?

At that time in my life, newly turned fourteen, I hadn't understood entirely the change in my father's attitude. He would become irritable when I wore my hair loose, and yet that was how I'd worn it for as long as I could remember. He didn't like the way I walked about with large long strides, even though this habit had resulted from trying to keep pace with him. He wouldn't let me shoot with him and his friends anymore, which was odd as most believed the older one got, the more responsible one was with a firearm, yet here was Father thinking it wasn't right for me to shoot as a fourteen-year-old but finding it just peachy at ten.

Fencing he still let me do. My education continued. And I was still allowed to visit Rafe in his room. Though even then Father had a strange obsession with keeping the door open wide.

And here was yet one more restriction. No more ambushing.

Drat.

"But it's fun when you attack me. Maybe if I was old and had a weak heart it might not be wise . . ." Rafe spoke energetically even though he was focused on the small clockwork pieces in front of him. He held one with a pair of tweezers and examined it through an eyepiece my father had bought him as a surprise for his most recent birthday. I wasn't entirely certain what it was he was inventing, something like a tiny self-propelling catapult I believed.

"I know! Exactly!" I flopped down on his straw mattress and stared at the stark white ceiling that sloped above me.

"My father's been getting on me too, but it's been all about my inventions."

"What about your inventions?"

"He wants me to stop 'fiddling about' and read those." He pointed at a stack of books on the small desk in the corner. I rose and crossed the room to read the spines.

"*War in the New Age*? *Strategy and Strength*? How dry."

"It's odd because he knows I'm just going to be a clock winder. But he says there's a war coming and thinks I'll be of age soon enough. I think he wants to prepare me—he even said I should learn to fence. But I think that, with the flying machines and the latest technologies, hand-to-hand combat is certainly a thing of the past."

"Isn't there *always* a war?" I asked, flopping back down.

"Oh, yes. There's always a war. If it isn't coming, it's going.

Father says it's what makes a boy a man, says that's what happened to him."

"I don't want you to be a man." What an awful thought. Oh! Imagine him with a beard. How frightening.

Rafe shrugged. "I think it's inevitable. Just like you'll become a woman."

"I most certainly will not!" I stood up and placed my hands at my hips. How dare he suggest such a thing.

Finally he looked up at me from his spot on the floor. "You can't *not* be a woman. That's what happens. We all grow up."

"You take that back!"

Rafe put down the clockwork piece and took the glass from his eye. He folded his arms across his chest. "I can't possibly take that back."

A woman was someone who had to sit around all day and talk about the weather. Who drank tea out of tiny cups that allowed for maybe two good gulps at best. Women nibbled at biscuits and left them half-eaten. Women wore tight uncomfortable corsets. I was not planning on becoming one of those.

I took another step towards him. "Take. It. Back."

The expression on Rafe's face was bewildered and frightened. "I . . . can't . . ."

I lunged at him and started to pummel him with my fists. He held up his arms to protect his face. Finally after several moments of struggling I managed to pin him to the floor. "Take it back, Rafe, take it back. Take it back or I'll hit you in the nose."

"I take it back, I take it back!"

"And promise me you'll never become a man."

"I'll never become a man."

"And you'll never go to war."

"I'll never go to war."

Finally, satisfied, I sat up, still straddling him, and pushed the hair out of my face. Rafe looked at me still concerned I might decide to give him a second helping. "Besides, you *can't* go to war," I said standing up. "You're too fragile."

Rafe sat up and started to collect his clockwork pieces that had been scattered about in the commotion. "Absolutely. I'd be ridiculous."

"Absolutely."

• • •

There is a tragedy that is inevitable when expectations run so high. It's a tragedy of great disappointment. It happened to me on the eve of my coming out party. I had turned sixteen an entire month before, but the season had been so full of other activities, and more than a couple of war fundraisers, that the party had been pushed back and back and back. But finally it arrived on the first cool day of fall. And as I'd sat staring at myself in the mirror, in a floor-length white gown, my sandy blonde hair piled high on my head, my waist cinched tightly in my corset, I felt as though all the years between this and the moment in Rafe's room had passed in a flash. That one moment I was vowing never to grow up, and then, in the next, I had.

"Drat," I said staring at myself hard. "Now how on earth did I let that happen?"

"Pardon me, miss?" asked my maid Silvia as she returned with some baby's breath for my hair.

"Oh, nothing, never mind."

Why was I doing this? Well, I knew why. I knew that I was doing it for Father. He desperately wanted me to realize that he loved me as I was, and not as the boy he'd originally wanted, and had spent my adolescence trying to make up for what he now considered a lack of propriety in my childhood.

Ironic because I'd so loved that impropriety. He insisted on a coming out party because he thought that's what I secretly wanted. Even when I told him it was not. So the odd turnabout of the thing was, I was doing this to make him happy, not the other way around.

And here we were. The ballroom aired out and ready for many unpleasant suitors to pass through its doors. Let us celebrate that Imogen is a woman. The one thing she never wanted to be.

I did my duty well. I took a turn about the room with all the eligible young men under the ever-watchful gaze of their attentive mothers. Some of these lads were rather striking in their uniforms, though I was careful not to share with them my distaste for war as a rather overzealous method of solving problems. No politics tonight. Father had been more than clear. No jokes. No complaining that your corset is too tight. Just smile. And turn about the room.

Rafe was there, of course. I'd spotted him in the corner, standing there in his suit. Father had generously had one commissioned for him. I liked how little Rafe had changed over the years. He was still a slight creature, though now finally taller than I. His dark hair flopped about as he spoke enthusiastically with our member of parliament. His face was always cheerful, always warm. And he was always there when I needed to exchange a glance or roll my eyes, with a bright smile.

Thank the heavens for darling Rafe.

"You were the prettiest girl tonight," he said as we sat at the edge of the lake dangling in our feet.

"I was the *only* girl there tonight," I replied.

"That's not true . . ."

"What? You think all those old biddies are girls, do you? You need to get out more."

"Can't you just take a compliment?"

"I . . ." No, of course I can't. Especially not from you. "Thank you."

"You're welcome."

Of course, Father had no idea we sneaked out like we did. He didn't know that we had met in this way ever since he'd forbidden my visiting Rafe's room. Both of us in our dressing gowns, down by the lake, hidden from view of the house by the hedge maze. As if we could give up on such a friendship. What a ridiculous notion.

"So," asked Rafe after a pleasant silence, "any of them strike your fancy?"

"Pardon?"

"Any of those blokes?"

"Don't be silly, Rafe." I shook my head. Who did he think I was? Didn't he know me better than that? Such interests were beneath me. Marriage was simply not something I was looking for. Such was the privilege of being the daughter and sole heir of a very wealthy man.

"Well, that's good," he said, then stopped himself short.

I turned to look at him. He was staring out across the lake, apparently with some effort. "What's good?" I asked.

"Nothing." He answered a bit too quickly. "No, it's just . . . it's good you didn't fancy them because they seemed right tossers. That's all. Shows you still have good taste is what I mean."

"Well, yes . . . of course."

"I think I'm going to head up. 'Night."

It was such an abrupt departure I sat rooted to the spot in surprise. He returned, of course, a moment later—"I say, do you need an escort back?"

"No, that's fine, thank you, Rafe."

But then he was off again at a quick pace.

I wasn't a fool, though I was hardly well-versed in such things. But I knew in an instant what had transpired.

Dear God, evidently Rafe was in love with me.

When had that happened?

Later he told me this affection had come upon him so gradually that he'd hardly noticed it himself. But when he'd watched me turn about the room that evening—an activity I had thought made me look rather the fool—he had found it enchanting. *Enchanting*. His word. Of course his word. He'd always thought I was pretty, but that night he'd found me beautiful. And he knew it in his heart.

Such a romantic.

For me, well, for me the moment caused a great welling of panic inside.

I returned to my room in a fluster and lay wide awake. I must confess my first thoughts were not about returning the sentiment but about anger. Anger? Yes. You see, I resented that in one indiscreet moment Rafe had totally changed the nature of our relationship. It would never be normal again, and the more he pretended it was, I knew, the more awkward it would feel. Rafe was the one person with whom I was always able to be completely myself. Say those ridiculous things my father chided me for, make strange pronouncements. He'd once taken back his prediction that I would become a woman. And he'd promised to never become a man. Who else but Rafe would indulge such a fancy?

But it had happened. And there we were. Could I feel safe with him, the same with him, knowing what I knew now?

My own feelings didn't come into focus until a fortnight later. Though I might have guessed at them. After all, why did it matter so much to me that our relationship was changed if the relationship hadn't mattered greatly to me in turn? It had been an awkward two weeks, for the both of us. Trying to pretend to be normal. We hadn't sneaked out once to meet, and though I was relieved not to be alone with him, I missed our conversations terribly. I missed most of all him sharing with me his latest inventions, which in recent years had moved on to life-sized versions of the models he'd made as a child. He'd even invented a communication system that ran through our house. A series of connected pipes that, with the push of a button, allowed one to speak to someone else in a room far off.

Once we ran into each other quite by accident in the music room. I'd forgotten a sonata on the piano, and he was winding the Waterbury clock. He'd taken to doing the rounds almost every day on his own, his father's arthritis getting worse by the year. Of course at this point in his life Rafe had more responsibilities than just those of a typical clock winder. Agents of the army had learned early on of his fantastic inventions, and had hired him to create weapon designs that he'd send along to London. It was an excellent situation, to be sure: he avoided going off to war by helping in the war effort in this way and got to stay at the estate while being paid rather handsomely by the government.

In any event, our meeting in the music room was awkward and brief.

"Oh, hello."

"Oh, hello."

Like that.

But then the thing happened. The thing that changed it all.

The thing came in the form of a young soldier about our age on horseback. He was in full dress uniform and took himself extremely seriously.

"Hello, sir," he'd said in a voice he forced low. "I'm looking for Mr. Rafe Wells."

My father had greeted the man in the foyer. Anyone from the army was of great interest to him. He'd have gone off himself, he'd always insisted, had it not been for his knee. An injury from another war that had been meant to be the end of all wars.

"Yes, of course," replied my father, and he went to fetch Rafe himself. I stood alone in the foyer then, the young soldier trying each moment to stand just a bit straighter until his head was so far back I could see right up his nose.

"I'm Rafe Wells," said Rafe, approaching the young soldier. He glanced my way briefly, but I had no expression other than confusion to share with him.

"Sir," said the young soldier clicking his heels together. "I have been ordered to deliver this to you. I ask you to gather your belongings and come with me immediately. It's a summons, sir." He passed over a letter, sealed with Her Majesty's stamp.

"Are you going to London, then?" I asked as Rafe read the letter. His expression was emotionless, but all color had left his face.

"No," he said looking up at me. "No, they want me at the front. Seems one of my inventions is acting up a wee bit."

"The front?" For the first time in a long while I felt as if I was going to cry. I never felt as if I was going to cry.

"Now, now, Imogen," said Father, sensing my heightened emotional state, "it's an honor to serve Queen and country."

"It is," said Rafe quietly.

"I must ask you to . . ." began the young soldier.

"Gather my belongings," said Rafe interrupting him. "I know." He turned as if in a daze and started the journey towards his room. I looked at Father wide-eyed, then at the young soldier. Neither of them bore any expression aside from that noble indifference that was meant to be stoic.

I turned and ran after Rafe.

"Imogen!" Father called out, but his shouting my name had never stopped me from doing anything in the past. That wasn't about to change now.

I caught up with Rafe on the servants' staircase.

"Rafe!"

He turned and looked at me, still with that stunned expression.

"You can't go," I said, panting hard.

"I have to."

"No, no, it's silly. You can't. I mean, you, on the front? It's absurd."

Rafe looked down. "I can take care of myself, Imogen. I know you think I can't . . ."

Drat. "No, I know that. I mean, you're no warrior, of course. But you are a capable . . . person. It's just, it's silly. You're not a fighter. You never have been."

"I'm not going to fight . . ."

"You could die!"

"We all die sometime . . ."

"You can't go!"

He finally looked up at me again, and I could see the fear behind his eyes. "I have to."

"But you promised me you wouldn't."

He furrowed his eyebrows. "When? When on earth?"

"In your room. Back then. I don't remember the day, but you did. It was the same day you promised you'd never become a man." I felt silly now; it wasn't really the best argument. "But . . . I guess you did."

"And I guess I have to go to war."

There was only one final argument that could be made. A realization that came in an instant of wondrous clarity. "You can't go . . . because I love you."

The way Rafe stared at me then made me feel even more ridiculous than when I'd reminded him of his childhood promise to me. Had I been wrong all along? Had that little slip he made at the lake been nothing more than what he'd said it was?

"You love me?"

"Maybe. I don't know. How would I know such a thing?" Adrenaline was surging through my body. I felt as if my skin was buzzing.

Rafe took a step down so we were standing level with each other.

"You know because you feel it," he said softly. "You think about the person every day, you can't wait to see them again, and when you do you're overwhelmed with excitement. You love their laugh, their jokes. And you think that no one on this earth is as beautiful."

"But you're a little funny looking . . ."

Rafe laughed at that.

Stupid Imogen. "You can't go then. Because I do love you. I do think about you all the time, and when you said what you did by the lake I was the most worried that I'd lose you somehow, that you'd be all different. And you were. And it scared me."

He took my hands in his. And even though we'd touched a thousand times before it felt this time unlike anything I'd ever experienced. "I have to go. It's my duty. And your argument, though wonderful, doesn't make sense. Most men have someone who loves them when they go to war. Now I'm lucky enough to be one of them."

He leaned in and I pulled back. I couldn't help it. How stupid.

"Sorry, try again," I said. I was doing this all wrong. I knew it.

This time Rafe moved much faster and I didn't have time to react. His lips were against mine, so soft and warm. So sweet. And all doubt in me washed away and was replaced by a feeling of complete certainty. As we pulled apart I knew what I had to do.

Rafe left an hour later, on a second horse the young soldier had brought with him. We waved and waved until we couldn't see him anymore, and still waved a moment longer.

"No tears, my girl," said Father. He didn't have to. I wasn't crying. I was determined.

Alone in my quarters, I re-read Rafe's summons. I'd asked for it as a keepsake, and he'd left it, most obligingly. The young soldier would take him where he needed to go and could serve as witness that he was indeed who he said he was. I, on the other hand, required this piece of paper.

My first act was to raid Rafe's room. I tore through his closet, eventually pulling out three work shirts and two pairs of trousers. His shoes were large on me, but I could stuff the toes with some scraps from my rarely used sewing kit. He had left his cap behind, so I grabbed that as well. I carried all of Rafe's clothing down to my room, tossing it on the bed. It was then that I took a moment's breath and doubt began to creep in. I couldn't really do this, now could I?

The plan was simple. Join the army and protect Rafe from certain death and so forth. The actualizing of it, however, was far more complex. The sanity behind it . . . possibly wanting. But it didn't seem that absurd to me. After all, I was far more physically fit than Rafe, and no one had found it odd he'd been recruited. And I had actual combat skills with my fencing and such. The thing of it was, I was a girl. Quite the obstacle to overcome. And there was only one way I could think of doing so.

Acting like a boy wouldn't be a big problem. Whether he liked it or not, Father's early support had meant mine was a boyish gait. Speaking like a boy might not be that tricky either as I had inherited my mother's low raspy tones. It was a voice that I'd overheard discussed by other girls my age as "inappropriately independent." No, the greatest difficulty would be my appearance.

That, and finding a way to sneak out of the house without Father noticing. I needed time to get to Dover, which might take a week at least. The summons had called on Rafe to board a dirigible at the Dover sky port to fly across the Channel on Sunday next. He was to stop over in London for a few days beforehand to meet with the war cabinet and give a presentation on the theories behind his inventions. Poor Rafe, speaking in front of crowds was certainly not his thing. But his extended stay on home soil would give me enough time to get to Dover under my own power. What, oh what to do, however, about Father?

This concern gave me pause. I needed a sign of some sort, something that would give me permission to go ahead with this scheme.

"I'm going to Manchester for a fortnight."

The words echoed around the grand dining room that evening at supper as Father made the pronouncement.

"Are you?" I asked from afar at the other end of the table, grateful this once for the distance between us. I was certain the beating of my heart would have been audible to him had I been closer.

"Yes, evidently there's some trouble up in one of the factories."

"When do you leave?"

"Tomorrow morning, first thing."

Well, if that wasn't a sign I clearly didn't know what such a thing was.

With Father gone for so long I could easily quit the house without bother. Yes, the servants would notice, but they would probably assume Father was aware I was leaving. Two full weeks gave me ample time not only to arrive at the sky port, but to take flight. By the time Father returned and learned of my absence, there would be little he could do aside from worry.

That did concern me a bit, Father fretting over me. It did seem unfairly mean to make him worry. But I had to do this. I had to protect Rafe who I had just discovered was the love of my life. Surely he would understand the motivation, if not the action.

My brain fought me every step of the way, but my heart was set to purpose. I kissed Father gently on the cheek as he left the next morning, and two nights later, I performed the last, and most unpleasant preparation before my departure.

I cut my hair.

My sewing kit had never had such use. That much was clear from my poor stitchwork on the hems of Rafe's trousers and shirt sleeves. Now I used the scissors, little ones meant to cut thread, to cut the long locks that hung down my back. One by one they fell to the floor, a pile of gold collecting at my feet. I kept my attention on the mirror before me, trying to remind myself that it would all grow back in time.

It was little comfort.

When it was done, I stared at the image before me. Concern for my lost locks was replaced by a deep fear that I, in no way, not even with the boyish haircut I had surprisingly managed, looked like a man. Nor even a lad.

I had an idea.

Quietly, though I supposed it wasn't really necessary as he wasn't home, I sneaked into Father's room and rummaged about through his toiletries. I removed the tin of pomade that he used to slick his hair and opened it. I applied it to my own hair, pushing the fringe back off my forehead. Without the hair to frame my eyes, my rather high forehead managed to make my features slightly more masculine. I turned to the side to examine my profile. I'd inherited my father's nose, strong and straight, not dainty and button-like like my mother's. The nose would help. Oh, most helpful nose.

I took the tin with me and added it to my sack of supplies. Though I'd packed food for a few days, a stop at an inn would be necessary. I had money enough for transportation and accommodation, though I didn't want to take too much along for the journey. Rafe's altered clothing fit me quite nicely. It was fortunate he was so slight that it was only the length of the garments that needed alteration. And since my figure barely filled out a corset (hateful thing) and was subject to derision by those same girls who mocked my voice, the lack of shape meant I needed only wrap a bandage a few times around my chest to remove any indication I wasn't what I pretended to be. With the cap on my head, I concluded I passed for a boy. But no more. There was no mistaking me for a man.

I left home just shortly after one in the morning. The thought that this might possibly be the last time I'd see my home hadn't even occurred to me until I was walking through the small hamlet that bordered our property on the east end. In all my concern over how I was going to manage my disguise, the thought that I was heading to a place where men die every day had quite escaped my thoughts. Strange, really, as my primary motivation had been to protect Rafe from just such a fate.

I wished in that moment that I'd said something more fitting in the short note I'd left Father. More than just a brief explanation and apology. I should have said something about how despite his constant concern over his part in my upbringing, I had always loved him for it. That he needn't have worried so much. That I'd lived a most lovely life. I knew he cared for me, and I needed little more than that. I might have written something about a job well done.

But I hadn't written any of that, and so I determined that I simply wouldn't die. It would save a lot of fuss and bother, and I didn't think Father could handle it. He'd blame himself, and the guilt that he already felt about my mother's death would be doubled. No, really, the only possible outcome was to survive.

I walked all night and took a brief nap beneath an old oak as the sun rose. Then I continued, eating my breakfast as I walked, until I arrived where the stagecoach picked up travelers in the larger town of Pontyville. I waited with an older couple for half an hour before the carriage arrived. The journey with them to Tuttman-on-the-Green was the first real test of my alter ego.

"I'm Nancy Smythe and this is my husband, George."

"Ian Wells," I said taking her hand and shaking it in a manly fashion. At least, in what I hoped was a manly fashion. The decision to take on Rafe's surname had been one of necessity. After all, I possessed his summons, which conveniently didn't mention his first name. But there was something rather nice about being a Wells, so I didn't mind pretending to be his relation. "Imogen Wells," I thought to myself. Then I inwardly rolled my eyes. Just like those girls who'd play pretend they were married to some bloke or other. Stop it, Imogen, you're going to war, not walking down the aisle.

"Where you off to then, lad?" asked Mr. Smythe.

On hearing his accent, I realized just how posh my own was. I endeavored to common it up a bit. "To the front, sir. Been called to duty."

Mrs. Smythe gasped, and her husband nodded sagely. "Bad business, war," he said, "but it makes a man outta ya."

"So I've been told, sir."

Mr. Smythe grinned then. "And you could use some manning up now, couldn't you, lad?"

I hoped that his joke at my expense had been made because of my youthful appearance, and not because he saw through the disguise.

"Yes, sir," I replied.

But if Mr. Smythe suspected anything, he made no mention of it. Instead, he happily regaled his wife and me with war stories of his own. I had to admit to myself there was a thrilling quality to them, though I wasn't sure if it was innate to the tales themselves or courtesy of the man telling them. A fine storyteller was Mr. Smythe, and I was wholly glad to have had the chance to share this long journey with him.

We made it to Tuttman-on-the-Green by ten that evening. The Smythes were picked up in a small carriage by their son-in-law, and I, after exchanging a few parting words, made my way to the local inn. My second test, I told myself. Let us see how this goes.

All was loud and cheerful and inn-like on the inside. The large room was filled mostly with men whom by this hour were well toasted.

I approached the inn keeper at the front desk and made my presence known.

"Well, hello there, young master!" he said in as cheerful a manner as any I'd encountered. A man truly pleased with his lot in life, and I envied him it for a moment.

"Hello, sir," I said. "I'm looking for a room for the night."

"Ah," he replied and examined me closely. "And where be you headin'?"

I wasn't sure it was his place to ask such a thing. But there was no harm in the answer. "Dover," I replied shoving my hands into my pockets so hard that, had my trousers not been held up by braces, I probably would have pulled them right off.

"Ah, a new recruit. They gets younger every year."

I nodded. And more feminine too.

"Well, I'm right full up, but there's some others of you staying out in the barn, if that'll do?"

"Others like me?"

"Headin' out to Dover like you. Quite a few pass through these doors see."

I nodded.

"Barn do?" he asked again.

"Yes, thank you. What do I owe you?" I asked reaching into my bag.

The innkeeper held up his hand. "Ain't nothin' for the new recruits. 'Specially stayin' out in the barn."

"Thank you," I said.

He showed me out back and introduced me to the three other fellows staying there. Two were brothers, the third their cousin. All had the last name Baker. Tim, Thomas, and Aeschylus.

"Did you say 'Aeschylus'?" I asked dropping my bag down on the straw mat the innkeeper had proudly pronounced mine before leaving us to our own devices.

Thomas laughed loudly and Tim snorted.

"Aeschylus. After the playwright," said the cousin with a sigh.

"The ancient Greek one?" I asked sitting down.

Aeschylus looked at me in shock, as did his cousins. I realized that probably they didn't tend to run into people quite so well educated as myself. There was so much more to this disguise business than just pretending to be a boy.

"Yeah, that's right. No one ever knows that," he said coming over and looming above me, leaning his forearm against a low hanging beam.

"Well, I do. And your parents did too."

"They did." There was a deep resentment in his voice then. "Call me Baker, though."

"Baker it is."

I didn't like the scrutinizing gaze and so stood up though he still towered over me. "I need . . . to relieve myself."

"You mean take a piss?"

I nodded.

"We've been going around back."

It was probably one of the most uncomfortable conversations I'd ever had, but it got me back outside and alone with my thoughts. There were so many things I hadn't taken into consideration. Namely sharing quarters with men. I'd never shared my room at all, let alone with anyone of the opposite sex. And there was the small matter of my bandaged chest. There was nothing else to do but sleep in my clothes. Pretend to some kind of silly modesty that would no doubt result in teasing, but it was better than revealing the truth.

I decided I might as well do what I had said I was going to—it was the first time, I must admit, I'd ever done so in such close proximity to men. Then I returned to the barn where the Bakers were all sitting around happily in their skivvies. I willed my face not to turn red and made my way to my mat, lay down, and drew my coat over my body.

They said nothing, thinking me odd in general, no doubt.

Sleep came. How, I had no idea, but in no time I was woken up by Tim with a shake. "Time to head out."

I looked at him for a moment, unsure of his meaning.

"You getting up or not? We gotta start walkin' if we're gonna catch the wagon."

"Uh . . . wagon?"

"There's a wagon picks recruits up from Boggington. Takes us straight on to Dover. Three days' journey. Thought that's where you were headed."

This was most fortuitous. "Oh, yes, *that* wagon. Sorry. Still asleep I guess."

"Well, come on."

I imagine they'd discussed me while I slept, came to some sort of conclusion to allow my company. It was good fortune, whatever it was, even though it made my life far more complicated, having to pretend to be Ian constantly. But this was what I'd signed up for. To be a man in the company of many men, in a war zone no less. It had to be what it was.

I was grateful to the Bakers for taking me under their wing, whatever the reason. They were fine company as we traveled the countryside. I talked little, trying to create a reputation of a quiet, shy fellow. They talked plenty, though. About growing up on the farm, about girls. They really did talk about girls a lot. It was quite obvious they knew little of our hearts. Then again how could I expect them to understand that by which I myself was confused?

It took a day extra to get to Dover. The weather on the second day was so foul we'd holed up in a small inn on the side of the road. There was just enough room for the lot of us. We'd made new acquaintances in the wagon, a dozen other lads, all young and rough around the edges. And the driver himself, old and world weary. Or, at least, weary of the likes of us.

That day we played cards and drank. Rather they taught me cards and I kept to my cider. I wasn't quite ready for a pint, though I was tempted. In all, it was rather pleasant. And my reputation as the quiet one served me well.

The day's delay was of little concern, however, as we still arrived a day before departure. Enough time to check in, I suppose, and get our uniforms. Possibly some basic lessons in weapons. I thought it astonishing we'd be sent to the front without a more thorough training, but Thomas explained that that would happen over in Europe. It seemed that men of our rank were not expected to train much. We would be taught how to take order and how to hold our weapons. Other than that, evidently, there wasn't much more to it.

I found that hard to believe. After all, we were fighting for Queen and country. Oughtn't there be more to it than just, "Have at it lads!"?

I was about to bravely make that point when Baker said, "Now if that ain't something."

I'd been rear facing on the journey, so I turned my body round to see what he was looking at. It was something indeed.

The cliffs rose up before us, white walls sheer to the Channel. White-capped waves crashed on the beach far below. And the green countryside through which we now traveled seemed even brighter for the contrast. At the point where the cliffs retreated out of sight was the most magnificent architectural structure I'd ever seen. Built up to the top from three quarters of the way down the white wall was a platform, reminiscent of the pier in Brighton. It jutted out into the sky, seeming impervious to gravity. As the intricate system of wrought-iron supports came into more distinct focus as we approached, I began to understand the science behind it. That was the fantastic thing about iron. It could be crafted to look as delicate as a willow branch but still have all the strength of an oak. In this instance, the platform's supports had been wrought to appear as twisting vines. The natural and the man-made creating a new kind of beauty.

Of course, I realized that most of the men in the wagon

weren't looking down at the supports of the platform but admiring the dirigible moored at the far end. It made sense. The airship could safely be estimated to be around three hundred feet long, and its body was painted the colors of the Union Jack. Truly quite hard to miss really. But I was a spoiled rich girl. I'd seen dirigibles before. I'd even flown in one to Paris for my thirteenth birthday. Clearly, I was the only one of my current company who had.

"Blimey, now that ain't natural," said Tim, taking off his cap and running his fingers through his hair. His brother agreed with a loud exhalation of air, and I felt it was my turn to express my awe.

"Impressive," I said because it was.

There was a general murmur of assent at that remark, and for the rest of the journey we were silent. Whether through fear or awe, I didn't know. I imagined probably a little bit of both.

The wagon eventually pulled up to the camp on the cliffs by the sky port. It consisted of several long single-story buildings around a large open square. There were men everywhere, some running drills and being yelled at by very scary looking men, others looking frantic for reasons of which I hoped to remain ignorant.

One by one, we clambered out of the wagon and stood awkwardly waiting for something, unsure of what that something was.

In the end, it turned out to be a short squat man with a magnificent handlebar mustache.

"Excellent! New recruits! Brilliant. Welcome, men." He did seem truly thrilled that we had arrived. "Get in a queue. First lesson, standing at attention." He showed us, and we emulated the stance. So far, so good. "Excellent. Now take your things. You lot are in barracks number three. Place your belongings in the cubby provided, then return with your summons and we'll get you outfitted. After that, some drills and basic weapons instruction. And then first thing tomorrow, we're off!" He said it all with great excitement, but the thought terrified me. I knew we'd be heading out soon. Still, the idea of war and actually facing it were two very different things.

But we obeyed our commander. We had no choice. I did all he asked, even though I rather fancied not. But I couldn't afford to stand out in the crowd. Not when I was so close to finding Rafe.

One by one, we handed our summons to our superior, got our uniforms, changed, though fortunately no one noticed I kept my shirt on. Then we ran drills. We were given a pistol and knife each, and taught how to use some of the more technologically advanced shotguns. Such as the one that could shoot off several rounds at once by holding down the trigger. That gun particularly terrified me. I hoped it wasn't one of Rafe's inventions. I was praised for my aim, which I knew was rather good after so many years of quail hunting. We were told the importance of keeping formation at all times. And then we were given half an hour for dinner and another hour before lights out.

It was a whirlwind experience, and I hardly felt ready to fight. At the same time, I felt as though I'd learned far more than I'd ever expected to. How was it possible that I felt like a solider when I'd been one for less than twelve hours?

I sat on my cot in shock.

"Ian Wells?"

At first the name didn't register.

"Ian Wells?"

Oh, right, that's me.

"Here, sir!" I turned and stood at attention as I'd been shown. My commanding officer approached.

"Come with me."

"Yes, sir."

I followed him out of the makeshift barracks into the early evening air. It was crisp and cool, eminently breathable. We walked south past all the buildings until we reached the pier of the sky port, and then we continued onto the platform itself. It was as sturdy as the ground, but it still felt odd knowing that we were walking hundreds of feet above solid earth. It was a wide pier that housed several buildings, with the large glowing shape of the dirigible looming at the far end. I longed to go to the edge, to look right down. But the way the air whipped around my head, I worried that I might be blown clear off the platform.

We reached the building nearest the dirigible, the entrance guarded by two officers who let us pass inside without question.

It took a moment for me to register where I was. The building consisted of one large room with maps strewn about a large table in the middle. Sitting around the table were several men. They all looked large and intimidating.

Except for one.

"Ian!" said Rafe, standing up quickly at the far end.

"Rafe." My heart was beating fast. What the devil was going on? How had he known my new name? I thought back to the moment that I passed off the summons to my commander, sharing with him my Christian name. Obviously news had traveled.

"Brother," said Rafe enunciating the word with extra emphasis. He walked around the table and extended his hand. "Good to see you."

I nodded and took his hand, unable to speak.

"I'm glad you got the message, glad you could join me. This is Colonel Fitzhenry." He gestured to the ginger man sitting at the head of the table. "Captains Carter and Dixon. And Lieutenant Williamson. Gentlemen, this is my brother, Ian. He is my assistant."

"Never said a word about this before, Wells," said Captain Carter, furrowing his thick eyebrows. Or rather, eyebrow, as it was difficult to distinguish two.

"I assumed you were all aware I . . ." Rafe stopped talking. He sighed. "I'm sorry. It's a surprise, I realize."

"It is. Pity you couldn't have brought him with you to London," said Captain Dixon.

"I couldn't get away until later this week," I said quickly, my voice shaking. "I'm glad I made it on time before lift-off."

"As am I, Ian, brother," said Rafe looking at me. I looked back. We looked at each other.

"Right," interrupted the Colonel. "I think we've got a basic handle on the plan to get you, and now your brother, to the machine. I think we should call it a night. See you at sunrise, gentlemen."

There was a general shuffling as the men rose and made their way out of the meeting room leaving behind me and my . . . brother.

"First," he said turning to me and grabbing my shoulders, "what the blue blazes are you doing here? Second . . ." He leaned in and kissed me. This time it was a much harder kiss than our first, almost a little *too* hard, but I didn't mind. We pulled apart.

"First . . ." I replied, "well, it's a long story. And second . . ." This time, I leaned in and kissed him. It was my turn after all.

There was a sound outside and we flew apart in an instant. The door opened. Captain Dixon stood before us. "I forgot my hat."

We nodded.

He got his hat.

• • •

Explaining to Rafe why I was there proved to be a rather emotionally fraught thing. For one, he did not appear to appreciate my intentions. For another, he became very angry that I was now in mortal danger. He said something about my being safe at home having been his motivation to continue in this beastly business when the chips were down, and now, evidently, I'd ruined all that.

"But clever about the whole brother thing," I said, trying to boost his spirits. We were sitting on a wrought-iron bench staring out at the water much like we always did. Though we'd never before been at such a height. With a large, glowing, flying machine in the distance.

"When they told me someone was here with my summons and surname . . . I knew it was you."

"Because I'm willful and spontaneous?"

"Because you draw ridiculous conclusions. What on earth made you think that disguising yourself as a boy and following me to the front was somehow for my own good?"

I sighed hard. "You needed protection."

"I *have* protection. I have an army to protect me. Trained soldiers. Not some girl whose father gave her fencing lessons and taught her how to climb trees."

He made a good point.

"Imogen, it's not that I don't think the gesture's marvelous. It's just . . . I don't want anything to happen to you."

"And I don't want anything to happen to you either. Which is why I came in the first place," I replied quietly.

Rafe said nothing in response. Then he reached over and took my hand. He held it low so that the action would not be noticed. We sat there for a moment in stillness listening to the waves crash far beneath us.

"I can't leave now," I said finally. "Not now that they think I've been officially summoned. It would be treason."

"And evidently I can't work without my assistant."

We looked at each other again. He was so nice to look at.

"So what's this device we have to fix?" I asked as lightly as I could.

Rafe leaned back and sighed hard. "It's a machine that fires a continuous stream of bullets as it moves on its own through enemy lines."

"What's happened to it?"

"It's gotten stuck."

"Where?"

"Behind enemy lines."

• • •

The next morning was upon us far too quickly. It seemed doubtful even that I had slept, though the hours had passed whether I had or not. Breakfast was a chaotic mess, and I searched frantically to find the Bakers at a far table in the corner. Just as I sat, I was called over by Captain Dixon to join my brother and the others. It was a small moment in time, a decision that made sense, and it was easy to follow Rafe to his table. But in doing so, I disassociated myself from the Bakers and the other fellows with whom I'd journeyed for the week. I was no longer in their company, and from that moment on belonged to Rafe's team.

The fact was, after losing the Bakers with a brief wave, I never saw them again. I do often hope that they survived and live on, farming and tending to the land happily with their families. I'd hardly known them, so, at the time, parting ways was no great loss. But these thoughts do occur to me every so often. People who have appeared in one's life for an important brief moment, and then are gone just as quickly.

Without ceremony.

Simply a change of seating arrangements.

And thus I was with Rafe from that moment forward. It was a good thing. First to be with the man I loved, but also to be with men of a high status whom not only ate better but got the best seats on the dirigible.

We boarded at seven in the morning. Orderly, as only the military could be. The inside was cavernous, divided in two so that the men were separated from their superiors. The section I was in was the nicer of the two. Plush and decorated in the modern style, it reminded me somewhat of Father's study. Dark walls, deep leather seats placed in sets of four around small tables next to the windows.

I sat by the window, and Rafe sat close. Though the windows were large and one could see the view from even the middle of the ship, he seemed very keen to lean into me so he might observe the world outside from over my shoulder. I didn't mind. Captain Dixon sat opposite, as did some other fellow I didn't know.

A hush fell, and a young man stood before us to explain safety procedures. There was absolutely no smoking allowed, four escape routes, and parachutes available in the sideboard by the bar. Oh, yes, drinking was almost a requirement, and I had my first Scotch that morning. It burned, but warmed me at the same time. Not an entirely unpleasant experience.

Then there was another announcement. This time a man's amplified voice projected over the room. It was time to take to the sky, and we were all to take our seats. It seemed to me an unnecessary instruction as everyone was already seated, waiting to go.

At first nothing happened. Then there was a lurching sensation and we clutched the arms of our chairs. Well, not Captain Dixon—he seemed utterly unmoved by the entire experience. Despite having flown previously, I still felt unsettled as I watched our cabin rise up from the platform. There were men on the outside, holding onto long ropes, easing them out through their hands until, finally, they let go and saluted.

We rose into the air and all within the dirigible were silent as we stared out the windows to watch our progress. The cliffs glowed in the early morning light, the water below a dark, even blue. The pier grew smaller and smaller, and the barracks on land looked little more than toys. Soon both retreated from view and all that remained below was the Channel.

Half an hour later, Europe appeared—green rolling fields, small farming villages. In time, though I'd never have thought it possible, the general company got a little tired of staring out the window and began to discuss plans for our arrival. Captain Dixon was to be our point man, and we were to follow him. We'd arrive at the camp, take a quick lunch, and then part ways. A small company would then be dispatched to track down the now broken machine.

And, indeed, after a slightly bumpy landing, this was precisely what we did. We were shepherded into an automated carriage, a contraption that looked much like an average carriage except it was made of a thick metal on all sides with slits for windows. Oh, and it wasn't pulled by horses. It seemed to move of its own volition, though there was a driver that sat on top. He worked a large wheel, and pulled at levers at his side. Each time he did, a jet of steam would explode from some pipe in the rear. The driver's position made him vulnerable, so another soldier, armed with one of those multiple-firing shotgun devices, sat up on the roof to protect him.

We traveled in the automated carriage for several hours until we hit no man's land and stopped. I took a peek out of the narrow window at the front. A thick forest stretched out before us.

"We'll set up camp here," announced Captain Dixon.

We were joined by half a dozen other automated carriages, and soon we'd created a makeshift town that felt remarkably comfortable. Rafe and I met with Captain Dixon in his tent, where the rest of the plan was outlined. They were pretty sure that the machine had stopped somewhere in the forest, south southwest. Rafe and I would go with a team, and once we found the machine, they would fan out to cover all sides. We'd be very well protected, he assured us, adding that he himself would be leading the mission. It might have been slightly arrogant of him to offer that as comfort, but I did feel better knowing he'd be coming along.

Soon enough it was evening. I'd noticed time seemed to go awfully quickly when one dreaded a thing. I ate little supper and spoke hardly a word. At one point, Rafe leaned in and whispered in my ear, "Once we fix this machine, we'll be off home." I nodded, trying to use the thought as comfort.

Eventually, it was time. Rafe and I and half a dozen other men stealthily made our way into the forest. It was difficult to be quiet. The time of year meant there were as many leaves on the ground as in the trees. And, of course, there were sticks and whatnot to trip us up as well. We walked for an hour. At least, I believed it to be an hour. It could have been less time, but my heart was in my throat, and I felt such a sense of terror with each step that the journey was interminable. My breathing was shallow, and every sound—the wind creaking the branches, a bird taking flight, some night creature scurrying away from us—made me think we were about to be attacked. Rafe took my hand once, but let it go quickly, realizing that the action was hardly appropriate to our make-believe.

Captain Dixon stopped finally and signaled for us. Rafe and I were at his side in an instant, and he pointed through the trees. Rafe nodded and gave me a look. Then, with a deep breath, we set out to take the last few feet on our own, while Captain Dixon and his men fanned out to set up a perimeter.

The machine sat waiting for us, purring. As Rafe took a tour around it, I stole a moment to understand what I was looking at. It was a large cube of brass on two thick wheels. Along the side I was facing were several winches and a large wheel that reminded me of something one would see inside a clock. It made sense, of course, the contraption having been invented by Rafe. There was a tube at the top, like a smoke stack. And I started when it blasted out steam all of a sudden as if it, too, was frustrated by its lack of motion.

For all the world, I had no idea how it worked, but it didn't seem broken.

"What's wrong with it?" I asked.

"The signal from home base isn't getting through," replied Rafe closing a latch on its side.

"Signal?"

"We've been using waves in the air to transmit instructions to it."

"You have? How amazing." And how miraculous.

"Yes, but see? The signal's blocked by the thick brush. We need something . . . we need . . ." He started to rummage around in his sack, and I could do nothing but watch. He pulled out a metal plate no larger than something one might dine on. Then there were some strange wires. I watched him work, as I had watched him work so often in the past.

I loved it. I loved how sure he was. Even in the midst of such peril, watching him now made my spirits soar. Then he suddenly looked at me, and I raised my eyebrows at him.

"So, Imogen," he said rising, "still fond of climbing trees?"

• • •

The plan was straightforward. We chose the tallest tree we could find in the vicinity. He, after a quick peck on the cheek, left me to my own devices and returned to the machine. I was to climb the tree and attach the strange plate to it. I'd then caw like a crow so he knew it was done. When the signal came through, he'd make a hooting sound. Like an owl, I supposed. I would return to him then. If he didn't make a sound, that meant I had to twist the wires a different way. Caw again. If that didn't work, then I was to shift the plate in the opposite direction. And if that too didn't work, return to him, and we'd try something else.

It was dark and silent. We were alone. And though I knew there were men protecting us, I could see no one. I was scared. Very scared.

There was nothing for it but to climb.

This I was good at. I was very good at. It was also a very good tree for climbing. I reached the top quickly and with ease, even with the small bundle on my back, and marveled for a moment at the view. The moon glowed brightly over the forest, and I felt as if I was staring over the ocean, the tips of the trees moving like waves in the dark.

The moment was just that, there was no time for any more. I had a job to do. I removed the plate from the bundle and tied the leather straps that he'd attached to it around a topmost branch, securing it as tightly as I could. I gave it a good yank, and it stayed firm. Then I cawed, feeling slightly silly. Nothing. I waited another moment. Still nothing. Right. Phase two. I took the two wires protruding from the middle and twisted them together. Another caw. Nothing.

Then an owl hooting. Or something close to an owl. I couldn't help smiling to myself as I began the climb back down.

I was halfway to the bottom when I heard the *snap*.

I froze in place, held my breath for fear it was louder than usual. The snap happened again. It was a slight sound. Very quiet, and I heard it only due to my proximity. It came from right below the tree. A boot breaking a twig.

Someone was there. I hoped upon hope it was Captain Dixon or one of his men. I couldn't see from where I was. And I had to see.

As quietly as I could, and that was quite quiet indeed, I slipped myself down a few feet to where the branches thinned, and I could see the ground below. I could also see the figure below. He was dressed in black and yellow, the colors of the enemy, and he was moving carefully step by step. His gun was before him, aiming at something specific. I followed his line of sight.

My God.

It was Rafe. He was the target. A perfect shot, clear right to him, as if someone had gotten rid of a row of trees expressly for the purpose.

My heart was racing. The soldier beneath me took another step and then kneeled down, aiming the weapon at Rafe, whose back was to us as he tinkered with the machine. I had to do something. And there was only one thing to be done. I had to kill a person. I wasn't sure I could. The thought terrified me beyond anything, but I had to try. It was either him or Rafe. With my chest constricting in panic, I grabbed my pistol, but my hand was shaking so that it slipped from my fingers through the branches of the trees and right to the ground next to the man beneath. The sound would have been enough, let alone the sudden appearance of a pistol. I saw the reaction. I saw him look up.

There was a moment when we both just stared at each other. And then each of us made a decision. He turned his weapon on me, and I grabbed my knife.

And I jumped.

It has come to my attention that you've been ambushing Rafe.

The memory flashed through my mind just as the gun went off.

I know little of what happened next. I was certain I landed on him. Where the knife went, I had no idea. I felt pain. Such pain. Pain unlike anything I'd ever felt before. Right in my chest. Through my heart. And a warmth, not unlike the first time Rafe had kissed me.

Then blackness.

Then peace.

"Young lady, it's time for you to wake up."

"It's no use, Captain, she's not typically one to take orders."

In and out.

"My girl, my poor baby girl, this is all my fault."

In and out.

"Imogen, my love, it's time now."

It's time now.

Time.

Rafe.

That was Rafe. Had he wound the clock? He must have, I can hear the ticking. Oh, good. I'll open my eyes then.

A white room came into focus, and two most familiar faces.

"Hello," I said.

"Hello," replied Rafe.

"And Father. Hello."

"Hello," said Father, tears streaming down his face.

I turned my head to the side to take stock of my room. Flowers were everywhere. That was nice. A couple of doctors stood off to the side. And my two men. Rafe and Father, sitting on either side of the bed. "What's all this then?"

"Well, you're in the hospital," replied Rafe.

"Yes, I suppose that makes sense. Did it work?"

"Did what work?"

"Putting the plate in the tree? Did it work?"

Rafe smiled at me. "Beautifully."

"Good." I smiled back. He was indeed a little funny looking. So wonderfully funny looking. "I tell you what, I thought I was shot."

One of the doctors chuckled at that. Seemed an odd thing to do.

"You were," said Rafe, giving him a vile look. How sweet of him.

"No, I mean, I thought I was shot properly. I thought I died."

Rafe and Father exchanged a glance, and then Father rose to his feet. "Let's leave them alone for a few moments," he said ushering the doctors out of the room.

"Tell me everything," I said, a panic rising up. I was missing something, I knew it. There was something I didn't know.

Rafe nodded. "I heard the shot, I came right over. You

were lying on top of a dying enemy soldier, a knife plunged deep in his gut. You yourself had been shot in the chest, the bullet grazing your heart. You were losing so much blood, and all I could think was that your heart had to keep beating. So I made it beat. I used my hands and I pressed on your chest, and then a medic came and Captain Dixon also, and they helped keep your heart beating. We got you out of there, and back to camp, and all along the way, I had this strange thought of a clock and the keeping of time and how the heartbeat is similar and . . . then I had this idea . . ."

He stopped the rush of words, words I hardly processed at the time. Up until that moment, I had stayed remarkably still, worried that the slightest move might cause pain. My body was still entirely covered by the white sheet. At his pause, I propped myself up on my elbows, and the sheet slipped away.

I looked down.

"I'm in a corset?"

Rafe nodded.

But it wasn't just an ordinary corset. It was made of a tough leather and covered in moving pieces. Winches and wheels, and leather straps holding it together. And over my heart was a forest of tiny gears in constant motion.

"Did you make this?"

Rafe nodded again.

"Did you make this to keep me alive?"

"In the camp, I made a machine that you were hooked up to. But I knew this wouldn't do in the long term—you needed to be free. You couldn't stay attached to something like a dog on a leash. I tried many different versions. I know you don't much like corsets, but in the end it needed to be tight to your body, and the shape made sense."

"All this, all this to keep my heart going?"

"All this. I'd have done more if I had to."

I looked at him. I didn't know what to say.

"You saved my life."

"Well," he said leaning in toward me, "you did save mine first."

I laughed a little, but it hurt, so I stopped.

We both looked down at the corset once more. The clockwork pieces ticked in perfect order, a moving work of art. And now my permanent fashion statement.

"You'll need to know how to take care of it," said Rafe. I could hear the excitement in his voice now that he was getting the chance to explain how his creation worked. "The most important thing to remember is to wind it once a day. Otherwise . . . well, otherwise, all will have been for naught."

I looked at him. He was still examining his work closely, and I smiled.

"I don't think I can do that," I said.

He looked up at me in surprise.

"You know me, Rafe. I'm all here and there whenever I feel like it. It's hard for me to keep to a strict schedule."

"Imogen, you have to," he said in disbelief.

"I just think I'd rather have a professional do it, if you don't mind."

"A professional?"

"Someone who knows how to properly wind clocks. There's an art to it, and I just fear I will never quite get it."

Rafe's expression finally reflected his realization.

"But that would mean you'd need someone to wind it every single day," he said slowly. "That's quite a commitment."

"One I'm willing to make, if such a person was also willing."

He took my hands in his. "Then, Miss Imogen, may I offer my services as your personal clock winder?"

"For as long as we both shall live? Because, you see, my life does depend on it."

"I fear my life rather does depend on it as well."

I smiled.

He smiled.

We kissed.

I loved how many times I'd already gotten to kiss him. How many more times that were still to come.

• • •

There are promises we make in moments of passion. Never to grow up. Never to go to war. Never to die. We can't keep them all. The son of the clock winder and the girl in the clockwork corset made many such promises to each other over the years. Impossible ones. Some were never fulfilled. But the most important of all was kept. Not just the practical one of winding a machine to keep a heart beating, though that was rather necessary. But the other one, about being there for each other. For as long as they both shall live. And, thanks to a remarkably well-designed undergarment, that was for a very long time indeed.

The Airship Gemini

BY JACLYN DOLAMORE

FAITH AND I had performed all over, but we'd never had an engagement like the Airship Gemini. Seven times now we'd crossed the Atlantic, fourteen times we'd taken the opulent dining room stage, but this would be our final voyage, and I would miss it. The Gemini felt special. Not just a mechanical wonder, but a being with a soul, a silver floating whale. It was unearthly to see something so bulky, yet so light. The very sight of it made me think of freedom, something I could only dream of.

The airship was operated by a branch of the Royal Academy of Mages, providing luxury transportation for the world's magical residents, whom were often looked at with fear and suspicion by the rest of the world—just like us. They had thought it a great lark, clearly, to engage Siamese twins to perform on a ship named after the twin constellation, and we had been happy to accept. For all the places we'd been, we'd never ridden in the clouds before. Auntie was terrified of heights, but she couldn't refuse the money.

Our quarters consisted of a small bedroom that had no windows and opened to the interior of the ship—Auntie preferred to spend her time here—and an equally small sitting room with windows that opened to the view, although we weren't allowed to open them until the ship was off the ground. Auntie didn't want anyone to get a free look at us. This is where Faith and I liked to sit, sneaking peeks between the curtains at all the people waving goodbye and gaping at the ship, which was longer than an ocean liner.

Auntie spent much of our passages looking ill and keeping to bed, which was ridiculous considering the airship was as stable as the ground itself, but it was always nice to have her out of the way. We'd rather spend time with the "Lizard Boy" any day.

For most of our lives, he was the only man we'd really known. Auntie didn't usually like us to associate with other "freaks," but he had managed to charm her and had been our opening act for many long years, and our French tutor besides.

He was not really a boy, but a man past thirty, with a taste for gaudily colored waistcoats and expensive port. His body was covered in fine gray-green scales, with little spines rather like whiskers around his mouth, and explanations for his appearance ranged from "magic curse" to "his mother was attacked by a crocodile while pregnant." He'd never told us the real reason, but we sensed it was sad and never asked.

We called him Uncle Marcel. Of course he wasn't our real uncle, but then neither was Auntie our real aunt. And at least we loved Uncle Marcel.

Today, however, he was the unfortunate bearer of bad news. "So, it appears the most illustrious mage in all of the civilized world is on the ship today," he said a bit sarcastically.

I made a slight, choked sound while Faith went rigid and gripped my hand. "Not Dr. Connell? Why would he be here?" she asked.

It really wasn't unreasonable that Dr. Connell should be

on the airship; he was a prominent mage and an investor in the line, but thus far our beloved Gemini had never been tainted by his presence.

"I just met him in the hall. He boarded at the last minute. He said he hoped he would surprise you." Uncle Marcel spoke gravely; he didn't like Dr. Connell any more than we did.

The last minute.

Now the beautiful ship was lifting off the ground, and the walls suddenly closed around us like a prison. For almost three days, we would be trapped above the Atlantic with Dr. Connell aboard.

"I know that Miss Weber"—So he called Auntie—"is all for this plan for him to separate the two of you—"

"He sees us as an attractive publicity stunt," Faith said. "Performing risky magic and unfounded science, claiming to do it for our well-being when it's obviously for his own glory. I'd rather die than let him separate us."

"I might be a man with the face of a lizard, but he is a pig with the face of a man." I always thought insults sounded more scathing with Uncle Marcel's slight French accent.

"Why was he speaking to you, anyway?" I asked, suddenly realizing how unusual that was. Dr. Connell referred to Uncle Marcel in such terms as "that horrible thing" and "that reptile creature"; he certainly didn't talk to him.

"I suppose he's realized you trust me. He told me that if I convinced you girls to agree to this separation, he'd shapeshift me, too. Make me into an ordinary man."

"Can he do that?" Faith cried.

"Well, he *is* the most skilled shapeshifter in all the known lands." Uncle Marcel's sarcastic tone was back, mocking Dr. Connell's own words. Dr. Connell was quite fond of superlatives.

How quickly this wonderful voyage was turning into a nightmare.

• • •

I had hoped this would be the trip where James proposed— a fitting end to our lighter-than-air summer on the Gemini. James had needed to travel a great deal this year, and the Gemini was his favorite conveyance, thanks to my presence. I didn't know how he managed it when ordinary humans weren't supposed to board, but he was charming that way. It was easy to sneak out of our room in the middle of the night to meet him while Auntie snored away. The presence of Dr. Connell, with his threats and promises, would make things somewhat more complicated.

We peered out the crack in the curtains, watching the people on the ground grow smaller, shrinking into the green field around them, but I was conscious of Uncle Marcel there, the ice in his drink rattling as he finished it off.

"If the man had a heart, he'd help you even if we didn't agree to be separated," Faith said softly.

"I'm not telling you this so you'll help me," Uncle Marcel said, although I detected pain in his tone. "I'm only warning you. I'd rather you hear it from me than him, before he gets you to agree to something you don't want."

"If Auntie really wants him to separate us, won't we have to let him?" Faith asked.

"Maybe not." Uncle Marcel looked fierce—and he was hideous when he was fierce. "All these years, I have stood by in silence because you were children. I am powerless to help you before you turn eighteen. But that time has almost come. You must only put up with Miss Weber's rules a little longer."

We always did as Auntie said. How could we not? Our own

mother had given us up, and Auntie was the only replacement we had known. But she didn't treat us like the kindly mothers you read about in stories. She had no qualms about subjecting us to medical inspections that would be published in the newspapers for money, nor did she hesitate to lash us whether we were naughty or not, leaving us to hold each other, console each other—two strange little girls in a world that seemed nothing but hungry eyes and snarling teeth, nipping off tiny pieces of our flesh. Somebody always seemed to want something from us.

Now it was Dr. Connell and his quest for fame.

"But . . . how could we manage, if Auntie was angry? What if she turned us out?" Faith asked. She seemed a little stunned. Uncle Marcel had never said such things before. We had always assumed we'd travel the world with Auntie as long as we lived unless we could find a husband willing to support us.

"You are dear girls. Someone will love you and take you away from all of this." Uncle Marcel's voice turned slightly rough, and our hearts broke for him. It couldn't have been easy to be known for your resemblance to a reptile. I never thought of Uncle Marcel as someone who could fall in love, but now I realized, like us, he must have sometimes looked out into the crowd and seen a face of beauty. He must desire to be loved just like everyone else.

"Dear Uncle Marcel," Faith said, dropping her hand over his scaled one. "We know you love us."

"Of course I do, but you know that is not what I mean."

"Uncle Marcel," I whispered. "What if . . . there was someone . . ."

"Yes?"

"A young man . . . who cared for me?"

He looked at me for a long moment, and said, "This

theoretical young man . . . how long have you known him? Has he any prospects?"

"He's a writer and a journalist. He speaks many different languages. Very clever. He's not rich, but he has a respectable income."

Uncle Marcel smiled. "I think a learned man would be a good match, very good. And what do you think of him, Faith?"

"Well, he is *theoretical*," Faith said. She smiled. "He's kind. A little soppy for my taste, but just fine for Patience."

"Does he seem fit to marry one half of a united pair? If you don't agree to Dr. Connell's operation, I suppose that you will remain conjoined." The medical doctors had declared we would need a magical separation by a very skilled mage if we were both to live.

I lowered my head, blushing fiercely at the thought of James, of how much I wanted to feel his lips on mine. "We don't want to be separated."

"We've always had each other," Faith agreed. "I don't mind if Patience marries James. I'll be fine. I just worry about you, Uncle Marcel."

I worried about more than Uncle Marcel, myself. I didn't think a man like James would engage in secret meetings with me while Auntie slept unless he had serious intentions, but would he ever propose? I had already expected him to half a dozen times, but I was still waiting. He'd never even kissed me, and I wondered if it was because we'd never really be alone, with Faith forever at my side.

I stopped at the sound of the door opening. Any hope that it might be an airship steward was quickly dashed as Auntie's ample frame stood in the doorway. She had grown rather fat, just over the past few years as the growing popularity of our act brought in more money, but current fashion flattered her lace-bedecked bosom. No fashion could flatter her face, however—the deep frowning grooves around her mouth, the small weary eyes, the fair hair slowly turning a hard shade of silver.

"Mr. DuBois, if you'll excuse us. I don't think we will be having any French lessons on this journey, busy as we shall be now that Dr. Connell is aboard." Uncle Marcel left, with a flash of a reassuring smile for us.

She shut the door behind him but remained pressed against it. She wouldn't get near the Gemini's windows for anything. Even sharing a room with them made her pale. "Now, girls, after your show tonight, Dr. Connell has asked if we might dine with him."

We sat very still and well-mannered, but Auntie frowned as if we had spoken out of turn. "You must promise to be on your best behavior. It's a great favor he's offering. Do you want to be exhibiting yourselves until your dying day?"

We were silent, sometimes breaking away from her gaze to stare out the window at the industrial landscape below us—a river winding through a shantytown, with factories belching smoke in the distance. The shadow of the Gemini fell on the treeless land like a stain.

"Do you want to be attached forever?" Auntie demanded. "It isn't natural."

She had raised us, but she still didn't understand us any better than the staring crowds. She didn't understand what it was like to be so close to someone that you didn't even need to speak most of the time—you just knew their thoughts. So close that you said "we" more often than "I," except when you talked to a certain young man . . .

I could tell Faith was close to speaking out against her. People thought Faith was the "stubborn twin"—sometimes advertisements for our shows even said so—because she couldn't hold her tongue. The trouble was, Faith gave in as soon as Auntie slapped her, and I usually got the back of Auntie's hand too, even if I'd said nothing.

Faith knew I didn't want her to speak, but she spoke anyway. "You didn't seem to mind, all these years you've made money off of exhibiting us."

"Because I had to do something to keep us all fed!"

"Oh, and to buy yourself furs, I suppose."

"Was that reptile putting these ideas in your head?"

I couldn't stand to hear her slight him like that. "Auntie! How can you say that about Uncle Marcel? He's been so kind to us!"

"Kind? Well, of course. Who else would be so kind to him as we are? Who else could he hitch his wagon to? Who in the world would want to look at him?"

I thought of Dr. Connell making Uncle Marcel into an ordinary man. We were silent again, but I suppose Auntie didn't like the way we looked at her. She finally left her place by the door and came at us, her voice low so no one would hear, but furious as a shout, "I should never have let you get so close to him. Now he thinks you're old enough he can fill your head with foolish ideas. Is that what he's been doing? Filling your head with trash?"

"No, Auntie, he just . . . He said nothing! You've . . . you've always liked Uncle Marcel," Faith stammered.

"Well, I've been thinking we've outgrown him. Your French is quite good. And if Dr. Connell will separate you girls, we can settle down in England and have some peace and quiet for once."

"England? So Dr. Connell can parade us all over the country and boast about himself and his skills?"

I knew that would set her off, and it did—she slapped our cheeks, one with each hand, a move she had perfected.

I always got it on the left cheek and Faith on the right. "He's a wealthy mage." She spoke through her teeth. "Don't forget, your own mother didn't *want* you. She gave you to me. I *could* have put you in a home for the simple-minded and infirm. You'll agree to his offer . . . or I'll agree for you."

• • •

We had first encountered Dr. Connell following a performance just outside New York City. The tall, dark figure with the refined British accent had approached us after the show with a handful of flowers. He told Auntie he had been so impressed by our sweet dispositions in the face of such adversity. She had heard all of this before, but then someone whispered his identity. He was Mitchell Connell, one of England's greatest sorcerers—a shapeshifter. Like all human mages, he could only work his magic on others, not himself, and a glimmer appeared in Auntie's eye before Dr. Connell even mentioned his plan.

He asked if he could examine us, and of course Auntie agreed. So we were made to stand before him in plain dresses with our connecting ligament bared, while Auntie watched and a man from the *New York Herald* made notes. Dr. Connell didn't use needles or tools like other doctors—he merely *touched* us, his fingers light. And Faith and I were frozen, trying to block out his presence, to merely endure this intrusion until it was over, as we did with all the rest.

I noticed the man from the paper—a very young man, with dark red hair and pale skin dusted with a few freckles on the nose—giving me an oddly sympathetic look. Just me, not Faith, even though we were identical and most people looked at us as a pair, and not as people at all. He smiled faintly when I met his eyes, and got back to scribbling.

"It could be done," Dr. Connell murmured, and then more confidently, "I have the power to separate them."

We had been told all our lives that we should only be separated if one of us was dying, for both of us might not live through the ordeal. But now here was Dr. Connell giving us a choice, and sometimes choice is the most terrifying thing one can have.

Or worse, maybe it wasn't a choice. Dr. Connell and Auntie went off to the next room to murmur. The man from the paper approached us.

"I'm sorry. Did I introduce myself? I'm James Martin." He shook our hands. "This wasn't supposed to be my story to cover, but my colleague has a bad fever, so they asked if I'd step in."

"Oh." We were both startled. James—well, I thought of him as Mr. Martin then—talked to us as if we were any two ordinary girls. We'd never been alone with a man besides Uncle Marcel. Any moment, I was sure Auntie would hurry back in and send James away, but she must have been so enthralled with Dr. Connell that she hardly cared what we were up to.

"I don't like the look of him," James whispered, leaning a little closer to me. He had a hint of a southern drawl that was somehow comforting after listening to Dr. Connell's precise British tones, even though I had always liked British accents prior to his. "Something about him. I've seen some unpleasant characters in my day, and he'll be added to the list."

I smiled, feeling as if a spell had broken. "I think so too."

We talked to James until Auntie and Dr. Connell returned. They both had a gleam in their eyes, looking at us as a predator looks on its prey. Of course Auntie wouldn't have agreed to the separation right away. She was a savvy businesswoman. She would have attempted to get as much of his fortune as she could before giving in.

Ever since that day, he had turned up at most of our performances, whether in England or stateside. He seemed to have unlimited means, and he always simply "happened" to be in Chicago or Boston or Edinburgh or nearly anywhere we traveled. We only escaped him in the American south, where they were suspicious of mages except their own. He would take us out to dinner on occasion, flatter Auntie and talk about our unfortunate condition and his wish that we could have the life of ordinary girls.

All the while, I was secretly exchanging letters with Mr. Martin—James. They had started as friendly little notes, but how quickly they had become outpourings of the heart, where I made my writing as small as I could to fill the page.

James felt like the first thing that had ever been mine.

• • •

On this, our last trip on the Airship Gemini, Uncle Marcel was, as usual, our opening act. We watched him from the wings of the opulent airship stage. The moment when he walked out from behind the curtain, the audience always gasped, and a lady or two would always scream, but Uncle Marcel took it all in stride. He strolled out across the stage like it was Sunday at the park, with his walking stick, black-and-white spectator shoes and well-tailored suit.

He always opened with several ridiculous jokes about his appearance, such as, "I just got back from visiting my mother in the Nile River, and my God I could use a drink." Or, "When I was young, I would ask my father, '*Mon père*, I can be anything I like when I grow up, can't I?' And he would look at me fondly and say, 'Yes, anything you like. As long as it's working with the blind.'"

The audience laughed as they always did, but Faith and I were clenching hands. We had never given much thought to Uncle Marcel's show before. We had never wondered how much it hurt him to make those jokes. But now we remembered the yearning he couldn't hide when he told us about Dr. Connell's offer, and we could hardly bear it.

"Poor Uncle Marcel," Faith whispered.

The jokes relaxed the audience so the ladies were no longer shrieking, but laughing. Then Uncle Marcel would say, "Now that I have made you laugh, I shall make you cry." A stagehand would produce his violin, and he would play music of such unexpected beauty that it would take everyone off-guard. I'd been afraid of Uncle Marcel the first time I saw him, like everyone else was, but when I heard him play the violin, he seemed touched by the very angels.

He always departed the stage to heartfelt applause, leaving the crowd in the proper state of awe and pity to fully appreciate our own act.

That evening, the audience consisted of magic practitioners and their families. They were mostly indistinguishable from ordinary humans, but were a more international crowd than we were accustomed to—a handful of fey with their instantly recognizable beauty, and perhaps even a few werewolves or vampires. We could only speculate. It was odd to be a curiosity among a crowd of people who were curious enough themselves. But my eyes searched only for a lone man with dark red hair and a lively face.

James was sitting alone at a small table near the wall. He caught my eyes and smiled, then discreetly lifted three fingers. I looked away before anyone could catch me staring.

Three a.m. A thrill ran down my spine. A late night visit would be risky with Dr. Connell on board, but I wouldn't miss it for the world.

Auntie finished her usual introduction, a weepy story of how she had cared for us all these years, along with a taste of the details audiences craved—how we had the appearance of being joined at the hip, but were actually locked together at the base of our spines, the ligament between us stretching enough to allow us to move side by side. She told them of how our clothes were specially made. How we claimed that we couldn't read one another's minds, but Auntie often wondered because of all the mischief we got up to! That always got a laugh. But it was a lie—she didn't tolerate much mischief from us before the strap came out.

We wore frilly pink dresses for the stage, still girlishly cut above our ankles even though other girls our age wore dresses to their feet. And our hair was still dressed in curls with bows, not in the sophisticated pompadours we wished for. We were small for our age, and Auntie wanted to keep us like children as long as she could.

We danced and played duets on a variety of instruments, including the Gemini's concert grand piano, and told fabricated, cheerful stories about our lives as conjoined twins. I was usually a fine actress, but just now I was so preoccupied with my hopes and fears that I almost missed my cue to make a witty quip in response to Faith.

I was so anxious to see James that every minute dragged. Even worse, I had to endure the dinner with Dr. Connell first. Faith was nearly in tears as we changed out of our performance dresses and back into equally juvenile sailor suits.

"I don't want to be separated," she whispered.

"I know."

"But Uncle Marcel . . ."

"He doesn't want us to go through with it just for him," I said. "We must be firm with Dr. Connell."

Auntie led the way to Dr. Connell's private cabin, which had a small parlor with the windows courteously curtained for the benefit of her nerves. We could hardly bear to meet his gaze. He had a trim little brush of a mustache and small, pearly teeth. Something about those teeth, perfect as they were, made our skin crawl.

"A wonderful show, girls, as always." Dr. Connell enunciated his words slightly more than other people, which was even worse than the teeth. "But I fear you looked a bit tired."

We shook our heads. Faith stirred her cambric tea noisily enough to verge upon rudeness.

Dr. Connell got straight to the point. "You girls are very fond of your Uncle Marcel, aren't you?"

"You know we are," I said.

"He is certainly skilled with the violin," Dr. Connell continued. "I imagine he'd rather be admired as a musician than have to stoop to the sad little act he does now. I imagine it must pain him that ladies scream at the very sight of him."

As he spoke, Auntie nodded sadly.

How I hated them! How dare Dr. Connell act as if he cared at all for Uncle Marcel, and how dare he use our affection for him to force us to break apart.

I had never thought about hating anyone before, and it made me feel more powerful than my small, girlish body, tethered to Faith, really allowed. Uncle Marcel had said we had to bide our time.

I didn't want to bide my time.

"Just think, it will be better for everyone if you're separated," Auntie continued. "It will make Mr. DuBois happy, and once it's done, you'll see it's much better. You'll be free to have normal lives and you shall no longer be gawked at, and I can stop hustling my old bones around the world."

"We–we don't want to be separated," Faith said.

Auntie gave Dr. Connell a knowing look. "They're just at that foolish age. Too young to understand what a gift you're offering them."

Dr. Connell patted her hand.

Auntie continued, "I've discussed it with Dr. Connell and we feel you should be separated before the Gemini lands."

"What?" Faith said. "On the Gemini? Shouldn't it be done in a hospital?"

"Mages don't need hospitals," Dr. Connell said. "There is an infirmary on the ship which will fully suffice. If I can't separate you, no one can. And I will. I will. I will go down in history as the greatest mage of the new century. I'm quite capable of handling the anesthesia as well, so you needn't worry about that."

The word "anesthesia" made it all sound real. They had a plan. Terror rushed through me, blocking my thoughts. I barely heard him speaking anymore.

"—when we touch down in New York, we'll be an absolute sensation. The country will be riveted!"

We were trapped. There was nowhere to even attempt an escape.

I pushed my plate away and shut my eyes, willing the world away. Uncle Marcel's warnings were useless. Even if it was true that Auntie couldn't force us to separate by law, there wasn't exactly a courtroom on the Gemini.

• • •

Usually we slept a little before meeting James, but that night we stayed awake, whispering.

"What if we told everyone onboard that Dr. Connell planned to separate us against our will? That would ruin everything for him, wouldn't it?" Faith said.

"Yes . . . but I don't know if anyone would believe us. He has lots of powerful friends. Besides, Dr. Connell is the only one who can help Uncle Marcel."

Faith sniffed. "What would it be like to be apart and alone? Have you ever tried to imagine it?"

Sometimes I imagined myself—not apart and alone—but with James. Just the two of us. "I don't like to," I said. Was I being truthful?

"Me neither." She hesitated, and then said, "But what about James?"

"James?"

"Don't be coy, Patience, I know you want to marry him. And I . . . I might be in the way."

"If he doesn't want to marry me as I am . . ." I trailed off, however. James had always treated us like normal girls, but he loved me, not Faith. Our relationship had mostly been conducted privately, through letters, but now that we were meeting all these nights on the ship, Faith was stuck sharing all our moments. And sometimes I know she didn't really want to leave her bed at three o'clock in the morning to accompany me to a rendezvous with James. Sometimes I resented her for it, deep down—but could I really hide these emotions from her forever?

We were no longer children, and I worried it could become even more complicated if Faith herself was to ever fall in love.

"I do hate Dr. Connell, but maybe . . . for Uncle Marcel's sake . . ." I ventured.

I couldn't even bear to voice the thoughts in my head— that I had never thought of Uncle Marcel as a man with feelings like other men until tonight, that I had never wondered about his hopes and dreams, that I felt ashamed for it. For years he had been there for us and we had taken it for granted. He told us stories. He even sat up with us when we had the flu.

"Maybe," she whispered. She nudged me. "It's almost three."

We opened the door and stepped out into the hall with our feet in slippers. The sight of James approaching, by lights kept low in the wee hours, melted all my apprehension.

"Good evening, Miss Patience. Miss Faith. You look a bit troubled."

"Dr. Connell is going to separate us," I said, dropping my eyes to James's worn but carefully polished shoes. "Tomorrow. On the airship. Before we land."

"Patience . . ." James took a step closer and cupped my cheek. His hand was cool and soothing. I lifted my chin and met his soft eyes, the blue just visible in the dim glow. I knew my own were gleaming with anguish.

"I suppose . . . it would make things easier . . . for us," I said. "But . . . I don't want . . ." I had trouble explaining my feelings to James.

"Of course not," James said. "All you know is what you are. The Bible may have been talking about marriage when it says, 'what God has put together, let not man tear asunder,' but I think . . ."

"No wonder Auntie didn't let us go to church," Faith muttered, although of course that wasn't the reason. Auntie simply didn't want fellow churchgoers to get a free look.

I flushed at the word "marriage."

James sighed. "I do need to talk to you about something." He propped his elbow against the wall to rub his forehead with the heel of his hand. My gut clenched. If he was going to break my heart . . .

"I've been trying to think what to say, but I just need to say it. I haven't been entirely honest with you. When we first started talking, well, I thought you could use a friend. Lord, the last thing I meant to do was fall in love, but before I knew it, your letters were the best part of my week. But . . ."

"But," I repeatedly bitterly, knowing now what was coming.

He frowned, his expression tightening. "I have something to confess to you. I'm a vampire, Patience."

I tried to say something, but instead only let out a little shocked breath.

"I can see why you don't want to be separated from your sister. I know how painful it is to become something . . . else." He was pacing, in what little room for pacing the narrow hall afforded.

He leaned against the wall again. "But I've been trying to think how I can ask for your hand in marriage. Because when a vampire asks a woman to share his life with him . . . well, it's no simple matter."

I was still trying to reconcile the thought. James—my unassuming James, a man of shabby suits and letters—a vampire. One of the world's most frightening hunters. With great strength and speed and keen senses. "How could you be . . .? I mean, vampires are . . . are cruel and dangerous. And the sun, and . . . and—"

"Now, surely you know better than to believe everything you read." A ghost of a smile crossed his lips. I'd complained to him quite a few times about the inaccuracies printed about Faith and me.

"But . . . could you be dangerous, if you wished to be?"

"I could be." He raised his eyebrows. "There are a lot of vampires out there who look unassuming . . ." He took my hand, a hand so small I could wear a child's gloves. "But on the inside, they're stronger than any human on earth."

I supposed I should have been shocked and should have

told him straight out that, of course, no sensible girl would want to become a vampire, and yet, I was not so appalled as I should have been. I was tired of being small and powerless, doing what I was told.

But it was no light matter to become a vampire. To leave my old self behind after a separation from Faith was one thing, but to agree to a death and rebirth was another.

"Are you really only twenty-two?" I asked, unsure I wanted to know the answer.

"1822 . . . is the year I was born," he said. "I was turned in 1845, and I had to leave home. They didn't look kindly on vampires back then, even more so than now. Went back home to South Carolina after the War Between the States to see if my little sisters were all right. They were old. Mothers of children about my age. I told them I was a cousin, gave them a little money . . . and I never went back again. So, it's not easy. But it has its rewards."

James released my hand, which was trembling a little. I didn't know what to say.

He glanced at his pocketwatch. "Well, you probably want to think about all I've said."

"Yes . . ."

"Will you be all right, though? With Dr. Connell?"

"We will," Faith said.

"Just do try and get a little sleep." He kissed my hand with lips I now knew had tasted blood.

"And here we were worried that Auntie would object to his being a Catholic," Faith whispered as he walked away.

• • •

"Dr. Connell," Faith begged, "you must help Uncle Marcel *first*. You promised!"

Auntie had ushered us, without breakfast, into the airship

infirmary still wearing our nightgowns, as we had no other clothes that left our connecting ligament exposed.

"I promise I will do what I can for that damned fruity lizard when we land in New York, but I don't have time for that now."

"Oh, please!" I cried, panicked that Uncle Marcel would miss his chance. "How long could it take?"

"Ladies first, that is my policy," Dr. Connell said firmly, pushing us toward the operating table. It was wide enough to accommodate us, small as we were, with leather straps to restrain two hands, two feet, one head. The table was cold through the fabric of my nightgown.

The entire room filled me with a deep-down dread—the machine housed in a wooden cabinet in the corner with a brass plate labeling it, "Dr. Iansbury's Patented Electrical Relief for Airborne Hysteria"; the open case of knives and hooks and other gleaming silver implements with usages I didn't want to think about; the small mounted cabinet of potions in brown bottles.

Among all these frightening tools of the medical sorcerer's trade was a framed painting of the Gemini itself, sailing serenely through the blue sky over modern buildings and chimneys spewing trails of smoke below.

Dr. Connell put his hands on our foreheads and pushed us down on the operating table. "Please. Lie still."

He fastened a leather strap around my right foot. When I tried to pull it back, he held me fast. On instinct, I kicked at him but he deflected me, shoving my foot down hard on the table. My heart was pounding.

"You don't have to restrain us," Faith said. "Where could we run?"

"This table wasn't made for two, but I don't need you wriggling around. It's for your *safety*." He made his way to my hand as he spoke, drawing another strap around my wrist. And now we *did* wriggle.

"Stop," Faith said. "I . . . I don't want to do this. I've changed my mind! *Help!*"

"Hush!" Auntie said. "I warned the staff you might scream, that it might hurt a little and you are of excitable temperaments. But they all understand it's for your own good. No one will come to help you so you might as well stop yelling."

Someone knocked on the door.

"Who is that?" she snapped.

When no one answered, the knock came more insistently. "It's the *Herald*. I heard about your groundbreaking operation, and I hoped to cover this fascinating story for the paper. It would be our cover story, of course!"

I smiled inwardly at the way James's drawl sped up when he was in reporter mode, but I wasn't sure whether to be joyous or dismayed at the thought of him entering the room and finding us in such a shameful position.

Dr. Connell opened the door a crack. "Oh, the papers will never leave me alone. How did you hear about this?"

"Why, Dr. Connell, sir, you are one of England's finest sorcerers. Did you really think you could attempt to separate the world's most famous Siamese twins since Chang and Eng and keep it a secret?"

"Oh, well. I suppose not."

"It'll be front page news, you just wait. I can already see the headline—'Dr. Mitchell Connell Works Miracle.'"

So Dr. Connell finally let James in. He looked quite official with his hat and notebook, but turned paler than usual when he saw us strapped to the table. He flashed me a brief look of concern.

"Do you need any sort of background on me and my accomplishments for the paper?" Dr. Connell asked James.

"No, no. I know all about your illustrious career, sir. You just . . . get started."

Dr. Connell pulled gloves over his hands in the same precise way that he spoke. He startled me with the sudden touch of his palm to my head.

"This won't hurt a bit," he said.

"You won't put us to sleep, will you?" I tried to turn and look at him, suddenly terrified. He shushed me, and I felt warm magic melting from his hand into my head. The room blurred. My panic fell into the background. I thought I heard faint piano music, and I realized it was a memory of Faith playing "Lily of Laguna." I could see Faith's little hands—the hands of a child, just the same as my own—feel the brush of her hair against my cheek, hear her heartbeat.

"'Let not man put asunder,'" I whispered, confused. I had trouble speaking. My strength was gone. But it didn't matter. Nothing mattered anymore.

I floated in that dream for a time, the soothing imagery somehow tainted with an undercurrent of distress and a metallic smell. Faith was here—Faith was here with me. But something was wrong. So wrong. I just couldn't remember what it was.

Suddenly, someone grabbed my hand, shaking my arm, shouting. "Why is there so much blood?"

"Don't touch her." That was Dr. Connell.

My dreamy images faded. James had my hand and my right side seared with pain. My nightgown was drenched with blood. That was all I knew before black spots filled my eyes. I could feel a tugging at my wrist—James was freeing me from the straps. I should have moved slowly, with Faith at my side, but instead I sat up. Alone. Too light, too free. Severed. Broken.

I didn't know it would feel like this.

I tried to cry out, I tried to grab at James's hand, the only thing I could seize at that wasn't pain and wrongness, but I had no strength. I was falling off the table, onto the cold floor. Faith was screaming my name.

"Hush. Hush. Let me—" James said. I heard scuffling between Faith and Dr. Connell. James got me to my feet.

"James," I managed to say, but maybe no one could hear me. Was I actually speaking or merely thinking?

Now another hand tugged at my arm. "You get your paws off her," Auntie snapped at James. "Dr. Connell! You've got to get over here. I think Patience is dying!" She almost sounded concerned for me, but I knew it was only because she saw her meal ticket slipping away.

"I've got to get Faith stabilized first! There's been a complication."

James shoved Auntie, yanking me from her grasp. His arms were around me, and my blood was everywhere. I could feel it hot on my arm—could smell it, even. Maybe it was Faith's blood too? "Faith," I choked as James dragged me away over the shouts of Auntie and Dr. Connell.

"James," I whispered. "I don't want to be helpless anymore." I reached for his head, digging fingers into his unfashionable long hair, the hair of 1845, and bared my neck for him.

"Is it . . . is it really what you want?"

"Yes. Hurry!"

"Forgive me," James said, moving his soft lips to the tender skin of my neck, making me shiver. "This isn't how I imagined it."

I had imagined it would hurt, to be bitten, but the pain of James's mouth on my neck was almost sweet compared to the horror of what Dr. Connell had done to me. I still heard shouting and scuffling, but all I knew was that my pain was melting away as James took my warm blood. I felt weightless. I imagined there must be nothing left of me between the separation wound and the bite.

He pulled away, and then he thrust his wrist at me, the pale skin gashed and bright with blood.

"If this is truly what you want . . . drink," he said.

For a moment, I didn't move. I felt weak, and half-dead already without Faith . . . and no other death could feel so beautiful.

But I wanted something for my own. A strength of my own, a love of my own.

I drew the red wound to my lips and drank his blood, drawing in the life and power that then flowed through me like a warm cup of tea on a cold day, my vision clearing. When I was done, I realized the commotion in the room had quieted. I heard Faith whimpering.

I broke away from James, touching the wall. Now I felt slightly drunk. Everything was sharper than before, colors brighter, sounds clearer. But the room was reeling. My teeth ached. The wound in my side didn't seem to matter anymore. I moved past James—shoved him, really, when my arms proved stronger than expected. I almost fell. I didn't know how to walk without the weight of Faith.

"Be careful, now," James said, slipping a hand around my waist, taking Faith's place at my side. "It takes time to change . . ."

He trailed off as we both took in the scene. Auntie flapping her hands and barking directions that no one was paying attention to. Faith was slumped in a pool of blood. And Dr. Connell was beside her, but his fingers were pressed to his temples as if he was deep in concentration. He wasn't doing anything to help her.

"What happened?" I cried. I tried to move forward,

stumbling, gripping James's lapel. "Is Faith all right?" I reached for Dr. Connell's shoulder.

Faith moaned.

"She's dying." I shook him. "Help her!"

"You've ruined everything. I would have had it all under control in a moment!" Dr. Connell said, shaking off my grip and standing, looking down his nose at me. "Now what are the papers going to say? It's all a mess! All because of you!"

He only wanted the glory of separating us successfully. He didn't want a report from the *Herald* that said he'd almost killed me. He wanted us to be little prizes he could show the world as proof of his skill. He probably already had a script to hand us, with weepy words about how he'd saved us from the life of freaks.

I looked at Faith's blood slowly seeping onto the carpet.

"Patience . . ." Faith's speech was barely a whisper, but my newly heightened senses heard every letter. "Just . . . be happy . . ."

She was willing to die. Willing to let me go.

I wouldn't give her up.

"You will heal her, Dr. Connell. Or I'll tear out your throat."

Dr. Connell snorted. "You? Tear out my throat? You must be mad if you think you can threaten me!"

He yammered on and on as my sister was dying.

I whirled on him—how fast I could move now!—and grabbed him by the collar of his suit. Even the finest wool was slightly itchy under my sensitive hands. I pushed him, dragging and yanking at his clothes, to the glass window that looked out to the ocean below. It was open just a crack to let in the cool Atlantic breeze. Auntie took a step back against the wall as I shoved aside the curtains.

"I wonder if your skull is thick enough to survive a fall." I spoke right to his face, something no well-brought-up girl would ever do, but I was no girl anymore.

I was a monster, sharp and hungry.

"Young lady, step away from that window! Is this really how you want to behave?" Auntie was horrified at my pertinence.

I snarled. "Dr. Connell, you risked our lives for your own glory. Now, it's simple. Save Faith or die."

My new fangs snarled my words. I knew the blood that covered my clothes and hands was starting to dry, brown and flaking, on my skin. And I knew Dr. Connell was afraid. He would never say so, I didn't expect that much, but he didn't need to. I could see it—I thought maybe I even *smelled* it, something rank and earthy like a mushroom turning slimy.

"And help Uncle Marcel, too," I added, pushing him closer to the open window.

"I will do . . . nothing of the sort! You dare throw me out this window and my friends will avenge me!"

"I'm sure you'll find that very satisfying from your ocean grave."

"Patience!" James was at my side, but I wouldn't let anyone talk sense into me. If Dr. Connell killed Faith, I would kill him. Still, James's presence rattled me, turning me back into a girl again, for an instant.

"Don't stop me, James." My eyes welled with tears.

"No, Patience. I'm here to help you," he said. He rammed his elbow into the window, breaking through the solid window glass with one thrust. Shards tumbled into the Atlantic. James grabbed a fistful of Dr. Connell's suit and, together, we shoved him further out the window, scraping his clothes on the jagged edges that remained of the glass. The cold waters rippled below him, as the cold air whipped at our hair and sleeves.

"What do you say now?" I screamed over the wind.

Somehow, it didn't take long to convince him after that.

• • •

"Maybe you should go," Faith whispered the words, for the first time in her life, "I just . . . want to be . . . alone right now."

We might be separated, but I was still beside her, had been at her bedside for the past hour, while she was silent, her cheeks pale. Dr. Connell had sealed her wounds and saved her, but she was clearly both physically and emotionally spent.

And now she was asking me to leave her alone.

As I hesitated, someone knocked at the door. "Girls? It's Uncle Marcel. I have Mr. Martin with me. We want to speak with you."

I let them in. Faith covered her face with a pillow. I suppose she'd had all the surprises she could bear.

The slim, dark-haired Frenchman with the pencil-thin moustache sounded like Uncle Marcel, acted like Uncle Marcel, but wore the face of a stranger—although he certainly looked better in Uncle Marcel's waistcoats.

He was followed by James.

"Girls," Uncle Marcel said. "I know we have all had quite the trip, and you will need time to adjust, but I've been planning for the day that I could give you a better life—and get you a bit of revenge. Trust me, not only will Miss Weber and Dr. Connell no longer interfere with your lives, but I do believe she will gladly share her jewels and furs to keep the vampires from the door. You have terrified her quite thoroughly, mademoiselle." He winked at me. "And now that I have this chance at a new beginning, I can work as a violinist, as has always been my dream. I wish to offer you both a home with me. I've always thought of you as if you were my own daughters." Uncle Marcel's eyes—still the same brown eyes—shone with emotion. "So, girls, what is your favorite city?"

I just wanted to be wherever James was. I'd never been a normal girl before. I'd never seen anything, really. Only visiting places in order to perform. I'd never had a choice.

"I'm living in New York right now, but I don't like to stay in one city for ever," James said. "I prefer it when my neighbors don't start thinking of me as the local vampire."

"Why don't you think on it?" Uncle Marcel rose to leave, but I didn't let him go without an embrace—and one for James, too. That one lasted just a bit longer.

• • •

Faith and I had no proper clothes that weren't attached, so I spent the evening cutting our dresses open and sewing them back together. Separately. It felt tremendously symbolic.

James stayed with me, but I didn't want to talk, so he worked at his writing. Or so he claimed. I caught him looking at me a dozen times.

Faith had remained quiet, even after Uncle Marcel's news, but when she fell asleep I knew she'd found a little peace.

Even past midnight, I didn't go to bed. I sat by the window and watched the moonlight shine on the water, once in a while spotting the jagged white form of an iceberg.

Just before dawn, Faith emerged from the bedroom, still wearing her bloodied nightgown, rubbing her eyes. Her gait, like mine, was unsteady, unaccustomed as she was to walking alone. She touched the walls for support.

"I fixed all your dresses," I said softly.

"*Our* dresses," she whispered, fingering the sturdy serge of our sailor suits. "You even fixed the pink frilly ones."

I shrugged. "We'll need something to wear."

"I hate these clothes. Sailor suits. Ruffles and bows. Other girls our age don't dress like this, they wear shirtwaists and things."

"Put their hair in pompadours," I agreed.

Faith looked at the window, and then at me, and the slightest twinkle appeared in her eye.

"You *wouldn't*," I said. "After all the hours I spent taking them apart?"

"You're the one who wanted a new life. Speaking of which, what do you think of Paris?"

"I think it would be a wonderful use of our French lessons."

She set aside our gray dresses with the black velvet trim, the best ones we had, and then she cracked open the window. The night air was biting. We filled our arms with the pink ruffles, the sailor suits, the skirts that only reached the tops of our boots, the hair bows, and watched them go, flying free beyond the walls of the Airship Gemini.

Under Amber Skies

BY MARIA V. SNYDER

I HAVEN'T SEEN my father in months. Not since I over-heard the rumblings of war in town. According to my mother, he has retreated to his basement workshop. Not to be disturbed. Every night, I fall asleep listening to the comforting sounds of metal clanking, machinery humming, and a hammer banging.

Every morning my mother makes me breakfast, using my father's Chef Helper device—a gleaming sleek cooker. Even with the kitchen gadgets, deep craters of exhaustion hang under her brown eyes, her pale face is lined with strain, and she moves as if an automaton. I offer to take a turn assisting father at night.

"No, Zosia. Your father is working to keep Poland safe from the Nazis. You will only distract him, and it is too vital. We all must make sacrifices during these uncertain times."

The Chef Helper beeps, then trundles over to my plate. It squats and deposits a steaming heap of scrambled eggs.

"But you go. Why can't I?" I try.

She ignores the question. No surprise as she's a firm believer in the children-should-be-seen-and-not-heard adage.

I gnaw on my bottom lip, debating if I should ask her

261

about Inek. He, too has disappeared, but for very different reasons. "Mother has Inek—"

"Zosia Jadwiga Nowak, you are not to mention his name to me again! Do you understand?"

"Yes, ma'am." My lip throbs. I taste blood from clamping down on what I really want to say to her.

"Good." Handing me a list of supplies, she says, "I need you to go into Leba today."

"But Father needs more amber—"

"And it will still be on the beach for you to dig for tomorrow." She snaps. "I don't know why Casimir insisted on decorating his inventions with that useless amber. It's impractical. I'm so glad he's now concentrating on *vital* machines. Poland will become a force to be reckoned with. Then the Nazis and the rest of Europe will be terrified of us!" Glowing with national pride, my mother hustles me out the door.

I could have told her why Father uses amber, but she never asks me for my opinion or wishes to have a conversation with me. Instead, she orders me about as if I'm a Polish soldier, sending me to fetch supplies. Mother has swallowed the war propaganda whole. I shouldn't be surprised. She's been a staunch patriot since forever. There had only been two queens of Poland throughout history, and my middle name, Jadwiga, was one of them. Anna was the other. If it wasn't for my father's protests, I would have been named Anna Jadwiga.

Perhaps if my name *was* Anna Jadwiga, I'd stand up to her. I'd refuse to be ordered about. I'd demand to see my father. But I'm just Zosia, named for my father's sister who died in the Great War.

Outside my home, I clutch the paper and a purse full of zlotys. Dark gray smoke pours from the chimney and stains the bright blue sky. Our wooden two-story house appears deceptively small as it huddles in the middle of our farm.

Although calling it a farm is being kind. Weeds choke the fields, the pasture fence is broken and rotted with decay. Our single cow has long since wandered away.

I fetch my wagon from the barn. The barn's roof droops at a dangerous angle, but it's quite safe. My father allowed the outer walls to fade into dilapidation while he strengthened the inner ones, keeping his workshop hidden inside. The windows even trick the eye, allowing light to enter, but, if you try and peer through them, all you'd see is black.

When the barn was deemed too small, he moved his workshop underground. Then my nights were filled with the scrapes of shovels, the chugging of augers, and the smell of damp earth while the barn was filled with mounds of dirt and rocks. I always wondered why he hid the piles.

A slight sound grates against the normal morning noises. I pause to listen and catch a flutter of squeaky wings. Scanning our farm, I search for the source. I've heard the Nazis have developed winged creatures to use for spying on their enemies. My pulse beats out a quick march, but all I see are real birds.

Unease crawls along my skin as I settle in the seat at the front of my wagon. I press the ignition button. Its small engine puffs out two tiny black clouds before settling into the quiet purr I'm used to. Since the day is so bright, I toggle on my umbrella. Sized just for me, the wagon resembles a miniature truck and is one of my favorite gifts from my father.

Steering the wagon, I listen to the buzz of its four tires over the dirt path. Every half mile or so, a bright flash of sunlight grabs my attention and I spot one of my father's machines working in the fields of our neighbors' farms. His Mole Plow digs deep grooves in the soil, a Beaver Saw's sharp whine cuts through the air as its blades cut through wood. Because of his equipment, our hamlet near Leba, Poland, is prosperous. I'm sure my father would have been content to create farm apparatuses for years.

Except the threat of war creeps toward us. And a few of our neighbors claimed to have seen the gleam of the Nazis' spy owls in the trees, and have smelled the diesel fumes from them.

We live on the very northern tip of Poland at the edge of the Baltic Sea. The supposedly Free City of Danzig is east of us—*supposedly* because the city's population is seventy percent German. And looming behind Danzig is East Prussia, also full of Germans. Across the narrow Polish Corridor to our west is Germany. We're almost boxed in by Nazis.

Jula's strident voice calls, jolting me from my train of thought. She waves me down. I brake. Her long ponytails bounce as she jumps in the back of my wagon. She talks nonstop during the rest of the trip to town. Rattling on about boys, fashions, and the war. I let her words flow around me like the hot August air.

Instead, I strain to listen to Father's Octopus Pluckers working in Teos' apple orchard. An odd clunk interrupts the cadence of the metallic pincers. If Teos fails to oil that joint soon, he'll be bringing one of the Pluckers back for repairs. Perhaps I should . . .

". . . I'm glad you're not helping him with his metal beasts anymore. Girls shouldn't have oil under their fingernails or know so much about hydraulics. You're sixteen now, you should be trying to find a husband before all the boys go to war."

"Jula, why do you think I'm not helping my father?" I ask.

"Because of the war."

"Why would the war matter?"

"So you don't see his new machines."

"What new machines?"

"War machines, of course," she says. "It's all hush-hush. The Polish government's involved, and they say once he's finished, the Nazis will be too scared to cross the border."

If it's all hush-hush, then why does everyone else know about it? Instead of pointing out the obvious to Jula, I concentrate on navigating over a set of deep ruts.

Eventually, the wagon clatters over cobblestones, announcing our arrival in the heart of Leba. Where the buildings are all huddled tight together as if they can't stay upright without the help of their neighbors. Townspeople fill the narrow streets with their loud voices, drowning out my wagon. Horses clop and carriage wheels thump and clunk. The rare automobile chugs by followed by an occasional lumbering truck. To me, the sounds are raw and unrefined. Just noise.

Jula and I part company as she heads to the pharmacist to purchase a tonic for her mother. The hardware supply store is a refuge of calm. Inside, the scents of sawdust, metal, and grease mix into a familiar aroma. The shopkeeper hustles to take my order as the other customers drift closer to see what's carried out to my wagon. I must admit to my own curiosity as each item is placed inside, wondering why my father needed that particular device or gadget.

". . . could be for a big trench builder for our boys," one man says about a stack of metal scoops.

"He's not going to dig trenches," his friend chides. "They're for a weapon. Maybe one that can run right through the Nazis."

"Those springs could launch bombs," another says.

"Or could help with suspension for a huge walking machine," says the first man.

Their guesses get wilder and a couple are physically

impossible, but I don't bother to teach them the laws of physics. Not that they would listen to me—a mere girl. At least my father never cared about my gender.

We would work together until late into the night, building fun gadgets like the Poodle Pooper Scooper. It resembled a poodle, with copper wires for hair, four metal legs, and it even barked. It ran around outside, but instead of leaving droppings, it cleaned them up with its wide tail. During those late-night sessions, he taught me so much until . . .

I shy away from thoughts of war. Instead, I notice one customer staring at me with a keen interest. I try to ignore him. But when I pass by to pay for my purchases, I smell the faint tang of machine oil. The hair on my arms stands up in warning.

After I receive my change, I bolt from the shop. Thankfully, the strange customer doesn't follow me. I wait for Jula at the place we parted. An odd creepy feeling slides up between my shoulder blades like I'm being watched. I search the streets, but see nothing unusual.

My father said my imagination would get me into trouble someday. I wonder if today is that day. Or is today the day I need to be smart? I run my finger over the clear crystal of my wristwatch. The numbers and hands are crafted from pieces of amber. Below the face, tiny gears spin, keeping time. It looks so delicate, yet the watch is thick and heavy on my wrist. My father gave it to me on my sixteenth birthday—May 22, 1939.

I remembered when he hooked his finger under my chin to pull my gaze away from his marvelous gift and said, "Zosia, this will tell you when it's time."

"Time for what?" I asked.

"Time to be smart. Time to stand up for yourself." He refused to explain any more, and the next day he disappeared.

Well, not completely—my mother claims he comes in late at night to check on me. And I have a collection of the little presents he occasionally leaves on my bedside table. Smiling, I recall the miniature amber statue of a girl with springs on her head instead of hair. The last present he left for me. I still haven't figured out how to turn her on yet.

Jula is slow returning today. The other shoppers don't pay me any attention. Although *my* attention is suddenly focused. Inek and his three younger brothers—all blonds—sit on the steps of the butcher's shop at the opposite end of the street. Probably waiting for their father to finish haggling over the price of beef.

Inek's family's cattle farm is about a mile away from our house. Inek used to work at our farm, helping me with the chores. That was before my father caught us kissing behind the house a month before my birthday. Father chased him off, yelling at him to stay away from me. At six foot four inches tall, my father is already impressive, but when he's waving a wrench and wearing an oversized pair of crystal and amber spectacles, he's doubly so.

Inek didn't come back, to my mother's delight. She never liked him and I suspect it's because he's half Swedish.

Inek catches me staring and frowns. I jerk my gaze away, but the damage is done. Even though I'm hurt that he hasn't tried to contact me this summer, my insides still twist tight. My mouth goes dry in an instant. I can't help remembering the impish spark in his sky-blue eyes, his sense of humor, his wide smile, or the way his long fingers tangled in my hair.

I tuck a few curls behind my ear, but know it's hopeless. Most of the long strands have sprung from my braid by now. My mother once claimed in exasperation that my curls were a force of nature. My father agreed, saying the color of my

267

hair matched the color of the Baltic Sea's amber. He then proceeded to use a few strands of my hair to build a very accurate rain detector.

I'm jolted from my memories by two men who block my view. One look at their black suits, fedoras, and dour faces and I know they're from the government. Problem is, which one? Germany's or Poland's?

The thin-faced man on the left says in German, "Miss Nowak, we'd like a word with you." The language isn't a clue as most people around here speak both German and Polish.

The suit on the right touches my elbow. He gestures to a side street, and I catch a glimpse of a Luger holstered on his belt. "In private," he says. His hand remains on my arm.

Now my heart is thumping for a whole new reason. There's nothing I can do as the men guide me to a quieter place. I catch a whiff of machine oil and fear rolls inside me.

Thin-face asks, "Where is your father, Miss Nowak?"

Surprised by the question, I reply in German, "At home."

They exchange a glance.

The man holding my elbow says, "No one is at your house. Where are the Poles hiding him?"

Cold sweat drips down my back. "My mother—"

"Gone, too."

Unable to comprehend, I stare at Thin-face. "But, they were there this morning."

His expression softens a tiny bit. "Did you see your father today?"

"No, but—"

"When's the last time you saw your father, Miss Nowak?"

He sees the answer in my face.

"How long?"

"Two, maybe three months ago," I say.

Elbow-man swears. His fingers tighten around my arm, digging into my skin. "Now what?" he asks his partner.

Thin-face studies me. His gaze lingers on my wristwatch. "We have his daughter. Perhaps we can use her to lure her father from his hiding place." He grabs my watch, ripping it from the leather strap.

"Hey," I say in response to both his actions and words. It's all I can manage before Elbow-man cuffs me, ordering me to be quiet. Pain radiates through my ear.

Holding my sixteenth-birthday present on his palm, Thin-face says, "This will provide the necessary proof."

It's almost as if my watch knows it's the center of attention. A strident clicking emanates from it and then an extraordinary thing happens. Metal legs unfold from its sides. The gears inside spin faster and faster. In mere seconds it transforms into a metallic crab, complete with two sets of nasty-looking pincers.

Thin-face is fascinated until the crab pinches his finger. Its claw cuts through his skin, exposing the metal beneath. A blue spark arcs through Thin-face's hand. He yelps and knocks the crab off. It immediately scrambles sideways toward Elbow-man and clamps onto his ankle. Again the electric hiss and blue bolt.

Elbow-man releases my arm to swipe at the crab. Thin-face is yanking at his own now unresponsive arm.

Inek appears in the midst of the chaos, urging me to run. I race after him. We weave through the streets and alleys until we're certain the *men* haven't followed us. Then we collapse to the ground, gasping for breath.

Inek recovers faster than me. "Were they Nazi agents?"

I connect the dots. "Yes," I puff.

"Enhanced?"

"Oh, yes."

Inek curses. "Did they capture your father?"

"No. They were looking for him."

"Good." Inek relaxes. "Someone in the village must have warned him."

Over two months ago. As my fear ebbs, my irritation increases. My mother has been lying to me. Then I remember what Thin-face said.

"Mother!" I jump to my feet, and run in the direction of home.

Inek catches up. "What about your mother?"

"The Nazis said she's gone."

"She's probably escaped with your father."

"No. My father's been gone for months."

Inek grabs my shoulders and stops me. "Wait a minute."

I'm struck by how tall he has grown since I saw him last. Inek's suspenders strain over his muscular chest, his white shirt is untucked, and stuck to his sweaty skin. The early August heat has been hotter than normal. I'm sweating as well, but I resist the temptation to wipe my brow.

"But I need to find her." I try to push his arms away, but they're solid muscle.

"I understand, but think about it. The Nazis know where you live."

His matter-of-fact statement sends icy daggers into my heart. They know where I live. Two separate pieces of information click together in my mind. The Nazis have been watching us, and my mother's been putting on quite the show for them. It explains all those nights of mechanical noises, the smoke puffing from our chimney, and her exhaustion.

Pride that she has been fooling them into thinking my

father was still at home wars with my anger over being kept in the dark.

"If you return home now, the Nazis will find you again," Inek says. "You need to hide until we can locate your mother."

He's right, but my desire to return to my house overrules logic. "What if she left me a message?"

He bites his lip as he considers.

"And I'll need a change of clothes and money." I would have to leave my wagon and supplies behind in Leba. "I'll go after dark."

"*We'll* go," Inek says. "You can't go alone."

"Why not?" I snap. "I'm quite capable of taking care of myself. It's not safe for your family. Or you. The Nazis are scarier than my father."

I know I've said too much when Inek squeezes my shoulders and anger flashes across his face. But he drops his arms. "You're not going alone. We'll cut through the fields while it's light and then wait until dark."

I open my mouth to protest, but a familiar clicking sounds behind me. Spinning around, I see the metallic crab, but not the Nazis—a minor relief until I realize the metal animal is heading straight toward me. *Fast*. I step back automatically as Inek hunts for a weapon.

Afraid of its dangerous pincers and electric shock, I hug my arms to my chest. My fingers brush the leather watch strap still on my wrist and I finally remember the crab was a gift from my father. Feeling a bit foolish about my panic, I crouch down.

"Get back," Inek yells.

"It's okay." I lay my hand flat on the ground.

The crab climbs to the strap. Humming and clicking, it retracts its legs and pincers and reverts back into my watch. I tug on it, but it has secured itself to the leather.

Inek stares at the watch. "And you wonder why your father scares me."

• • •

After we make sure the Nazis didn't follow my watch-crab, Inek and I hike through the fields. I hold up my skirt and I'm careful not to crush the plants with my work boots. We keep out of sight. There is no breeze, and the heat presses on my skin. My tunic is soon soaked with sweat. Insects buzz around my head, and our footsteps seem overly loud.

Something's wrong. I stop, gazing at the rolling countryside.

"Did you see someone?" Inek asks.

"No. It's just . . . Too quiet. That's it!" Another sweep of the neighboring farms confirms my theory. "My father's machines are gone."

"Nazis probably stole them," Inek says. "You can't be too surprised. His machines are efficient, compact, and don't require a heavy combustion engine or diesel fuel. They probably want to tear them apart and see how they work."

He pauses, and I wait for the inevitable question.

"Do you know what fuels them?" he asks.

"No." I lie to him because my father swore me to secrecy after I figured it out on my own. He worried the Nazis would learn the secret. My father refused to tell my mother or anyone else. When asked, he deadpans that it is the sea air—the Baltic's very own electrons that power his equipment.

"Can the Nazis figure it out?"

"I've no idea." Which is true. My father rigged the power block on his machines to incinerate the fuel when it was tampered with, but I didn't know if it worked or not.

Inek and I walk for a while in silence. My stomach growls, and I long for water. When we reach the woods that border my home, we stop and wait for dark. It's hard for me to sit there doing nothing. Worry over my mother's disappearance churns inside me. And where is my father? Does he know the danger he put us in? Does he care?

I search my mind for any clues to his whereabouts. Suppressed memories of my parents arguing bubble to the surface. My mother insisting he help the war effort, his quiet response, and Mother using my name as a weapon. I also recall my mother flinging his Catfish Rug Sweeper—his vacuum cleaner invention—into the kitchen wall. Unable . . . or rather unwilling to explore those memories further, I ask Inek about his family.

Inek chats aimlessly about his brothers and how their antics have gotten them in trouble. I realize I've been so pre-occupied with my own problems that I forgot that Inek abandoned his brothers to help me.

"Will your family be worried about you?" I ask.

He shrugs. "Probably not."

"I guess they're used to you running off without saying a word."

Inek's expression flattens. He gives me a cold stare before he stalks away.

• • •

Alone with my thoughts isn't fun. I try to think of happier days. Like when I mastered the installation of the reticulating gears needed to move a four-legged device. Or when my father beamed with pride after I designed my first gadget—a page-turning music stand. Or when I spent hours and hours on the beach with both my parents. As I played in the sand, my father would collect amber while my mother dug for clams. My heart lurches as I remember the day when I was eight-years-old and a green crab bit my toe. I yowled and begged my father to build a metallic fish to eat all the crabs in the sea.

Instead, he drew me into his lap. Beads of salt water clung to the ends of his short curls, and grains of sand peppered his beard. "Zosia, the crab didn't bite you out of meanness or anger," he said. "You were probably going to step on her and she was defending herself."

"Or her babies," my mother chimed in.

"Yes, that's it," he said. "Mothers are very protective, and she didn't want you hurting her family. You see, they're planning a very long journey to Finland to attend the wedding of the king of the crabs." Then he proceeded to tell the most outrageous story about the mother crab's trip across the Baltic, and how, in the end, she protected the future crab queen from a giant herring.

I touch my watch, trying to imagine the protective mother crab's shape in the gears, but am unable to focus due to the tears in my eyes.

● ● ●

Inek returns a few hours after he stormed off. He brings sugar beets and a jug of water from a neighbor's house. The beets taste delicious.

"Mr. Sobczak said the Nazis have been posing as Polish officials and going house to house asking questions about your family, and confiscating your father's machines," Inek says. "No one has seen your mother. And he thinks the Nazis have left the area, but it makes sense that they would leave someone or a few of their spy owls behind to wait for you. You're going to walk into a trap. Come to my house. My mother will—"

"No. I need to see for myself. I know it's dangerous, and I appreciate your help and the beets. But you've done more than enough. Go home, Inek."

"No." Inek sits down. He leans back on a tree trunk and crosses his arms.

It takes a long time for the sun to set this far north. A long time of sitting in an uncomfortable silence. Complete darkness finally descends after midnight. The chirp and trill of the nighttime insects help fill the emptiness, but as we approach my house from the back field, the silence is eerie.

No lights shine. The doors are closed. No smoke from the chimney. The place already has an abandoned feel.

Inek remains outside to watch for the Nazis as I sneak toward the house. The moon is three-quarters full and gives off enough light to illuminate the steps to the back door, which is unlocked.

I slip into our kitchen and stifle a gasp. The floor is littered with broken plates and glasses. Drawers hang open or have been flung to the ground. Careful not to step on any debris, I look for a note or some clue as to where my mother has gone. Our table has been broken in two and most of the chairs smashed into splinters. The rest of the house is in the same state as the kitchen. Outrage and fear churn in my stomach as I realize the Nazis have taken all of Father's kitchen machines.

In my room, I gather a few things from where they had been carelessly flung and shove them into a knapsack. Except for the statue of the amber girl, the Nazis have taken all my father's gifts from my room. My hand brushes a hard lump in one of the pockets of my bag. They left one. A bug light—one of Father's gadgets. It's the same flat round shape as my watch, but it's bigger than my palm and amber covers the entire face. When I twist the bottom, the amber glows with a soft orange light.

Throwing the knapsack over my left shoulder, I clutch the bug light in my right hand as I go down to the cellar.

My father's workshop is a mess. What couldn't be taken has been destroyed. A quick look around confirms that all his tools are gone. The amber I collected for him last month has been strewn about. There was more amber left than I'd expected, but when I considered that my mother has been down here making nothing but noise and smoke, it made sense.

I spot a stack of papers half hidden under an overturned workbench. Odd. I yank it free. The papers are tied with copper wire. My name is written on the top in an unfamiliar hand. I take the bundle with me as I return to the kitchen.

The drawer where my mother keeps her purse has been upended, but underneath I find her purse still bulging. Another oddity. That the Nazis would leave the money behind.

"Zosia," Inek whispers from the doorway. "I heard voices. Let's go!"

I turn off the light, shove the papers and purse into my knapsack, and join him. We press against the back wall, listening.

"I saw a light," a man's rough voice says in German. "Check the house, I'll go around the back."

Boots crunch on the gravel. My heart slams in my chest, beating a frantic rhythm. Inek points, and we slip around the side. More voices call out, growing louder. Lights fill my house. If we stay here, we'll be caught. I gesture to the barn. Inek nods.

The desire to run pulses through my legs, but we keep an even and quiet pace. Every inch of my skin burns as I strain to listen for the shout of discovery. We reach the barn, and I thank my father for keeping all our hinges well oiled. Or should that be my mother?

Inek and I climb up the side of one of the many dirt piles

and crouch behind it. My hope that the Nazis give up searching when they find the house empty shatters with the shuffle of footsteps.

"Gimme that light," a man orders.

A yellow glow fills the barn and casts a shadow on the wall.

"She has to be here," another voice says. "Footprints."

My whole body is shaking, but I don't want Inek to get caught. "Stay here," I whisper to him. Then I rip off my watch, drop it, and before I can chicken out, I step into view. Holding my hands wide, I flinch when they shine the light on me.

"Don't shoot. I surrender," I say.

"Come down nice and slow," one of the men says.

"Told you she'd come home." His companion smiles.

I slide down the pile. The noise of my passage masks the sound of my clicking watch.

Except . . . the clicking grows louder and is joined by more . . . and more.

Dozens of metallic crabs erupt from the dirt pile. They swarm toward the two Nazis, whom yell and shoot at the skittering mass.

Inek grabs my arm and pulls me from the barn. Soon we're running full out. Shouts and shots follow us, but we don't stop. We're half a mile away before we slow to a walk. I'm amazed I still have my knapsack.

"That was . . . incredible," Inek says. "Those crab things give home security a whole new meaning. I'm glad you knew they were there."

I don't bother to tell him they surprised me as well. It's yet another reminder that my parents have been keeping secrets from me. What else have they hidden?

Inek leads me to his home. I'm too exhausted to protest, but I plan to leave in the morning. Light glows from the living room, and Inek's father and mother are at the door before us. Mrs. Adamczuk hugs her son while his father demands an explanation.

"Nazis," Inek says.

I let him explain. His mother doesn't hesitate. She takes me upstairs, lends me one of her nightgowns, and tucks me into Inek's bed. I haven't been tucked in since I was six and my mother chided my father for babying me.

"You're welcome to stay as long as you like," she says, sweeping a stray curl from my eyes. "Inek can sleep in Marcin's room."

After she leaves, I breathe in Inek's musky scent on the pillow as the day's horrid events swirl in my mind. I don't think I'll be able to sleep, but I do.

• • •

When I wake in the morning, I notice my watch has returned during the night. It's creepy and comforting at the same time. The watch is covered with dust, and even after traveling a mile to find me, it still keeps the correct time. I wonder what my father meant by knowing when it's time to be smart. My mother fooled me for months, and the Nazis almost captured me.

Not very smart.

Getting out of bed is difficult—I'm stiff and sore from running. Mrs. Adamczuk's nightgown reaches the floor. She's tall and thin like her husband and sons—all blue eyed. Unlike my family. We all have darker coloring, but I inherited my father's gray-green eye color and his cursed hair.

I sit on the floor of Inek's room and sort my meager possessions. Money, a clean blouse, my favorite green skirt, the amber statue, the bug light, and the stack of papers. I untwist the copper wire and realize the papers are letters. Perhaps my mother or father has left them to explain everything to me. But instead I learn about something completely unrelated to the Nazis and the war.

When I finish reading the last one, tears flow down my cheeks. The letters started out so sweet, then became confused, and finally angry. Not that I blame the letter writer. I'd get upset if my letters went unanswered, too.

Conflicting emotions overwhelm me. I want my mother to comfort me, and I want to yell at her for concealing these letters. After a few minutes, the tightness in my throat eases. I wash, change into my clean clothes, and search for Inek's family.

The six of them are sitting around the kitchen table, finishing breakfast. The affable chatter ceases the instant they notice me. Inek's three younger brothers stare as if they've never seen a girl before. Their mother musses their hair and shoos them out to work.

"Sit, Zosia," she says. "You must be famished." She bustles about, filling a plate for me.

I sit across from Inek, who is beside his father. The resemblance is striking, and it's like seeing into Inek's future. Inek's hair is sleep-tousled, but his gaze is hard. I drop mine to the table. I hope I can talk to Inek in private and explain about those letters.

Mrs. Adamczuk cooks the food herself. Their kitchen is free of anything more complicated than a manual can opener. She sets a dish full of scrambled eggs in front of me. The smell causes my stomach to growl, and I can't seem to eat fast enough.

"The gossip in the village is at full steam," Mr. Adamczuk says when I finish shoveling eggs into my mouth. "Most of it is pure nonsense, but I'm pretty certain no one has seen your

279

mother, and she's not hiding with one of our neighbors. And the Nazis don't have her."

"That we *know* of," I say. "They could have grabbed her while Inek and I were hiding."

"True. Do you have family nearby?"

"No. My parents are from Warsaw, and what's left of their families live there." My father couldn't stand the city. According to my mother, he dragged us all out here for peace, privacy, and the sea. I think about my mother's family. Most of them died in various wars and battles.

"Let's assume she's free," Mr. Adamczuk says. "Do you know where your mother might go?"

I imagine that I'm her and have just escaped from the Nazis. What would I do next? I groan at my idiocy. "She went to town to find me. And so did the Nazis!"

Mr. Adamczuk says, "Unless she witnessed your escape, she might believe they have you."

I jump to my feet. "I have to go back to Leba."

"No. You will stay here, and I'll go," he says.

Inek straightens. "Her mother or father might even be able to find her here." He points to my watch. "There must be some sort of homing device in the strap."

As he explains to his parents about the crab, I'm remembering the others. How they crawled from the piles of dirt. How my father delighted in camouflaging his gadgets and fooling the eye.

"Then it is settled," Mrs. Adamczuk says. "If some metal crab can find Zosia, then her family can as well. She will stay here."

But I'm far from feeling settled. Even after Inek and his father go to town just in case my mother is there. I help Mrs. Adamczuk, marveling at their uncluttered and quiet house. And the poor woman has to do all the housework herself! No devices or gadgets to help her.

She seems happy, chatting and paying me more attention than my own mother, asking me questions and commenting on how nice it is to have another lady to talk to. But I'm only half listening. Instead, I am imagining that my mother has returned to our house to search for me or to confront the Nazis about her missing daughter.

We're sorting piles of laundry when it hits me.

Conservation of mass. The piles of dirt and stone in the barn were much bigger than what could have been dug from the basement workshop. Either my father hid more devices under the dirt or there is another hidden room under our home.

If there is another workshop, then my mother could be hiding there! Or perhaps my father is there as well and my mother *hasn't* been lying to me all these months. The room could also hold all those vital machines my mother talked about. Machines that could help Poland.

By the time Mrs. Adamczuk and I hang all the wet sheets out to dry, I'm determined to return to my house that night and seek out that room.

Inek and his father arrive with the news that no one has seen my mother or has any clue as to her whereabouts. The lack of information only increases my desire to go home. I'm well aware Inek and his family will refuse to let me go, or Inek will insist on coming with me. But his family is so . . . caring. Their house is a home and not just a building full of gadgets. They love each other, and I will *not* endanger them or bring them any pain. If anything happens to Inek, Mrs. Adamczuk would be devastated.

Once the sun is fully set, I creep downstairs in stockinged feet, carrying my boots. I leave a note, thanking them for their hospitality and explaining that I do not want to cause them trouble. I'm very glad that I never had the chance to talk to

Inek in private. It would have just complicated everything, and this way, he'll stay safe.

The back screen door creaks as I open it. I pause, but when the house remains quiet, I slip outside. Pulling on my boots, I shoulder my knapsack and head home. The moonlight is brighter tonight, and I worry my green skirt and light-brown blouse are too visible.

I'm careful to move without causing undue noise so it takes me twice the amount of time to reach the woods around our farm. Then I all but crawl. I stumble over a metal pod and realize it's one of the Nazi's spy owls. Dropping the hand-sized device, I back off. But the thing thumps on the ground—lifeless. Upon closer inspection, I find scorch marks. It was zapped. I glance around but don't spot any of my little crabs. However, moonlight gleams off a few more dead metal owls.

When I reach the edge of our back field. I stop. Crouching low, I wait and watch as my heart taps a fast beat.

At first the farm appears deserted, but a light shines from our kitchen window. When I'm sure there is no one lurking around the house, I step from my hiding place.

All of a sudden, an arm wraps around my chest as a hand clamps over my mouth, muffling my cry of surprise.

"It's me," Inek whispers.

I relax, but he doesn't let go. His chest is pressed against my back.

"I knew you'd try something stupid. I just didn't believe you would be *this* stupid." He sighs. "Can you at least answer a question for me before you're caught by the Germans?"

Curious, I nod, and he removes his hand. "Did you get my letters?"

My heart rips in half as I say, "Yes."

He lets me go and steps away. I shiver as cool air touches my warm back.

"Why didn't you answer them?" he asks.

Glad he couldn't see my face, I close my eyes and say, "Letters are a coward's weapon. If you really wanted to be with me, you would have stood up to my father."

The silence eats at my resolve. I suppress the urge to spin around and tell Inek the truth.

Finally in a low flat voice, he says, "Good luck with the Nazis."

There's a slight rustling, and I know he's gone without having to glance behind me. I swallow my emotions and inch closer to the house. Angry voices reach me first. Then the unmistakable thuds of a scuffle, followed by a crash.

Wild, horrible scenarios fill my mind and, after what feels like a thousand hours, I peek in the kitchen window. As I feared, my mother sits on a chair. Her lip is split and bleeding. Bright purple bruises dot her face. Six men—enhanced Nazis—surround her, asking questions about my father, but she keeps quiet. The Nazis stand stiff-limbed and awkward, probably still recovering from the encounter with my crab helpers last night. I recognize Thin-face and Elbow-man, but not the other four. I note Thin-face's left arm is still immobilized and Elbow-man is balancing all his weight on his right leg.

Thin-face asks my mother where he can find my father, but she refuses to answer. He strikes her. I marvel at her strength as I fight the desire to rush to her. Getting caught isn't on my agenda, and would only add to her misery. Pushing the fear aside, I concentrate on the reasons that brought me here. I sneak over to the barn and slip inside.

Once I'm certain no one is hiding there, I twist on the bug light. The piles of dirt are undisturbed. The crabs have erased their marks. A few broken ones litter the floor. I touch the face of my watch with my left index finger—the same finger my father used to draw my attention on my birthday—and whisper, "It's time."

A pulse of light erupts from the face. Bug lights glow from the walls as crabs push out and crawl from the dirt. Working together, they dig a tunnel into the piles. After digging down a couple of quick meters, they uncover a large metal pipe. I peer inside and see a distant orange glow. Who can resist the light at the end of the tunnel? Not me.

Perhaps my father is there waiting.

The pipe is more than big enough for me to crawl through. I'm four meters in when a yelp echoes behind me.

The Nazis. Half of the crabs following me reverse direction to attack the intruders. *Good.* I keep crawling.

Except the next curse sounds familiar. Scrambling back, I poke my head up out of the hole in time to see Inek cornered, his legs covered with pinching crabs.

"No!" I say. They keep climbing. "Stop." They listen too well, simply clinging now to Inek's trousers.

"Come here," I try that command and it works. They surround me like soldiers, waiting for orders. Handy. Could I send them after the Nazis beating my mother?

"Thanks," Inek says.

"What are you doing here?" I ask. "I told you—"

"I was halfway home when I figured it out."

"Figured what out?"

"You lied to me. I saw your confused expression last night when you were sorting through the rubble of your kitchen. It just took me a while to match it to what you held in your hand. My stack of letters."

"Letters from my father to my mother," I say. "Go home, Inek."

"And that was my other clue. You've been trying so hard to protect me and my family. What better way to send me away than to tell me you don't care for me." He edges closer, careful not to step on the crabs, our saviors. Who seem to be ignoring him now.

"Go home," I say again. "Or I'll . . ."

"What? Send your little metal army after me?"

"Yes."

"Go ahead."

I point at Inek and say, "Attack." Nothing. I almost laugh at Inek's shocked expression. "En guard." Nothing. "Charge." Nothing.

"You were—"

"Testing to see which commands they obey," I say.

By now he's close enough to touch, and the crabs are still motionless.

"Tell me the truth, Zosia." Inek wraps his arms around my back. "Are you protecting me or do you really wish me gone?"

"I can't . . . The Nazis have my mother."

"I'm truly sorry."

"You need to—"

His stops me with a kiss. Heat spreads through me, and I'm the one deepening it. Inek pulls me tight against him. Just for a moment, I forget the Nazis and my mother. Forget we are two separate beings.

He's the first to stop and draw back with an impish smile. "I was right."

"Yes, you solved the puzzle. Now go." I shoo.

"Not before *we* help your mother." He presses his lips together, jutting out his chin.

Too stubborn for his own good, fighting with him will just waste more time. "Fine. You can come along. But don't blame me if you get yourself killed." Returning to the pipe, I crawl inside without waiting to see if he follows. My crab army is at my heels, though. Their metal legs clink and clatter behind me.

The tunnel ends at a set of stairs. Bug lights glow as I step down. By the time we reach the bottom, the entire room is lit. It's easily four times the size of the basement workshop.

This must be where my father built his war machines. Lethal-looking devices and gadgets line the shelves, schematic drawings cover the far wall, and prototypes sit in neat rows on the ground. Tools and supplies are scattered as if my father left in a hurry. All the way at the back of the room is a jumble of half-completed farm equipment, as if carelessly discarded. The pile is next to a patch of bumpy ground. I wonder what is hidden beneath. More crabs? Another invention of my father's? Something just as wonderful?

"Wow," Inek says. "If this is what he left behind, imagine what he'll create to fight the war."

I scan the room, searching for a device or weapon that could help free my mother. Finding a promising long-barreled gun, I pick it up and toggle the power button. Nothing happens. It remains dead in my hands. Odd. I walk around the lab, examining the items. Something feels . . . off.

Part of the far wall slides back then, revealing my mother. On seeing me, she covers her gasp of surprise with her hand. Her face resembles raw meat. Before I can react, four Nazis rush in. My loyal metal army scrambles toward them. The men aim their Lugers at Inek, me, and my mother. They order me to stop the crabs or they will shoot us.

"Stop!" I yell. The crabs halt at my command.

Fear swells. Simple subtraction means there are two more Nazis waiting upstairs. Dread churns in my chest at the same time. "Zosia, what are you doing here?" my mother demands.

"Rescuing you," I say.

The Nazis find my answer amusing. The man pointing his Luger at my mother's temple says, "Drop your weapon."

I forgot about the useless device in my hand. Dropping it to the ground, I realize with a heart-lurching certainty that there is no way we can escape. We no longer have the element of surprise on our side.

Thin-face strolls around the room, inspecting the weapons. He tries a few of the smaller devices with his right hand. They're all like the long-barreled gun—powerless. He returns. No one has moved or spoken.

"Miss Nowak, your mother was . . . kind enough to show us your father's secret workshop, but she claims ignorance about what fuels your father's machines. What leaves behind that black oily residue. Perhaps with her daughter's life in jeopardy, she will be more cooperative," Thin-face says.

"I swear, I don't know," my mother cries. "No one knows except Casimir."

Thin-face exchanges a look with Elbow-man. I step forward as the loud report of gunfire fills the room. Inek flies back into the wall. A bright red stain spreads on his chest as shock spreads on his face. He slides to the floor.

I rush over. Kneeling next to him, I press my palm over his wound. "Damn it, Inek. Why couldn't you just go home."

Dazed, he peers at me for a moment before he smiles. "Because you care."

"Mrs. Nowak," Thin-face says. "One last chance or *Miss* Nowak's next."

"I don't know!" Mother yells.

I stand. "She doesn't. But I do. Let my mother take Inek to the doctor and I'll tell you everything."

"Zosia, no," my mother says. "Our whole country is at stake! *Millions* of lives."

"I don't care," I say.

"I'll let your mother live," Thin-face says. "The boy won't make it to the doctor."

He's right. Inek coughs up blood. Color leaks from his face. Why couldn't my father invent a healing machine? Instead of these machines of war.

And . . . *click*. Two thoughts lock together. I realize why these weapons felt wrong. My mind races. My gaze lingers on the crab army built by my father. Built to protect me.

"What is the fuel?" Elbow-man demands.

"It's Baltic Electrons. Also known as Jantar. It's a black oily rock found only on the shores of the Baltic. My father stores it upstairs."

Thin-face taps his Luger on his thigh. "We didn't see it."

"Did you check the attic?" I ask.

"There isn't one."

I shake my head as if amazed by his stupidity. "Haven't you figured it out that my father loves to deceive the eye? The barn, this workshop . . ." Thankfully, Mother remains silent.

He gestures with his gun. "Show us."

I hesitate. "Can you give me a moment alone with Inek?"

Thin-face considers. He sends one man to climb the steps to the barn, guarding the exit—my only escape. "One minute."

They pull my mother with them into the other room. I crouch beside Inek. Eyes closed, he's slumped on the floor, gasping for breath.

I take his hand in mine. "You were right. The first time I read your letters was this morning. I'm sorry."

He squeezes my hand. I lean close and kiss him on his cold lips. Then, in desperation, I point to the hole in Inek's chest with my left index finger. "Heal him," I order, but my army remains still.

Think! Father created them to protect and help me. "Fix him," I say, and the four closest crabs scramble onto his chest,

288

clicking as metal gadgets unfurl from their bodies as if they are the Swiss Army knife of crabs.

No time left. I run from the room with my insides turning to ice. I know those metallic creatures can't really fix a living being. Even my father isn't that smart. They will probably just increase the speed of poor Inek's demise. But it's a fairy tale I cling to in order to get through the next ten minutes.

I lead the five Nazis upstairs. We do have an attic. It has multiple entrances—all hidden except one. We squeeze inside the master bedroom's closet, which is bigger than it looks. The cord hanging down from the ceiling appears to be connected to the light bulb, but the switch is located on the wall. Before I yank the cord to lower the ladder, I ask Mother where Father is.

"He's in England," she says.

Thin-face huffs in surprise. "Not in Warsaw?"

"Too risky. He is safe in London, helping our allies."

I meet my mother's gaze. "Those weapons below aren't his inventions are they?"

"Decoys to make the Nazis believe he was still here."

She's lying. They were too well made to be mere decoys. Her left eye is almost swollen shut by the bruises on her face. Yet there is a defiant hardness in her gaze. My father wouldn't make war machines, but she would. Except she didn't know how to power them.

I tug on the cord, grunting with effort, pretending it won't budge. I rub my arms and ask for help as my finger brushes my wristwatch. One of the younger Nazis yanks the rope with all his strength. The well-oiled door flies open and all the precious amber stores pour out, taking everyone but me by surprise.

Pushing against Thin-face in the commotion, I grab his Luger and aim it as his heart. He freezes in shock. The young

Nazi is buried in mere seconds. Mother wrestles the gun away from Elbow-man then shoots him in the head with quick efficiency. I blink in surprise.

More gunfire cuts through the hissing of the steadily falling amber as another Nazi's forehead explodes under my mother's cold skill. Then the clattering of my army of crabs soon adds to the confusion.

The crabs zap and disarm the last enhanced Nazi, destroying his circuitry with their shocks, but my mother calmly executes him anyway. The next bullet pierces Thin-face right between the eyes before I can scream at her to stop, horrified at her killing.

"It's war, Zosia," she says before rushing off to dispatch the other Nazi at the barn exit.

She's back by the time I reach our ruined kitchen. Ringed by my protective crabs, I stand amid the debris, reluctant to see Inek's body, but knowing I should. Mother puts on her apron and bustles about making tea as if this is a normal day.

"How did you know the attic was booby trapped?" she asks.

I don't answer her. Instead, I ask, "Where is Father?"

"Probably in America by now." She waves her hand dismissively. "The Nazis have no reason to fear him. He ran away like a scared little boy." She huffs. "He asked *me* to abandon *my country*. All so he could build better plows instead of better tanks and airplanes." Her tone is harsh. The images of the executed Nazis float in my mind.

"He built these crabs," I say in his defense.

She tsks. "Toys really. Mother Crab's Children he called them."

"They saved me."

"We'll use them to bring the bodies to the basement. I'll contact the Polish authorities in the morning. They'll have to take me and my weapons seriously now. Your father wasn't the only creator in the family. The government will move us back to Warsaw, but I'll make sure I bring wagon loads of Jantar along so I can invent and fuel more armaments for Poland."

She sounds so rational, yet I'm stunned by her words.

"Zosia, sit. Have some tea." Handing me a cup, she gestures to the ceiling. "I assume the Jantar is hidden in the attic along with the amber?"

I stare at her. Jantar is the old Slavic word for amber. The Greek word for amber is electron. Baltic Electrons are just pieces of amber. Easy to find along the Baltic coast. It's amber that fuels my father's machines. But she is oblivious.

I fetch a clean bedsheet and go down to the basement labs. My crabs follow me, and I idly wonder how to turn them off.

Inek is lying flat on his back. His skin is gray. One crab has remained on top of him like a stubborn pet who refuses to leave its dead owner. I shoo it off.

Sitting by Inek's body, I'm too numb to cry. I stare at the dirt floor. It's smooth as glass, except for that patch near the back wall, which is scuffed and lumpy.

Unfolding the sheet, I lay it over Inek and decide there is nothing holding me here anymore. After he is buried, I'll leave and search for my father in America. Mother can figure out the fuel source without my help.

"Zosia?"

I'm startled to my feet. The sheet moves and I back away.

"Still trying to get rid of me?" Inek squirms, uncovering his face. "Shouldn't you have checked my pulse first?"

I rush over and hug him tight as joy fills me.

"Easy." Pain laces his voice.

I relax my grip. "Sorry. I was just . . . But you were . . . How?"

He tries to sit up, but winces before sinking back. "Those damnable crabs of yours."

I pull the sheet off and inspect his chest. The wound is off-center, about an inch and a half from his heart. The torn flesh has been stitched together with . . . I laugh. I can't stop the giggles until tears stream along my cheeks.

"Are you going to tell me what's so funny?" Inek asks.

I suck in huge gulps of air to calm my emotions. "The crabs have used fishing line to close your wound."

Inek appreciates the irony. "I wonder what else they did. I passed out soon after they started."

Glancing around, I spot a flattened bullet.

"I think they dug out the bullet, and fixed your lung."

"Think?"

"We should take you to the hospital."

He refuses. I help him upstairs instead. Covering the ruined cushions with the sheet, I settle him onto the couch. My metal army scurries under and over the furniture, waiting for me.

Exclaiming over his recovery, Mother dashes to the kitchen to fetch him tea. Which, it seems to my mother, is the cure all for encounters with Nazis. After all that shooting, she didn't try to comfort me, or hug me, or even ask if I was all right. No. She handed me a cup of tea.

I sit on the edge of the couch, holding Inek's hand. His family will be so worried about him. Inek is sound asleep by the time Mother returns. She stands in the threshold of the living room with his cup, and stares at my crabs with a wicked gleam in her eyes.

I frown. "They're mine," I say to her in a whisper. Although I doubt anything less than a thunderclap will wake Inek.

"Don't be silly, Zosia. They can help with the war effort."

"Then make your own. I'm taking Inek home tomorrow, and then I'm leaving for America."

"No, you're not." Her stern tone warns that she won't tolerate an argument.

Too bad. She's finally going to get one. "Yes, I am. Did you even consider the danger to me and our neighbors when you decided to trick the Nazis?"

"Of course it's dangerous. It's war."

An easy excuse. "Why didn't you tell me what you were doing?"

"To keep you safe."

"Wouldn't I have been safer in America with Father?" I demand.

"You belong in Poland."

"And Father agreed to this?" I ask.

She hesitates. "Eventually. He wouldn't agree until those . . . crabs were ready. I begged him to stay. Pleaded that he should build giant crabs to defend against the Nazis. This is his homeland! But he wouldn't listen. And he refused to tell me about the Jantar. Baltic Electrons, pah! What utter nonsense."

Mother clutches the tea cup in a tight fist. Her anger still raw even after three months. I remember how eerily calm she was when shooting the Nazis. How she seemed willing to let Inek die. Yes, in wartime saving millions of people in exchange for a single person is logical, yet . . .

I remember her words. *The Polish authorities will now take me seriously.*

"Where is Father?" I ask.

"I told you—"

"Where in America? It's a big country."

She glances at the floor. "I don't know. He didn't tell me."

"Surely he sent you letters? Or me? Did you hide them like you hid the ones Inek sent?"

Frowning, she shoots Inek a disgusted look. "Don't worry, Zosia, you'll soon forget him and we'll find a . . . better suitor in Warsaw. We all have to make sacrifices for the war."

I stare at her. When did she turn from patriotic to psychotic? "Why did you save Inek's letters if you want me to forget him?"

Her hands twist around the tea cup. "The letters reminded me of another . . . boy." Mother's expression softens into . . . I don't know. I've never seen her look this way before. Maybe love. Regret perhaps.

"Fredek Lisowski and I were to wed in the fall of 1920. He was a soldier and he sent me a letter every week. Fredek was killed in the Battle of Warsaw." Once again anger flares. "I met and married your father a year later. His genius attracted me, but his useless devices . . ." She put the teacup down and wiped her hands on her apron. "I tried to get him to make more useful things like weapons."

"Did you marry him for love or for Poland?"

She won't answer. But deep down I know. With such different views of the world, it must have been difficult for them to be together.

"Why didn't you leave him?" I ask.

"It was my duty to my country. If I had succeeded, we wouldn't be worried about another war."

"Why didn't he leave you, then?"

A strange wry smile twists her lips. "He wouldn't leave you, Zosia."

Her answer reminds me that she didn't answer my other question. "Has Father sent you any letters?"

"No."

Her answers don't match. If Father wouldn't leave me then why was he in America? Unless . . . I stand on weak legs. My mother calls to me as I pass her and stumble down to the basement.

Kneeling by the rough patch of dirt, I cry. *What has she done?*

"Zosia," Mother says behind me. "What are you doing?"

I whirl around. "You killed him." It's not a question.

"He was a traitor."

"Are you going to kill me, too?"

"Why would I do that?"

"Because I'm leaving." Fanned out behind her is my crab army. It's almost as if they know they should keep a respectful distance from us.

"Don't be silly. You're staying with me."

"Why do you want me to stay?"

"You're creative and can help me design weapons."

She says nothing about me being her daughter. Nothing about love. Nothing about family. "Did you make that statue of the girl with springs for her hair for me?"

Confused, she's slow to answer. "Yes."

"Why did you make it?"

"To keep up the ruse. To make you think your father was still here. He was always making you worthless things."

I close my eyes for a moment as pain rolls through me. The statue was part of the deception. Not a gift to comfort me when I was lonely and missing my father. "I'm taking Inek home and then I'm leaving."

"No. You're not. You're going to go to your room. I'll take care of Inek." Her cold tone coats my shattered heart in a layer of ice.

"Like you took care of Father and the Nazis?" I shudder. "No."

When I fail to move, she pulls a Luger from her apron pocket and aims it at me. "Go to your room. Now."

I gape at her. By the set of shoulders, I knew she'd kill me for being a traitor. She has only one love. And it's not me or my father.

My crabs sense a threat. Silent on the dirt floor, they overwhelm her in mere seconds.

She yells my name, but I turn my back on her.

Her shrieks follow me as I climb the steps to check on Inek.

Like she said, it's war.

King of the Greenlight City

BY TESSA GRATTON

THE SUMMER THAT Everest Aleksander the Younger—called Ever by his many friends—set the housekeeper's apron on fire was the summer his parents sent him to the family seat out on the Pearshire cliffs. It was the summer he met his intended, Alys Greentree of the Chenworth Niobes, the summer he turned seventeen, and the summer he cut off all his dark red hair. It was also the summer he fell over said Pearshire cliffs, after a bit too much champagne, plummeting off the iron staircase toward the tooth-like rocks below.

Fortunately, Ever could fly.

• • •

It wasn't such a shocking thing, given that every member of the Zephyr clan could also fly. What was shocking to Ever, and would have been to anyone else he decided to tell, was that Everest Aleksander the Younger was not an Air Worker, but the heir to the council seat of the Prometheans—the Fire Workers.

Ever was supposed to be able to call fire with a glance, or snap his fingers to set logs—and aprons—ablaze. And he could do all those things quite well. Well enough that it had been said in court he'd surpass his father's skills by the time he was twenty.

297

When he fell, Ever experienced a moment of sheer panic, where none of his muscles worked and he merely dropped like a tailor's dummy. But then some instinct gripped him, and he swooped out his arms. His fingers caught onto something not so firm as earth, but slippery and thin as garden snakes. This something wound through his flailing fingers and he closed them into fists. His body slowed, and the tendrils he grasped tightened. Soon he rested akimbo in the dark night sky, feet dangling five horse-lengths over the crashing waves. Looking up toward the stars, Ever realized he held on to nothing but air.

The realization was nearly his undoing.

Wisps of air slipped away from him and he fell again, only jerking to a stop when he closed his eyes and imagined the air growing thick and visible as vines.

Carefully, he lowered himself onto the narrow crescent of beach, where he huddled in a ball, holding his knees tight against his chest. The anxiety lasted only a moment, however, before Ever was on his feet, staring up the jagged side of the cliff, his breath puffing out of him in thick ropes. He pursed his lips and blew, imagining that the air from his lungs crawled up the rock face and hardened into a ladder. Of sorts.

Ever gripped the first rung and pulled. He dragged himself upwards slowly, unable to keep the air-ladder formed after releasing it with his hands, so that his legs had nothing but cliff to scrabble against.

By the time he'd climbed to a point where he could access the iron staircase bolted into the rock, it had been nearly an hour. He was covered in bruises, his breath felt like fire in his chest, and even his bones seemed to shake with fatigue. Ever lay sprawled over the steps, metal cutting into his back, and watched gray clouds take away the stars.

He dragged himself back into his bedroom by dawn and slept for thirteen hours. His tutor, Paul Primus, woke him after sunset in order to make certain the young prince wasn't ill.

Ever sat, ran to the washroom, and vomited into the tub. He came out and ordered Primus to ready their things; it was time to return to the City of Light.

• • •

Alys Greentree of the Chenworth Niobes was generally bored with life. Not that she wished for an end to it, but rather she looked at her family as they sent her off to the City that same summer and wondered what was the point. Three younger sisters, hair swept up with flowers; a mother too clean to garden; a father interested in political ties, not familial ones; two aunts with husbands and daughters dressed, for all intents and purposes, identically to Alys's sisters.

As her horse broke into a gentle—too gentle—canter, and her nurse and four Earth Hand bodyguards fanned out behind her, Alys relaxed into her seat, put her heels down in the stirrups, and imagined what her Promethean husband would be like.

Full of temper, disregarding of her cares, and no doubt, boring. She suspected the young prince to be ugly, for why else would he not have been sent to collect her himself?

So it was with a delicate scowl that Alys came to the crossroads an hour's ride south of the City of Light, and met with Ever, who careened past on a dun gelding, his cape flapping and his mouth open to yell at them to get out of the way.

Alys's horse reared, and to her credit, she did not fall. Instead she wheeled around, calming her poor mount, and held her chin high.

Ever, to *his* credit, paused. A flush overwhelmed his Promethean freckles, but he bowed from the saddle and made his apologies. Alys barely managed to respond, demanding this churl's name, before Ever shouted a nameless apology and charged on.

• • •

They met more formally that night.

The City of Light glowed with new electricity, a crescent of earthly starlight bowing around the eastern banks of the River Acrimony. On the west bank crouched the Greenlight City, dull and pale like a sore against the world from the green gas lamps lining its crooked streets. From an island in the center of that river, seven towers rose: Promethean, Zephyr, Niobe, Amphytrite, Animator, and Thanatos. In the center, connected to all others by arching bridges, was the Seventh Tower in which the six royal families held council.

From the window of the library in the Promethean Tower, Alys could see the crown of the Seventh. A giant model of the solar system turned there with an audible *tick-tick-tick*. The planets were gilded and silver-cast, glowing in the sunset all the colors of blood. A scattering of glass stars hung from the clockwork and caught the light, too, dazzling her eyes. Each was the size of her skull, but from this distance seemed little more than pinpricks against the sky.

Alys ran a finger down the windowsill, coaxing tiny green tendrils out of the stone. Her skin warmed; the leaves unfurled to the size of one of her teeth and turned toward her as if she was the sun. The greenery calmed her, though it was unable to entirely soothe away her anxiety. She'd asked to be left alone until her fiancé arrived to escort her to supper, and as she contemplated her final moments of freedom, Alys thought perhaps she would one day climb to the top of that

Seventh Tower, walk out along the steel supports, and collect one of the stars.

At least, planning such a ridiculous scheme would keep her occupied over long afternoons regretting her marriage.

In his rooms, one story above, Ever continued staring at himself in the bronzed mirror that hung between two wardrobes full of court jackets. All his family had freckles and dark red hair. But while his mother and aunts, and even his six-year-old sister, covered theirs with rice powder, and his uncles sought to draw attention away from them with bright cravats and feathered hats, Ever had always rather liked his.

To him, the scatter of dots on his nose and cheeks were dark embers, points of fire that billowed up from inside his heart and pushed out. The fire was so desperate for life that it cut through his skin and emerged in small, burning spots.

He was a Promethean. Fire was his.

And yet. And yet he had flown.

• • •

Ever entered the library wearing crimson and black, an appropriate but utterly uncreative choice. The red of the jacket clashed with his hair; when he bowed, uneven chunks fell into his eyes and Alys wondered if it had been cut with a hacksaw.

She had chosen a simple split skirt in mauve, in case she decided to run, and covered it with a long jacket colored similarly to the pea soup her nurse used to bring her when she was ill. Not a poetic association, but it made her feel better. She hadn't let them put flowers into her hair, and instead it was bound only by a string of ribbon that loosely gathered it at the nape of her neck.

"Hello," Ever said as he rose from his bow. All the extended and polite greetings he'd been taught since he could walk had slipped out of his head when the air slipped through his fingers.

Yet Alys didn't mind. His eyes were the color of mud—rainy and murky and reminding her of her garden. So much not what she'd expected that it took her a moment to recognize him as the youth who'd nearly killed her on the road that afternoon. Her lips parted, but instead of the measured salutation Ever expected, she said, "Damn you, my horse nearly broke her ankle!"

Ever gaped at her, never having heard a lady curse before. Swiftly, he shut the library door behind him, and began to laugh.

Horror at herself made Alys touch her lips, smearing the carefully applied pink paint meant to make them appear larger and fuller. The moment her fiancé began to laugh, she lowered her hand and laughed, too.

Soon his hands were around hers and they supported each other in their merriment. Ever wondered that such a lovely and shocking girl had shown up to marry him, and found further amusement in the thought that his own mother had chosen a girl so very different from herself. Alys's relief that her intended hadn't run from her, wasn't ugly, and seemed, in fact, the very opposite of boring, bubbled up inside her and transformed into heady delight.

Before either had managed another word, their lips met.

• • •

That night instead of bathing and readying himself to retire, Ever stood at his bedroom window and stared out toward the glowing green lights across the river. Unlike the City of Light, which shone silver and gold from the new voltage lamps, the eastern shore was lit by eerie gas lamps that burned green. It was said that Titan did not allow electricity in his domain.

Smaller and squatter than the Seventh Tower, but still hulking over the green radiance, the Titan's Tower on the eastern shore had been there for generations. Its many windows winked in all the colors of the rainbow, and Ever stared at the uppermost square of red.

It was said by nurses and old grandfathers to their wards and children that Titan had lived a hundred lifetimes, that his control over all six types of magic gained him immortality and power as strong as all the ruling families combined. *Never go to the Greenlight City*, they whispered, *for there are all the monsters and criminals, living together under the Titan's protection*. And it was said by Ever's own father that 328 years ago, a truce of sorts had been set between Titan and the Seventh Tower—that Titan should never cross the flowing waters of the Acrimony, but keep himself and all his mischief and mayhem on his side. In return, the ruling families would turn a blind eye to small trading and the forbidden, unclean progeny of Titanic magic. *Never go to the Greenlight City*, Ever's father ordered, *for the wizard there is a king of crime, a king of mischief, and a king of lies*.

In the City of Light the understanding was only one magic from one hand. But Ever had discovered two magics in his blood. No one under the Seventh Tower could teach him, or even explain. If he tried, he would find only censure and fear.

Titan was the only creature he could turn to for answers.

Although he should have been exhausted from the long day of travel, followed by a rather blissful evening in the company of his future wife, Ever's body hummed.

When he'd kissed Alys, he'd felt her breath inside his own mouth. Ever had wondered if she tasted his, too, and could tell that he'd discovered how to fly. A part of him had wanted to confess it to her, just to that one person, the girl he was supposed to marry. But the smell of her hair and the sweet, slippery flavor of her lip paint had stopped him. He hadn't wished to ruin the moment.

Pushing open the window, Ever climbed up onto the narrow stone sill. His rooms were on the seventh floor of the tower, and at this time of night the courtyard far below was a black nothing. The river, though, sparkled like a ribbon of sequins, and beyond it, the green ocean of gaslight.

Wind brushed at his hair, curling around his face and neck, tugging at Ever, cajoling and playful. He reached out to grasp at the strands of air. They whipped around his wrist, and before Ever could decide otherwise, he stepped off the sill and into the night.

• • •

It was only because she'd happened to shove open her own window to let out the candle smoke that Alys saw Ever leap over her head two stories above, and take off in an arc both graceful and sudden, toward the river.

He was merely a red and black shadow, but Alys knew it was him by the tenuous connection already linking her heart with his. Her fingers dug into the stone casement, causing tiny furrows that sprouted yellow flowers. She lost her breath, and watched him until he vanished into the darkness between the stars.

• • •

Over the river the wind turned sharp and hungry.

Ever struggled to maintain his control. He was buffeted and tossed about like a leaf in autumn, and only his fierce determination kept him from being shredded.

He landed on the far bank, boots clomping down onto the docks hard enough that he fell to his hands and knees. All around were the smells of river-rot, fish, and gear oil from the barges. Laughter came with the wind and the soft lapping of the water against wood. He heard music pouring out of gambling houses and the call of women from the fancy rooms. Here, in the Greenlight City, the night was a living monster, sticky and ecstatic and reeking.

Making his way through the green-tinged shadows, Ever kept his eyes on the black silhouette of Titan's Tower. It blocked out stars and moonlight, and he could see it over all the buildings. The cobbles at his feet shimmered sickly as the gaslights sputtered. It wasn't green light, he realized as he paused to gather his bearings beneath a tall iron streetlamp: the glass enclosing the tiny fire was mottled green. As he watched, the lamp went dark. A clicking noise drew his attention to the next lamp, which suddenly flared into life.

Ever moved between lamps, counting off the moments they ticked on and off.

The lamps were on a timeline, and all, it seemed, part of the same giant network. In the City of Light, it would take a massively coordinated effort spanning each of the different families of magic: Animators to bring the gears to life, Prometheans to charge the flames, Niobes to create the gas pipes, and Zephyr magic to move the gas.

But here in the Greenlight City, all the credit lay entirely at the feet of Titan.

• • •

The tower door was small as a cupboard, and had no lock so far as Ever could tell. He knocked once, and then again. Green light shone off the polished stone and silver of the building from a perfect circle of gas lamps, creating a round courtyard between the tower and the ring of shops and churches.

When no answer came to his knocks, Ever twisted the intricately carved knob. A rattle of gears and shaking of tiny metallic parts echoed through the thick wood, and a low gong rang through the tower. The sound shivered through Ever's bones, and he called upon that ferocity of spirit that had allowed him to pick himself up at the base of the Pearshire cliffs and climb his way to safety.

The door swung outward, forcing him to step back.

A young woman appeared, wearing a pink dressing gown with tattered hem. Her thick ash-bark hair fell in snake-like curls around her shoulders, and when she spoke she showed off perfect rose-petal lips. But the thing that made Ever's breath thin and disappear were the plump violet berries where her eyes should be.

"Welcome, young sir." Her voice was liquid and thick as perfumed oil.

He recognized the simulacrum for what she was, though such a creation was not supposed to have been born for more than a hundred years because it was a task that took a variety of magics perfectly woven together.

Something Titan could do with ease, Ever thought, raising one hand to his chest and bowing. Both polite and kind, it most conveniently allowed him to avert his eyes from her beautiful, alien face.

"My thanks, lady," Ever managed in a whisper.

When he glanced up, the rose-petal lips had broadened into a smile. "What is it that you need this evening?" Her small white hand gestured widely, spreading before him all the room, with its shelves of potions and dried flowers. Ribbons and knives and candle wax covered a worktable, and dripping from the rafters were a hundred tiny glass hearts. The simulacrum continued, lifting perfectly groomed eyebrows coquettishly. "A love potion? Something for virility? Or perhaps a tonic of forgetfulness."

Wiping his sweating hands down the legs of his trousers, for he was much too nervous to be particular about his behavior, Ever said, "No, I must speak with Titan."

"Oh," she said, raising perfect hands to her silk-covered bosom, "a great request indeed. I'm afraid Titan does not take sudden visitors lightly or well."

"Nevertheless, I must."

"Perhaps if you leave your name, and return in a week, he will see you."

Drawing a breath from deep inside himself, Ever blew a string of air that curled around the simulacrum's neck, tickling with the pressure of ten invisible fingers. He followed it immediately with a snap of his right hand, and ten tiny yellow flames flickered in a spiral over his palm.

As if he had pulled off a mask and revealed himself to be a salamander or sylph or unnatural monster, the simulacrum's entire demeanor shifted. No longer coy and sweet and flirting, the lines of her body fell into seriousness, and she inclined her head as a great queen might have, in the days there had been queens in the City of Light. "I shall take you to Titan at once," she said, and turned with enough swiftness to cause the tattered bottom of her gown to billow out like a blossom.

• • •

Titan, despite the perception of his countrymen, was only a man, and had once had a man's name. He hardly thought about what it used to be, as he had been Titan for nearly a hundred years. And although Titans tended to be longer lived than those with skills in only one kind of magic, they were not immortal. In fact, Titan's immortality was merely a ruse perpetrated by the line of men—and very occasional women— who were born naturally inclined to all forms of known magic.

It suited them to have the populace at large afraid, and so they lived under the pretense of all having been the same powerful wizard.

But this particular Titan was getting on in years, and had yet, despite two decades of hunting, to find a suitable heir. Which is what caused him to receive the boy Everest Aleksander the Younger more cordially than he was typically inclined.

Ever was greeted in the wizard's show room, the most impressive level of the tower, where Titan kept all of his worldly and otherworldly acquisitions. Fountains of fire and water; metal birds flitting back and forth across the cavernous ceiling; a pair of automatons sharing a game of chess; a tree shaped like a woman, made of glass and light; a life-sized clockwork horse with a silver mane and chips of green glass for eyes. Some of these things one Titan or another had obtained, some he had created with his vast power and curious nature. Many were the result of bargains he'd struck with the wealthy or desperate from the City of Light. They came to him for aid, and sometimes he helped; other times he tricked them out of self or life. Because he was cruel or lonely or merely bored.

A perceptive person would notice that the walls and domed roof should not have been able to fit in Titan's Tower, but Ever was too engrossed in the person of Titan standing before him to detect the difference.

For Titan was not a large or tall man, but in the graying hair pulled back from his temples, in the creases about his eyes, and the way his lips dragged down at the corners, Ever saw years of weariness and a complete lack of malice. It surprised him, and so he was softer and more polite than else he might have been.

308

"Show me what you came to show me," Titan said in place of greeting.

And instead of speaking, Ever obeyed.

"I don't know, sir. Can you help me learn?"

Titan walked closer to the boy, taking deliberately slow steps. He loomed close, and although sweat broke out along Ever's hairline, he did not quail, nor back down. It satisfied Titan, and the wizard smiled. Thin tendrils of smoke coiled through his teeth, and Ever felt his heart stutter. But Titan said, in a coaxing, gentle voice, "Most certainly."

• • •

Alys waited all night long for her intended to return home, and it was only as the sun threw pale orange scarves of light over the rippling water of the Acrimony that she noticed Ever's red and black form hop off one of the river taxis and down onto the stone landing of the Tower island. He turned around to pay the poler before dodging though the shadows in a swinging, jagged line toward the Fire Tower.

Wrapping her dressing gown more tightly about her waist, Alys tiptoed past her snoring nurse and skirted the door beyond which her Earth Hand guards slept in rotation. Out in the hallway, Alys dashed for the outer staircase, praying to her ancestors that she'd guessed correctly which Ever would use. She slipped into the well and pressed her back against the cold wooden panel wall. Closing her eyes, she listened for footsteps. She let her hands rest flat against the wood, and listened to the lines of grain singing so quietly they were only vibrations under the pads of her fingers.

Ever came quickly, skipping two stairs with every step. When he noticed Alys standing against the curving wall, he checked himself so abruptly he nearly fell backwards. She reached out and grasped his lapel, and they managed to find a balance. Alys's face tilted upwards, and Ever found himself leaning into her.

"You smell of the river," she whispered, reveling in the wild scent of industry and thick water. She meant it as a mere statement of fact, but Ever jerked back, chagrin pulling at his features. "Sorry," he whispered back.

Putting her hands on the sides of his face, Alys pulled him gently down. She skimmed her lips across his cheek and said into his ear, "I saw you fly."

All of Ever's body tightened, and he sank down to kneel on the step below her. "Do not tell anyone, Alys."

She let her knees bend, curling down beside him. Her hands slipped under his red and black jacket, resting over his heart. "I will keep your secrets, Ever, if you promise me one thing."

He let his own hands find her hips, and his fingers curled into the folds of her dressing gown.

Gasping for breath, Alys said, "Tell me everything."

• • •

As courtships go, the one shared by Alys and Ever was rather mundane. They attended well-chaperoned parties together, went for walks in the Oriental Market, had a picnic in the grass near the Ginger Step Fountains, and Ever touched her hand once when the mechanical awning outside Rucker's coffee bar unfurled just in time to block out the afternoon sun that streamed fresh between the Ostrelands Bank building and a solicitor's office.

But every third night, Ever flew across the Acrimony River to visit Titan, and when he returned home just before dawn, he would float up along the smooth outer wall of the Fire

Tower and settle onto the balcony attached to Alys's room. There she waited with leftover tea and as much cake or bread as she could manage to get hold of without arousing suspicion, for, after a long night of performing for Titan, Ever tended to be quite famished.

Once he had eaten and gulped several cups of tepid tea, Ever would regale Alys with every detail he could recall about Titan, about the magic, the simulacrum—whose name, he'd learned, was Melea—and all the wonders inside Titan's Tower.

He told her of the way the woman-tree shook her glass leaves when he approached, and of the repellent, piercing noise made by the clockwork horse as it feasted upon scraps of copper and chrome.

He told her that although the City of Light assumed Titan to be ancient and so set in his wizarding ways that he was distrustful of the new electricity, the true reason Titan held tightly to the gas lamps in the Greenlight City was because he refused to consider allowing workers from the City of Light to cross into his streets and lay the necessary line. The gas lamps Titan could control, the electric lines, never.

He told her of Titan's quiet smile as the wizard led him to a shallow pool of clear water on the third visit. Of how Titan asked Ever to dip his finger in and feel the flow of liquid, instructed him to imagine the water running in threads similar to the flow of air. That, if only Ever might grasp the tendrils of water, he would be another step closer to mastering all the elements.

Ever, though, had not found that place inside his lower organs that had instinctually rescued him the night he fell off the Pearshire Cliffs. Titan, looming closer, had ordered Ever to close his eyes.

The next moment, Ever found his entire head—though he remained standing in the center of the marble floor—enveloped in water. He'd tasted it on his tongue and thrown his arms out in panic. Staring through a bubble of water, he saw Titan backing away. Ever held his breath, ran after the wizard, but quickly became disoriented. He could not breathe—and as he related this part of the tale, Alys grasped his hand and held it so tightly, as if she, too, could not breathe. Ever had sunk to his knees on Titan's floor, reaching through the water with his hands as if he might strip it away drop by drop. His eyesight turned gray and he heard a constant *tick-tick-tick* in his ears.

Then finally—*finally*—he opened his mouth and drank in the water. He thought of Alys, of never kissing her again, and of his parents who had not known his secret. He closed his eyes, thinking perhaps it would have been better if he'd fallen to his death two weeks ago instead of living through this hope and promise and new love, only to lose it all.

And then Ever realized he was not dead.

He breathed the water. It filled him as heavily as too-thick cigar smoke and pinched his lungs uncomfortably, but he did live.

The water bubble shattered, splashing to the marble floor. And Ever, on his hands and knees, lifted his head to stare at Titan. The wizard said, "Thus you prove your water-working."

Here, Alys shifted her body on to Ever's lap and kissed him and kissed him, as if she might find drops of water still in his mouth, as if she might breathe the water with him. Ever returned her enthusiasm, knowing all those long moments of terror and drowning had been worth it—not for the magic, but for the reward of Alys's passion.

• • •

Titan was distressed.

Although he had determined that the young wizard Ever was proficient with fire, air, water, animation, and even the sensing of ghosts, no matter what torture or impractical invention of stone or dirt was thrown at him, the boy had no gift with earth.

After nearly five weeks of effort, Titan concluded that despite this lack of Niobe's touch, and even in the face of Ever's rather unfortunately public position as the heir to the Fire Seat, he was, in fact, the only possible successor to Titan's own name.

And so, one night at the end of several hours of lessons on the weaving of water into ice, the wizard drew Ever to the table, and as Melea served them roasted hen and candied berries, Titan proposed a full apprenticeship.

Ever stopped eating, with his tiny fruit fork hovering between his mouth and the dish of cream. "You wish for me to what?"

Hands folded elegantly and resting on the edge of the heartwood table, Titan repeated himself. "For you to leave your life in the City of Light and join me here. I will make you into a Titan, boy, and raise you up to heights of magic of which you can barely dream."

"But, sir, I'm to be married in less than a week."

Titan did not move, except to lift one silvering eyebrow.

"I can't leave my life," Ever said.

"Because of marriage? Because of your family? I assure you, boy, being a Titan will serve this land and city far more precisely and well than political capital or a convenient marriage ever could."

Ever set the fruit fork into the dish. "I want to marry her."

"At the expense of all this?" Titan spread his hands. The

clockwork horse stomped one silver-shod hoof. The mechanical birds swooping about fluttered their wings to catch light in a hundred shades of gold and copper.

Ever pushed away from the table. "Sir, I don't know what to say."

Standing, Titan gathered his power to him, drawing air and fire, earth and water into a swirling sphere that danced and spun around him. "Is this not," he said, in a voice soft and deadly, "more beautiful than any pair of simpering eyes or any smooth flesh?"

Caught in the sudden ferocity of magic, Ever stared at the colors, at the lights and sounds and shifting, tingling energy. It reflected in his muddy eyes, flashing demonic.

Titan pressed. "The elements will be your lover, holding your heart and soul and body more kindly than any woman. You will marry the universe if you study with me." The wizard could hear Ever's heart thrashing about, pumping hard and fast. Even when the boy slashed an arm through the air as if to banish Titan's magic, even when he turned and fled, Titan smiled.

The boy would return. He would look into the face of his intended and find her entirely lacking.

• • •

That dawn, as he climbed over the rail onto Alys's balcony, Ever's chest felt as though it had been bound in straps of iron. Shallow breaths were the best he could manage.

Alys, too, was having difficulty breathing, because Ever had never been so late before. The sun already touched her face, gilding her eyelashes and turning the raw green silk of her dressing gown into emeralds and light. It dazzled Ever the moment he saw her, and knowledge settled in his heart and freed his lungs from the iron grip.

314

She was more beautiful than any magic.

She rushed to him and he caught her hands, kissing her fingers again and again. "I love you, Alys," he said, in a quiet, resolute fashion, quite unlike the passionate and demonstrative declarations of love Alys had always imagined took place during secret rendezvous such as this. Yet she found she did not mind. His certainty was as calming as a healing ointment over red burns, and as it seeped into her bones, Alys shared the knowledge which Ever had so recently discovered: she would be with him for all time.

"I love you," she returned and kissed him more gently than she had before.

"But Alys," he said, holding her close, putting his cheek to her temple and closing his eyes against the dawn, "Titan wants me to abandon all this, to go live with him, to be his apprentice. It is the only way to know the magic."

"You will not abandon me," she murmured, a smile teasing at her lips.

"No, I won't. I can't." In Ever's voice were a hundred tiny pinpricks of longing, and Alys was not immune. She had seen him make fire dance, felt the swirls of his air-fingers tickling down her neck and up her ankles, listened to the fall of rain as he pulled water out of the sky to sprinkle over her face. She had borne witness to his first mechanical animation, a delicate copper rose he fashioned from flakes sawn off a clock in his bedroom, which he gave power with a kiss so that whenever she touched the third leaf from the bottom, the blossom opened full as if her face were the sun. And once, five nights ago, she had stood beside him the moment his body stilled with death and a passing ghost flitted through his eyes quicker than a thought. She could not ask him to give all of that up, any more than she was willing to forsake their marriage.

For Ever was the very opposite of boring.

"Take me with you," Alys Greentree of the Chenworth Niobes said. "We'll go together."

• • •

And so it was that Everest and Alys climbed onto the rail of her balcony off the Promethean Tower, held hands, and stepped into the sky.

• • •

"You have lovely eyes," was the only greeting which Melea the Simulacrum offered to Alys, leaning close to the Niobe girl and peering with her violet berry-eyes.

Alys curtsied, drawing her dressing gown about her with a regal temper, as though she was dressed in all the layers of finery a lady could afford. "And yours are more unique than any I've seen," she returned.

Ever drew his intended onward, up through the winding staircase built like a boring beetle's tunnel into the walls of the tower. They emerged into Titan's showroom, and though she had heard again and again of the wonders present, Alys sighed, brushing her hands over her mouth as if to collect the magic of the space and hold it close.

With his arm about her waist, Ever introduced her to the wizard, who sat in an ornately carved chair under the spreading branches of the glass tree. "Here is my wife-to-be, Titan. If I am to stay with you, she shall as well, for we would be one."

As Alys curtsied again, Ever gave up her whole name. Titan, who had been at war with himself over whether to accept this rather unprecedented turn of events, focused his attention solely upon the girl the moment it came to light that she was of the Niobes.

"You brought your own earth," Titan said, standing and weaving his fingers together before him. "I am well pleased."

Ever laughed. "Yes, I suppose that I did. Together, we are a complete Titan, are we not?" As the wizard nodded, Ever slid his happy gaze to Alys's face. She, too, was surprised and pleased to think that her magic—her very being—so perfectly completed Ever's own.

"Very well." Titan paced toward them, opening his arms in a fatherly fashion. "Face each other closely, for there are vows I require of you."

Bodies touching from collar to toe, Ever and Alys obeyed. Their hands clasped, their lips hovered ready, as if they knew a kiss would seal this darker, more intimate marriage.

Neither noticed Titan's fingers flickering swiftly as he wove a net of air. He stepped close, and before the two could protest, flung the knotted strands of wind around them. Ever yelled and Alys struggled, but the magic was too strong as it tightened and pulled them against each other. "What are you doing?" Ever demanded.

"Marrying you," the wizard answered, and the words became a laugh that filled the space from marble floor to domed ceiling. The clockwork horse stomped and tossed its mane, the glass tree shook and moaned, the metallic birds dove and darted in spirals, clinking their wings together in a tinny cacophony. And Titan continued to laugh.

• • •

Alys felt it begin.

The magic pulled at her skin and cracked her bones. Her head lolled and despite Ever's cries and attempts to catch her, Alys's knees weakened and her fingers fell slack. But the web of air did not allow her to fall. It pressed her against him, and three tears squeezed their way out through her eyelashes. They did not drop onto her cheeks, however, but were drawn sideways inexorably toward Ever.

The tears splashed onto *his* face, and Alys's heart shuddered. Her skin became pink as blood rose to the surface, and all she could do was gasp his name before the pain of her disintegrating body claimed her.

Ever thrashed and reached with the new powers he had, but they were powers Titan had taught him, and they were no use against the old wizard.

There was not a thing Everest Aleksander the Younger could do as his body absorbed the tiny particles of his never-to-be wife.

• • •

Ever felt it end.

He stood alone as Alys's green silk dressing gown pooled at his feet, empty and flat.

A cool fire burned in his chest, flaring as his fire always had, but soothing his tight muscles and caressing the twisted pain gathered in his stomach. It filled him, and it even embraced him. It strengthened his knees and gave power into the bones of his hands.

Her.

Earth.

Niobe.

Ever lifted his head, and Titan's laughter cut off as the wizard saw three marks under the boy's right eye—green stains as if some artist had dropped ink onto the skin.

"You have given me her power," Ever said, in a quiet, resolute fashion.

Titan nodded. "You are a Titan now."

But Ever disagreed. "No, sir, you taught me that the title

passes from one to the next. Never have there been two." The boy raised his hand, palm up, and from his skin a small tendril of a living tree sprouted. He did not notice the pierce of pain as it drew energy from his own blood.

"Even so," Titan said, nodding again and pleased at the boy's final graduation into all forms of magic. He intended to say more, but something caught in his throat. Something bulbous and thick, crawling up over his tongue.

Everest Aleksander the Younger smiled as a vine burst out of Titan's screaming mouth.

• • •

For five generations of wizards, Melea the Simulacrum had held the tower for her masters. As companion, as slave, as lover, as mother, and even as daughter. All these things she had been at one time or another, for Titan, ever since the day she'd been rescued by the first and given the freedom of her own will. She had used that will to remain at Titan's side, no matter whose side it was.

It was not without sorrow that she observed her current wizard being consumed by vines and flowers. But Melea had her own history with love, with needing and power and death, and she understood what it was to have the person you adored, whose heart you shared, destroyed by your own magic.

As Titan fell, curling on the marble-inlaid floor in a swarm of yellow and pink flowers, with thick and thin vines coiling like snakes in and out of his papery skin, Melea entered the showroom. She waited as the boy Ever sank down to his knees and closed his eyes. She waited as he shook, as he hugged himself and whispered the girl's name. As he pushed his fingers into this legs so hard they flashed white and ghostly.

A mechanical bird landed on the tangle of vines, poking at a pink flower with its silver beak. The clockwork horse pranced closer to the center of the room. Melea waited still.

Finally, the boy put his hands to the floor and pushed up. He stood, wobbling, and drew in a breath long and hard enough to suck the wind from all the edges of the room. It curled through Melea's ash-bark hair and fluttered the tattered hem of her dress.

He saw her, and his eyes widened only slightly. In them, Melea saw all the colors of magic.

"Welcome home, Titan," she said.

• • •

As the sun set that night, Ever gathered his strength and in one tremendous burst, leapt to the Seventh Tower across the Acrimony.

He had been sitting at the crown of Titan's Tower through the long, bright day, and as the last rays of sun bled into the world, they caught the stars hanging from the clockwork universe that surrounded the central tower.

And a strange new thought slipped through his dull, tired mind: *I want one of those stars.*

Never before had he given much thought to them. They were bright and hung prettily to catch the light, but they were only glass. Only a simulation of the brilliant fires of heaven.

Yet now, the longing pinched at his breath and before he knew it, he'd flown over the river and beyond his family's home, to land upon one of the arching steel beams propping up a giant yellow planet with rings of blue and purple glass.

Below his feet dangled one of the skull-sized stars. The points gleamed, and Ever crouched. He touched his finger to one. It was sharp, but refreshingly so. The quick pain shot through his arm and tingled in all his bones. Alys would have loved this, he thought, and with a weaving of air and earth, he plucked the star from its binding of wire.

In his arms, it continued to catch the dying sun.

The Emperor's Man

BY TIFFANY TRENT

FOR A LONG time, I could not remember how I came to be in the Imperial House Guard. There was a vague sense of shame, a sense that I was possessed of a dark past. I felt that if anyone knew what I'd been, I would be ejected from my position, and it was all the more troubling because I myself could not remember. The fear that someone would discover my past to be every bit as horrible and incriminating as I imagined was great indeed.

The only thing that banished these fears was the Imperial Tonic I took daily along with the rest of my regiment. The Emperor, who was a great inventor, had developed it to protect us from magical incursion. And while we soldiers jested with one another about sylph sickness and pixie infestations, we all knew that as long as we took the Imperial Tonic daily and adhered to the Scriptures of Science we were safe.

It was not so in the Forest that reached its knotted fingers toward our walls. In its depths hid all manner of Unnatural beings, and the depravity and danger they posed to us mortals was a constant threat to New London's safety. It had been this way since the Arrival, when Saint Tesla's Grand Experiment accidentally transported so many of us from Old London.

322

Though we could never return to the place from which we came, His Most Scientific Majesty reminded us that we were the vanguard of a glorious new Age of Enlightenment for this benighted land, that we alone had been given a grand opportunity to force magic and all its irrational power into the service of progress.

And if I woke in the night from vivid dreams of the Forest beyond New London's walls, if I dreamed of a life wild and howling under the tangled branches, I fervently whispered the Boolean Doctrine or the Litany of Evolution as revealed by Saint Darwin until I became calm. I was the Emperor's man, after all.

What then did I have to fear?

Athena would teach me soon enough.

I knew of the Princess Royal, of course. I saw her often at a distance, sitting in a window seat, her nose deep in a book while the other nobles played bridge or gossiped. I saw her at various functions speaking at length with Scholars of the newly founded University of New London. Her father's courtiers looked on with barely concealed sneers. While they fluttered about like perfumed and bejeweled peacocks, she stood apart, a drab peahen proud of her drabness. I felt a grudging kinship with her at those times. She was the only person I had ever seen besides myself who could be surrounded by people and yet still be so terribly alone.

When I was assigned to her during the Imperial Manticore Hunt then, I wasn't overjoyed, but neither was I indignant as many of my regiment would have been. We waited in the Tower courtyard for the Huntsman and his hounds to arrive. I was mesmerized by the leashed werehounds as they came—their knowing, malevolent eyes, the white brushes of their tails, the way they crouched when their master passed them. Something about them made me shudder and turn away.

And then I was looking straight into the Princess Royal's eyes. She regarded me steadily, gravely, her gray gaze more piercing than any pike or bayonet in the Imperial arsenal. She rode astride, much to everyone's horror, and was dressed in a plain but perfectly serviceable habit, devoid of lace or jewels or the plumed tricorns those around her favored. Her dark gold hair was pulled back severely and bound up in a white snood. Despite her unfashionableness, she looked every inch the Empress she was destined to be. And then I realized why.

She knew who and what she was. She had no need to compete or dissemble. And I envied it of her sorely.

"This is Corporal Garrett Reed, Your Highness," my Captain said, gesturing me forward. "He will serve as your escort on the Hunt."

"Corporal." She nodded.

"Your Highness," I said. I lowered my eyes so as not to have to meet her gaze. There was something unnerving in the way she looked at me, as if she knew things about me that even I didn't know. As if she knew my worst fear. My stomach tied itself in intricate knots.

The Captain left us then to introduce the other nobles to their escorts.

"I expect you to stay as far from me as your duty will in good conscience permit," she said. Her gloved hands tightened on the reins. "I have no need of escorts, and no desire for them, either. I intend to continue my studies of the denizens of this Forest. You may find it dreary in comparison to the excitement of the Hunt you will surely miss."

"I am at your service, Highness," I murmured.

"Hmph." She turned her mount away from me then and rode out behind the others.

I followed at what I hoped was a respectful distance, far enough to honor her request, close enough should danger arise. I would be lying if I said her disregard didn't sting, but it was no more than I expected.

We passed down through the winding streets of New London, and the greenish cloud drifting from the newly built Refinery dulled the glitter of our cavalcade. The Emperor's Refiners had recently developed a new energy source called myth that was mined far to the north and brought here for refining. Using myth to heat homes and keep everlanterns lit throughout the City would save many from the madness and enchantment suffered so often by those who gathered wood in the magic-laden Forest. The Refinery had also spawned a multitude of new inventions, among them the myth-powered, iron-clad wyvern the Emperor rode. People lined the streets, and the women threw hothouse roses or embroidered kerchiefs, which were soon shredded beneath the wyvern's iron claws.

I ignored those thrown to me.

In the Fey Market, gray sylphs flitted back and forth in their cages, careful of touching the nevered bars that kept their destructive magic from infecting their human captors. I swallowed the sudden, strange feeling that rose in my throat when one sylph shivered mournfully into dust, and I whispered a prayer to Saint Newton instead. I saw something in Athena's face sag; I would have sworn a tear glittered at the corner of her eye. She dashed at her eyes with a gloved hand, and then her face became stone.

Apothecary shop assistants distributed broadsheets advertising sirensong syrup to aid with coughs or nulling powders to extricate parasitic pixies. Over the River Vaunting, the Night Emporium spanned the entire bridge, its brothels, gin palaces, and gambling establishments crouching between haberdasheries, millineries, and antiquities shops. I glanced at Athena through it all, trying to gauge her reaction to the silk bolts spun from shadowspider webs, the fascinators and hair combs bedecked with the plumes of feathered serpents. But after that one moment, her expression never wavered.

My comrade-in-arms, Bastian, rode in close, nodding his head in her direction.

"Minding the mad witch, are we?" he asked. His round face was open and empty as the moon.

"You ought to show a little more respect," I said. I sat taller, using my height as yet another way of embarrassing him into silence.

"It's only what everyone thinks, Garrett," he said. "Besides, she can't hear us anyway."

He gestured toward the Princess. We had passed through the City gates, and the Forest raised its thick, twisted tangle against us. Princess Athena had sent her horse ambling under its eaves off the main track and away from the rest of the party.

"Saint Darwin and all his apes," I muttered under my breath. The Forest was filled with evil, irrational, mind-corrupting magic. Anything could happen to her, and I would be held responsible. And yet, I felt a twinge of uncertainty. Should I do as she bid and leave her to her studies? The Emperor expected us to stay on the track, to let the Huntsman do his work.

But if something happened to the Princess Royal on my watch . . .

Bastian laughed.

I spurred my horse forward as Athena disappeared through the trees, trying to ignore the crash of the iron wyvern's claws or the feeling that I was somehow betraying my orders by following the Princess.

"Your Highness!" I called after her. The Forest swallowed my voice. Yet it opened before me, leading me down its overgrown avenues. I glimpsed her ahead—here, the feathered fetlock of her mare, there the white curve of her snood against a dark-clad shoulder. She passed through light and shade like a dream, a ghost of herself. And where she passed, the Unnaturals of the Forest followed.

Filled with light, the sylphs came, dancing through the summer leaves, dayborn fireflies. Their wings whispered and chimed like little silver bells, so very different from their caged cousins in the market. When I looked up, white faces peered at me out of the mottled trunks of sycamores and dark faces frowned from the hemlocks and pines. I whispered Saint Darwin's Litany of Evolution as a dryad peeled herself away from the bark of her tree and followed the princess.

They were all around me—sylphs and sprites, gnomes and hobs, and many others for which I had no name. I tried to remember that the Imperial Tonic protected me, that I wouldn't be enchanted by anything, but I couldn't help my uneasiness. Just when I realized I'd become more engrossed in looking at the sylphs than seeking my charge, I saw the Princess's mare wandering riderless, grazing along a tiny stream. I spurred my gelding toward the clearing ahead, my heart crowding my throat.

I found the Princess seated on a mossy stump surrounded by toadstools.

And Unnaturals of every kind and description.

"Princess!" I shouted.

Some of the Unnaturals slunk away, but others hissed and bristled, their colors changing from soft pastels to angry vibrancy.

She looked up at me with eyes like ice. "Stop," she said.

"But, Your Highness, you're in great danger! You must . . ."

She transferred the quill and book she held to one hand. She held up the other for silence.

"On the contrary, Corporal," she said at last. "It is you who are in grave danger. Now go back the way you came and let us be."

I stared at her for a moment, trying to discern if the worst had already happened, if she had already been bespelled, and wondering how it could be. Did she not also drink the tonic her father had developed to protect us? Then my gaze wandered, drawn by the rustle of a leaf, and I saw what she meant. Little, taunting faces thrust out of the vines and branches. Little hands held darts that glimmered with poison in the morning light. If I so much as moved, I had no doubt the pixie army would turn me into a human pin-cushion in short order. I also had no doubt their darts were deadly.

I straightened my spine. "You know I cannot do that, Your Highness. Your father, the Emperor . . ."

She laughed then. She looked me full in the face and laughed. The sound of it caused the angry colors of the sylphs to fade, and soon all the Unnaturals were giggling with her, too. She laughed so hard that the book fell to the ground next to her foot, and tears streamed down her face. I thought for a moment she would fall off the stump.

"The Emperor," she finally said when she could catch her breath. "You know, every time someone addresses him that way, it's all I can do not to burst into laughter. And right now, I can't be bothered to care!"

I could do nothing but stare. Perhaps Bastian was right, after all. Perhaps she was a mad witch.

"Oh, I am most certainly a witch," she said, as if I'd spoken aloud. "But I'm not mad."

I gaped at her.

She pulled the book she'd dropped back up into her lap. "Truthfully, I think I'm the only sane person left in this world. Aside from you all, of course," she said to the Unnaturals at her feet. The Scriptures of Science dictated that I should be repulsed by the Unnaturals and the threat to rationality they represented, but here I was—fascinated by the color chasing over their faces and through their wings. And their expressions! So rich, so varied, so full of life in ways I'd never imagined in that dull Tower . . .

I shook my head. I shouldn't be thinking these thoughts. The Unnatural magic was corroding my logic. How was that possible?

I focused on the Princess. "I don't know what you mean," I said coldly.

"Let me ask you this, Corporal. What do you remember before coming to the Tower?"

I blanched and looked down at my gloves. How had she been able to pinpoint the one worry that gnawed most constantly at my heart? I wished that I had just obeyed her and gone back the way I'd come. I didn't want to know where this was leading.

"That's about what I thought."

I glanced at her. "Your Highness, I hardly think my past . . ."

But she cut me short with something she held up in her hand. It glimmered darkly—a tiny, all-too-familiar vial held between her thumb and forefinger.

The Unnaturals around her drew back, muttering.

"What is this, Corporal Reed?" she asked.

"Imperial Tonic, Your Highness. But I fail to see . . ."

She glared me into silence. "And you take this every day, yes?"

"Yes, Your Highness."

329

She sighed. "Oh, stop that nonsense. My name is Athena."

I'm sure my eyes went round as dinner plates at that. What royal in her right mind would permit—nay, demand—a lowly guard like me to use her familiar name? But I swallowed and nodded.

"I stopped taking this eight years ago," she said. "And when I did, I realized a few things. Or remembered them, I should say. First, I remembered where we came from—the real London. I remembered that my father was nothing more than an astonishingly well-read butcher from Cheapside who liked to invent things when he wasn't killing them. He had always fancied himself a man of science, and he seized power in the chaos that ensued after the Arrival. I don't know entirely how he did it—I have my theories—but the main point is that my father's power comes at a great price—the lives of the Elementals whose world we've stolen."

Sylphs, pixies, and dryads all nodded around her.

My lower jaw very nearly hit my pommel.

"You *are* mad," I gasped.

"Oh, yes?" she asked. She got up from her stump, and stalked toward me, stepping over the toadstool ring as if it had no power at all. "Who are you really, Corporal Reed? Why are you so afraid of your past and yet you can remember none of it? And if these beings, these . . . Unnaturals, as you so rudely call them, are so evil, why are we both still alive?"

She stood just at my knee, and I looked into her furious face. Her eyes flashed like icy lightning, and a hectic glow spread across her cheekbones. Little sylphs flitted to and fro around her head in a chiming halo. She was, in that moment, the most beautiful woman I'd ever seen. I forgot everything but that, lost in amazement at how much could change in the span of a few hours. She was absolutely bewitching, but not at all in the way I'd been taught to expect.

"Corporal Reed?" I finally heard her say. "Are you even listening to me?"

I could see quite clearly that she knew what I'd been thinking. I coughed, feeling suddenly constricted by my uniform. "*Ahem.* Yes. You were saying, Your Highness?"

"Stop taking the tonic," she said. "It's a potion meant to make you biddable and forgetful. When you do, you'll see who is truly mad, I promise you."

I opened my mouth in what I was sure would be a weak retort, but the only sound that came was that of a distant braying.

The horns of the Hunt.

The werehounds bayed, a ghostly howling that set my spine shivering. They had cornered their quarry.

Athena's face instantly changed. It was as though someone had slammed the shutter over her inner light. Panic was all I saw in her face as she called to her mare.

"The Manticore is in danger!" she said over her shoulder. "We must hurry!"

"But Your Highness . . . Athena," I said, "isn't that why we're here? To kill the Manticore?"

"I didn't truly think he'd be able to find her!" she said as she climbed into the saddle. "She's very powerful—she should have been able to hide. Something is very wrong!"

The lights in the trees dimmed all around me. The sylphs, colorful and laughing only a moment ago, dimmed to dusty browns and grays. Dryads slunk away like slices of shadow. There was a restless fear and sorrow that I inhaled with each breath.

"What will happen if she's killed?" I shouted at Athena's back, as she urged the mare forward. If the angry mutters and gestures were any indication, none of us would fare well.

"They will all ultimately die without her magic. Her power feeds theirs, from what I understand. If they can, they will try to stop that from happening. That's why we must go!" she called over her shoulder, slowing her mare enough that I could hear.

Then she spurred her mount onward, and I was racing my own horse just to keep up. As she galloped, ducking branches, her snood came unbound and fluttered to the ground like a wounded dove. Her hair uncoiled in a long curl behind her. I followed it like a golden semaphore through the trees, avoiding the Unnaturals—Elementals, she'd called them— that flowed alongside through the undergrowth and between the trees above.

The Emperor's wyvern had cornered the Manticore. The monster shrank from the Emperor's mechanical mount, weeping tears of blood in her fear. The Huntsman affixed a strange gauntlet to his hand, a weapon so powerful that its numbing chill froze everyone around it. The Elementals fell back from that miasma of icy horror, but it slowed many of the smaller ones, such that they were unfortunate enough to be snatched up by observant courtiers and stuffed hurriedly into their saddle panniers. A new pet, a little extra money at market didn't hurt.

I caught myself feeling sorry for them and gritted my teeth. I shouldn't be sorry for them at all. I vowed silently to drink another vial of tonic as soon as we returned to the Tower.

If we returned.

The Manticore begged for mercy in her silver voice, even as the Huntsman advanced on her.

The Emperor ignored her and gestured that the Huntsman should finish the job. "Bring me its heart, if you can," he said.

The Huntsman, eerily hooded like an executioner, nodded.

I watched the Emperor on his wyvern and couldn't help but wonder. Much about him suggested what his daughter had said. He had a craggy nose that looked as though it had been broken, and his eyes were narrow and hard. He was not a big man; in fact, he seemed pinched somehow at the edges, as though something ate at him from the inside out. Still, he had the charisma of a leader, the sharp command of someone destined to rule. Was he really only a butcher, as his daughter had said? Was everything I'd been taught a lie?

And then Athena edged her mare forward, her unbound hair causing the ladies-in-waiting to chatter and giggle. Some looked sidelong at me in amazement, and it occurred to me that they assumed we had been engaged in some sort of dalliance. I sat as tall as possible, looking neither right nor left, and hoping my face was stone.

"Father!" Athena called, as the Huntsman readied his knife. "I beg you to spare this creature's life."

A hush so deep descended that a single falling leaf seemed to crash into the Forest floor. Even the Manticore dared not breathe as she waited on the Emperor's reply.

He looked at his daughter with the shrewd glance of a man who believes everyone schemes against him, even his own flesh and blood.

"And why would you have me do that, Princess?" he asked.

Disdain etched the faces of all his courtiers. I will never forget how we all sat there, like statues in the vortex of the horrid weapon in the Huntsman's hands while the trees wept leaves all around us. I will never forget the battle of wills, of calculation, that passed between the Emperor and his daughter as we all waited for her reply.

"A matter of scientific study, Father." She looked at the Manticore, and the flash of her eyes belied the cold facts of her words. "We know so little about the Greater Unnaturals; this is a perfect opportunity to understand them better. I'm sure the University would . . ."

"For what reason need we understand them?" the Emperor cut in.

"Surely," she said, ever so calmly, "His Most Scientific Majesty does not question the Doctrine of Logic to which we all ascribe?"

I couldn't help but smile. Well played, Princess, I thought.

She looked at me then, and her small smile hooked me straight in the heart. All she had to do was tug. If I had felt the first stirrings of admiration when she flashed her anger at me in the clearing, it was nothing compared to now when her gaze stripped me bare to the bone.

I cast my eyes down to my pommel, certain she had bespelled me in that moment.

Through the ringing in my ears, I barely heard the Emperor reply, "Take this Unnatural thing to the dungeons. It is very nearly my daughter's birthday; I shall acquiesce to her desires as a gift to her."

The Huntsman bowed his head and sheathed his knife. He unlooped a coil of silver chain that hung across his saddle.

Athena dismounted. "Let me," she said.

She went to the beast, who had ceased weeping. She whispered something I couldn't quite catch, and the Manticore bowed her head and allowed the Princess to slip the chain lightly over her neck. I thought I saw Athena's hands tremble, but when she turned and led the Manticore toward her mount, her face was as impassive as always.

There was murmuring. The Emperor seldom gave gifts, especially not in public, certainly not to his eldest daughter.

What was he thinking? Were the winds of favor shifting? I could see suitors who had given a lackluster performance rethink their strategies. Others mumbled that she had now gone beyond the barriers of good sense and enchanted her own father. All the while, I wrestled with the knowledge she'd given me, wondering what to do with it and why she'd trusted me. And whether I could believe her.

There were no easy answers, and I followed the procession as it wound back to the City with the Manticore at its heart, trying to ignore the trees that wept at her passing and followed us on the suddenly chill wind.

• • •

The Manticore was taken deep into the Emperor's dungeons. I refused to think about it or anything else I'd experienced in the Forest. I resumed my duties, as usual, ignoring the whispers of witchery, fending off the jibes of my regiment about my involvement with the mad witch. I drank and diced, did my drills like any soldier, and hoped for the promotion that never came. Every morning, despite the princess's admonition, I drank the Imperial Tonic. I was the Emperor's man, after all.

And if I fancied that I heard the Manticore's silver voice raised in dirges of mourning on the border between waking and sleep, if I dreamed of running through the Forest on four feet instead of two, what of it? What soldier didn't wake in the night, hearing the croaking of the Tower ravens on the sill, and wish he'd chosen another path every now and then?

Every fortnight, we rotated through a night watch. I was grateful when my turn came, hoping it would banish my increasingly frequent night terrors. If I wasn't meant to sleep, at least I could be doing something useful.

Again, it seemed that Fate, if the saints aren't to be believed, had a hand in my assignment. I was to patrol the Throne Room and Main Halls. I cursed myself for wishing that I'd been assigned to the Imperial suite. I still saw Athena's face as it had been in the Forest—open, alive, full of light—and I wanted that back. But did I really think I would see her this late at night? It wasn't as if I had access to her bedchamber. At most, I might glimpse a shadow of her behind her bed curtains or in her easy chair by the fire. I would certainly not see or speak to her. And even if I did, what then?

I tried to banish the flutter in my stomach at the mere thought of her name as I paced up and down the echoing marble halls. This was ridiculous, and I knew it.

Clocks lined the walls, squatted on little tables and loomed in cabinets everywhere. The Emperor was deeply curious about Time, so it was said, and he had made it part of his personal study to explore the Horological Arts. Why he needed so many clocks to do it was a mystery, but their numbered faces glared at me as I passed with my everlantern and pike. Their ticking measured out my worries in discrete units of consternation.

I had just returned for the sixth time that night to the notion that I should request a transfer to some outpost on the edge of the Copernican Wildlands, when something whispered across the stones at the edge of my light.

"Halt!" I said.

Click. Creak. Whoever it was refused to heed me.

The hallway was lined with doors, and the few everlanterns that circulated in the high ceiling made pools of light and shadow as they passed.

A whisper of white, the edge of a bare foot. A ghost? I ignored the tingling on the back of my neck, but raced forward and slid my pike between door and frame before the door could be shut and locked.

"I said, *Halt!*"

I thrust my lantern into the unlit room.

It would have all been much easier if I'd seen who I expected instead of who I'd hoped. I'd expected a petty thief—perhaps some member of the house staff pilfering candlesticks, that sort of thing. I'd hoped foolishly for Athena, even though I couldn't imagine why she'd be roaming the halls at this hour, even though I didn't know what I would say to her. Why should she even remember me?

Athena glared at me from the circle of light.

She was in her nightgown, a darker dressing gown wrapped loosely around her. Her feet were bare, and I couldn't help noticing the fine arches, the perfect fan of her toes against the marble.

"Are you going to stand there gawking at my feet or help me?" she asked.

I think I must have blinked before I found my voice. And even then, I couldn't think of a single thing to say beyond, "Eh?"

"Just . . . get in here," she said.

I stepped inside the room, trying to muster up what was left of my dignity. "Princess, you shouldn't be here. I'll escort you to your chamber now, and we'll pretend like none of this happened . . ."

"We will do no such thing," she said.

I opened my mouth, but that piercing stare shut it for me.

"I could make you go with me," she said, "but I don't think I've misjudged you that badly. Will you help me?"

I swallowed all my questions, except one. "What are we doing?"

"Why, freeing the Manticore, of course," she said. "You truly aren't that thick are you, Garrett?"

Then she did something completely odd.

She leaned forward and sniffed me.

I frowned. "Does something offend you, Highness?"

"You're still taking that blasted tonic, aren't you? I can smell its stench on your breath." She sighed.

I wanted to cover my mouth, but my hands were full. Flushed with shame, I nodded.

"Look around you," she said. "And tell me that I've played you false."

The Emperor's Cabinet of Curiosities was generally kept locked. I had never seen inside it, though there was much speculation about its contents. It was the sort of room you'd find tucked under a staircase or in the eaves of an attic. The sort of room I'd never been in, I suddenly realized. The floor yawned beneath my feet. It was as if I was standing here and running across the Forest floor—fleet, four-footed, furred—all at the same time.

"Garrett." She bit the end of my name so hard it brought me back into the lantern light.

I blinked.

Portraits, newspaper clippings, books, cases of strange insects . . . All were scattered willy-nilly. There was nothing especially out of the ordinary about any of it at first glance, but as I looked closer, the marble floor tilted under me again.

A portrait entitled *Butcher Vaunt*, of the Emperor in his bloody apron, holding up a freshly killed goose, with a little girl beside him who might have been Athena. A picture of Saint Darwin, looking terribly ordinary in a suit and bowler hat, rather than the green, vine-covered robes held up by apes in the stained glass of the Church chapel. Newspaper clippings with the wrong dates and mentioning places and people I'd never heard of. A globe with countries I'd never seen, and a battered map spread on the wall that was of an unfamiliar city also called London. A book under glass that only said "Holy Bible," rather than "Holy Scientific Bible" as all bibles did.

"What is all this?" I said.

"These are all things from the real London. Things my father doesn't want anyone else to see. Things he can't bear to get rid of, even though they incriminate him for the fraud he is."

My eyes wandered the chaos of the long, narrow room, trying to take it all in. One piece drew my gaze and wouldn't let go, a softly glowing thing that throbbed like a beating heart in its case.

I went to it, spreading my fingers on the glass. Its power seeped through to my fingertips, buzzing up my arms and into my skull. It looked very like a heart, but none that I had ever quite seen, comprised of metal and light and whirring parts that I had no names for.

"And that is how we got here," Athena said over my shoulder. "The Heart of All Matter."

"How?" I said. I couldn't take my eyes off of it, even to look at her face.

"Tesla used it to power a secret experiment to create wireless electricity," she said. "He never realized that the Heart is much more powerful than mere electricity. It ripped a hole in space and time. It brought us, along with buildings and artifacts from all of London's history, here. Our ancestors from the real London called this place Fairyland, Arcadia, Elysium, Shangri-La, Tir Na Nog . . . any number of names. They apparently weren't sure it existed. But it does. And now we're trapped here."

"But . . . surely . . ." I was so mesmerized by the Heart's pulsing light that I could barely think to form words.

"No," she said. "No one knows how to use it. My father, of course, has tried. That's why he founded the University, after all. He thinks his scientists will find us a way home."

I tore my gaze from the Heart. "And you don't?"

She shook her head. And then came that sardonic smile that made my insides flutter. "I surely hope not. Leave all this to become a lowly butcher's daughter again?"

With so few words did she remind me of her station. And of how far below her I truly was. "I suppose not. You will be Empress, after all," I said stiffly.

She swatted at me then, and I looked her in the eyes.

"I was joking, you ninny!" she said. "You know I don't care a fig for being Empress. But it's true I don't want to go back. This world is so fascinating, so thrilling, so very beautiful. I want to explore it. I want to find out everything about it. Don't you?"

Truthfully, I had never thought about it. I had done my duty every day, and the Forest beyond the City walls was something strange and awful I seldom contemplated, except in my nightmares. All I could think about now was that if there was anything beautiful or thrilling or fascinating about this world, she was standing right in front of me. And as much as I wanted to find out everything about her, I knew that it could never be so.

I also knew that she heard exactly what I was thinking. Her lips parted, soft and shining in the light of the pulsing Heart.

She reached, as if she would touch my cheek, as if she was trying to decide if I was real.

But then her face hardened and her hand fell back to her side. That icy resolve returned to her eyes, and she said, "Fetch your lantern and pike, and follow me."

She opened the case that held the Heart and gently lifted the thing into her hands. Instantly, its pulsing grew faster, its light stronger.

"What are you doing?" I asked, unable to take my eyes off its light, unable to take my mind off of the moment that had just happened between us. What had happened to alter it?

"You'll see."

She led me to the end of the room. A portrait hung there of a woman I didn't recognize but felt I should—a young queen sashed and crowned with white roses. The plaque beneath the portrait read "Victoria Regina."

Athena slipped her hand along the edge of the portrait and the wall slid away seamlessly, very nearly soundlessly.

Marble stairs curved down into darkness.

"Leave the lantern here," she said.

I was about to protest that we would surely need light, but as her foot touched the first stair, Athena's hand blossomed with the Heart's light. She smiled at me then, and that swift hook tugged me after her down the stair.

I wasn't surprised that the Emperor had his own secret access to the dungeons, but the fact that the passage saw frequent use definitely made me wonder. There were no cobwebs, no signs of disuse. Doors were well oiled; the marble treads were quite well worn. The possibilities of what he did here were unnerving in the extreme.

Athena had no caution about her whatsoever. She hurried ahead of me, pushing through doors and rooms as if an invisible string drew her deeper into the labyrinthine prison. Any good soldier worth his salt knows that you don't go charging headlong into an operation like the one she was undertaking. I tried to hang back, but she urged me onward with a raised brow and a gesture of her flame-ridden fingers.

At last she came to a door that required a bit more muscle to open; it was a sealed hatch with great gears and pressure valves. It reminded me of the entrance to a boiler. I approached it with foreboding.

"Help me," she said, setting the Heart down in an alcove nearby. Its light went out of her hands and danced in little currents through the still air as she tugged on the door.

"Where does this lead?" I said. "Shouldn't we consider what might be on the other side? Do you know if your father keeps guards stationed down here?"

"I thought you would know that," she said. "Clearly, my plan to use you for ill gain has failed."

I stared at her, and then realized she jested again. I had never quite expected her to have a sense of humor.

"I can feel the Manticore beyond this door," she said. "I hope we're not too late."

I dared not think about what the Elementals in the Forest might do if we were. Or what would happen after we helped the Manticore escape. Instead, I put my hands near hers on the wall affixed to the door and turned. Her arms curved under mine; her shoulders pushed against my chest. The top of her head was just at my chin, and her hair smelled of cloves and oranges, of holidays long forgotten. We fit together so perfectly, like pieces of a puzzle finally coming together, that I wanted to put my arms around her and stay.

She coughed delicately. "Corporal Reed, you'll recall that I can hear your thoughts."

I pulled hard on the wheel and stepped away. "Yes. Sorry." The heat in my face was from exertion, I told myself.

I saw an amused flash in her eyes as the door swung open. She retrieved the Heart.

The deep well of the chamber echoed with labored breathing. Something below, I knew, was in terrible pain.

I put a hand out to warn Athena, but she had already begun creeping down the curved stairs. A glow rose from the floor, and then the stairs turned enough that I could see.

The Manticore lay across a long slab of table. A great machine squatted over her, its hoses and needles like the searching tentacles of some oceanic horror. Though the beast was secured at various places by silver chains, it was the machine that truly kept her bound, its needles nosing into her flesh and drawing out her shining blood and replacing it with viscous ichor. The machine throbbed and hummed like the demonic twin of the Heart in Athena's hand. Steam escaped from its joints with each pulse.

Behind the machine stood the Emperor, working its levers and checking its dials, while the Manticore struggled to breathe.

Athena stood staring, a trembling hand raised to her mouth, the Heart's light abruptly doused. Then she raced down the remaining stairs, her bare feet slapping the stones.

"Athena!" I hissed. But she ran on, heedless of my warning.

"What are you doing to her?" she cried. "Stop this at once!"

The Manticore tried and failed to raise her head. *Child, you must not.* Pain tarnished her voice.

I saw only half of the smile that sliced the Emperor's face, until he stepped from around the machine to confront his daughter. He hadn't yet seen me, and I hoped he hadn't heard my warning. I slid slowly down the stairs, keeping as close to the wall as possible, praying my pike didn't rattle and give me away, but my hands shook almost uncontrollably. I couldn't bear to contemplate what I might have to do to protect Athena. Was I not the Emperor's man?

"Whatever do you mean?" the Emperor asked. "Was it not you who said we should use her for scientific experiments?"

His smile was the ugliest, most self-satisfied smirk I'd ever seen.

"I only meant . . . I didn't mean . . ." I could hear the tears in her voice.

"I know," the Emperor said. "You thought you would buy her enough time until you could figure out some way to help her escape. Look well upon what you've wrought, daughter. There will be no escape from this."

I could see the Manticore's head and chest. Where there should have been red velvet fur, muscles over ribcage, there was a gaping hole of darkness.

The Emperor had taken her heart.

Athena ignored him. "We're getting you out of here," Athena said to the Manticore.

Leave me, the beast said.

"And just how do you think you'll do that?" the Emperor sneered at Athena. "If you unhook her from my machine, she shall surely die. And we will have lost valuable understanding of the Unnaturals. You were correct, daughter. They are well worth our investigation—the properties I have discovered in her blood alone! They are worth so much more alive than dead. I shall bring all I can here into the dungeons. We shall create a world more rich than any we could possibly have imagined before, and when the time is right, we shall force the gate back to the old world open. London, Britain, the Earth itself will be ours."

I gaped. So, what Athena had said was true. I crept down onto the floor, every muscle shaking so hard I wondered how I could stay standing. Anger, bitterness, and grief chased one another in a vicious circle through my chest.

"Not without this," Athena said. She raised the Heart in her hands then so the Emperor could see it, and it burst into eerie flame.

"No," the emperor said. His voice had an edge keen as my pike. "Foolish girl, to think you can handle such power."

He moved toward her. A dagger coalesced in the shadows of his hand.

I scarcely dared breathe and certainly didn't think as I crept up behind him. Athena, wise witch, gave no sign that she knew I was there. I prayed the Emperor couldn't hear my thoughts as she could.

I dug the tip of my pike into his lower back. He wore no armor, no protection whatsoever. I could slice him in half as easily as look at him. "How do you dare, Sire," I said, "to threaten the one who might save us all? Or shall I call you Butcher Vaunt instead?"

He stiffened.

"Drop your weapon," I ordered.

He laughed. He half-turned to look at me. "You shall regret this deeply one day, Corporal," he spat. And then, he disappeared in a thread of stinking smoke.

I cursed. "Hurry," I said to Athena. "I'm quite certain he'll be back."

Athena set the Heart down, and her hands roamed over the wires and tubes snaking in and out of the Manticore. She looked over her shoulder at me as I came nearer.

"Help me," she hissed.

She started unhooking and pulling things, but the Manticore cried out in pain. I reached for Athena's hands. Her fingers were cold and shaking.

You cannot release me, the Manticore said. *I shall die for certain.*

"Why?" Athena whispered. She had always seemed so much older than her years, so sure of herself, but now she was little more than a child. I longed to comfort her, but there was no soothing away this hurt.

My heart is gone, the Manticore said. *This machine keeps me alive.*

It was then that the tears came. Athena's shoulders shook with them and she kneaded her fingers through the Manticore's belly fur, for all the world like a nursing kitten, save for her howling grief. I took her in my arms without a word, and she folded herself there against my heart.

Children, the Manticore sighed at last. *You should go while you still can. He will return. I am content with my fate.*

At that, Athena turned from my arms, wiping her face with the edge of her robe. "I'm not," she said. "I'm not letting him win. All those afternoons . . . all you taught me . . . I proposed this to save you, not torment you!"

She heard my unspoken question, for she looked at me and said, "I used to sneak out of the Tower and ride to the Forest to meet her. She taught me everything I know about magic, about how what I'd been brought up to believe wasn't true. She taught me so much. I can't just leave her to die."

"Forgive me," I said to them both, "but you may have to. Your father will return soon. Do you have magic enough to fend off his entire guard?" I glanced down at the Heart, glowing softly where she had placed it on the floor.

"Of course I don't," Athena said. "But there must be some way to undo this . . ." She paced up and down, glancing occasionally at the devilish machine. I tried to listen beyond the sounds of her pacing and the Manticore's labored breathing. Was that the turn of a key in a door? A shift in the movement of an everlantern?

I was about to urge her again to hurry when she stopped. She stood so still for a moment that I wondered if the Emperor had secreted a Basilisk in the chamber. Athena was like stone.

Then she grinned.

"What?" I said.

She had knelt down to touch the Heart of All Matter.

"What will you do with it?" I asked, though I was fairly certain I already knew.

"Put down that pike and help," she said.

I set my pike carefully on the stone floor, and put my hands on the Heart, alongside hers, to lift it up. It had grown strangely heavy, and seemed to grow heavier the closer we got to the Manticore. The rhythm of its pulsing grew faster, like a heart waking into action after a long sleep.

Child, the Manticore said to Athena. *You mustn't. Your father . . .*

"We both know my father will use this for evil someday," Athena said. "I'd rather he didn't have the chance. I'd rather you were able to live free."

But it isn't mine to possess . . .

The Manticore's protests were subsumed in a field of glittering light as together we placed the Heart in the beast's chest. A flash and a low concussion knocked us back from the table.

When I could see again, the Manticore stood, her spiked tail twitching. With one swipe of her red paw, she sent the Emperor's horrid machine flying across the room. The Heart in her chest clicked and purred as it knitted itself between muscle and bone.

Then the great beast's eyes met mine.

Come here, child, the Manticore said.

The inexorable pull of her voice sent shivers across my scalp.

I went.

Kneel.

She loomed above me. The great, smiling mouth with its triple row of teeth was just above my head. I wondered for a

347

moment if she would take me as her first free meal, and she must have heard that thought, for she laughed, a sound like deep silver bells ringing.

I am going to give you something, she said.

She bent her head and breathed on me.

Remember, she said.

The curtain over my mind shredded. It was as though someone pulled a shroud from over me, and I could at last breathe in the light. I remembered who I had been in the Forest. I remembered that I ran away to become a guard because I was ashamed. I remembered that I was a wolf.

"I am . . ." I couldn't quite form the words. The idea was so strange, so forbidden, that I hardly understood how to comprehend it, except that I knew in every bone and muscle of my body that it was true.

One of the Were, yes, the Manticore said. *Welcome, little brother.*

Then it was my turn to weep. For the pack I'd lost. For the wolf-brethren I'd forgotten. For all I'd never known.

"If you're done blubbering," Athena said, "I could use some help. This door is heavy!"

I gathered my pike up and turned to see her pulling frantically at the door to the chamber.

"Figured it out finally?" she asked, as I approached. She was in complete control again; the vulnerable child I'd held in my arms had vanished.

"You knew?" I asked. "You knew and you didn't tell me?"

She looked at me sidelong. "Would you have believed me? I hardly think one should tell one he's a werewolf on first meeting, do you?"

I couldn't help but laugh. "No. I suppose not."

I rested my pike against the wall as we scraped the great iron door open together. There was no one on the other side, but somehow I knew the Emperor would return. Every moment wasted was a moment we might lose for ever.

"Now let's get her out," Athena said.

I had no idea how we would sneak a Manticore out of the Tower and down through the City in the middle of the night with the entire Imperial Guard after us.

Use all your senses, the Manticore encouraged.

I hated the thought that we might have saved her life only to botch her escape.

• • •

I stood in the doorway and sensed with all of my being. It had been a long time since I'd done anything like that. I was amazed that I still knew how. Worms and other insects crept through the foundation of the Tower all around us. Guards murmured in a distant dicing game. I smelled mold, stone, the remnants of torture. And then a thread of river air, a ribbon of freedom twining underneath all the rest.

"This way," I said, nodding toward the ground-level door.

Athena stopped me. "I doubt I can hide all of us with magic. But we may be able to hide in plain sight."

"How so?"

"We'll just pretend that we're transferring her somewhere else. I'll be the handler and you be the guard. Hopefully, we'll get out before my father returns."

The Manticore nodded her approval. Athena slipped a length of silver chain over her neck, murmuring an apology.

I watched as Athena magically altered her dressing gown into a hooded robe that hid her face and most of her body. I shifted my pike into position, glad of its familiar weight in my hands.

Together the three of us entered the corridor. I prayed to every saint I could think of that the Emperor had not yet put the entire dungeon on alert. I also hoped that no one would look too closely at my house uniform.

As it happened, there was no one on our corridor. We wended our way past prisons packed with hopeless victims, past torture rooms that my rediscovered senses told me I didn't want to explore. We came at last out into a great hall of sorts, a cavernous room hollowed from the living rock. There were cages there, mostly empty, but the Manticore paced past them sadly nonetheless.

This place should not be, she said. *Great harm will come of it.*

"We must get you out of here," I said. I didn't want to think about anything beyond seeing the Manticore to freedom.

We were nearly under the eave of the cavern wall and into a corridor that would lead us to the river when the word I'd dreaded came.

"Halt!"

A regiment of dungeon guards hurried across the shadowed floor, their pikes gleaming as they came.

I could think of nothing else to do. The guards were obviously already aware of the devastation in the Emperor's laboratory.

"Run!" I shouted.

Athena and the Manticore bolted past me, the silver chains slipping from the monster's body, while I took up rear guard. I had no idea how long I could hold the soldiers while the Princess and the beast worked at the door that would give us our freedom.

And then I felt him. The Emperor. And with him was a power so terrible I nearly dropped the pike I held. But then I gripped it tighter. If my death could delay him long enough for Athena and the Manticore to get free, then so be it.

The soldiers fell back as the Emperor approached. On his

hand, the nulling gauntlet that his Huntsman had worn in the Forest gleamed darkly.

"I told you that you would regret your insolence, Corporal," he said.

"I regret nothing," I said through gritted teeth. "Except that I ever bent the knee to you."

"Is that so?" he asked.

He stepped forward, and I nearly swooned under the influence of his fell magic.

"Then, you shall die at my feet," he said. His smile was sharp as a knife.

I lifted my pike. He shattered it with a word.

My regulation dagger was in my boot. I waited until he came closer. One step. Another.

Then I heard the sound I longed for—the door behind me scraping open.

The light of the full moon poured in, turning the Emperor and his guard to skeletal shadows.

"Garrett!" Athena screamed. "Come, now!"

I half turned. The river gleamed under the moon; its voice was deep and loud and I understood every word of its song.

And in that moment, as the cold light touched my face, I was no longer human but wolf. The Manticore roared behind me. Several spikes from her tail felled guards in the mouth of the tunnel, and several lodged in the left side of the Emperor's body—his face, his shoulder, his knee. He fell, bellowing in agony, curses leaking from his paralyzed lips.

I leaped to Athena and crouched before her. "Climb up," I said, my voice rough as the stone on which I stood. She climbed onto my back, digging her small hands in my ruff.

"Go!" Athena cried, as the guard advanced. "Go!"

I went. And the sound of my claws on stone was music. And the feel of her body against mine was delight. And the moon was nearly as bright as the Heart that burned in the Manticore's chest.

I followed the Manticore into the river, the Emperor's man no longer.

Chickie Hill's Badass Ride

by Dia Reeves

The more Sue Jean Mahoney listened to her boyfriend wax poetic about his newly remodeled 1958 Ford Thunderbird—his glasspack muffler and his whitewalls and his fancy-schmancy Motorola radio—the more she wanted to hop into the driver's seat and run him over.

She'd rushed here to the garage where he worked, upset about her parents and needing someone to listen to her, but Chickie only had eyes for his T-bird. Eyes and hands. The flash of heat that ignited Sue Jean's blood as she watched him stroke his gorgeous white and candy-apple red car felt weirdly like jealousy.

Chickie had popped the hood to show Sue Jean his rebuilt engine. "The steam doesn't power the car," he said as she scowled at the pistoning brass cylinders and glass tubes white with vapor. "That's just for effect. Look." He reached through the car's window and fiddled with something, and Sue Jean leaped backward as steam chuffed from the grille.

"See that?" he exclaimed. "When I'm racing her, I want it to look like she zoomed straight outta hell, like she's breathing fire and brimstone. Plus I put in a bunch of other dragster-worthy modifications." He herded Sue Jean into the passenger's side and pointed to the center console, which contained numerous antique brass knobs and dials that, like the fantastical steam engine, seemed out of place in his modern, newly remodeled masterpiece. "There's the usual stuff," he said. "Like, you turn that knob to raise and lower the windows, and that knob turns on the air conditioning. But! When you turn *that* knob, flames shoot out of the—"

"Chickie Hill, if I hear one more word about this silly automobile, I will have no choice but to *set it on fire*." Sue Jean punched the center console and was about to punch it again when Chickie grabbed her fist.

"Careful! You almost hit the compass. It's very delicate. Very . . . special."

"*You're* special," said Sue Jean, and meant it. Chickie had qualities no one else had, certainly no one else in his family, who in the past had done their best to downplay his exploits. Like the time a five-year-old Chickie "fixed" the TV and made it impossible to watch American stations—only European ones. Or when, at seven, he fashioned robot legs for his pet frog, Mr. Hoppers, who leaped into the air in 1952 and nine years later still hadn't landed.

But the day Chickie built a time machine in his closet, the day he had gone to lunch a ten-year-old and to dinner the same day as a twelve-year-old, his parents decided to stop ignoring his abilities. They put him to work in the garage hoping to keep him too busy to get into any more trouble.

"The most special boy I know," Sue Jean repeated, "but you're so shallow. Why are you more concerned about this car than about social injustice?" She pushed out of the T-bird, but didn't feel any less oppressed outside. Their town of Portero, Texas, was heavily forested, and the trees loomed over them at all times, hemming them in like prison bars.

Chickie said, "Was that today? That thing?"

"The *freedom ride*!" How could he call the most exciting trip ever a "thing"? People from all over, Sue Jean's parents included, were caravanning to Washington, D.C., and from there, riding buses into the Deep South to protest against segregation. The most exciting trip ever, and yet everyone was slouching along the busy street totally unconcerned that history was about to be made.

"My folks just left," said Sue Jean, ignoring Chickie's wince when she slumped against his precious car, as if she were the one wearing greasy coveralls. "I tried to talk them into taking me, but they didn't think it was 'an appropriate venue for a girl my age.' They're so . . . *parental*. I have just as much of a right to protest as some old fogey."

"It's 1961 not *18*61," Chickie said. "I don't need anybody to fight for my rights."

"So you like having to sit in the colored section and being told where you can and can't go?" When Chickie rolled his eyes and walked into the garage, Sue Jean followed him, willing to sacrifice her pristine saddle shoes to the grimy floor in order to make him care. "You know what we should do? Organize a sit-in! Just like those kids up in Greensboro and Nashville."

"We don't have a Woolworth's in Portero."

"There's Ducane's Department Store; we can start there. We can do so much!"

"Or . . ." Chickie peered around the garage to make sure they were alone before pulling her into his arms, "since your folks are out of town, we can go back to your place and neck all night long."

Sue Jean pushed him away. "Shallow!"

"What? I'm just being realistic. You know how tricky it is upsetting the natural order? Let's just keep everything nice and simple and go make out."

"The natural order? What's natural about being treated like second-class citizens?"

Chickie waved away Sue Jean's ire. "I don't mean segregation in particular. I mean any situation, in general, where you upset the status quo can have unintended consequences. Like the French. They were inspired by the success of the American Revolution to revolt against their aristocracy, right? So thousands upon thousands of people got beheaded, governments rose and fell, and families were destroyed or displaced all because a handful of cheapskate American bastards didn't want to pay their taxes. What people do, even little things, can have huge bloody consequences. But what *you* wanna do ain't little. *You* wanna change the world."

"For the better," said Sue Jean defensively. Just when she thought Chickie couldn't be more frivolous, he turned into a college professor.

Chickie laughed. "The world according to Sue Jean Mahoney: a bunch of uptight missionaries doing good deeds. Uptight missionaries with long silky legs." He lifted her circle skirt up to her thighs and got a playful smack in the face for his efforts.

"Get outta there." Sue Jean straightened her skirt as he reached across the workbench against the wall and switched on the oily Zenith transistor radio. When he heard the song "Mannish Boy," he cranked the volume. It was definitely Chickie's theme song; he could be so adult about certain things (he had stolen an extra two years from the universe, after all) but a five-year-old about everything else.

"You just don't understand, Chickie. I don't want to wait around and do nothing. I don't want to hope things get better. I want to *know*."

"Knowledge is power," he said gravely, rubbing his cheek, "but power corrupts."

"Why do you always use wisdom to irritate me?"

"Beneath all this grease lies a complicated man. A *main*," he emphasized, like the song on the radio. His untried schoolboy voice was so unlike Muddy Waters' worldly growl that Sue Jean couldn't help but giggle. This time when Chickie put his arms around her, she let him. Irritating mannish boy indeed, but he was *her* mannish boy.

"So you wanna make the scene at the Old Mission tonight?"

Sue Jean agreed, not just because she planned to talk him into helping her organize a sit-in, but also because she really liked making out. She had only recently discovered that she was very good at it, and Sue Jean liked doing things she was good at.

"Cool, mama." Chickie kissed the side of her neck and let her go. "Lemme just lock this dollhouse away in the back." He grabbed a large, tarp-covered object from the workbench.

"A dollhouse?"

He laughed. "Look at the way your eyes just lit up." He set the dollhouse back on the bench and removed the tarp. "You gals say you outgrow dolls and stuff, but it's all lies."

"It's beautiful," Sue Jean exclaimed, admiring the gables and the wraparound porch. "But it looks just like Mr. Peterson's house."

"Yeah, this is his kid's dollhouse. He asked me to electrify it for her birthday." He undid the latches and opened the house so Sue Jean could see the interior. "See the switches in all the rooms? Flip one."

She did, and *ooh'ed* when the little doll kitchen flooded with light. "I would have died for that when I was ten." Sue Jean was dying now as a matter of fact, but she wouldn't give Chickie the satisfaction of admitting it.

"Did you see the dolls the kid keeps in it?"

There were three dolls, one in the bathtub, one on the

couch, and one standing in the corner in the master bedroom, like a child that had been naughty. All three dolls were hideous, as tall as Sue Jean's hand, bald and nude with gnarled skin. They looked like creatures out of a gross horror flick where old men had mutated into tiny trolls.

But this wasn't a drive-in. This was real life. And in Portero, reality was unnaturally thin. In addition to battling social injustice, Porterenes also had to confront the occasional monster or two that slipped through the thinnest places. Sue Jean preferred the monsters to the bigots, though; monsters were more easily destroyed.

She picked up the doll from the bathtub. "My neighbor found one of these things in her mousetrap last week," she said.

"Maybe the kid found them roaming in her backyard, scooped them up in a jar, and made Mr. Peterson stuff them for her amusement."

"Morbid kid," said Sue Jean as she put the doll back in the tub.

"Morbid yourself. I remember when you put your Chatty Cathy's head in a vise."

"That doll was defective. Or possessed. She wouldn't shut up." Sue Jean grimaced at the memory. "Ever."

Chickie tweaked her chin. "You're a tough little mama, Sue Jean. Lucky for me I like—" He frowned and moved her aside so he could peer into the dollhouse.

Sue Jean was about to ask what was wrong when she saw it herself. The light in one of the doll bedrooms was flickering. Chickie reached in to test the switch in that room, and the doll standing in the corner turned and launched itself at his hand.

Chickie screamed as blood streamed down his arm. He tried to fling the doll away, but its jaw was clamped tight.

Sue Jean scanned the workbench and picked up the first tool she saw—a pair of scissors. She grabbed the doll and neatly snipped its head from its body. The head was still clinging to the back of Chickie's hand, though, so she had to dig it out like a stubborn thorn. Finally she placed the head and body back in the naughty corner.

"Think the other dolls are still alive?" Sue Jean asked, using the tissues in her pocket to clean the blood from Chickie's wound.

"I don't aim to find out." He shooed away her attempts at first aid and closed and latched the dollhouse. He covered it with the tarp and carried it outside to his car. "This is going back to that kid *today*. That thing almost ate me!"

"Your pinkie is bigger than its whole body," Sue Jean scoffed, moving aside the toolbox he kept in the trunk of his car so he could set down the dollhouse. "Coward. Why did I ever get mixed up with someone who fails the test so miserably?"

"What test?"

"My ideal mate test," she said, just to provoke him. "There're only five criteria—twenty points for each one. You scored abysmally. Looks: ten—"

"Ten? Out of *twenty*?"

"Intelligence: twenty; bravery: zero; social conscience: zero. Even if you aced the passion criterion, you'd still fail."

"I'll show you passion." Sue Jean thought he was going to grab her, but there were too many people on the street. Instead he lowered his voice. "Just wait till we get to the Old Mission. I'll melt the starch outta your petticoat."

"Don't be vulgar." But Sue Jean couldn't wait to see what would happen to her petticoat.

"You like that I'm vulgar." Chickie leaned close to her, indecently close. "That's the real reason you hang with me."

The proper thing to do in public would have been to step back and maintain her distance, but Sue Jean didn't want to be proper. She wanted a kiss. So she stole one and said, "That and your car."

"I thought you said it was shallow."

Now that all of his attention was on her, Sue Jean was no longer jealous of his T-bird but admiring. She remembered when he'd brought it in from a salvage yard a year ago, wrecked and practically smoking from the accident that had mangled it. And now it was a work of art, a red and white confection gleaming in the spring sun.

"I said *you* were shallow. Your car, on the other hand, is seriously righteous."

. . .

The Old Mission had been abandoned by Spanish priests centuries ago and now its ruins lay sprawled in a clearing deep in the woods. It had found new life as a popular make-out spot, and several cars were parked there, including Chickie's. Moonlight glinted on passion-fogged windows as far as the eye could see.

Sue Jean checked her makeup in the rearview mirror and fluffed her hair. She had cut it recently, and it was short and incredibly chic, like Dorothy Dandridge in *Carmen Jones*. She hated the vanity in her that made her care about such things as cute hairstyles when there were so many problems in the world, but she didn't see any reason why she couldn't help her fellow man and look good at the same time.

"Why're you doing that?" Chickie asked, switching off the interior light. "I'm about to undo all that primping and preening and mess you up in a big way, mama."

"Don't speak to me like that, Chesney Albert Hill."

"Hey!" He actually looked around as if he expected to see

360

the ears of his cronies pressed against the windows. "*Ix-nay* on the *Chesney* business."

He thought he was so cool. Chickie's own normally soft, curly hair was slicked into a ridiculously greasy pompadour. He'd exchanged his coveralls for black jeans and a T-shirt and his prized red letter sweater. She prized it too. If Chickie ever got around to asking her to go steady, she would get to wear it, and everyone would know they were a serious couple. But it was hard to get Chickie to be serious about anything.

"Sorry, daddy-o," she told him. "I'd hate to think I was ruining your reputation."

"When you call me daddy-o," said Chickie, sighing in the dark, "I wish you wouldn't sound so ironic."

A Studebaker pulled up next to them—right next to them, totally ignoring make-out spot etiquette. They realized why when the Studebaker's windows creaked down, flooding the clearing with Little Richard's raucous rendition of "Tutti Frutti" and Chickie's basketball teammate's incredibly loud voice.

"Chickie Hill!" Nate screamed, leaning past his girl, Peggy, in the passenger's seat. "What's buzzin', cuzzin'? Still trapped in the old wage cage?"

Chickie rolled down the window and said, "Sadly, yeah, but I got time off for good behavior."

"So you can practice bad behavior?" Nate winked suggestively at Sue Jean, who rolled her eyes.

"You know it, but what's with Junior?" Chickie nodded at the little boy in the backseat of the Studebaker who was wearing a cowboy hat and scowling. "Y'all giving him pointers?"

"Very funny, peabrain," Peggy said, offended. "It's just that I have to babysit now that our folks are joyriding across the country."

"Joyriding?" Sue Jean asked. "Did they go to D.C.? For the freedom rides?"

"Yep."

"Couldn't you just *die*?" The sense of unfairness washed over Sue Jean anew.

"Yeah." Peggy looked wistful. "Be nice to stick it to the man just once."

"I'm a man," Nate told her. "Come stick it to me."

"This is grody," said the little boy in the backseat, as Nate kissed his sister's ear. "Can't we go to the zoo?"

"The zoo's closed, Shrimp," said Nate.

The little boy turned to Chickie. "You're the one who got stuck in a closet when you was five and came out all grown up."

"That's me."

"Don't lie to him," Sue Jean said.

"It's not a lie," said Chickie. "It's a legend. Don't hate me because I'm a legend."

"I like legends," said the boy. "Peggy, tell me the legend of Sleepy Hollow."

"Peggy's busy, kid."

Peggy pushed Nate away. "Whyn't you go play hide-and-seek, Leo?" she said. "That way you can have fun and me and Nate can have some privacy."

"No." Leo looked out of the window at the ruins, wide-eyed. "It's haunted here."

"Betcha it's not," Peggy said. "Come take a walk with me, and I'll prove it."

"You oughta take Sue Jean," Chickie told her as she helped her brother out of the backseat. "She's not scared of anything. This monster tried to attack me in my dad's garage and she saved my life."

Leo grabbed Peggy's waist tight. "A monster?"

"It was this big," said Sue Jean reassuringly, holding her thumb and forefinger about an inch apart. "If you see it, just stomp it like a cockroach."

"Come on, Leo," said Peggy. "Ain't any monsters around these ruins. Everybody knows the Old Mission counts as hallowed ground."

"That's why you hear so many people screaming, 'Oh, God, yes!'"

"Little pitchers have big ears, Nate." Peggy shot her boyfriend a speaking look and then led her brother off toward what remained of the Old Mission.

Sue Jean was hoping that Nate would turn off his interior light and mind his own business now that Peggy was gone, but he seemed content to keep jabbering at her and Chickie.

"So you're Miss Bravery, huh?" he was saying as he popped the cap off a soda. "Ma's always asking me to kill spiders. I can't stand spiders and she knows that, but she always wants me to kill 'em when they get in the house. Here's to brave chicks." He lifted his soda bottle and drank.

"You're the brave one," Chickie told him. "Driving around in that skuzz bucket. Want I should jazz it up for you? Just say the word. Got my tools in the trunk."

Nate gave him the finger. "Climb it, Tarzan. Not only is this baby a classic, it's a chick magnet. You know how much action I get cruising in this—" He looked at Sue Jean's disapproving face. "I mean, how much action I *got* before I started going steady with Peggy."

"Obviously the car's not the only skuzz bucket," Sue Jean said, turning the knob on the console that raised the windows.

"Don't let him spoil the mood, mama."

"It's not spoiled."

And it wasn't. They were alone now and it was dark and

"There's a Moon Out Tonight" was playing on the radio, one of her favorite songs. As far as Sue Jean was concerned, the mood was finally set.

"Let's get in the back, okay?"

She followed Chickie into the backseat where they could cuddle without the console getting in the way.

She put her face in his neck and inhaled his warm scent. "You should really change your mind about doing a sit-in with me."

Chickie groaned. "Not that again."

"It would be just like this." She squeezed him tight. "We'll sit on the floor of Ducane's and cuddle and sing songs of protest."

"Until they sic the dogs on us."

"Are you afraid of dogs, too, you big coward?"

"No. I'm afraid of being *eaten* by dogs. I never showed you my glove box, did I? Whyn't you check it out."

"I'm sick of gushing over your car, Chickie."

"There's something in there for you. A present."

Sue Jean leaned forward and rummaged around in the glove box while Chickie attempted to caress her rear end through her many layers of crinoline. Buried beneath *A History of the Necronomicon* and old issues of *Hot Rod Magazine* was a pink, beribboned box just big enough to hold a ring. Sue Jean squealed and sat back against Chickie, tearing open the gift.

"What's this?" she asked disappointed, staring at the ring in the box. She had been expecting his *class* ring, a sign that they were going steady—an even better sign than wearing his letter sweater—but this wasn't a class ring.

The band was cobalt-blue glass, and above it spun a dime-sized replica of the planet Earth. Sue Jean had seen satellite photos of the Earth on the news, but all anyone could see on

364

TV were grainy black-and-white images. Chickie's Earth, though, was shockingly detailed. Colorful and gorgeous.

"Amazing." Sue Jean held the ring to her face and tapped it. And the Earth moved. Not the one spinning over the ring, but the *real* Earth beneath her. She felt a rumble like someone was beating a dozen timpani in her belly. Even the moon, visible through the sunroof, seemed to shiver.

"Did you feel that?" Sue Jean fisted her hand in Chickie's T-shirt. "Was that an earthquake?"

"Maybe a small one." His heart wasn't even beating fast.

"*You* did that?"

"Just to remind you how powerful you are." He removed her hand from his shirt, and slid the ring on her finger. "I know sometimes you feel helpless, which I don't get at all because . . . you're the strongest person I know. You could wrap the whole *universe* around your finger if you wanted. You can do anything."

Sue Jean melted against him. "You know how you've been wanting to get to third base?" she murmured. "Batter up, Chickie."

"Really?"

She smiled. *Now* his heart was beating fast. "I guess I'm not that strong. Say nice things to me and I turn into mush."

"I like mush."

Sue Jean studied the blue orb spinning over her finger. "But I'm scared of this. What if I break it and the *whole world* breaks?"

"Touch it again."

She prodded it with her finger, but nothing happened.

"That initial quake was just me showing off."

Only he would think creating a ring that could jostle the Earth was "just showing off."

"You're very unusual, Chickie Hill."

"I'll say. You just gave me the all clear to head for third base, and I'm sitting here like a wet firecracker. Come here."

He pulled her close and—

"*Nate!*"

They jerked apart, startled—not by the sound of Peggy's voice, but by the tone.

Peggy raced to Nate's Studebaker and clawed open the driver's side door. "Leo's been kidnapped!"

Nate leaped out of the car and grabbed her. "By whom?"

"The Ku Klux Klan!"

The name brought the other couples out of their cars in a way even the earthquake hadn't been able to. Sue Jean pulled Chickie out of the T-bird to join the disheveled crowd.

"Peggy?" Nate was saying. "Are you sure?"

"Yes! I was walking Leo around the ruins, showing him how safe it was." Her sudden hysterical laughter made Sue Jean's skin crawl. "And then he told me he had to whiz. So I waited while he left the ruins and went into some bushes near the forest. A minute later Leo screamed my name, and I saw them coming out of the trees—a whole crowd of them. The Klan!"

"That doesn't sound right," Chickie said. "If you'd said they burned down your house and hung your brother from a tree, that I'd believe. But kidnapping?"

"*I know what I saw!*" Peggy shrieked, as Sue Jean elbowed Chickie in the side. "Those horrible white costumes, the long pointy hats. They stole my brother!"

"Call the sheriff," someone suggested, a boy originally from up north judging by the accent and the naïveté.

Nate gave a grim laugh. "Sheriff Ramsey's *in* the Klan." He pulled a rifle from the trunk of his Studebaker. "*I'll* get Leo back."

Peggy took his arm. "I'm coming with you."

"So are we," Sue Jean added.

"No." Nate blocked Sue Jean's way. "This is personal. But if something happens, get help."

Peggy and Nate ran off, and as they disappeared through the ruins, the northern boy said, "A full moon, an earthquake, and now the Klan? I say we split while the splitting's good."

"You're not even going to *try* to help?" exclaimed Sue Jean when everyone headed back to their cars.

"Help how?" The headlights of the exiting cars illuminated a girl with lipstick smeared across her cheek. "With what? You got rifles in *your* car?"

"Nope," said Chickie.

"Well you can bet the Klan does. Nate—he's delusional going after them with a peashooter."

"What he is," said Chickie, "is vengeful. The KKK burned down his uncle's store last summer, remember? Nate obviously thinks it's payback time.

"Well, leave me out of it," said the girl as her guy dragged her away. "If my dad finds out I was up here tonight, he'll kill me a lot worse than the Klan ever could."

In less than a minute, Sue Jean and Chickie were the only ones left at the make-out spot.

"Cowards!"

"They're not cowards for not wanting to get lynched."

"But it's 1961 not *18*61. Remember? Why would anyone be afraid of getting lynched in this glorious day and age?"

Chickie sighed. "Again with the irony."

A gunshot sent the two of them leaping into each other's arms. At least temporarily. Sue Jean broke free of Chickie's embrace just as another shot was fired and ran toward the sound.

"Sue Jean!" Chickie chased after her into the ruins, past

broken stone and teetering archways, past the bushes and then finally into the woods.

It was very dark beneath the trees with no moonlight to brighten the way, and several times Sue Jean ran face-first into low-hanging branches and slipped in what felt like slime. The darkness, however, was unexpectedly broken by the light of a campfire.

"Peggy? Nate?"

But at the campsite, instead of her schoolmates, she found two other people, a man and a woman near the fire. Both dead. A clear substance coated their faces, like a beauty mask, only there was nothing beautiful about their expressions, which were frozen in terror.

Sue Jean heard Chickie curse beside her. She turned and saw him kneeling on a sleeping bag next to Nate's body. His rifle had been wrapped around his broken neck like a bowtie. And less than a foot from Nate lay Peggy, still alive and tugging frantically at the hard clear mask that covered her face, blocking her nose and mouth and any ability whatsoever to draw a single breath. Sue Jean fell next to her and broke her fingernails on the mask trying to pull it off. But it was as hard and unyielding as concrete.

Chickie shoved her aside and smashed a branch against the mask to break it, but the branch broke instead, shattering into a million splinters. Peggy's eyes glazed over, and she went limp, her struggles over.

Sue Jean shot to her feet, hands over her mouth to keep the screams in.

Chickie was more in control, studying all of the bodies with a cool detachment. "Peggy was wrong," he said. "This wasn't the Klan. The nine-lived did this. They steal boys, young ones like Leo, and drain their lives. It's how they survive." He stood and brushed the dirt off his jeans.

"My cousin's son was stolen by them years ago. When she tried to fight them off, they spat on her face. She suffocated just like Peggy did." He nodded toward the man and woman. "And like they did. Notice how there's three sleeping bags? I'm guessing they had a son out here with them. The nine-lived have him now—him and Leo. Sue Jean, we gotta go and warn people."

"I'm not leaving those boys in the clutches of some monster."

"Mon*sters*. Plural. There's only the two of us against who knows how many of them. And remember what I said about consequences? If we save those boys, the creatures'll just search for *other* boys, maybe killing more people along the way."

"You can reason your way out of this if you want, Chickie Hill, but I'm staying. I'm tired of being told I can't make a difference—"

"Sue Jean—"

"—and if the world explodes as a result, then so be it! God, don't you see? This is *our* freedom ride. Our chance to charge into battle and save the day." She watched Chickie struggling with himself and couldn't begin to guess what he was struggling with. When people needed help, you helped them; when things were wrong, you righted them. It could not have been more clear-cut. "Is there nothing you won't take a stand against?"

Chickie stared at Sue Jean for a long moment, the firelight snaking across his unhappy expression. He said, "The slime trail leads that way. Let's follow it." As Sue Jean hurried past him, he grabbed her arm. "But when everything goes to hell," he said, "remember that I tried to warn you."

· · ·

They traveled a short way through the woods and came out into a smaller clearing just big enough for the large, weathered house sitting on the property.

"Look." Chickie pointed to a green light glowing in the basement window of the house and the misshapen shadows passing before it. As they watched, the light changed to a normal yellow, and moments later, the nine-lived exited through the front door of the house.

Maybe from a great distance, if you needed glasses, they looked Klannish, as Peggy had thought, but they were worse. What looked like long white costumes were their bodies; the long, pointy "hats" were their heads, and their eerie, ghost-like glide was definitely non-human.

"Where're they going?"

"I'd guess to find more boys," said Chickie. "That road leads into town."

When the nine-lived had disappeared down the dirt road, Chickie and Sue Jean ran across the yard to the basement window and peered inside the dimly lit space.

"I don't see the boys. Do you think—"

Chickie shook his head. "No, they're inside there some-where. Nine-lived keep the boys they steal sometimes for years, the way farmers keep cows. When the last boy's life is drained, they go out and round up some more. I need to get my car so we don't have to make our getaway on foot in the dark with who knows how many kids. Stay here."

"No way! Splitting up is stupid. In the movies that's how people end up dead."

And so they both double-timed it back to Chickie's T-bird and then drove to the house up the same narrow dirt road the nine-lived had traveled down. Chickie parked the car close to the house, out of sight of the road and as near to the basement window as he could get.

The damp East Texas climate had eroded the wood of the house and rusted the screen, which screamed as Chickie used his tools to remove it and then pry open the window. He slipped inside and Sue Jean handed him the toolbox before crawling through the window herself. At least, she *tried* to crawl through.

"Come on," Chickie said, reaching up and taking her by the waist.

"You try crawling around in a corset," she said breathlessly. "Besides, my skirt is too wide for this window. If only my folks would take me shopping for those new, straight skirts, I wouldn't need all these petticoats."

Chickie finally pulled her through, despite her petticoats; she felt like a cork being yanked from a wine bottle.

"Why are you wearing a corset?" he asked, as she caught her breath.

"It's a shaper. It trains your body to conform to a proper womanly shape."

"Underclothes can't alter genetics. Besides, there's nothing wrong with your shape."

"Don't flirt with me now, Chickie Hill; I'm *trying* to be a hero."

He let her go so they could begin their search in earnest.

A cuckoo clock hung askew near the window above a moldering box full of daguerreotypes. An overturned fainting couch lay dank and rotting in a corner, and a crank wall phone was shattered at the bottom of the basement stairs. But what overwhelmed the room was a black, cast-iron stove that was taller than both Sue Jean and Chickie.

It was a real antique piece adorned with copper filigree and scrollwork. The transparent door ballooned outward in the center of the stove, but instead of a fire glowing through the glass, there were boys, six in all, sitting glumly together like sheep in a pen. There weren't inside the stove, but rather, they were able to be seen *through* the stove, as though it were a giant television broadcasting the boys' whereabouts. Sue Jean recognized Leo right away in his cowboy hat, tears on his cheeks.

Chickie kicked aside a gentleman's bowler hat that had become a receptacle for mouse droppings and knelt before the stove. He tried to open the door, but it wouldn't budge.

"Boys?" Sue Jean beat against the glass, but wherever the boys were, they didn't seem able to see or hear her. "Is that the sun?" she asked, gawking at the boys' surroundings.

"Yep."

"Why is it sunny where they are and nighttime where we are?"

"Because," said Chickie, "they ain't in Kansas anymore."

Sue Jean turned away from the stove before her mind cracked from the weirdness overload. "I don't care where they are. We need to get that door open. You got an ax in that toolbox?"

"Nope. But I don't need one. I'm the kinda guy who likes to keep things simple. So all this is"—he slapped the stove—"is a locked door. We unlock it and, *bam*, we get the boys back. The only thing I need to unlock a door is a key." He snatched the cuckoo clock from the wall, cannibalized it for its clockwork mechanism, and discarded the remains; a blood-red cuckoo lay among the springs and bellows and splinters of wood like road kill. Then he rummaged through his toolbox for wires and screws, batteries, and a pot of glue. "See if you can find a long piece of wood around here," he said absently, already absorbed in his task.

Sue Jean didn't like that Chickie was doing all the work to save the day, and so she was glad to have a way to contribute, even a very small way. So she searched the basement.

A single naked light bulb hung from a chain overhead and did little to chase away the shadows. Sue Jean wandered toward the stairway and peeked into the darkness beneath it. An old crate with the word FRAGILE stenciled across it caught her eye.

She reached for it . . . and heavy, warm breath swooshed against her bare arm. Two red dots, like twin drops of blood, peeped at her, hovering high in the nothingness. Sue Jean backed away on legs she could no longer feel. A giant white blob followed her, oozing out from under the stairs, gliding along on its snake-like lower body; its pointy head scraped the ceiling. It had long, upsettingly human arms that it used to grab her and pull her up to its face, to its slimy hole of a mouth. It hissed something at her, like it was trying to speak. But Sue Jean didn't want to be spoken to.

All Porterenes understood that they lived next door to monsters, but *understanding* hadn't prepared Sue Jean to come, literally, face-to-face with a creature straight out of the depths of a nightmare.

She smashed the crate against the creature's head, and before she knew it, she was sailing across the room. She hit the ground hard next to Chickie who was squatting next to the stove.

"The hell?" Chickie looked down at Sue Jean and then up at the creature. And up and up. "Damn." He rose to his feet.

"No!" Sue Jean jumped up and waved Chickie back down to his gears and tools and tossed the remaining bits of crate at him. "Work on the door. I'll handle this part."

Any other boy would have shoved her aside and shouted, "No! This is man's work!" and then launched himself at the creature. But, though Chickie had many fine qualities, bravery wasn't one of them.

"I just need five minutes," he said, and then settled back to his arcane work.

Five minutes, thought Sue Jean, grabbing a crowbar from the toolbox. That was nothing. Surely she could outlast a monster for five—

The creature sped toward her, so fast she almost didn't have time to dive out of the way. It hit the wall near the basement window, pivoted, and then sped back toward her. Sue Jean was ready this time and waited until the last minute to dodge aside, swinging the crowbar at the creature's midsection as she did so.

But it jerked away, taking her crowbar with it, stuck in the deep layer of slime protecting its body. It wheeled on her and made that sound disgusting boys made right before they hawked loogies onto the sidewalk. She ducked just as a wad of slime came flying at her.

Sue Jean dashed behind the creature, leaping over its tail, and pulled the crowbar free with a squish; she hadn't even made a dent in the creature's hide. It grabbed at her, but she feinted left and then right. As it whipped its head around, trying to keep her in sight, it came into contact with the naked light bulb dangling from the ceiling. The sound it made as the bulb scorched its flesh black could have peeled the paint off the walls. Maybe the creature's hide was thick with slime, but its head was—

The *head*.

Sue Jean jammed the business end of the crowbar into the creature's shiny, blood-drop eye. It roared in pain, its tail lashing the floor. Sue Jean pressed her advantage and smashed the creature in the head until it fell lifeless. She stood over it panting and listening to *everything*: her blood's heated swish through her veins, Chickie's efficient hammer blows, even the moon's icy skirl across the sky was audible.

Everything was clearer than clear. And so when the creature lying dead at her feet began to inhale—a harsh, mucousy rasp—Sue Jean heard that too.

It rose from the ground—its head healed and all of a piece—and towered over her, its two bright, healthy bloody eyes gleaming with malice and remembrance. Staring at her.

It attacked. Sue Jean turned to run up the stairs, but the creature slammed her between the shoulder blades and she went sprawling. It got her by the hair and yanked her upright and then tried to pull her head back so it could spit in her face. Sue Jean swung the crowbar blindly . . . and lost her grip *yet again* when it stuck to the creature's slimy body.

She reached out and grabbed the creature's arms, to steady herself, and then threw her legs up, kicking the creature in the face with the hard heels of her shoes. The crunch of the impact traveled up her legs as the creature fell backward, flipping her over completely so that she landed on top, pinning it to the ground. She leaped up and drove both her feet into its face again. The creature convulsed once and then was still.

Sue Jean pulled the crowbar free of the creature's body and waited. As soon as she saw its long, pointy head begin to heal itself, she jammed the crowbar into its mouth, skewering it. She waited again, but it must have used up all of its lives because this time, the creature stayed dead. Its chest, however, split apart and released a blinding ball of light, which rose high and disappeared through the ceiling.

"You see how it rose upward," said Chickie, startling Sue Jean, who had forgotten he was in the room with her. He looked beautiful, like a fairy creature. Even the scurry of rats in the walls was beautiful.

"Upward," he said, "like it was going to heaven. I think I'm gonna start worshipping Cthulhu."

"Before you go insulting God, do you mind waiting until we're not quite as close to death?"

"What death? You whaled on that thing."

She plopped down beside Chickie, who grabbed her and held her tight until she slumped against him and shivered. Sue Jean could have slept right there in his arms, that's how tired she was. So tired . . .

"I knew you could take that thing," Chickie was saying. "You really are the toughest mama I know. And I'm the smartest daddy-o you know. See?" He waggled his hand in her face, forcing her to pay attention. "I finished the key. Look."

She followed his pointing hand to the huge stove. He had fastened gears to the draft controls below the bulging glass door, and at the stove's copper base he'd glued the piece of wood—Chickie's idea of a key apparently—which contained a large battery and a switch. Wires connected the battery to the draft controls, and when he flipped the switch, the gears began to spin and the entire stove rumbled and shook like a Gay Nineties rocket about to blast into space.

Chickie pulled Sue Jean to her feet and they backed away just as the glass door sprung open. Warm green light—the sun there was *green*?—spilled from the stove and filled the basement, and now the boys were able to see them as well.

"Come on out," Chickie said, causing a stampede as everyone tried to be the first out. It was like watching a hundred clowns pour out of a tiny car at the circus. When they were free, the boys crowded around Chickie and Sue Jean, wanting hugs and reassurance. When Peggy's brother, Leo, gave Sue Jean an especially hard hug, she realized there was no time for her to flip her wig or feel tired. And certainly no time to feel awed that Chickie had figured out in five minutes how to open a door to another dimension. Or that she had killed a creature—not once, not twice, but *thrice*—in the same amount of time.

Well . . . maybe there was time for a *little* awe.

The key on the stove dinged as the switch flipped back into position, like a timer, and the gears stopped spinning. The glass door swung closed, and the green light vanished from the basement with the suddenness of a light turning off.

"Come on, boys," said Sue Jean. "We need to get you back home safe. So follow us and do what we say, okay?" She steered them away from the dead creature near the stairs and toward the basement window.

"I'm gonna go out and pull you guys up one at a time," Chickie said. He shoved the toolbox through and followed after it, then leaned in the window and called, "Who's first?"

Sue Jean gave each boy a boost up to Chickie, who pulled them out and directed them into the backseat of his T-bird. Leo, the fourth boy to go through the window, pointed and said, "What's that?" just as he was getting into the car.

Chickie backed away to look . . . and froze. "Get in the car," he snapped at Leo, "and all of you be quiet." He hurried back to the window and said, "We need to hurry."

"What's wrong?" Sue Jean asked, helping the fifth boy through.

"That one you killed?" he whispered. "The light it left behind is *hanging over the house*. Like the bat signal from those old Batman and Robin serials I used to watch when I was a kid. It's—" He paused and looked over his shoulder, motioning for her to wait. So she did, the last boy in her arms.

Chickie disappeared for a moment—*forever* it seemed to Sue Jean—and then reappeared. The panic on his face was not pleasant.

"They're back."

Her stomach dropped. "With more kids?" She would take on the whole group if necessary, though the thought made her want to find a hole to crawl into.

"They didn't come back with more kids. They came back because of that damn signal. We gotta get outta here now!"

Sue Jean was helping the last boy through when she heard something heavy and wet slithering above her on the first floor. Chickie helped her climb through the window, but once again, her skirt was too wide. The door burst open behind her and a roar echoed through the basement as Chickie yanked her free, ripping her skirt in the process. A long white arm shot through the window and grabbed at her feet, but the monster was much too big to follow them.

Chickie and Sue Jean raced to the car and sped away. Sue Jean blessed the universe for every foot of road the car put between her and that house. "Okay," she told the boys crowding the back seat. "We're safe now. Just—"

A loud splintering crash silenced her as a white fist broke through the rear window. The boys screamed, and Sue Jean wanted to scream too when she saw the nine-lived, all of them, streaking up the road. Right on their tail.

Chickie stepped on the gas and peeled down the road in a cloud of steam.

"Charlie Brown" was blasting on the radio. Such a fun, silly song, but after that ride, Sue Jean would never be able to listen to it again without breaking out in a cold sweat. The nine-lived rolled alongside the car, ramming their fists into it. Spitting at it.

"There goes my paint job," Chickie muttered, and then turned one of the antique knobs on the console. Flames shot from the back of the T-bird. Several of the nine-lived caught fire and so did the forest when the monsters slid blindly off the road and into the trees.

But the T-bird was still being followed closely. Too closely. The car jerked as one of the nine-lived grabbed hold of the tailfin and reached through the rear window to snatch Leo by the back of the shirt. The other boys held him inside the car while Sue Jean grabbed a utility knife from the toolbox at her feet. She climbed into the back and slashed the blade across the creature's eyes. It screamed and released Leo, and they left it in the dust.

Sue Jean clambered back into the front seat as Chickie sped onward onto a bridge that spanned the creek. They were going so fast, she almost didn't see the BRIDGE OUT sign.

"Chickie, did you see that?"

"I saw it," he said grimly, the gaping hole in the bridge growing closer. "Boys! Crouch down as low as you can." He looked at Sue Jean. "You too."

"What're you going to do?"

"This."

Chickie turned the knob beneath the compass, and Sue Jean's cheek slapped against the window as the car went sideways. The world disappeared for a moment, Sue Jean's brain floating weightlessly in her skull, and then the world came back, and Chickie's T-bird squealed across a paved street and slammed into a trolley sign.

Sue Jean gaped at Chickie. "What just happened?"

"I told you that compass was special," he said, petting it like it was his favorite dog. "You can use it to travel in more than just the usual four directions. But there appear to be . . . side effects."

Severe side effects.

Sue Jean knew what street they were on—Seventh Street— but she only knew because the street sign said so. All the buildings within one hundred yards of Chickie's car were gone, reduced to smoking rubble. But even further down the derelict street, several other abandoned buildings were on the verge of collapse, listing to and fro with an ominous groaning sound. And then, an even worse sound:

"Monsters!"

One of the boys was pointing out of the rear window at the onrushing pack of nine-lived. They were quite far behind them, but at the speed the monsters moved, they wouldn't be far behind for long.

Chickie started the car and pulled away from the trolley sign but could only limp down the street.

"What's wrong?"

"The tire's blown. We gotta run for it."

He grabbed his toolbox, and he and Sue Jean hustled the boys out of the car and ran down the dark street toward the only beacon of light—a diner called Smiley's. They willfully ignored the WHITES ONLY sign in the window.

The few people inside the diner stood at the windows watching in awe as the buildings down the road collapsed, but they weren't so awed that they didn't notice the arrival of eight colored children onto the premises.

A surly woman at the window nearest them yelled, "Get outta here. You don't belong in here." Sue Jean could barely hear her over the jukebox blasting "Tutti Frutti." The Pat Boone version, of course. They didn't even allow colored *music* in the diner, let alone colored people.

The boys huddled together behind Sue Jean and Chickie, scared and uncomfortable, knowing they weren't welcome.

"See why we need to have a sit-in?" Sue Jean hissed.

But Chickie wasn't paying attention. He grabbed a screwdriver from his toolbox and then jumped onto the counter and started to unscrew the shiny brass carriage clock mounted on the wall above it. A little boy sitting at the counter with a milkshake in front of him said, "Daddy? There's a colored boy standing on the counter. How come you don't ever let *me* stand on the counter?"

A bespectacled man in an apron came out of the back wearing a name tag that read "SMILEY" and a shocked expression at the sight of Chickie on his counter. "What the hell're you doing?" he yelled, as Chickie jumped to the floor, the clock already half dismantled. "Get outta here 'fore I call the sheriff."

"We're being chased," Sue Jean explained. "By monsters."

"Is that why the buildings're in ruins?" asked the woman at the window. Even bigotry took a backseat to monsters.

"Yes," said Sue Jean. Better they blame monsters than Chickie's weird navigational abilities.

"Wait." The woman squinted out the window. "That's just the Klan."

Sue Jean said, "No, it's not."

"Is so," said Leo. "They're white and pointy and scary. My Daddy said they were."

"Leo?" A colored man, a fry cook judging from his hat, came out of the kitchen.

So it wasn't really whites only. Smiley didn't mind colored people working for him; he just didn't want them as customers.

"Uncle Jimmy!" Leo ran into the baffled fry cook's arms.

"Why aren't you at home with Peggy?"

"Peggy's dead!"

"What?" Uncle Jimmy looked to Sue Jean for confirmation so she nodded, sadly.

"The Klan killed her," Leo cried, "and then took me and put me in a place where the sun was green."

"I don't know what y'all're involved in," said Smiley, "but I don't want any trouble in this place."

Uncle Jimmy gave Smiley a look.

"What do you want me to do?" Smiley exclaimed, his cheeks bright red. "If the Klan wants them, there's nothing I can do about it."

"It's not the Klan!" Sue Jean screamed.

"Oh my God," said the woman at the window. "She's right. It's—" She scrambled backward just as the nine-lived burst into the diner.

They slid straight for the boys, all of them, including Smiley's son at the counter.

In the commotion, Sue Jean blocked the entrance with tables; the nine-lived might have the boys now, but she was damned if they'd leave with them.

"Bash them on the heads!" she yelled. "That's their weak spot." She grabbed Chickie's trusty crowbar from the toolbox and followed her own advice. "And don't let them spit in your face!"

The diners fought with chairs, napkin dispensers—even the salt and pepper—doing their best to wrestle the boys from the monsters' grip. But it was difficult, as Sue Jean well knew, particularly with an opponent that kept regenerating.

"Daddy!"

Sue Jean turned just in time to see Smiley get thrown across the diner by the creature holding his son. She ran forward to ram the crowbar into its eye, but before she could, it spat in her face.

She dimly heard the crowbar clatter to the floor as she tried to wipe her nose and mouth clear, but the stuff had already hardened. She fell to the floor; the spit on her face like a weight, dragging her down. Her eyes were glued open; the fluorescents buzzed overhead, and "Tutti Frutti" blistered her ears. She prayed to God that she wouldn't die listening to Pat Boone.

And then, instead of fluorescents she saw Chickie standing

over her holding the carriage clock he'd modified, the hands spinning backward, faster and faster.

Until she could breathe again.

Sue Jean gasped and sucked in a huge gulp of air. The slime that had been a hard suffocating mask a second ago now hovered wetly over her face, but only for a moment before it flew back into the mouth of the creature who'd hawked it up. The monster dropped Smiley's son and stood bewildered, clutching its throat and choking on its own spit.

"Good!" said Chickie. "It works." He wound the clock and, as he did, the red mechanical bird that Sue Jean had last seen in the basement was now perched on the carriage clock's ornate handle. When Chickie lifted the clock over his head, the bird began to cuckoo shrilly.

Sue Jean got to her feet as the bird's calls silenced the diner. The nine-lived froze and watched the carriage clock, watched the hands spinning, not backward this time, but forward, so fast that after a time the hands seemed to disappear altogether. As quickly as the clock was spinning, so were the nine-lived aging, shrinking into dried, withered husks. They released the boys and when the cuckoo had called twelve times, as one, the creatures fell over dead. And this time, they didn't regenerate.

As the cuckoo spread its red wooden wings and flew away through one of the diner's newly broken windows, Sue Jean waited, looking for bright, bat-signal lights to burst from their bodies, but when none did, she finally relaxed.

When Smiley hobbled over to his son and swept him into a bear hug, Chickie tucked the clock under his arm and said, "When we came here for help, you were willing to turn us over to our enemies. But when you and your boy were threatened, we helped you without being asked—Sue Jean, because she's a good person, and me because if I had just walked out of here, she would have ragged me about it for the rest of my life."

"Shallow."

"Shut up," Chickie told her. "I'm making a point."

"Save it, kid," said Smiley tiredly, rocking his son in his arms. "I get preached to on Sundays."

"Can *I* have a sundae, Daddy?" asked Smiley's son brightly, looking no worse for wear. "A milkshake won't cut it this time."

"And that," Chickie exclaimed, "is my point. I think we could *all* use a sundae." He sat at the counter and pulled Sue Jean down beside him. "What do you think, Mr. Smiley?"

Smiley looked around his mangled diner, at the young faces. The old ones. The dead ones. "Sundaes for everybody," he said, sounding surprised to hear the words issuing from his mouth. "On the house."

And that's how Chickie and Sue Jean and six little boys became the first coloreds ever served in Smiley's. Sue Jean thought there should have been fireworks to mark the occasion, but there weren't. Just the fire spreading outside and the fire trucks.

But it would do.

• • •

Chickie and Sue Jean waited until the parents came to claim the boys before going back to Chickie's T-bird. She watched him change the tire, noting how dinged up and windowless his car had become. But for all its battle scars, it was still a sweet ride.

After changing the tire, Chickie sat on the hood and surveyed the destruction he'd wrought: the fire coloring the sky in the distance, the wreckage of several historic buildings. "I told you everything would go to hell," he said. "And yet, I feel kinda good. I guess sometimes God dresses heaven in hell's clothes. Just for a laugh."

"Ice cream and blasphemy," said Sue Jean, resting her head on his shoulder. "The perfect end to the perfect date."

"Your sense of irony pains me, Sue Jean. Wait here a sec."

He left the car and smashed the carriage clock he'd modified under his shoe and kicked it into the gutter. Sue Jean had always known Chickie had a bit extra. Tonight she had learned just how much extra. When he came back to her, she said, "If you were a Martian, you would tell me, wouldn't you?"

"Of course not." He gave her a shocked look. "That's the kind of secret you take to your grave. And for what it's worth, humans are just as capable of destroying things as aliens. But I'm not in a destroying mood. I'm in the mood to right wrongs. To fight for Truth, Justice, and the American Way."

"The ideal if not the reality," she said, knowing a few sundaes at Smiley's hadn't magically rid her town of hatred and inequality. Though it was a step in the right direction.

"I feel like *altering* reality," said Chickie rubbing his hands together as if he meant to tear the world apart and stitch it back together right then and there.

Since he could do just that, Sue Jean thought it prudent to turn his wondrous mind to other things. Odd, but getting Chickie Hill to be selfish wasn't something she thought he'd ever need help with.

"Know what *I* feel like?" she asked, and then kissed him.

"Okay, to hell with reality." He pressed her back against the hood, right in the middle of the street, and really planted one on her. When her thighs had turned to jelly, he said, "What's the score now?"

"Still zero for bravery, but full marks for passion and your newly developed social conscience. So seventy." It really wouldn't do for Chickie to become conceited.

He removed his letter sweater and helped her into it.

"Finally!" Sue Jean squealed, rolling up the sleeves and luxuriating in the rich red warmth of his love. "Now that we're going steady, I'll award you an extra five points."

"Five points? Is that all my love is worth?" Chickie kissed her again, and this time, *everything* turned to jelly. "Now what's the score?"

Sue Jean stretched against the hood, smiling sensuously, steam rising from Chickie's T-bird and quite possibly from her own skin. "One million." So what if he developed a big head; he deserved it. "The Earth moved. Did you feel it?"

"Yeah." He looked around. "But that was because a couple more buildings just collapsed. I mean, it wasn't *me*." He pulled Sue Jean to her feet and opened the car door for her.

"That's why you're squeamish about upsetting the natural order, isn't it?" she said. "I talk so lightly about changing the world, but you really could, Chickie Hill. You really could save or destroy the world."

"Sure I could," he said matter-of-factly as he got in the car and cranked the radio. "Speedo" was playing; he loved that song. "And so could you. So could anyone." Chickie laughed. "But screw it, mama. Let's just see where the road takes us."

Sue Jean settled back, caught in his orbit, not upset about the past or worried about the future. Content, for once, to simply enjoy the ride.

The Vast Machinery of Dreams

BY CAITLIN KITTREDGE

Matt Edison is the author of such serials as Lord Van Helsing, Witch Hunter *and the* Commander Cloud, Steward of the Skies *stories, which remain the most popular tales ever serialized in this volume. Matt became this magazine's youngest writer at fourteen-years-old, and hasn't stopped since. To write to Matt, address letters c/o* Strange Adventures Magazine, *Box 2, 112 Derleth Street, Lovecraft, MA.*

THIS IS WHAT happened:

Matt Edison met the love of his life at fourteen. Her name was Clarice, and they met in the way of young people, slowly and by torturous inches. Matt was attending a lecture given by one of the last living men to survive the Storm, one of the last men to have seen the world as it was, before witchcraft and aether and the advent of the Great Old Ones. Matt wanted to be a reporter, to go and see all these things for himself. Clarice was attending the lecture as well, and miraculously she talked with him, even though he was a townie and she attended the Lovecraft Academy.

Matt and Clarice were inseparable from that first night, when the silvery-blue glow of aether lanterns danced across the maps of the world that their speaker smacked with his pointer. It was 1915, and newsreels blared the surrender of France to the German Empire, and more fantastically, news about the shadowy, inhuman creatures that Kaiser Wilhelm held at his disposal. Necro-demons, the scientists of the Proctor Bureau called them. Human flesh twisted and remade.

The monsters interested Matt more than the dull politics about a war he was old enough to fight in, but could not discuss with his father without getting his ears boxed—though Clarice hid her eyes. She never got over her squeamishness—not until after she'd graduated from the Academy and they'd married, and she gave birth to their first child.

Matt was away, covering this and that, a stringer for the Lovecraft dailies. They named the boy Clarence Matthew, after his mother and father. They moved away from Lovecraft to the great city of New Amsterdam when Matt's article on Al Capone's trial for witchcraft attracted the attention of the *Times*.

They had more children. They grew old together. Clarice never looked at Matt without love in her eyes.

• • •

This is what happened:

Matt Edison is fifteen, not fourteen. Fourteen came later, when his editor, Mr. Messer, decided that, "Fifteen, hell, you're old enough to be shot by the Kaiser. Ain't nothing impressive about that. Fourteen, that's something that'll get people buying issues. Too bad you can't pass for thirteen, not with those whiskers."

Matt Edison has just been fired from his third job in as many months, as a bicycle delivery boy for the greengrocer's near his father's apartment. His bruises from falling off the enormous wheeled contraption mingle with the ones he got when George Edison, fresh from his shift as a steam ventor in the Lovecraft Engine, discovered Matt scribbling on the back of his *Saturday Evening Post*.

Matt doesn't know where he goes when he drifts off, just that the stories come up and they take him down, down into a drowning pool of other places and other times, people and things he's created, faces only he recognizes. He got fired from his job at the Western Union office when his boss discovered him typing up "The Adventure of the Iron Peril" on the company steno machine.

He thought of a story, about a girl who finds a garden maze behind a house—no, her grandmother's house, that she's just inherited—a rose garden overgrown and sweet with fragrance, and she steps into the maze and wakes up one hundred years in the future, a trick of the Great Old Ones, or maybe the grandmother is still alive and a heretic witch. She's saved by handsome Proctor agent Jimmy Slater, a recurring character in Matt's stories. Jimmy Slater is a loose cannon, not afraid to get into a slugging match with a warlock or drink a poisoned tea that will send his mind outside his body in order to rescue a dame.

Matt already knows he'll never *be* Jimmy Slater. He's skinny and pale, his forehead is too wide, his eyes are too small. He bleeds when he gets hit, and he can't talk to a girl without managing to stare at his shoes rather than her face. Matt will have to be satisfied with writing about Jimmy Slater, about enchanted gardens and haunted mansions, and he is.

He could start a new story with his free afternoon: "The Adventure of the Screaming Skull." He's wanted to use that title for a while. He keeps a list on an old Lovecraft jitney service map in his pocket. If his father finds it, he'll light it up with one of his cigarettes and that'll be the end of Matt Edison.

There is a letter waiting for Matt when he gets home:

Dear Mr. Edison,

I read with great interest "The Black Catacombs of Buried London," but I'm afraid at this time Strange Adventures *is moving away from ghost stories and into serials like* The Shadow *or* Allen Quartermain. *Please keep us in mind for future work.*

Best wishes,

H. Messer, Editor

Matt crumples the letter, then thinks better of it. Cheap paper, but the back is blank.

He decides he can't face telling his father he lost the delivery boy job. He'll try to find another one before George wonders where Matt's weekly eleven-dollar paycheck is.

He wanders the streets of Lovecraft, Old Town, where the townies like him go. Uptown is for rich people and Academy students, and Matt is neither. He was expelled for daydreaming in class—and for failing half of them because of the daydreaming.

He sees that the old Glimmerlight Theater, which used to be a real vaudeville stage but is now a movie house, is playing the sorts of movies banned in uptown. War movies in which the hero dies at the end; cheap, racy adventure serials; farces featuring women with fat lips in dressing gowns and either a very fat or very thin actor, who's supposed to be hilarious. Matt doesn't get it.

He sees Clarice—no, her name's not Clarice. She could never be called Clarice. *Isabelle.* That's her name. Belle for short, or Izzy, if Matt's in the mood to tease her. She's beautiful. Her hair is black, and the light from the screen turns it into a fathomless, shimmering oil slick surrounding her white, white face.

She shouldn't be here. The Glimmerlight is a bad spot in a bad part of town, and Matt can already see Lenny Hastings, the meathead from down the block, elbowing his buddies and staring at Isabelle like she's meat and he's hungry.

Matt Edison makes the one move of his young life that could be considered brave. He sits down beside Isabelle and says "Hello. I'm Matt."

She says, "I'm sorry, do I know you?" Drawing back. Too late, he sees her pressed navy dress, the red tie at her throat, the red scarf draped on the back of her seat. Academy girl. What the hell is she doing in Old Town?

"I just . . . you shouldn't be here." All the Jimmy Slater is gone. Now it's just Matt Edison again, stuttering dunce Matt Edison. "There's some bad types, and . . ."

Isabelle smiles. Her lips are red as her scarf. "And you thought you'd protect me?"

Matt knows he's turning colors, can feel the blood beating through him screaming, "*Retreat!*" before he gets the Proctors called on *himself* for molesting an Academy student.

"I don't know what I thought," he admits. Isabelle turns, bold as brass, and stares at Lenny Hastings. And for some reason, rather than waggling his tongue or making obscene gestures, Lenny Hastings looks away. He folds into himself, like he's hollow. A moment later, he lurches from the theater, holding his stomach.

Isabelle looks at Matt. She smiles. Her teeth are perfect. She is perfect. She says, "Won't you sit with me for the rest of the picture?"

• • •

This is what happened:

Matt did meet Isabelle that night, except it was *she* who came to sit by *him*. He saw her hair and skin in the silver light, and he knew right then he'd write a story about her. They barely talked, whispers he couldn't recall for the life of him, and when she slipped her hand into his, it was as if his eyes were open and he could see all the corners of the universe, planets and galaxies turning like clockwork about the bright spindle of Isabelle's eyes.

He could see things he shouldn't see, like the creeping hands of Lenny Hastings under Marjorie Thompkins's blouse. He could hear things he shouldn't hear, the click and whirl of the lantern projector, the whisper of a man and a woman not his wife two rows down and five seats over.

Matt asked Isabelle, as his stomach lurched and his heart clenched, "What are you?"

Isabelle just smiled.

When Matt gets home he fishes his pens and a year-old copy of his father's Engineworks handbook out of his mattress and writes in the margins. He's never written a story like this before. It's full of blood and madness, inscrutable oracles and gods that drift through the icy reaches of the stars. There is a beautiful girl, who leads the hero to a pool in the forest, a pool that will tell him the truth. He looks in, and what he sees there causes him to throw himself in. The truth is too horrible to contemplate. Matt is awake until four in the morning. His job has him up at five. He writes. He gets a letter. It is dashed off by hand, and the ink is blue, not black. It bleeds like a water stain.

> *Matt,*
>
> *Thanks a bunch for sending me "The Tale of the Black Pool." This is what I'm talking about. We're putting together an all-Elder Gods issue, and I'd like to run this. Pay is sixteen dollars plus a comp copy of the mag. Drop me a line if that's acceptable, and I'll put a check in the mail.*
>
> *Hiram Messer*

Matt Edison is speechless. All he knows, as he goes about finding a clean sheet of paper and walking to the post office on legs like stumps, is that he has to find Isabelle. He hasn't really slept since he typed and mailed his story. That was a week ago. He can't feel the skin on the small parts of himself—fingers, nose, ears. There's a constant hum in his ears. He's hungry but food won't stay down.

He goes back to the Glimmerlight, up and down every street and alley in Old Town. He wanders, feet heavy, and there's a wetness in his sock that lets him know his toes are bleeding. He's walked for hours. He doesn't dare venture into Uptown looking like this. He'll be taken for a heretic—arrested, interrogated. They'll take away his paper and pens.

Matt knows if he could just touch Isabelle again, all of it would stop. The very Earth would stop on its axis, and he'd be well.

And then like a ghost, she's there, coming out of a hat shop on Blackinton Close. Matt tries to call to her, but his throat has dried up. Still she turns. Sees him. Says, "I'm so sorry, Matt."

He says again, "What are you?"

Isabelle dips her head, and under the shadow of her new school hat her eyes are infinity, starlight on deep water. "I'm sorry, Matt."

"What did you do to me?"

Matt can see Isabelle wants to run away very badly. Her feet shift and her fingers twitch and her lithe, white body sways. "You did something to me," he whispers, because talking scrapes his throat raw. "I wrote about you, but I can still see you."

Isabelle makes her decision, moves, and takes his hand. Matt knows at that moment he needs Isabelle, will always need her, and knows also—because he's not as stupid as his father thinks—that he was a marked man that night in the Glimmerlight. A schmuck, sitting alone, watching a stupid adventure serial when he should have been out sneaking drinks and picking up girls, like Lenny.

Matt decides he doesn't care. She came back, and now the stories bursting out of his head can be born. He can almost hear another voice, entirely separate from his own, coarse and gravelly like Slater's.

The drowning girl came in his dreams, and dragged her warm wet finger across his lips. She whispered, and told him everything he never wanted to know.

His fingers start to itch and he needs to write, needs to replace his blood with ink on paper.

"Come with me," Isabelle says, and leads him from the crush of Old Town down to the rotted parts by the Erebus River, where nobody lives anymore. Not since the Proctors burned the ghouls and critters out of Lovecraft with their great machines.

"I can't answer you," Isabelle says when she reaches the last house before the river, its bulk leaning to the left, a turret spiking a rusted finial into the sky. "You asked what I was and I can't tell you, but I'll show you."

She opens the door, and the last thing Matt Edison hears before he's forever lost to the noises of the wide-awake world is the ticking of great, hungry clockwork.

• • •

This is what happened:

Matt Edison doesn't die, not right away. He did not meet Isabelle by happenstance but found her waiting for him on his stoop when he stumbled home, finally—feet bloody and fever raging through his bloodstream.

He's not so happy to see her. "What the hell did you do to me?" he demands. Still, he can't help but notice she's beautiful, pale and dark at the same time, and that her eyes are so deep, like that black pool in the story he's just sold that morning.

Isabelle looks at her shoes. "It's complicated."

Matt has never had a girl interested in him, never mind one on his front stoop. He's fifteen. Isabelle looks even younger, but at the same time, he knows that she's already older than he'll ever get. She moves as if the air parts before her, like she could leap across distances and hit her mark effortlessly.

He's mad as hell, but she's still beautiful. Matt is human. He notices.

"Uncomplicate it," he says. His throat is on fire and he's coughing up globs of green and blood. There's no money for a doctor, and he's not sure he wants one anyway, because they'd make him explain the things he's been seeing, and then he'd get carted off to the madhouse. Just another victim of the necrovirus. Madness in the blood, the cause of all the world's ills. So the Proctors say.

Isabelle is at his side, as if she never moved. She looks him over, and she's not beautiful in that moment. She's hard, searching. "Can you walk?"

"Been walking, ain't I?" Matt says. Horrible grammar, and in front of a girl—a well-bred girl at that. That should show how sick he is.

"You weren't supposed to run out of the theater," Isabelle says, and she takes him by the coat and gets him moving. "You were supposed to offer to walk me home."

"I got nervous," Matt admits. "You're . . . you're out of my league."

"You have no idea," Isabelle agrees, and they walk.

To the rotting house. To the front door. Where Isabelle turns to him and says, "I'm going to show you something very few see. I don't bring people home."

Even her way of speaking is old, her accent melodious, and Matt is gripped by the story-voice all over again, only this time it's the inhuman whisper of cold space and deep oceans.

The drowning girl will rise at the end of the world and tell you everything you never wanted to know.

Not a bad opener, as far as they go.

Matt Edison knows one certainty—that Isabelle is not a girl, and that he will follow her into that house because he can't not follow her. He needs her now, needs her touch to awaken the story voices. On a much deeper level, needs her touch on his skin, on his scars. Needs to touch her in return—that pale smooth ivory that has no human tissue or veins beneath it.

Needs. *Needs.* In a way that he thought only existed in the stories he wrote and read.

Isabelle says, "It's dark. Hold my hand."

Matt Edison steps over the threshold. The house smells bad, the acrid stench of dry rot and the choking damp of mildew in his nose. Everything is wrapped in sheets, and the walls are massively cracked and patched. Dust is so thick the air is yellow-gray before his face.

Isabelle is a vapor in the near dark. All he sees is the glow of her skin.

When Matt touches her hand, he gets a rush, a rush of blood and a rush of whispers in his ears, whispers that cannot possibly be real, because he and Isabelle are the only people there. He feels that if he doesn't write down some of the snippets of phrases and babbling, his skull might explode.

He tries to just breathe, and Isabelle takes him into the kitchen. It hasn't been used in recent memory. Thick furry mold creeps black out of the sink drain and the icebox stands with the door hanging open. A few rusted tins of wartime rations linger on a dusty shelf, but that's it in the way of comfort. Someone has cut cardboard and propped it in all the windows, so only the thinnest razors of light leak in to slice designs on the filthy, encrusted tile floor.

"It's not much," Isabelle says, "but it's my home."

"I think it's swell," Matt lies gamely. "You get to live here all by yourself?"

She looks at the toes of her shoes. She reaches for his hand again, but before she touches him, Matt feels a pain in his back teeth, like somebody's blowing a dog whistle. Isabelle looks up at the water-stained plaster, fallen away in chunks, making a map of a world nothing like their own.

"I have to go upstairs," she says, and for the first time her face is something other than perfectly serene. "Matt, you have to stay here. Promise me you'll sit in a chair and you won't move from this spot."

"I . . ." Matt starts, and she grabs his shoulders. He can see all of her small, white teeth, as she grimaces in panic.

"*Promise* me."

"I promise," he says. Truthfully, Matt is baffled. This place, this dirty house, Isabelle's panic—it's not what he imagined for a beautiful creature like her.

Isabelle disappears up the stairs, and Matt sits, listening to the clock above the coal-fired stove ticking off the seconds, then the minutes, then the hours.

• • •

This is what happened:

It was pretty much as Matt wrote it. Although the whispers weren't as ethereal as he makes them out to be. In the part of his mind that didn't balk at the idea, he was pretty sure that the whispers were coming from other rooms, directly to his ears, like voices over the aether waves.

And Matt is a teenage kid. He doesn't stay put for more than eight or ten minutes after Isabelle leaves. He starts with just poking around the kitchen, looking in the cabinets and finding only chipped plates and cups, the occasional bent spoon or a fork missing half its tines.

He remembers thinking, *What does she eat?*

He doesn't want to go back down the dark hall, where wallpaper peels and hangs like dead moss from the branches of trees. He waits. He taps his foot. It seems like a long time, but really, it's seconds.

Matt knows he's going to open the door before he actually does so, the door that Isabelle had gone through, the one that leads up dark stairs to a cramped hall lit only by the orange of a single oil lantern. The house is so old it's not even got aether piped in for light and heat and all the things a person needs to live.

A *person*, Matt thinks. But not Isabelle.

His footsteps creak and crack, but nobody opens any of the thin, water-spotted doors to scold him. None of the rusty knobs turn. The house is silent, even of whispers.

In the manner of all old houses built across decades, the hallway veers. A thin pair of double doors greet him. Matt knows he shouldn't snoop, should turn around and leave while he still can, but even then he's not sure he could find his way back, out onto the street and to the places he's known before as "real."

He wouldn't turn back in one of his stories. Wouldn't even think of it. And what good now is the real Matt Edison? He's a dumb kid, a coward who can't even tell his own father to lay off him, who can't talk to beautiful girls. He'd do better to become one of his stories, to disappear into that world where men are brave and women need rescuing and everything always works out in the last paragraph.

Matt pushes open the door. He thinks the room might have been a library once. There're empty shelves and snowdrifts of yellowed paper and empty moth-eaten book spines. The light here is that pale yellow-green of approaching storms; a kind of light he's only seen once before, when a hurricane was blowing up the Erebus River from the Atlantic.

That sound, the one that caused his teeth to ache, comes again. Matt can see the source now. The room is taken over with clockwork. It spews and sprawls and climbs up the walls, in every crevice, every crack. Gears and rods bite into plaster, bolts gouging out large chunks of masonry. The entire room is a great device, and he sees clear glass pipes running amongst the iron. In the center, suspended from delicate wires so thin and silver they are nearly white, is a glass globe large enough to house a small child in the fetal position.

The globe is half-filled with viscous pale-green fluid, and within the cradle of glass and gear and effluvia, something moves. The shriek grows and blossoms in Matt's skull, and all he can think of are words, too many words, that spill from his brain until he's worried it will be more than words, that it will be him, lost to the howling creature suspended in front of him.

Matt falls on his knees and a square nail bites into his flesh. He bleeds, from his skin and from his ears, and while he bleeds he sees a warm place, a place where such creatures float in a primordial sea, sharing only their thoughts with one another. He understands this one is very old, and trapped here in Lovecraft. He hears its story, and it terrifies him, that it has survived this long, built this contraption from the bones of a house to sustain itself. He understands they lure the susceptible, the ones they can touch in dreams, to the shores of the sea to drown and feed themselves.

He understands it is not a sea, but a graveyard, populated by scavengers.

Matt understands all this before he runs from the house, bleeding and half-deaf, but alive and sane. He will meet a girl, he will dance with her, and he'll write Isabelle off to a nightmare, though for years after he'll write stories about a dark-haired, pale-skinned woman, always bad, but never quite bad enough to stay away from.

$$\bullet \; \bullet \; \bullet$$

That isn't how it happened.

Matt does run, and when he comes home, his father—in a voice betraying a small amount of actual concern—asks where he's been and why he's all bloody.

"You look like hell," Mr. Edison says. "Eat something, why don't you?"

Matt realizes he can't have seen what he saw. Clockworks don't masquerade as houses, do they? Things suspended in glass bulbs don't talk? Only in your mind, they do.

Isabelle must be playing a joke on him. Maybe in league with those guys from the neighborhood. They found some old flophouse and decided to play with his mind.

So he writes a quick, choppy, nasty story about a neighborhood bully who gets his just desserts from the jaws of a night-jar, one of those predatory, viral creatures who crawl around Old Town. He mails it off to the magazine, even though he's dizzy and feverish and can barely make it to the post box.

Two days later a letter arrives.

Matt, I thought we were through with the kid stuff. Try again. M.

Matt tries again. And again. Writing spikes pain through

his skull. When he sleeps, which isn't often, all he sees is the room in the rotting house, and all he hears is the grinding of gears and the hiss of the life-giving fluid through the pipes. Where does it come from? *Who* does it come from?

On the sixth night of no sleep—food turning sour the moment it touches his tongue, and stories refusing to come from his pen in any form other than dull, trite, and broken—Matt sees Isabelle standing in the street below.

There is river fog around her ankles, and she wears a black dress that bares her arms and throat even though frost has crawled all over the windowpanes. He breathes clear a circle of glass and stares down at her. Isabelle lifts her hand and beckons. Matt feels his guts roil and hears the familiar whispers.

He goes to her. He has no choice.

Isabelle doesn't try to touch him. "You ran away. I told you not to move."

"What *was* that?" Matt doesn't waste time. Has no time to waste. Just being near her makes him feel as if he's on fire. He'd do anything to touch her, to recreate what he felt the first time he laid eyes on her.

"That was our father. Our maker," Isabelle says.

Matt asks the important question. "What are *you*?"

Isabelle does reach for him then. "Please come with me, Matt. Let me prove I'm not what you think."

"I can't . . ." Matt winces as the memory of the creature in the rotted house rises to the surface. "I just can't."

"Father won't hurt you," Isabelle whispers. She brushes sweaty hair off of Matt's forehead, a gesture that ignites the fever he feels for her anew. "He wants to keep you. None of us want to hurt you, Matt."

"*Us?*" he rasps. He feels as if he's swallowed glass. Still, he lets Isabelle lead him through the streets, back to the house by the river that is not a house but a nest, a nest of nightmares. The alternative is to burn away to nothing, his mind crumbling like ashes.

Isabelle stops in the front hall, the hall of whispers. She strokes her thumbs over the back of Matt's hand. "Where we come from, it's cold and silent," she says. "We feed off the living things on the shore, and we speak to each other in dreams."

Matt has read stories about this, but never written them. He thinks they're creepy. The idea of a thing that drinks blood borders on heretical. "Vampires?" he guesses.

"We don't feed on the body," Isabelle says. "We feed on the energy, the thoughts and the emotions. It's like drinking warm honey, but it always fades. Except, once in a great while . . ."

She pushes open a door that rolls back on soundless hinges, and shows Matt a boy about his age, strapped to an operating table. Tubes and wires connect to a collection point near his head, and steel pins drill directly into his skull. Electrodes and wires travel back into the larger clockwork. The boy is asleep, and he thrashes a bit before he trembles and goes still.

"I don't understand," Matt says. He's not brave now. Not the hero of anything. Isabelle is his only ally here and she's one of *them*. One of the things he saw.

"There are some dreams that are strong and bright, and some that are dark and terrible. There are some we can feed on again and again, some we can exchange dreams with," Isabelle says. "We need them, especially in this place." She looks Matt in the eye. "We need you."

"No." Already, he's trying to run, but he can't, transfixed by the eyes of his love. And he does love her. Even though he's young. Even though he can't talk to a girl to save his life.

Isabelle is in his blood, and he has to love her, or go insane from wanting to be near her.

It's not perfect, but it's the closest thing Matt Edison has ever felt to real love.

"No, you don't understand," Isabelle whispers. "You and I, we can share our dreams, yes. But we want you to share yours with the world, Matt. We want you to turn your pen to us. Make everyone in this world dream of us, so we can feed."

Matt's first instinct is to refuse. There's no way he can allow the thing upstairs into the dreams of the people who read his stories.

But *nobody* reads his stories. His life is going nowhere. He could grow up, meet a girl, marry her and be happy for a while. He could start drinking like his father, grow older and bitter with memories that can never be slaked by the face of anyone but Isabelle.

"Everyone will know you, Matt," she whispers. "And you will never want for worlds and people and places to write about. That is the bargain. Your role is that you will be one of ours. You and I will have dreams, forever."

Everyone. Everyone will read him, everyone will know him. He can go to a university and maybe move out of his neighborhood. Isabelle will sustain him.

Isabelle will love him.

It's not a good choice, but it's the only choice Matt Edison can make. So he nods.

"I never want it to be anyone but you, Isabelle. I don't want to know about this. Any of this. I just want to write, and have you. That's all I ever wanted."

In response, Isabelle stands on her toes, and pushes her lips against his. It is a kiss that Matt will never forget, and the last one he will ever receive.

The kiss soothes his fever, the whispers in his mind. Fills

his brain up with the images of the calm green sea, and him and Isabelle, floating forever with their shared dreams.

• • •

This is what happened later:

> *The magazine regrets that as of next month's issue, Matt Edison will no longer be contributing serials to our fine publication. We wish him luck in his future endeavors, and will be publishing a final stand-alone tale entitled "Isabelle" in a special farewell edition. Mr. Edison is no longer contactable by letter or telegram. All inquiries about Mr. Edison's work must be directed to the Bureau of Proctors.*
>
> *With thanks to all our loyal readers,*
> *H. Messer*

Tick, Tick, Boom

BY KIERSTEN WHITE

THE PROBLEM WITH explosions is they nearly always wreak havoc on one's hair. And when one has to spend one's entire morning having one's hair pinned and curled and twisted just so, having it go up in flames is to be avoided at all costs.

However, this is not on my mind as I readjust my goggles and lean in closer to the watch casing. It ought to be, but it's not. Instead, my mind is spinning with vitriol, spewing brimstone curses in the direction of one Franklin Greenwood. Franklin Greenwood and his simpering, inane, sycophantic love for my father.

And his never-ending efforts to extend that love to me.

Of course, the worst part of all is that his surname lends itself so poorly to manipulation. I haven't yet been able to come up with a good rhyme for it. Thus far the best I've done is Franklin Well and Good, and I'd hardly say it achieves the appropriate level of mockery. It's vexing.

So vexing that as I lean over the delicate gears to put the wire *just right*, I scrape my tweezers against the side, and before I blink, the powder ignites and a whoosh of flame burns my fingers as choking smoke engulfs my head.

I scream and back away, the acrid scent of burning hair assailing my nose. I swat at my head. "Blast it all," I mutter, angry tears stinging my eyes. I pull off my goggles and, trembling, go back to the tiny mirror on the wall of the dim workshop. My face is nearly black, save the two shockingly white circles around my eyes. I raise my trembling and burning fingers to my hair and survey the damage. One curl in the front is burned beyond repair, but with a little tucking and pinning it should be unnoticeable. It could have been worse. At least I hadn't added the chemicals yet, and no lightning bugs were wasted.

My fingers are a bigger problem. Biting my lip against the pain, I dip them in a basin of water beneath the mirror. "Kitty, you glock. You absolute glock," I whisper. How could I have been so stupid? All of today's work up in smoke. The wires'll have to be dinged, maybe even the whole casing. And the gears are irreplaceable right now; I cannot possibly justify getting more until next week.

Tonight's buyer will be disappointed. Nothing to be done about it. Probably best to skip the meeting altogether rather than show up empty-handed.

I pull off my heavy leather overshirt, sighing in relief that at least my dress was spared damage, and scrub my face until it is stinging and pink. Metal shears serve to clip away the offending bit of melted hair, although the action hurts my fingers something terrible. No amount of scrubbing will hide that damage.

Heaven help me if Father sees. But Heaven may yet be on my side, and I thank whatever saints I can think of that gloves are so firmly in fashion. I pull on my favorite brown leather pair, biting through the pain to do up the row of buttons at either wrist.

A large grandfather clock that ticked its last tock years ago is tucked up in the corner. I gather my supplies—mournfully cataloguing the ruined pieces—and haul them over there. Three times around with the hour hand to rest at 2, twice around with the minute hand until the clock reads 2:42 and—with a small whirring sound and a gentle click—the face panel springs open. The interior of the clock crackles and sparks with energy from the jar of lightning bugs within, and my hair stands on end from the charged atmosphere. I breathe a sigh of relief that the bugs still have enough food. There is no way I could pry open that lid right now.

I hang the various pliers and tweezers in their places, carefully replace the leftover powder in its container, and line up the ruined watch beside its pristine siblings. Only two left. Looks like a visit to the market for more churched pocket watches from my favorite duffer.

I roll my eyes. I hate having to visit Locksby. And now I'll have to do it tomorrow instead of next week. I close the door, give both clock hands a twist to reset the locks, and my work there is done. The cluttered wooden worktables are left as I found them, my used overshirt hung back on its peg.

Now I haven't even a single clandestine meeting tonight to justify sneaking out of Father's party. And it is all that big nancy Franklin Greenwood's fault. Well and good, indeed.

• • •

"Ouch!" I jump as something sharp is jabbed into the exposed skin of my upper back. Nurse stands behind me, glaring, still holding the incriminating fork.

"Stop slouching. And smile."

I rub my neck, pouting. "Couldn't you have at least stabbed me a little lower, where this accursed corset offers some protection?"

"Aye, or in your thick head where nothing gets through. Lord Ashbury's been askin' after your daytime activities. If you want your freedom, I suggest you don't draw his ire."

I bare my teeth at her in my best approximation of a smile and swish my way out of the darkened eaves and into the center of the ballroom, curtseying and batting my eyelashes and demurely holding a fan in my raw, gloved hands. It is a sea of suits and silk, perfume and perdition. My nose stings from the cloying, overwhelming competition of scents, and I look anxiously through a glazed doll-like expression for my father. One curtsey—evidence of my obedience—and I can slip outside where I can breathe.

A woman cackles, her laughter shrill and grating as she waves a cotton handkerchief in time to her convulsive shrieks. For all their powder and wigs and finery, the upper class is far uglier than all the dirt and sweat of Manchester's workers.

But there! In the corner, Father, holding court with the local magistrates, their bellies straining at satin waistcoats. One of them sloshes wine all over himself during a particular emphatic gesture. I sidle my way through the crowds until I am close enough to hear the conversation and wait for Father to make eye contact with me.

". . . with the new Factory Acts, the negative consequences to men of business cannot be emphasized enough. And why should we punish the great men among us, the men funding the development of our glorious nation?"

I sigh and resist the urge to roll my eyes. Anyone who uses terms such as "our glorious nation" is either a liar or a fool. And usually in nepotistic government positions. Regardless, I care nothing for this conversation. It is the same conversation they always have—why it is our right to subjugate the lower classes in horrific working conditions, why the notion of children toiling in cotton mills is not only just but merciful, why men like my father can impede progress in the name of profit.

My father, Lord Ashbury, looks up and meets my eyes. I instinctively erase my glare and replace it with a dutiful, mildly happy expression.

"Catherine." All of the men turn as one when he addresses me, tipping their heads and giving paternal smiles. Except the fattest one; his smile has a leering quality that dips far past my face and into the white skin spilling out my corset top.

Collins. That's his name. I shan't forget it.

"My Lord," I answer with a curtsey.

"Are you enjoying yourself?" Father asks.

"Always."

And that, as ever, is all the conversation he can muster for his only acknowledged child. I am dismissed with a nod when he turns back to his gaggle of fools. Already my toes twitch in my tiny shoes, anticipating a change to sturdy boots and a quick climb out the library window to the freedom of the night. Maybe I can still get to the meeting place in time to inform the buyer of the delay and set up a new exchange? I have nearly an hour, after all. This is our first dealing, but he came through the right channels, referred to me by the underground network of social revolutionaries that Richard led me to. I would hate to lose his business. And a small part of me hopes that maybe he'll be the elusive Wilcox—union leader, rabble rouser, and general thorn in my father's side. We've never met, but I'd dearly love to make his acquaintance.

I am almost out of the room and already walking the dark alleyways in my mind when another voice softly speaks my name.

This time a real smile pulls apart my lips. "Mister Cartwright." He sits in a chair in a dimly lit corner of the ballroom, a book open but unattended in his lap, glasses balanced on the tip of his narrow nose.

Those glasses always amaze me with their ability to remain perched there no matter what the circumstance. The only time they ever came close to falling off was when, after I studied his plans for a pocket watch-timed bomb, I shocked him with my own design for a bomb entirely contained by the pocket watch itself. He told me he'd never been prouder of a student. I blush with pride now just thinking of it.

If only I were Richard's daughter, or he were thirty years younger and could be a suitor. What a pair we'd make.

"Come sit with me, child."

I take the chair next to him and raise my eyebrows. "I see Father let you out tonight."

"Oh, yes. He likes to remind people now and again how powerful he is. He can make anyone disappear, he can make anyone reappear. Lord Ashbury is quite the magician."

"At least you didn't get the boat."

"There is that, I suppose. I doubt the climate in Australia would agree with my constitution."

The thing I like best about Richard Cartwright is that he is both the most brilliant and the most devious man I know. Brilliant because he never came up with ideas on his own—he simply figured out how to steal other men's plans and improve upon them. Nearly every development in factory machines in the last ten years has come from him (or those he stole from). His latest round of inventions eliminated the need for most workers by mechanizing cotton production. Alas, that had meant that soon everyone else would have been able to compete with my father, who holds a monopoly on all cotton in England.

My father was not fond of this development.

Thus, Richard was put under house arrest and declared a criminal, which was technically true but never bothered my father before. Now the only man who has access to his mind is my father.

I do not get involved in politics; I am merely a supplier to those whose goal is to make my father's life more difficult. It may be that the only *man* who has access to Richard is my father, but the only girl who has access to him is me.

"And how are your . . . side projects going?" he asks. I pull off a glove and show him my fingers. He tsks. "This is why you should hire people to assemble for you."

"And give up the best parts? Never. Besides, a secret shared is no longer a secret."

"Too true, my dear. Too true. Do try to be careful with those clever hands of yours, though. I can't have my smartest protégé crippled, now can I?"

"Of course not. Oh! I have been meaning to ask if you know any churchers besides Locksby. I've bought from him two weeks running and—"

"Catherine!"

Were my spine not held so rigidly in place by my corset I would no doubt slump in despair as my visions of dim, mysterious, salamander-lit streets melt away.

I turn, not even pretending to smile. "Franklin."

Oblivious to the waves of hatred I am sending his way, he reaches down and takes my bare hand in his to kiss it. He frowns at my angry red fingers, the tips still black.

"Whatever have you done to your fingers?"

I pull my hand out of his and hastily shove my glove back on, trying not to wince. "Salamanders. They are such sweet-looking things, I always forget how long they hold heat."

He shakes his head, his voice its usual dull and even tones. "I shall have my physician send over some salve immediately. We cannot have those delicate fingers of yours damaged."

"I don't see how 'we' fits into this problem, Franklin, as my fingers are not of your concern."

He smiles, his teeth perfectly white under his thin mustache. The mustache is a new development—perhaps an effort to blend in better with my father's men; he's not yet twenty. I hear the maids sometimes, gossiping about him. Alas, not even they can give me any terrible stories of broken-hearted laundresses or hidden bastard children. Franklin is as clean as his immaculate clothing, as upright as his handsome round face and deep brown eyes would imply.

He is also a complete glock and a half-wit. Any man who thinks my father worth emulating is no man at all. And now I will be his captive for the rest of the night, subjected to idiotic questions about my father's business and inquiries after the health of various relatives whose names I cannot remember, but Franklin seems to have memorized.

"Would you be so kind as to introduce me to your friend?" he asks, glancing at Richard, and my heart leaps at the thought of foisting Franklin on my poor captive friend and making my escape. But at that moment a wincing maidservant whispers something in Richard's ear. He sighs and stands, bowing to me before leaving the room.

"Perhaps another time," I say, devastated at the loss of Richard. I am now entirely at Franklin's mercy.

Thus, I am shocked when he bows. "I beg your pardon, but I've a previous engagement. I do hope to call on you later in the week and inquire after your health."

And, just like that, the man who never misses an opportunity to talk me into a coma of despair walks out of the room.

Curious.

• • •

Breeches are glorious things. Give me a pair of black breeches, sturdy boots, a long coat, cap, and scarf, and the person slinking down the steaming, dark cobblestoned street is a young boy instead of landed gentry. I quite like being a young boy. My vocabulary options expand to include a whole world of vulgarity, and I become invisible.

I suppose I am invisible in my normal life, but this is the invisibility of freedom rather than that of confinement.

Behind schedule, I walk faster, keeping to the shadows as I pass the Rookeries, slum homes for the city's factory workers. More lights are on there than usual, and a vague roar of noise floats on the sharp air. I frown, wondering if I'd overlooked some sort of holiday. Nothing comes to mind; usually the workers have drunk themselves into a stupor by now or are home sleeping off their last shift.

Soon enough, though I get to my alleyway, thankfully ahead of the buyer. I do a quick check of the switch and cables, tugging to make sure the pulley above me is secure, then hook it to my suspenders beneath my coat. It's a precaution I have yet to need, but a comfort nonetheless. A few weeks ago a buyer thought I ought to donate my wares to his cause, and for a tense moment, I nearly had to use my escape route. Fortunately he decided I was worth paying.

Of course, this only added to the humor when my father and I were greeted by an explosion of noxious green smoke upon leaving our manor the next day. A peril of the trade, I suppose. My inventions keep finding new ways of blowing up in my face.

I give a black smile to the night. Ironically funny, and it was worth it, if only to see the way my father cowered for a few brief seconds. Perhaps I should ask about buyer intention in the future, though. Had it been a more lethal bomb built by someone else, my brilliant career would have been cut tragically short.

A dim, warm light arrives at the head of the alley. I scowl. I hate it when they bring lanterns. His lamp flickers as the glowing salamander inside scampers up and down the sides, frantically trying to get out. No matter. I applied liberal smears of charcoal to my face before leaving.

The man wears a long black coat and a bowler hat that obscures a face hidden by a short beard. Although the coat is old and the hat has seen better days, his shoes are better suited to a Swell. No one meeting me here should have such nice shoes. I wonder who he blagged them from. He's also definitely not Wilcox; from what I've heard Wilcox is an ox of a man, barrel-chested and broad-shouldered. This man is lean and tall.

"I haven't much time. The wares, please." His voice is curt, forceful.

"Oy, 'bout that. Me duffer had to ding the lot. 'E says come back next week."

"What?" He steps forward, looming over me, and I throw my shoulders back in false bravado, as I imagine a street boy would. The cable at my back is reassuring.

"'S not me fault. Duffer says next week."

"You've wasted my time on a very important evening." He takes another step forward, menacing, his voice cruel and sharp as the spring night air.

"Next week. Cain't be helped. You on the randy? I can mebbe find you a nice dollymop, warm friend for a cold night." This is a lie; I know of no prostitutes in the area, but if he threatens me any more I can give him the address of a very large thief who won't take too kindly to being woken up.

He swears under his breath and backs up a step. "No, boy, I have no interest in any friends you can introduce me to. Tell your duffer that if he fails to deliver next week I will take my business elsewhere."

We both turn as shouts sound down the street. Figures run by, panicked, and someone screams. There's light out there now—much too much light. "What the—"

A young man turns down our alley and yells, "Nommus! Nommus, quick! Punishers!" He races past us, and the buyer swears again, tipping his lantern over and kicking at the salamander so it scurries away from us, leaving sparks in its wake.

I reach behind myself, trying to unlatch the hook. Running is probably my best option. The buyer turns to go, but two hulking men enter the alley, each carrying a club the size of my leg.

The buyer pulls out a cane with a solid silver handle and twirls it once through the air, setting his legs in a fighting stance. "Run, boy."

I shake my head, exasperated. I was all set to abandon the nasty bloke, but now he has to go and redeem himself by protecting me. "Grab me shoulders."

He turns to me, eyes narrowed in confusion. "What?"

"Now! Grab my shoulders and hold on as tightly as you can!"

The punishers are nearly to us, but the buyer throws his arms around me, and I trip the hidden switch with my foot. We're both yanked into the air, flying up the side of the building as the counterweights crash down. The suspenders pull so hard with the extra weight that I yelp, and I think surely my pants will rip but they don't. Somehow the buyer manages to hold onto me.

We hit the top of the loop as the weights smash to the ground. One of the punishers cries out in pain and I would relish the moment more could I actually breathe. "Cable! Above your head! Grab it now!"

He does, and I swing wildly for a moment with the loss of his weight. He pulls me in, and I grab the cable, too. Now we are in real trouble—the roof is too far a drop, and I only placed one ring on the pole next to us. The buyer is between me and my swift ride to freedom.

"What now?" he asks, bewildered.

"Behind you," I say, still gasping for breath. "A metal ring on a peg. We hold on to that and ride the cable to the end of the line. It's several streets away, so hopefully we can avoid any company. But there's only the one ring, so you have to take me with you."

I hold my breath, hoping that his benevolence hasn't reached its end. He could just as easily knock me to the ground and escape alone. My arms are already trembling, my burned fingers screaming in pain from gripping the cable.

He reaches back with one hand and unhooks the ring, then gestures to me. I gratefully wrap my arms around his neck and my legs around his waist. "Wait!" At the last moment I remember to unhook the cable attaching me to the rope with the counterweights. That would have been a painfully short trip.

"Go!"

He lets go of the cable and puts both hands on the ring. We immediately start forward, the cable on an incline as it passes over roofs. When I practiced this alone it was exhilarating, but wrapped around a stranger and unable to see our progress, it's terrifying. I never accounted for extra weight in terms of cable strength and sag, and don't dare look down for fear that any moment we will slam into the side of a building and have our lives snuffed out like a crushed lightning bug.

My cap flies off into the night just before the ring catches on the end hook. Our momentum and combined weight is too much. The hook snaps. The buyer lets go and we fall to the roof beneath, my breath smashed out of me as he lands on top and then rolls off.

I cannot breathe. My lungs refuse to pull in any air, and an odd creaking noise is all that escapes my lips. Finally, when I think I will surely faint, my lungs resume working and I gasp, coughing and curling into a ball. Everything hurts.

"Are you . . . are you okay?" The buyer is sitting, stunned, a few feet away from me.

"No," I moan.

"Do you need help?"

"No."

He's quiet for a few moments, and then what he says takes my mind off of the pain. "You are no street urchin. You're a woman." He says it as fact, but there's a twinge of wonder in his voice. I ready myself to spring up and run, so when he breaks out into barking laughter I'm stunned into stillness. "You're a bloody woman!"

"Thanks for that, you big glock."

He continues with his irritating laughter. "And you just saved my life."

I stand, groaning with pain, and wipe some of the soot off my clothes. The angle of the roof is shallow, so standing isn't difficult. Or it wouldn't be, if my entire body wasn't trembling from pain and fatigue. "Yes, well, try not to make me regret it."

He stands. "So are you the duffer, too? Who are you? Why are you involved with this?"

I am glad that the darkness is so complete up here he cannot possibly make out my features any better than I can his. "Yes! Let me tell you all my secrets. Why, let's have a cup of tea while we're at it, and you can meet my family."

He takes a step closer, holding up his hands to placate me. "You saved me. The least I can do is allow you your secrets. We all have them."

I sniff. "Thanks for that. But if you blow me to my other customers—and I *will* know—I'll take a shiv to your Nebuchadnezzer." I'm glad he can't see my blush in the dark. It is an absolute bluff, but I had wanted to threaten a man with that ever since I heard it in a fight between two drunks.

He laughs, which is somewhat deflating. "Fair enough. One more thing?"

"Yes?"

He leans in and kisses me full on the lips.

• • •

My fingers hold the tweezers and betray none of my rampaging emotions as I lower the lightning bug into its tiny compartment. With a quick flick, it's trapped and I breathe a sigh of relief and triumph. Perfectly executed, and my hair survives unscathed.

I double check the gears and the powder level, then close the watch face and pull off my goggles to admire my work. It's a deviously ingenious design, as Richard himself said. Because the bomb is the pocket watch itself, there's no chance for detection. The amount of damage is limited by the size of the bomb, which is why I use a mixture of powder that emits a noxious gas cloud for further disruption. That was Richard's suggestion. And if the watch isn't wound twice within three days to release the lightning bug, the powder is never ignited, the lightning bug dies, and the pocket watch merely becomes a broken pocket watch.

Today, thankfully, my work is flawless. Which means that tonight I meet my mysterious buyer. The thought makes me tingle from my toes to my lips.

I should be more careful. After all, I still know nothing about him, and he holds very dear secrets of mine. However, the memory of his lips on mine, rough and soft at the same time, runs through my head with the fury of a steam engine. I could feel the smile at the corners of his lips as he laughed before disappearing into the night.

I realize I've closed my eyes and am clutching my hand to my chest—my hand that still holds the watch. Now there is a terrible thing waiting to happen, Kitty. One kiss and I've become an absolute ninny. I wrap the watch carefully in several layers of handkerchiefs and place it in my silken handbag. All set then.

I clean my materials as quickly as possible and check for flaws or tell tale signs in the mirror, but I am once again Catherine, foolish doll-child of Lord Ashbury. Which is my role for the day, and I switch into character as I pin my hat on over my curls. Usually this would leave me in ill spirits, but not even a lunch with that simpering nancy Franklin can ruin my mood or take away the fluttering of my nerves.

Tonight, tonight, tonight.

I walk through Market Street in a daze, barely noticing the vendors that call out to me in wheedling tones, the children who beg in unnatural whines. My gloved fingers hold a handkerchief to my nose to filter the ripe scent of too many bodies and too little spring rain. I reflexively pass along coins where coins are needed, and it's not until Locksby calls out that I focus.

He stands behind his makeshift stall in the corner between two stoops, somehow finding shadows even during the brilliance of day. "My Lady Ashbury," he says, his voice an improbable combination of oily and grating; when he speaks I half expect the stench of burning gears to rise from his mouth.

"Good sir." I paste on a vacant smile and walk over to his booth as though I've no idea he sells stolen goods, as though

I cannot understand the vile things he says about me in slang when one of his assistant thieves is near.

"I've some very nice things for you today, very nice indeed."

"How do you always come up with such fine wares!" An eyelash bat for good measure, I think.

"I knows the good places to look, my dear." He sees someone behind me and suddenly shouts, "Oy! I need some fresh tea leafs! Get the word out!"

I turn to see a seedy, scrawny-looking boy on the verge of a growth spurt that may or may not happen given the company he keeps. He nods hungrily and runs off. "Tea leaf," rhyming slang for "thief." It would appear Locksby is in the market for new help.

"Do you drink a lot of tea, sir?" Ah, how he loves it when I remind him what a fool I am and how easy it is to pull the wool over the eyes of the upper classes.

"Love the stuff, me duck."

I bristle, my spine straightening and my eyebrows raising. I will allow him to think he's fooling me in secret, but someone of my rank would never allow him to be so familiar. Besides which, he's a slimy wretch, and I can find stolen watches elsewhere. "Perhaps I am not in need of any gifts for friends today. Thank you, sir."

As I walk away, he lets off a string of curses and I smile my own true smile. I am no one's "duck."

• • •

My fan drifts a lazy breeze over my face as I flick it to-and-fro, to-and-fro, as steady as the ticking of a pocket watch. Fortunately today's tea is outside, which makes it much easier to tune out the prattling of my father's worshippers. By some miracle of seating, I am on the far end of the table away from Franklin, which allows me to relax at least a little.

Until, however, Collins' voice breaks through with something about the Rookeries. I sit a bit straighter and look out into the gardens, angling my body away but my ear closer.

". . . cannot allow this. Soon the masses will think they should have some say in business practices. How can a dumb, illiterate factory worker who could no more scrawl his own name than understand the economics of this country presume to tell the Lords of industry how things should happen? The workers should be grateful for roofs over their heads and food in their bellies, and be content with drinking and siring their filthy children."

"At least their children can fill future spots in the factories." I do not bother looking at Franklin when he says this, although I want most passionately to fling my tea in his face.

"What of Wilcox and the union men?" Franklin asks.

My heart twists painfully in my chest. If I thought there were anything I could do to help Wilcox, I'd do it in a heartbeat. That these men could sit, idly eating lunch, while a true visionary sat awaiting his fate in jail . . . I jump, startled, as the delicate handle to my china cup snaps under my tense fingers.

My father waves dismissively. "The police raid on the Rookeries put an end to that. Without Wilcox they will crumble, as always."

"Wilcox is dead, then?"

My father sets down his silver fork, done eating and obviously bored of the conversation. "No, his trial is this week, after which he will get the next boat to Australia."

So he is as good as dead. I was half in love with merely the idea of Wilcox; now not only will I never meet him, but Manchester will lose its greatest hope for change. I grind my teeth, looking away from this table of privilege and trying to keep my face blank. What a marvel of justice, when the men in charge have decided a man's fate prior to any semblance of a trial. My father is nothing if not efficient.

"And what of the machine parts?" Collins asks, realizing a moment too late that it was the wrong sort of question to ask. I am unable to resist watching my father cut him down with a single knifing glare.

"The factories run as they have and as they will; I suggest you keep your thoughts to things that concern you. Such as ensuring that we have no more talk of unions or men charismatic enough to inspire the sheep."

Father stands and the men stand with him. As he turns to go into the house, Franklin speaks. "May I have a word in private, my Lord?"

A curt nod is his only answer, and Franklin follows my father into the house like a lovesick puppy.

I get up without excusing myself and wander into the garden hedge maze to find my favorite bench. Today's tea was better than unbearable, at least. No conversation with Franklin and a bit of information on what happened at the Rookeries last week.

Nothing to be done for Wilcox if he got the boat. For all my tinkering, I cannot openly affect anything, and what I do must be done in secret. My very small part is all I can play in what is and always will be a man's game.

The images of faces, tiny hollow faces with cotton in their hair, flash in my mind and I close my eyes against them, against the pain, against the hopelessness and despair that has never been my own and so weighs that much heavier on my soul. A bit of luck, a different mother, and I was raised in silk and lace, privilege and plenty, with a home and a future.

Sometimes I loathe myself with more passion than I loathe my father.

I push my handkerchief fiercely against my eyes. I have no right to cry. I will gouge out my own eyes before I allow myself a moment of self-pity. I think of the pocket watch ticking upstairs in my chambers and try to match my heartbeat to it. It had better be put to good use or I will have to come up with a new way to be helpful.

"Miss Catherine?"

I startle, blinking my eyes against any remaining tears. How did Franklin find me here?

"Oh, dear. Something has upset you. Is it too warm? Females have such delicate constitutions. Shall I call for your nurse?" He sits next to me, his voice devoid of any emotion.

I hate him. I hate him, I hate him, I hate him.

"Please don't trouble yourself," I say, gritting my teeth and twisting my handkerchief between gloved fingers. Would that it were his neck.

He sits, silently, his sole purpose in life to aggravate me.

"Did you want something, Mr. Greenwood?"

"Ah, yes. I was wondering about that gentleman you were speaking to the other night at the party. Whether you and he have any . . . connection."

I frown. "Richard Cartwright? What do you mean?"

"In your familiar manner of speech, I felt you two may have a mutual affection, or perhaps—"

I let out a harsh laugh, far from my usual fake titter. "With Richard? Mr. Greenwood, he is old enough to be my father. He's merely a permanent guest of the house, and as such we have become excellent friends." Also, he instructs me on how to navigate the underbelly of Manchester and the finer points of lightning-bug assisted explosions. But idiot Franklin hardly need know about that.

He nods, apparently satisfied. "I would be gratified to be introduced to him, in that case. Perhaps on my next visit." He pauses. "I spoke with your father today."

"You've a talent for stating the obvious."

He looks at me then, surprise bringing his usually dull and distracted eyes to life. I give him a blank smile, trying to counteract the sharp edge of my previous statement. He's not worth the energy, Kitty. Play the dumb heiress, the smiling glassy doll. He shakes his head and moves on, apparently dismissing my brief show of spirit.

"You've grown into a fine woman."

My stomach clenches icy cold. I am sixteen. I should have at least a couple of years before figuring out how to dodge this issue. Maybe I should have let my father ship me to the continent for finishing school after all. Or perhaps I could still claim to be passionately in love with Richard.

Franklin has continued on, unaware of my internal panic. ". . . advantageous to both parties, and with my newly secured position and your father's permission I would like to begin calling on you formally."

"I . . . I . . ." How could a day that started out with such promise turn into this? My mind fires thought after thought, none connected, none offering a solution to this monstrous new development. "I . . . I'm afraid I do feel faint, Mr. Greenwood. The air, and the, the heat, and the . . ."

He pats my hand. "I understand you are quite overcome with emotion, as am I." His tone is even and utterly lacking any feeling whatsoever. His fine features are untouched by anything resembling love or affection. I wonder if anything has ever excited passion in him, if he has ever cared for anything other than securing a position among Lords. "I'll get your nurse."

Watching him walk away, I hate him. I would sooner leave my entire life behind than face one with him at my side.

I touch my lips in memory; maybe I can do just that. Tonight, I meet with a real man.

• • •

I am a bundle of nerves as I wait in my dark alley. I'm in costume as usual, but instead of it hiding me I feel exposed. He knows I am a girl—he knows more about me than I do about him. I wish I had my cables and pulleys reset, but there hasn't been time to do it myself or contact one of Richard's boys. The day's anticipation has turned into nervous fear. Comfort comes with the knowledge of the knife in my boot, the iron filings in my pocket. I can take care of myself. I just hope I won't have to.

A soft glow at the entry to the alley draws me out of my musings and steals away my breath. He carries his silver-topped cane and walks with far less urgency than at our last meeting.

"Evening," he says, his voice low and hinting at a smile I cannot make out in the dim light.

"Evenin'," I answer, glad that the darkness also hides my smile and burning cheeks.

He leans forward, closing much of the distance between us. "I trust there were no supply problems this time?"

"So long as you have the payment."

He reaches forward and takes my hand in his, lingering far longer than necessary before dropping a small, heavy purse in it. After I purchase supplies, the rest goes immediately to three families with small children, a private salary I pay to keep at least a few kids out of the factories.

I tuck it into my coat pocket and pull out the handkerchief-wrapped package. "Use it in the next three days. Wind it twice, then you have about sixty seconds to get away."

He takes it out of my hand and slips the watch inside his coat. "Aren't you curious what I want it for?"

425

"S'long as it causes problems for the men who run the factories, I approve." The last one put an end to a very important meeting of local magistrates. Others disrupted factory shipments or stopped trains carrying in scabs; then, of course, the one that showed up on my doorstep.

I expect him to move now that he has the package, but he leans in even closer. I can see the dark outlines of his beard and mustache, the black intensity of his eyes barely lit by the glowing salamander held between us. "I still have questions." His voice is low, and I don't think I've ever been addressed as intimately.

"I don't doubt it." I tilt my face up to his.

"Questions can wait, though." He puts a finger under my chin and leans in, kissing me again, less quickly than before but I still taste the smile on his lips. I should know his name, I should question who he is, but I care about nothing so long as his mouth talks to mine. Then his hands are on my hips, pulling me closer; my arms are around his neck, wanting more, more, more of him against me.

A harsh scream breaks through the night, and we pull apart. I gasp for breath, my lips tingling and numb. "What—"

The scream sounds again, followed by the same woman's voice shouting . . . something indecipherable. My mysterious buyer runs in the direction of the noise, and I follow, almost as fast on my feet. A couple of turns and we're in the labyrinthine passages of the Rookeries.

He slows and I do, too. Then, to the right—"Stop! Gerroff me! I said no!" Her shrill shout is suddenly muffled.

We race around the corner to find a portly gentleman pinning a woman against the wall, his arm against her throat. His other hand is doing things my mind refuses to register.

My buyer does not hesitate. Raising his cane, he brings it hard against the man's back. With a shout the rapist turns to face my buyer, and the woman falls to the ground, scrambling on her hands and knees before getting up and running.

"How dare you!" the fat man growls, and with a shock I realize I know the voice. Collins. Collins here, in the Rookeries, attacking a young woman.

"How dare *you*." My buyer's voice is low with menace as he swings again with the cane. But Collins surprises me with his reflexes, ducking out of the way and knocking the cane to the ground as he pulls something out of his belt. A knife. Collins has a knife. And someone who would do that to a girl would certainly have no problem shivving my buyer.

I dart in closer and reach into my pocket, grabbing a handful of iron shavings. "Oy, Collins!" He looks over at me, surprise widening his eyes just as I fling the shavings into his face.

He screams, clawing his eyes. The more he blinks the more it will hurt, the more it will scratch at his delicate corneas. I am surprised by my cold, unfeeling calculations as I watch him. He will probably be blinded.

I cannot summon the pity to care.

"How do you know him?" There's a strange tone to my buyer's voice.

A shout from a nearby alley interrupts us. "Time to go," my buyer says, running in the opposite direction of the voice. I reach down, pick up his cane, and spare one last look at the loathsome Collins before taking a different path into the freedom of the night.

• • •

"Yes, but there isn't any point in our waiting for Father, is there?" I am irritable and hot, my fine lace parasol doing

427

nothing to lessen the baking heat radiating up from the stones of the main square.

Nurse folds her arms over her ample bosom, heaving a sigh. I will get nowhere with this argument. If Lord Ashbury requests tea with his beloved daughter after the trial, then his beloved daughter will obediently wait outside for him as long as it takes.

I hate his beloved daughter.

A man bumps into me as he walks by and mumbles an apology under Nurse's glare. I look around, suddenly aware the square outside the courts is far more crowded than is normal for this time of day. There are no definable groups, but there does seem to be an unusual amount of people milling about and talking with vendors. Curious. I would worry, but even my trained eye cannot pick out any weapons beneath the men's open-necked shirts.

"Mr. Greenwood!" Nurse calls out, her face brightening. I curse inwardly; I think the old bat fancies him. That, or she hates me. Likely both.

He turns, interrupted in his purposeful walk toward the courthouse. A brief flicker of something—annoyance?—passes over his face before he sets it into his usual blank, bland smile and walks over to us.

"Good afternoon." He tips his hat to Nurse and takes my hand to—blast him—bring it against his dry, passionless lips. It is all I can do not to rip it away when I notice that, in his other hand, he clutches a pocket watch.

A churched pocket watch.

A churched pocket watch that was, until two short nights ago, in my possession.

I look up, horrified, into his face and picture him with a short, false beard—picture his eyes in the dark, animated with passion. I imagine his flat voice infused with urgency and harsh with determination.

And his lips. How could I have not recognized those lips?

"Miss Catherine?" His eyes, that I now see hide just as much as mine, consider me. "Are you well? You seem to have gone quite pale."

I pull in a breath that leaves my corset straining against my breast. Biting my lip against a smile, I nod. "Quite well." He smiles and turns to go.

"Oh, and Franklin?"

He turns, raising a single eyebrow at my informality.

"Do give my regards to poor Mister Collins. Such a tragedy. But perhaps you could call on Richard Cartwright and myself later this afternoon? I believe I have something of yours. A certain cane with a silver top." I bat my eyes at him and admire his ability to betray only the slightest hint of shock through widened eyes. "Are you well? You seem to have gone quite pale."

He recovers more quickly than I would have expected, a secret smile pulling up the corner of his lips. I have tasted that secret smile, and I intend to again. "Quite well. This afternoon, then."

I wave demurely as he strides off into the crowd, turning and glancing back at me at least three times. As for me, my world has shifted on its axis. And so it is that, two minutes later, when they bring out the union leader Wilcox, I am utterly unsurprised by the cracking, echoing bang that sounds, or the choking billows of foul green smoke. I step politely out of the way as the masses shift and congregate to add to the confusion, and conveniently use my parasol to trip several soldiers as they run toward the courthouse.

I've no doubt, as Nurse rushes me away, that Wilcox will have mysteriously escaped custody before being put on that boat to Australia. And I've no doubt that my buyer will become a regular customer. And much more . . .

Franklin Greenwood. *My* Franklin Greenwood.

Well and good, indeed.

Acknowledgments

"Rude Mechanicals" © 2011 by Lesley Livingston. First publication, original to this anthology. Printed by permission of the author.

"The Cannibal Fiend of Rotherhithe" © 2011 by Frewin Jones. First publication, original to this anthology. Printed by permission of the author.

"Wild Magic" © 2011 by Ann Aguirre. First publication, original to this anthology. Printed by permission of the author.

"Deadwood" © 2011 by Michael Scott. First publication, original to this anthology. Printed by permission of the author.

"Code of Blood" © 2011 by Dru Pagliassotti. First publication, original to this anthology. Printed by permission of the author.

"The Clockwork Corset" © 2011 by Adrienne Kress. First publication, original to this anthology. Printed by permission of the author.

Author Biographies

Ann Aguirre is the national bestselling author of urban fantasy, romantic science fiction, apocalyptic paranormal romance (as Ellen Connor, writing with Carrie Lofty), paranormal romantic suspense (as Ava Gray), and dystopian young adult fiction. Before she began writing full-time, she was a clown, a clerk, a voice actress, and a saviour of stray kittens, not necessarily in that order. She grew up in a yellow house across from a cornfield, but now she lives in sunny Mexico with her husband, children, two cats, and one very lazy dog.

www.annaguirre.com

Jaclyn Dolamore has a passion for history, thrift stores, vintage dresses, drawing, and food, only some of which appear in her novels. Her debut, *Magic Under Glass*, was a Junior Library Guild selection and received a starred review from *Booklist*. She is hard at work on the sequel, or so she tells herself, and in the meantime her next book, *Between the Sea and Sky*, will be published. She lives in Orlando, Florida, with her partner, Dade, and two naughty cats, Tacy and Oskar.

www.jaclyndolamore.com

Tessa Gratton has wanted to be a palaeontologist or a wizard since she was seven. After traveling the world with her military family, she acquired a B.A. (and the important parts of an M.A.) in Gender Studies, then settled down in Kansas with her partner, her cats, and her mutant dog. She now spends her days staring at the sky and telling lots of stories about magic and monsters. Her debut novel is *Blood Magic,* which is followed by its companion, *Crow Magic*.

www.tessagratton.com

Frewin Jones is the author of the fantasy series The Faerie Path, in which a sixteen-year-old girl finds that she is in fact the seventh daughter of King Oberon and Queen Titania of the ancient and Immortal Realm of Faerie. To date, there are five published books in the series, with more to come. Frewin is also the author of the Warrior Princess series, set in seventh-century Wales, which chronicles the adventures of Branwen, a fifteen-year-old girl who becomes entangled with the Shining Ones—a quartet of Old Gods from back in the mists of time. After publishing his first book in 1987, Frewin became a full-time writer in 1992. He lives in South London with his wife, Claudia, and their elderly and very pampered cat, Siouxsie Sioux.

www.allanfrewinjones.com

Caitlin Kittredge is the author of the Iron Codex trilogy, a Lovecraftian steampunk adventure. The first volume is *The Iron Thorn*. Caitlin is also the author of two bestselling adult urban fantasy series. She lives in Massachusetts with three cats named after comic book superheroes, and does pinup modeling and photography in her spare time.

www.caitlinkittredge.com

Adrienne Kress is a Toronto-born actor and author. Her middle-grade children's novels are *Alex and the Ironic Gentleman* and *Timothy and the Dragon's Gate*. She is a theatre graduate of the University of Toronto and the London Academy of Music and Dramatic Arts in the UK. Published around the world, *Alex* was featured in the *New York Post* as a "Post Potter Pick," as well as on the *CBS Early Show*. It won the Heart of Hawick Children's Book Award in the UK and was nominated for the Red Cedar in Canada. The sequel, *Timothy*, was nominated for the Audie Award in the U.S. and the Manitoba Young Readers Choice Award in Canada, and has also been optioned for film. Her debut YA is *The Friday Society*.

www.adriennekress.com

Lesley Livingston is the award-winning author of *Wondrous Strange* (winner of the CLA YA Book of the Year Award) and *Darklight* (shortlisted for the Indigo Teen Read Awards). A writer and actress living in Toronto, Canada, she has a Master's degree in English from the University of Toronto, where she specialized in Arthurian literature and Shakespeare. Captivated at a young age by stories of folklore, past civilizations, and legendary heroes, Lesley is a Celtic mythology geek—especially when it comes to stories of the Otherworld, Faeries, and King Arthur—and an unrepentant egghead (a character trait that somehow doesn't interfere with a love of shoes and shiny things). The concluding volume of the trilogy is *Tempestuous*.

www.lesleylivingston.com

Dru Pagliassotti is the author of the debut *Clockwork Heart*, which was one of the first published books in the rising new genre of steampunk romance, winning *Romantic Times'* Best

435

Small Press Contemporary Futuristic Novel, and named by *Library Journal* as one of the five steampunk novels to read in 2009. Her second novel, *An Agreement with Hell*, features one night of horror that briefly puts angels and demons on the same side against a threat from beyond. She is a Professor of Communication at California Lutheran University, and has raised two iguanas named Hemlock and Belladonna.

www.drupagliassotti.com

Dia Reeves is the debut author of the critically acclaimed young adult novel *Bleeding Violet*, a nominee for YALSA Best Fiction for Young Adults. She lives in a suburb of Dallas, but her family grew up in East Texas, a mysterious area that has inspired many of her stories. She is a librarian with a wild imagination, and in order to make her life less boring, she enjoys writing stories of monsters and doorways to absolutely anywhere else but here.

www.diareeves.com

Michael Scott is the Irish-born *New York Times* bestselling author of the six-part epic fantasy series, The Secrets of the Immortal Nicholas Flamel. He began writing more than twenty-five years ago, and is one of Ireland's most successful and prolific authors, with over one hundred titles to his credit, spanning a variety of genres, including fantasy, science fiction, and folklore. The fifth book in the series is *The Warlock*.

www.dillonscott.com

Maria V. Snyder is *The New York Times* bestselling author of the Study series (*Poison Study*, *Magic Study*, and *Fire Study*) about a young woman forced to become a poison taster. Born and raised in Philadelphia, Pennsylvania, Maria dreamed of chasing tornados, but lacked the skills to forecast their location. Writing, however, let Maria control the weather, which she happily does via a Stormdancer in her book *Storm Glass*. Her first young adult fantasy is *Inside Out*.

www.mariavsnyder.com

Tiffany Trent is the author of the acclaimed young adult dark fantasy series Hallowmere, which was an IndieBound Children's Pick and a New York Public Library Book of the Teen Age. A former instructor at Virginia Tech, Tiffany has three Master's degrees, in English, Creative Writing, and Environmental Studies. She currently lives in the Outer Banks of North Carolina. Her new YA steampunk novel is *The Unnaturalists*.

www.tiffanytrent.com

Kiersten White is *The New York Times* bestselling debut author of *Paranormalacy*, the first book in a new trilogy. She has one tall husband and two small children. They live in San Diego near the ocean, where Kiersten stays inside on weekends to write and is thus far paler than any Californian ought to be.

www.kierstenwhite.com